EMPEROR'S FATE

ALSO BY AJ WALKER

Upcoming in Rulers of Tarmigan Series

Shepherds of Fire

Shattered Dragons

In the Bond of a Dragon Series

Zahara's Gift

Secrets of the Sapphire Soul

Fall of the Kings

Rise of the Dragonriders

Bond of a Dragon Prequel

Dragon Wars: The War of the Magicians

(Available through newsletter sign up.)

Bonnie Glock Mystery Series

Into the Mixed

Finding Justice

Exiled and Forgotten

Dark Fae Rising

Soul Harvest

EMPEROR'S FATE

THE RULERS OF TARMIGAN SERIES

A J WALKER

For Bubba,
A best friend
A loyal companion
Always young at heart
The first pet and the best dog

ACKNOWLEDGMENTS

Writing Emperor's Fate has been such a journey! From creating an entirely new world with so many unique aspects to hunting out typos, this book is my best work yet. And I couldn't have done it without a lot of help from my publishing team.

Thank you to my editor and the person who works the closest with me on these books, Susan Penner. As always, your willingness to assist me with my writing has shaped this story into a great work of fiction. When you offered to read my first draft of *Zahara's Gift,* I had no idea that we'd make it this far, wrapping up a tenth novel together!

When writing this book, it was easy for me to get sucked into the world I'd spent so much time creating. I felt a need to share all the details of everything I was visualizing. Susan helped me prune this massive story into a book I'm very proud of. When embarking on a story this big and epic, it's hard to see the forest for the trees, but with Susan's help, we've created something truly wonderful. She keeps my writing voice true to itself, helps me find my characters' motivations, and enhances my writing to a new level. This story wouldn't be the same without our collaboration. Thank you, Susan.

Beyond the written words on the many pages of this book is the outstanding illustration that Cristiana Leone created. After giving her a prompt of the characters, as brief a description of the setting as possible (which wasn't that brief), she's created a visual representation that suits my story extremely well. Cris has been so much fun to work with. Thank you.

Thank you to Hoskins Cartography, who brought my world into a visual representation I'm thrilled with. The Tarmigan map is amazing! I saw Josh's work posted on an indie author group and I loved what I saw. I contacted him and we started work together the next day. His work in making Tarmigan appear like a real world on the page is excellent. I'm very proud to have his art displayed in my book. Thank you.

The clarity of my story improved through honest input from my beta reader team. Thanks to Starr Waddell at Quiet House Editing and Heidi for your work on my story. The book is much improved as a result.

And, always, a big shout-out to my support group, aka my family, friends, and dogs. My wife, parents, grandparents, extended family, in-laws, friends from Montana and beyond, and our two big hairy dogs that always believe in me. You're all my rocks and I thank you all for encouraging me to follow my dreams as an author.

Special thanks to:
Susan Penner – Copy and Development Editor
Cristiana Leone – Book Cover Design
Hoskins Cartography – Fantasy Map Cartographer
Quiet House Editing, Starr Waddell, and Heidi – Beta Reading
ARC Team Members

CONTENTS

Prologue ... 1

1. Shylo ... 9
2. Death's Bells ... 26
3. The New Observer ... 43
4. The Last Order ... 48
5. The Scaled One ... 56
6. A Rude Awakening ... 65
7. Flushed ... 77
8. The Yellow Stone ... 92
9. Galterius-Brex ... 105
10. Jermanus' Fate ... 124
11. Not Alone ... 140
12. Hatching a Plan ... 152
13. Outside the Walls ... 163
14. Burnt Hopes ... 179
15. Noble Reasoning ... 194
16. The Bad Men ... 207
17. Marxius Ovando-Kai ... 215
18. The War Room ... 226
19. Finding the Messenger ... 243
20. The Tsuga Tree ... 253
21. Jexsanna ... 265
22. Total Control ... 277
23. Different Lives ... 295
24. Yaak ... 308
25. The Dirty Shame ... 320
26. Smoke ... 339
27. Brismil Scale ... 355

28. Opposing Forces   369

29. Volurem Burning   378

30. New Armor   395

31. Isik   406

32. From Ai to Kai   421

33. Majority Rules   436

34. Ivory Room   453

35. To Ash   471

36. A Night to Remember   488

37. Backburn   502

38. Fire and Smoke   517

39. Taken   534

40. Perdigon   542

Epilogue   551

Seeking Out Connections   559

Ordered to Lie   567

Digging for Details   573

Unforeseen Options   594

The Blue Light   615

Leave a Reivew   621

Newsletter Sign-Up   623

About the Author   625

TARMIGAN
ZECHRIU
State of Anhisen
Lake Fosse
State of Derasos
Mosgar
NEW RHYDENAR
OLD RHYDENAR
Ocean
Couro
Ocean
Maelstrom
Ocean
Brimn Bay
Malsa Bay
State of Apsar
State of Sdryo
Nardan
State of Chorein
Flamps Bay
Flamps Bay
VOLOURIUM

Rosebud R.
Shield
Trick Falls
Mountains
PERDIGON
Pryor R.
Esuga R.
fort of Perdigon
Yauk
Apsar Forest
Cardwell
Shield Lake
Brism Bay
Lake Pryor
Sularo
Florebs
OLD RHYDENAR
State of Apsar
Plains
Shield R.
Palus Rim
Saypo
State of Saypo
State of Naydan

"And when Tourome, last dragon and surviving Creator of Tarmigan, left this world, he shed a single scale. A scale unlike those of lesser dragons, for he was one of The Creators. He left this piece of himself behind to act as a signal, a warning that magic could return. Tarmigan, the world Tourome helped create, was no longer a home for dragons. He'd won the war against the other Creators, making this world as he wanted it, free of all other magical dragons. And so, he left this world to the magicless beings that now inhabited it, until the time when his scale signaled a rejuvenation of the power he dismantled." – The Final Page of The Dracolyth

PROLOGUE

PEOPLE OF THE FIRE

Commander Rhydan Gathrius, third in command of the Unburnt Army, defenders of his people, felt the surrounding heat intensify. The fires of their enemy suddenly rose over the forest, the flames licking a smoke-filled sky.

Commander Rhydan called for his troops to retreat, "The Pyrignum, it is coming! Get to the wall! Defend the city walls!"

A thick layer of smoldering ash plumed under Rhydan's feet as he backed away from the enemy, a hellish race of people on fire. Rhydan and his countrymen couldn't bring themselves to call their mortal enemies a race of people. People didn't sprout from embers, catch fire, and spread their flames with a vengeance. People didn't live in the fire, intent on destroying everything their flaming bodies touched. These two-legged creatures shared a silhouette eerily similar to Rhydan's own people, broad-shouldered and muscular. Only, where Rhydan's skin was light brown, theirs was a charcoal black, cracked and glowing with brilliant red magma. Where his straight black hair hung flat around his head, theirs appeared to be flames dancing atop their spiked skulls along with the same orange flames that emitted from entire bodies. Where Rhydan's grey eyes glinted in the sun, theirs burned ember red. The Volurem were a people of the flames that scorched the earth and warred with Rhydan's people. And the Volurem soldiers were making a run through the burnt trees directly toward Rhydan's position. Volurem foot soldiers, those who appeared to be men fully engulfed in flame, couldn't burn for long once the trees in the forest were scorched to ash. Not on their own at least. They needed a conjuror of magic for tactical warfare. This conjuror was a unique type of Volurem. It used an opal gem called the dragon's heart to channel magic and influence the soldiers' fire behavior. Rhydan's people called these Volurem conjurors, Pyrignum.

A Volurem foot soldier lunged at him. The bright orange and yellow fire bursting from the soldier's body battered Rhydan's leather surcoat before their blades even met.

Rhydan blocked the Volurem's inky-black blade. Sparks showered over Rhydan with each deflection as the soldier attacked with increasing speed. Rhydan ducked, the practiced motion of a seasoned legionnaire. He spun under the burning soldier's sword. His steel struck true, and he rose back to his full height in time to see the damage he'd inflicted. Rhydan cut through the Volurem soldier's leg at the knee, adding one more charcoal limb to the pile of ash where the last of his people defended their city. The Volurem fell with a missed step. As Rhydan continued his retreat to the safety of the city walls, he watched the front lines of Volurem foot soldiers ignite with increasing intensity.

The enemy influencing this army's flames had a powerful and devastating gift. Believed to be bestowed from the dragon gods, the very creators of the world, each Pyrignum had the ability to channel the elemental force of its people's fire. Protected at the center of the Volurem army, the Pyrignum channeled the dragon's heart. Bolts of white light arched out from the conjuror's opal gem imbedded at its chest, passing energy into every flaming soldier within range. The entire length of the battle front flashed hot, growing in intensity and size as the Volurem soldiers exploded with blue flames. Rhydan had never seen so many Volurem affected by one Pyrignum. Rhydan had hoped to confront an enemy less well organized. He'd hoped there wouldn't be a conjuror and that the Volurem army would dwindle in the burnt trees. Now, facing an enemy on fire led by a strong Pyrignum, Rhydan's army would be lucky to survive the battle. If they fell, their city would burn. The hope for his people to survive above ground would die if the Volurem breached their city wall.

Roaring wind surged within the forest. A thick cloud of smoke engulfed Rhydan. He sprinted as fast as he could to catch up with the other soldiers of his legion. The flaming blue inferno coming off the Volurem bodies was so intense that it burned his skin through his standard army surcoat devolved from dragon leather. Beneath the heat-resistant leather he wore a protective wool tunic for added insulation and padding. Rhydan had only felt such overwhelming radiant energy once before.

As he feared for his life, something tugged at his subconscious. The sensation blossomed into a burning desire to grab the relic he had attached to his sword belt: a fossilized dragon scale from north of the Shield Mountains.

Rhydan's skin blistered in the heat as he desperately searched for some sign to support his instinct about holding the dragon scale. Rhydan's last glimpse of Perdigon, his home and the single remaining city for his people, disappeared in the dense plume of smoke. The sky darkened around him, highlighting the backs of his infantry soldiers in a burnt orange glow. Perdigon's walls were still a hundred strides away. Rhydan felt his skin bubbling from the heat penetrating his leather surcoat and wool tunic. The smoke grew too thick. He could no longer see the backs of his cohort. He was going to die like the rest of his legion.

As he fumbled with the leather pouch on his sword belt, his vision blurred. The cloud of smoke made him sick, but he didn't slow to retch. His lungs burned. No matter how hard he set his mind to force his body to move, he knew it was failing. Rhydan fell to his knees. The wild flames closed in on him. Rhydan knew his skin would fry when he took off his glove, but the sensation he felt to open that pouch overpowered his reluctance. He screamed as his flesh charred, blistering in the radiant heat as an army of flaming people descended on him. Somehow, he knew the dragon scale was his last hope of survival. He opened the leather pouch and plunged his hand in.

An instant later, he touched his burned fingers to the fossilized scale. The stone felt impossibly cold. Rhydan didn't understand how, but he realized the burns no longer hurt. He watched in horror as Volurem soldiers rushed past him. Their intense blue flames rolled off their ember-colored bodies, setting everything in their path ablaze, including Rhydan. Yet, he didn't burn. Not his flesh. Rhydan's leather surcoat, wool tunic, and padded wool-blend shirt dripped away from his body like resin from a burlap torch. He looked in his hand. He still held the fossilized scale, but it was no longer a dark grey stone. The scale gleamed in the firelight like molten pewter. The metallic sheen spread from his hand, up his arm, and across his entire body. The shining layer molding perfectly to his body was textured with scales, like the single scale he held tightly with his hand. Before Rhydan thought to react, a Volurem soldier hit him from behind. The searing air rushed from his lungs as Rhydan tumbled through the ash covering the battlefield. He dropped his broadsword, clutching tightly to his lifeline, the dragon scale.

He expected a deathblow to come next. Rhydan felt it, the burning black blade striking him across his back. Yet he felt little pain. Only a dull ache lingered where the soldier had hit him.

Rhydan scrambled to his feet, scale in one hand, no sword in the other. His protective leather was gone, only the dragon-scale armor that spontaneously encased him when he touched his bare skin to the dragon scale remained.

More Volurem soldiers surrounded him. Rhydan had never seen them this closely. They stood two and three times taller than him. Their charcoal bodies now burned with jet blue flames, influenced through the Pyrignum's magic. These flaming soldiers wore no armor like Rhydan's people. The Volurem's corded muscles bulged under their continually shimmering ember essence. The Volurem appeared to be built much like people, but born of ash and charcoal. Their bodies were a constant shimmer of rolling black and red like a burning log. Fire emitted from them, blazing bright and licking the air above their bald heads. Despite the similarities Rhydan's people shared with the Volurem in bone structure and muscle tone, no person of Rhydan's race could survive the heat that these abominations carried with them. Yet, Rhydan stood among them, unburnt.

One Volurem, a soldier twice Rhydan's height, attacked him. Rhydan reacted, blocking the goliath's glossy blade with his scaled arm. Where the black weapon would've bitten into his protective layers and cut through his flesh and bone, the metallic-scaled armor produced by the dragon scale protected him. The Volurem's glowing red eyes widened when he saw his weapon failing to deliver a killing blow. The moment's hesitation didn't last. The Volurem attacked with renewed intensity, showering Rhydan with embers.

Rhydan blocked each strike with his protected forearms. His energy seemed to match the merciless speed of the Volurem soldier. Rhydan took hold of his attacker's sword arm, stopping the soldier mid-swing, and punched. He punched with all his might, sending the fist that held the dragon scale into the Volurem's burning chest. Rhydan had always been able to kill a Volurem soldier with a powerful strike from his steel broadsword, but now, when his fist hit the Volurem's chest, it passed clean through. The blue fire of the soldier burned out, its charred black corpse collapsing to the ash-covered battleground.

Rhydan suddenly noticed it. Every Volurem within view stopped moving to watch this duel. Rhydan spotted a single-handed broadsword lying next to the burning body of a fellow legionnaire. This man was dead. He didn't need the metal weapon anymore. Rhydan hefted the broadsword, surprised by the chill of the metal grip in his scaled hand. He noted how light the broadsword now felt to him, he had no issue wielding it with one hand as his other clutched the dragon scale. Keeping his movements quick and choppy, he blocked and fell the next Volurem attacker. Rhydan fought with an increasing strength that he'd never felt before. Had he had time to think, he would've realized that he fought with a power that could've only come to him through the dragon's scale. In the heat of the battle, he used this new strength to snuff out the Volurem soldiers around him. The smoke momentarily lifted. He saw Perdigon's walls still standing.

When the guards atop the walls spotted the Legion Commander standing among the fires of their enemies, they cheered. The cheer was so loud that it sent a hush across the remaining Volurem soldiers.

A bellowing battle cry sounded from the Volurem mob sprawled out before the city. Rhydan turned to face it. A Pyrignum stood amongst the mob, its bright white flaming hair rising from its molten scalp. The Volurem conjuror pointed an ash-white arm at Rhydan in challenge. Arches of magic surged from the dragon-heart in its chest, passing into every Volurem foot soldier between Rhydan and the Pyrignum. Rhydan swelled with a determined sense of pride. Even if these soldiers overcame him, tearing the palm-sized dragon scale from his grip, he had given his people something they hadn't had in centuries. He'd given them hope. But Rhydan would give them more than hope. He would fight through the Volurem, regardless of the strength of the Pyrignum's influence over its soldiers' fire. The blaze didn't hurt him now that the dragon scale protected him. Rhydan would not stop fighting until the Pyrignum was dead by his sword. If he didn't cut that opal gem out of the

Pyrignum's chest and stop the attack, his people wouldn't survive. Killing the Pyrignum meant more than saving his city. It meant saving his entire race. If his city withstood this attack, his people, the Terra people, could endure. Perdigon would become the capital city and stronghold that birthed a new age in Tarmigan.

Rhydan gripped his sword in one hand, the dragon scale in the other, and barreled through the enemy to usher in a new era; one that would forever be known in the Terra people's history as the beginning of The Rulers of Tarmigan.

SHYLO

The Day Before the Emperor's Death

A column of dark smoke plumed on the horizon. Shylo gulped, trying to clear his suddenly dry throat. Thoughts of burning soldiers storming across the Imperial State of Apgar took over his thoughts. He tried to imagine enemies he'd never seen producing fire from their bodies, setting the fields and forests ablaze across the southwestern-most region of Rhydenar. All crops and food sources for the Rhydarian capital destroyed in one expansive burn. That's all it would take for the nearly one million people within the walls of Perdigon to suffer. The citizens in the capital would not burn from the fires of battle. Perdigon's walls were too thick and too tall for the Volurem to breach. The capital city of the Rhydarian Empire would survive the blaze.

No, it's too early for them to be this far north, Shylo thought.

Shylo felt a vague sense of comfort, however, that Perdigon had previously survived the Volurems' blaze in a much more unstable time, when Rhydan of the Unburnt Legion turned the tides of war in their defense against the Volurem. Rhydan's sacrifice to kill the Pyrignum spurred Rhydarian expansion into the empire Shylo now hoped to serve one day. An empire spanning the continent from the northern reaches of Zethril and south into northern Volourium at the Fringe. And though Shylo could feel a cool spring breeze on his face, seeing a smoke column this far north before the fire season had even begun was cause for concern. Like all Rhydarians, Shylo understood that when the crops burned, people starved. He was lost in thoughts of the possible repercussions of that haunting column of smoke when his reverie was broken by a man stating firmly, "Penti." The man addressed him by what they called all entry-level trainees on Capitol Hill.

Catching his leather sandal on the sandstone landing, Shylo nearly fell. To his embarrassment, when Shylo straightened he found himself standing before Senator Rembert Didimo-Kai, a Noble of Perdigon and head of the House Didimo. Only the Akai, members of the Imperial family, were above the Kai, the Noble Class citizens. Shylo prepared to hear a reprimand from the New Rhydarian Noble. As an Eso, a common citizen, Shylo instinctively expected to be reprimanded, even if the middle-ranking Noble was his host. House Didimo had only granted Shylo's application to train in Rhydarian politics because of his uncle's personal relationship with Senator Didimo-Kai's advisors. With that connection, and Shylo's mother's ability to foot the cost of his tuition, he was in his Penti level of training.

"Senator," Shylo said out of surprise, instantly recognizing his failure to observe the proper etiquette while in the presence of a Senator. The Senator hadn't asked him a direct question, which in a Penti's case would have allowed him to offer a response. Only third level trainees could freely address a Senator while in the trainee program. Even worse, Shylo had failed to acknowledge the Senator's honorific as a Noble, something a common Eso was expected to do. "Didimo-Kai," he added after a pause.

Conflicted about whether speaking out of turn as a Penti or not saying the Senator's full title was worse, Shylo saw his dream of becoming a Senator's advisor slipping away; a dream that surpassed something achievable for most Esos, as advising a Senator was the highest a commoner could rise in Rhydarian politics. Only the Noble class, the Kai, could serve in the Senate. He waited for the Senator's reply.

Please don't send me home, back to Florens, Shylo thought. *Oh, what would my mother say? This was as much her dream as it was mine. She was the one who pushed for uncle to submit my application. And my father, he would be validated.* A foul taste formed in Shylo's mouth. *Father expects me to fail. To come home with my tail tucked between my legs, having to go back to work for him in the tannery. I'd almost rather join the legions, a death sentence for someone like me who would rather pick up a book than a practice sword. No, please don't let this experience be over after only half a rotation.*

"Each Senator, and those who advise Senators, have all started right where you are, as a Penti," Senator Didimo-Kai said.

Shylo thought to close his gaping mouth. He wasn't expecting his host Senator to speak so naturally to him.

"If you want to continue as a trainee in the Novi and

Medi levels, then I suggest you stop daydreaming and focus your attention on making it through this rotation. It only gets harder in the second half," Senator Didimo-Kai continued.

As he faced the Senator, Shylo realized he'd never really taken in the Senator's Noble presence.

It's not the expensive robes, but how he carries himself that give him his Noble presentation, Shylo admired.

Like the Senator, Shylo was Rhydarian, but of the southern region, Old Rhydenar. He stood a full hand-and-a-half shorter than his New Rhydarian host. Being New Rhydarian, Didimo-Kai's dark brown skin and tightly curled black hair was a classic confirmation of the northern Rhydarian region. Where the Senator's eyes were green, flecked with a yellowish-gold, Shylo's were storm grey. Shylo's nose was more pronounced than the Senator's and his skin a lighter shade of brown.

Senator Didimo-Kai embodies everything in a Noble politician that I one day hope to assist, Shylo told himself. A lofty goal, he knew, but Eso citizens like Shylo had to serve the Noble class, the Kai. *It's either serve the Kai or earn a living in Rhydenar's Imperial Army,* Shylo cringed.

The life of a soldier had never appealed to Shylo as it had to most Eso boys he knew. Some Eso soldiers gained fame and wealth to rival the Nobles, but most died young, burning in the continual war with the Volurem. What Shylo lacked in brawn he made up for in his studying. His devotion to learning set Shylo apart from other Esos his age. Even in his youth he had his sights set high and couldn't be bothered to maintain the failed friendships he'd had with the Esos in his hometown, Florens.

"Sorry, Senator Didimo-Kai," Shylo said, bowing low. "The smoke on the eastern horizon surprised me. It's spring, and early in the year's rotation to see a column of that size."

As the Senator's gaze fixed on the eastern horizon, Shylo's thoughts lingered on the potential destruction if the Volurem reached the Rhydarian supply chain before the Rhydarians were prepared. From this spot atop the stairs that descended below the Senatorial Chambers on Perdigon's Capitol Hill, they could see over the city walls. A thick forest blanketed the sprawling land as far south and east as they could see. To the west, the vast Maelstrom Ocean and to the north, the snowcapped peaks of the Shield Mountains. For a long moment Senator Didimo-Kai's gaze lingered on the grey column of smoke.

Breaking his gaze, the Senator glanced around the stone façade. Shylo followed the man's searching, noting that no one of interest was lingering on the steps or around the massive sandstone columns behind them.

"I expect out of the fifteen or sixteen rotations you've been alive, only a few of them were dry enough to see the Volurem burning this far north in the spring. Do not fear it, Penti Trainee Shylo Conserra, that column of smoke must be beyond the Apgar Forest. Burning in Saypo on the High Plains this time of year is common enough. There is little Imperial presence in that grassland wilderness. It will burn itself out before long, and if it doesn't, the Imperial Army Corps will handle it. The Hundred and First Legion patrols our imperial state. Those Volurem will not reach us here."

Shylo could hardly believe his ears. This was the most any Noble, regardless of rank or political standing in the Rhydarian capital, had spoken to him. In the half rotation since arriving in Perdigon for his training, he hadn't received so much as a single question from any Senator. That Senator Didimo-Kai knew Shylo's full name and social rank shocked him. Shylo remembered his manners and stood tall, folding his arms behind his tunic. He wore the forest-green short tunic and black trousers of House Didimo. The yellow belt around Shylo's waist marked his Penti trainee status. His lanky physique and smooth skin gave away his youth. He had black hair, like all Rhydarians, but unlike New Rhydarians, Shylo's heritage provided him with straight hair.

"I have a task for you," the Senator said, placing his soft hand on Shylo's shoulder. "Collect the quills and parchment left over from today's discussions in the Assembly Chamber. I've noticed an increased demand for documenting supplies as of late. House Didimo needs to cut down on waste until we hear High Noble Benton Querci-Akai's supply report."

Shylo knew he shouldn't question his Senator, but a Penti wasn't allowed unaccompanied inside the Senate Assembly Chamber.

"If anyone asks why you're there after hours, give them this and direct them to me," the Senator said, slipping a copper bracelet from his wrist and giving it to Shylo.

Shylo noticed the bracelet had the House Didimo symbol stamped into the copper, three conifer trees. The crest was singular to House Didimo. Shylo suspected the Senator likely gave the direction to turn Shylo's attention away from the smoke column in the east. Whatever the case, a task assigned by a Senator and head of the house that hosted him wasn't an opportunity Shylo intended to waste.

"Take any leftover supplies back to the villa. Turn them and my bracelet over to Medi Trainee Kinsey. Is that understood, Penti?" Senator Didimo-Kai said.

Shylo nodded, pressed his leather-soled sandals to the stone landing and headed toward the Senate Chambers at a swift pace. The noisy chatter of Capitol Hill vanished behind the thick sandstone walls of the iconic Perdigon building. Walking with his head politely angled down and moving with purpose, Shylo passed through the sparsely populated main entrance, skirting around the Center Rotunda. He jogged up the left side staircase, accessing the Senate Assembly Chamber through the southwest entrance on the balcony. Without stopping to offer anyone the opportunity to question him, Shylo pulled open the wood-paneled door and entered.

The Assembly Chamber was a long rectangular space, two stories tall and west of the Center Rotunda. The Senate Assembly Chamber hosted three-hundred-and-sixty-nine active Senators when the Assembly was in session. The theater-style bench seating on the balcony formed an arc encircling two-thirds of the Senate floor. Below the stone balcony, the Rhydarian Senate acted as the ultimate repository for executive power. Within these walls the Senate debated and adopted legislation that governed Rhydenar. The ten most powerful Senators among them served on the committee that advised the emperor. As he took in the expansive room, Shylo envisioned that one day he could be a link in the chain of power leading the empire. His mother's words popped into his head, "A Rhydarian Senator is only as good as his or her team of advisors." That belief had driven Shylo's ambition. It drove him to aim for the lofty goal for an Eso.

The Assembly Chamber, at a glance, appeared empty of lingering politicians. Shylo located House Didimo's symbol among the rows of bench seating on the balcony. Three green pine trees with long black trunks represented House Didimo. A small flag marked where Senator Didimo-Kai's assistants sat while documenting Senate proceedings. A stack of loose parchment as thick as Shylo's narrow thighs and three pheasant feather quills blackened with ink rested on their section of the wooden bench. Shylo surmised that leaving the writing supplies behind was commonplace.

"What's an ashen Eso like you doing in here?" a distorted voice swore from the entrance directly behind Shylo.

Shylo whirled, dropping the collection of parchment on the stone floor. A fresh worry rose to the surface. But when he saw who was speaking, his fear subsided. His fellow Penti classmate stood in the doorway, head tilted, a grin spread from ear to ear.

"Blazing fire, Wilsall. You scared me half to death," Shylo said, feeling his face flush with embarrassment. No doubt, everyone in their class was going to hear about this by morning, how Wilsall put the fear of ash into the snooping Eso. "How in the blazes did you do that with your voice?" Shylo asked, feeling annoyed at his friend. Shylo didn't have many friends back in Florens, and of the few, none acted like Wilsall. None of them were positioned to become Kai either. Wilsall was a Minor Noble, but would eventually become a Noble, given his inheritance.

Wilsall pressed his hand to his throat, pinched, and spoke in the same ghoulish voice he'd used a moment before, "I did it like this."

Shylo frowned as he bent down to collect the parchment he'd scattered.

"What are you doing? The day's work was over hours ago," Wilsall said, stepping all the way through the balcony threshold and letting the wood door close with a hollow thud behind him.

"Senator Didimo-Kai gave me orders," Shylo explained.

Wilsall chuckled, crossing his arms on his chest. He

wore the same style of short tunic and trousers as Shylo, only his were a more expensive lightweight wool blend, crimson with white trim embroidered on the collar. A Rhydarian infantryman with spear and shield was featured on the front as House Sarapio's symbol.

"Didimo gave you an order to pick up blank papers?" he asked mockingly.

"That's right," Shylo replied, rising with the collected parchment and quills held against his side.

Wilsall curled his upper lip, crinkling his thin mustache with a look of disbelief. "Anyway, some of us are going to the Canteen. Are you going to come?"

"I told you," Shylo said, exiting the Didimo bench. "I have orders."

"Ismay will be there," Wilsall said, eyebrows rising as he bounced in place on the balls of his feet.

Shylo hunched forward, glaring at his New Rhydarian classmate, "Last time you told me that, she never showed."

"Yeah, because I was lying to you last time," Wilsall said with a chuckle. "But this time I'm being honest. I swear to The Creator."

"Wilsall Sarapio-Ai being honest?" Shylo teased. "I'll believe that when Perdigon burns."

"Which reminds me, have you seen it yet, or were you too busy pretending to follow orders from your Senator so you could snoop in the Assembly Chamber?" Wilsall asked.

Shylo balled his fist around the used quills.

"I saw it right after you ran into the entrance. Didimo and several others were discussing it on the stairs."

"The smoke?" Shylo asked.

Wilsall nodded, only then seeming to want to stop and take in the grandeur of the Senate Assembly Chamber. The Penti trainees toured the Senate Chambers on their first day but were only allowed to view the Center Rotunda. They weren't allowed inside the Senate Assembly Chamber. The building was a prominent symbol of Rhydenar's Empire and one he treated with awe.

"I'm surprised to hear you say Senator Didimo-Kai was gawking. When I pointed out the smoke column to him, he acted as if it wasn't anything out of the norm," Shylo said.

Wilsall's attention turned back to him, "You're lying out your ass. The Senator, a Third Class Noble, did not speak plainly with you about a column of smoke on the eastern horizon."

Shylo bit the inside of his lip to keep himself from cursing. This was not the time nor the place for such an argument, and Shylo knew it.

"I'm headed to the Canteen. Join us when you can," Wilsall said, turning to leave.

Shylo made to follow him when a door on the first floor creaked while opening. Wilsall paused. Shylo nearly bumped into his classmate.

"What are you doing?" Shylo whispered as adult voices filled the previously silent space below them.

Wilsall pressed his finger to his lips and widened his round, green eyes in warning. Silently, he dropped into a crouch and started removing his leather sandals from his white stockings.

Seeing fully robed Senators walk into view on the Assembly floor, Shylo dropped behind the nearest row of benches alongside his classmate. "Are you crazy? We'll be expelled if we get caught," Shylo whispered.

"Who's going to catch us? Everyone has left and all eyes are on the smoke in the distance," Wilsall replied, his voice barely audible from less than an arm's length away.

"Whatever they're talking about isn't meant for our ears. Blazes, we're Penti trainees Wilsall," Shylo cursed.

"If you get up and leave now, they'll hear you for sure and we'll both be scorch-out-of-luck. Shut your stupid mouth and do as I say, you Eso," Wilsall demanded nearly silently.

The insult cut Shylo deeper than his classmate's foul language. Shylo attempted to come up with a reply, but the blatant classism stunned him into silence. Wilsall wasn't even that much higher up in social class, but by the laws of Rhydenar, Esos were lower ranking than the Minor Nobles.

From where the two Penti crouched on the balcony, Shylo could see only a few of the adults on the Senate floor. From the sound of it, a small group of Senators and assistants had gathered. The stone balcony railing blocked most of their view, but Shylo recognized one man: the most famous Eso man Shylo knew of, Galterius-Brex, High Commander of an Imperial Brigade and second in command of a Division in the Imperial Army. Shylo knew of Galterius primarily from reading about his military career. Galterius-Brex was an Eso who rose from humble beginnings and worked his way through the Legion's ranks. He had become an important leader in one of Emperor Jermanus' three preferred legions chosen to protect him while campaigning against the Volurem. Every Eso in the Empire knew his name. High Commander Galterius-Brex surpassed most Kai and even some High Noble-Akai with his wealth, landholdings, and fame. Though he could never hold political office, Galterius' opinions directly influenced the Senate's military decisions. The famous Eso had broken the ceiling of what was possible for Esos three rotations earlier when he was invited to leave his station on the battlefield, come to Perdigon, and advise the Emperor as a member of the Imperial Defense Committee. Shylo recognized two others as Senators, Noble Kai, but all the rest were out of sight, and he didn't want to risk being shamed by the Eso hero.

Wilsall tugged at Shylo's tunic sleeve. He pointed, mouthing the word, "Look!"

Shylo thought his classmate was ogling over Galterius too, but when he adjusted his position, Shylo caught a glimpse of what Wilsall had noted. Standing between Galterius and an Old Rhydarian Senator stood a muscle-bound soldier. His skin shone with the metallic glint of form-fitting brismil-plate armor.

"That's got to be brismil scale," Wilsall whispered.

"No doubt," Shylo replied with awe. Brismil was rare, and expensive even for Nobles. A single brismil scale was rumored to give the wearer super-Terra strength and speed and was nearly impenetrable. The lightweight and maneuverable fit of brismil-plate armor allowed the soldiers who wore it maximum freedom on the battlefield. It was much harder than steel and protected the wearer from extreme heat. Anyone wearing brismil-plate armor could survive a Volurem's blaze and fight the Ignis creatures from the south without worry of being burned. As long as the brismil scale remained in contact with the wearer's bare skin, the soldier was extremely difficult to kill, even for a Volurem infantryman.

"My uncle says that brismil scales come from ancient dragons. They're found most frequently on the Volourium and Old Rhydarian border," Wilsall whispered.

"I heard the armor has magical properties and all it takes to don it is to touch your bare skin to the scale. When you do, it instantly forms to perfectly mold over your entire body," Shylo said.

"My uncle says the scales give the soldiers who wear them increased fighting strength and speed. It would be like a Terra person from the south, like an Agunzi from Volourium, that went north to Zethril, where the gravity is two-thirds lighter than what they're used to fighting in," Wilsall said, grinning with enthusiasm. Judging by his excitement, it was also the first time the Minor Noble had seen brismil-plate armor. "I wonder if he's got a brismil blade? They're said to be forged from dragon bone fossils. Just like the scales, the fangs, claws, and spines that were broken or chipped off a living dragon retained magical power. Apparently, the blade, once drawn, will vanish when dropped and reappear in its sheath. And if the brismil blade comes from the same dragon as the brismil scale, they don't even need to wear the sword to summon it into their hand. It just needs to be within range of the matching scale, but those are exceedingly rare."

Shylo strained but was unable to see that low on the armored soldier without risking being seen. If he had a sword belted to his side, it more than likely was not a dragon's blade.

"I'd wager that's Galterius-Brex's guard. That's the famous Eso standing there next to him," Wilsall said.

"No," Shylo said quietly, but firmly. "Galterius-Brex doesn't part with his brismil. Not the scale or the blade. His soldiers need to earn their own. I read that he doesn't force anyone to wear brismil-plate armor. Not even on the battlefield."

Many rumors surrounded the brismil-plate armor, but one thing everyone understood was the danger of wearing the scale for too long. Rhydan the II, the First King of Apgar, was the first known victim of the armor's costly illness. The cancer resulting from wearing it took him before his time. Other soldiers also fell victim to the painful disease. It wasn't until the last few centuries that the Terra people of Tarmigan learned the cancerous effect of wearing the armor for long periods. The Nobles and high-ranking soldiers lucky enough to have a brismil scale or have the armor issued by their superiors wore it sparingly these days, typically only when they knew they were heading into a potentially deadly encounter.

"Regardless, I bet that soldier has faced the Volurem more than once," Wilsall said.

The thought of fighting people who constantly burned everything made Shylo shiver. As the voices continued to outline the potential for supply shortages if the Volurem made it this far north and their need to issue more soldiers to the south, Shylo's attention piqued when he heard a deep, distinctly feminine voice mention his hometown.

"Reports have been coming into Florens stating new columns of smoke are cropping up more regularly from across the Fringe Waters," the woman said.

"Let the ashen Volurem burn their land right up to the water's edge. It makes no difference to the Empire," another responded.

"Spotting embers have the potential to float across the Fringe and into Rhydenar-controlled land," a different woman replied.

"They wouldn't make it all the way to Apgar. The embers die when they reach an altitude high enough to float north. I've never heard of anything near the surface blowing this far up from the South. Volourium draws surface winds from the north, driving the elemental forces to extremes in the equatorial regions. But like you said, if spotting embers make it high enough in the atmosphere to drift north, they extinguish," Galterius-Brex replied.

"We're all aware of your experience in Volurem behavior, but how do you explain the burning in other Old Rhydarian states, Saypo and Nandan? We must send more legions to protect the Fringe Barrier," a man Shylo couldn't see said.

"Cracks forming in the Empire, that's how," Galterius said. "Local widebacks want to regain control."

Shylo frowned, never having heard the term 'wideback.' He understood when the woman with the deep voice asserted, "They prefer to be called Agunzi, Galterius."

"To ash with that," a nagging male voice said. "The southern Terra people know they're better protected under the Rhydarian Empire."

"They would be, if the Rhydarian Army was supporting them," Galterius said.

"The Empire supplies support to its borders from the western coast, across the southern imperial states, to the eastern shores," the woman said.

"They certainly pay for it, but do they actually see any legion support?" Galterius asked.

"That's treasonous talk, Eso King," a man said.

"I've devoted my life to fighting for this Empire," Galterius spat.

"Then what are you suggesting?" the woman asked.

"That we send an entire division to the southern border at the Western Fringe. And another to the south-central border. The Imperial States of Saypo and Nandan. Give the Agunzi tribes who live there our support where the border wall needs the most protection. This season is already shaping up to be a scorcher, and the Navy can hold off the coasts until end of spring," Galterius responded without hesitation.

"Sending that many legions south will delay the supply chains across land to the ports," a man said.

"Without a sturdy military defense, there won't be any cross-country supply chain," Galterius said.

"We can at least run numbers with our Zethrillian counterparts," another man said.

"Do you need to run everything by them? You know they can't fight and most have never been south of Perdigon. They don't have the experience to make an informed decision," Galterius said.

"Need I remind you that I am standing right here," the woman with the deepest voice said.

Shylo wondered which Zethrillian was on the Senate floor.

"Maybe it's time we sent one of your kind south. Test the theory that what a Zethrillian lacks in physical strength they make up for with increased intelligence," the venomous male voice said.

"Was that a threat directed at Isik?" Galterius asked.

"Put your petty differences aside. You've made your point, High Commander. The Emperor will make the final decision. Thank you for your time," a man said, speaking for the first time to the group.

Shylo suddenly understood that this must be the Imperial Defense Committee. He waited with Wilsall until the sounds of footsteps exited the Assembly Chamber and the doors closed behind them.

"I can't believe we just saw a soldier wearing brismil-plate armor," Wilsall said, rising from behind the bench seats.

"Who cares about the brismil, did you hear what they were talking about? The Empire is fracturing. The Volurem could burn farther north into our lands."

"So? The Senate has this argument every year at the beginning of fire season. It's nothing to worry about," Wilsall said.

"What about the crops? Everyone knows the best cropland is along the Old Rhydenar and Volourium border. If the fire burns the crops, they won't grow back. We'll have no food," Shylo said.

"This isn't something you or I need to worry about. We're too low-ranking to make a difference. We're safe in Perdigon, so come to the Canteen, drink a few bottles of sizzle, and maybe you'll finally work up the courage to make a move on Ismay. That would at least prove to everyone that you weren't just making it up about sleeping with that Eso girl," Wilsall said.

Shylo burned with anger. He would not be made a fool of by Wilsall, not again. Shylo only lied about going all the way with the older Eso girl in the Novi trainees because he knew Wilsall wouldn't bother to go asking her about it.

"Okay. I will," Shylo said through gritted teeth. They left the Senate Assembly Chamber by walking down the balcony stairs, across the Center Rotunda, and passing through the front doors. Dusk colored the sky above Perdigon's massive urban sprawl. The horizon glowed violet as the orange hue of the setting sun sank beyond the Maelstrom Ocean to the west.

"Hey Wilsall. Don't spend all of your allowance before I get there," Shylo teased as the two Penti classmates parted ways.

DEATH'S BELLS

The Day of the Emperor's Death

Shylo entered House Didimo's darkened villa. He stopped to adjust his grip on the loose parchment he'd collected. Instantly, he noticed the absence of the Didimo Guardsmen who usually glared at him judgmentally. The abandoned courtyard lacked the villa's daily hubbub just before supper was to be served. Normally in the evening, at least one visiting harquice-drawn carriage stood in the Senator's courtyard, while an Eso servant tended to the four-legged equine to keep it from grazing on the gardens. Slaves typically could be seen foraging in the raised bed gardens, hunting for fresh ingredients for the Senator's supper.

Shylo hesitated, funneling his attention to each of his senses. The hairs on the back of his neck stood up. None of the peristyle lumistone columns surrounding the courtyard glowed. Just one room on the second floor was lit with the soft yellow lumistone light. A light breeze tickled his face; he realized that he didn't smell any food cooking on sunstones in the nearby kitchen.

The courtyard appeared to be empty, though Shylo couldn't see into every cranny in the darkness. He listened for movement of the staff and slaves. He heard none. Even Didimo's family quarters on the second floor opposite the courtyard entrance offered no chatter. The only noise he heard was a faint hissing from the sunstones simmering water in the bathhouse.

Shylo heard distant voices of jubilation from neighboring villas on the lower west side of Capitol Hill, above the wealthy Eso homes that circled the Noble class neighborhoods. Since first arriving in Perdigon half a rotation ago, Shylo had never seen House Didimo so quiet. Something about the entire estate seemed off to him. Worried, he hustled to the right, cutting across the gravel courtyard. He passed the first several lumistone pillars that propped up the clay-shingled roof covering the peristyle walkway. Shylo continued, sandals scuffing the stone slab path as he swiftly passed the Penti and Novi living quarters. He stopped at the third plain wooden door, the Medi living quarters. The shutters on the window to the left of the door were closed. He saw no lumistone light through the cracks. Shylo rapped on the door, announcing his presence.

While he waited for someone to answer, he continually checked over his shoulder, taking in the desolate villa. Across the courtyard and beyond the adjacent peristyle, Shylo examined the servants' rooms. No soft yellow light glowed through the cracks in the closed shutters there either. While its residents often spent late nights at the

Canteen, the servants' quarters had never been this dark this soon after sundown, and he'd never seen the courtyard and entryway empty of lightly armored guards assigned to protect the villa and its community.

As thoughts of what Wilsall warned Shylo during their first week of Penti training leeched into his mind, he brushed aside the idea of the Noble Houses playing a deadly game of political control behind closed doors. House Didimo didn't have any outspoken rivals as far as Shylo knew. And if they were being *taken care of,* as Wilsall had phrased it, Shylo assumed the aggressor Noble House wouldn't go after the slaves, servants, and trainees. Yet there was no sign of anyone at the Didimo Villa.

Did I miss something important? Shylo wondered. He'd just been in personal contact with Senator Rembert Didimo-Kai. A matter as important as the clearing out of the entire villa's residents, staff, and slaves should've warranted mentioning. *I wonder if the Senator took his family, the older students, and his servants to another villa?* Shylo wondered. *They must be at another social function,* he convinced himself. That might explain why Didimo took the House Guard with him, to protect so many people. Certainly no low-ranking Eso, or Penti trainee for that matter, should expect to represent House Didimo at a social gathering. It would explain why the Senator decided to give him his task of retrieving supplies. To make him feel needed. If that were the case, Shylo wasn't so foolish to see past it. *But where are the slaves?* he wondered, espying their darkened shutters. *They must already be asleep in their bunks,* he decided. *And any remaining servants are taking advantage of their night off.*

When no one answered at the Medi trainees' room, Shylo shifted to the next door, closer to the entrance. A single soft yellow light shining within the cracked shutter panel settled his nerves and confirmed his suspicions that House Didimo was attending a social function in force. After he knocked twice, the door opened.

"What in the flaming ash do ya want, Penti?" the older teen girl asked with unexpected aggression.

He swallowed hard. Shylo recognized her as belonging to House Didimo, but he didn't know her name. The New Rhydarian teen had answered the door in her low-cut undergarment. Shylo struggled to avoid staring at the trainee's exposed cleavage. "Senator Didimo-Kai asked me," he started, his speech slowing slightly as his eyes drifted down. "To return these materials to Medi Kinsey," he finished.

"Do I look like Medi Kinsey to you? Is this the Medi quarters?" the New Rhydarian girl asked. The young woman facing Shylo stood a full hand shorter than him. Her hair was longer than styles worn by most fashionable New Rhydarian women. Her black curls crowded the door-way. She wore a low-cut, sleeveless, white undergarment of simple design that hung loosely around her full-figured body, ending a few finger-widths above her knees.

"Medi Kinsey isn't in his quarters. None of the Medi are," Shylo said, forcing himself to stare above the older girl to be polite. Shylo guessed the Novi trainee to be at least two rotations older than he was, making her eighteen or nineteen.

"And you expect me to believe Didimo-Kai gave ya a direct order? Hang on, I know who you are," she said.

Shylo lowered his gaze to show her the copper bracelet the Senator gave him, unintentionally allowing his eyes to drift past her face. The older teen broke his concentration,

"What are ya looking at, Penti? Never seen a woman in a smock before?"

Shylo averted his attention again, peering at the door frame.

"Don't you like it?" she asked, suddenly changing her voice to a pleasant pitch.

From his peripheral vision, Shylo could see her arching her back slightly and leaning forward with her shoulders pinched together. He didn't have any opportunity to express his interest romantically with any of the young men or women from his hometown before coming to Perdigon. There were several people his age he found attractive, but he'd never worked up the courage to say anything to them other than a passing, hello. Most of his fellow Penti trainees were pleasing to the eye, but one captured his attention more than the others. A female. Seeing this young woman now confirmed his preference in physical attraction. Seeing her so exposed and standing right in front of him.

Shylo couldn't help it. He looked at her, all of her.

For an instant, she cracked a devious smile, her teeth bright in contrast with her dark skin. Her smile turned into a snarl. "Who told ya you could look at me like that?"

"I'm sorry," Shylo said in a panic. "I..., I didn't mean to."

"Didn't mean to what, lie to your Penti friends about sleeping with Jexsanna?" she accused.

Shylo blinked, stepping away from the Novi's room.

"Didn't think word got out, did ya?" she said, snatching the quills from Shylo's loosened grip.

He flinched, expecting the older teen to strike him, though she didn't. She took the stack of parchment too, leaving him with the bracelet.

"And now you're standing there, lying to me about the

Senator giving you a direct order so you can look at me in my underwear. How would you like it if I told my Novi classmates that I wanted a taste of what Jexsanna got, but I was gravely disappointed?" she asked threateningly.

Shylo stammered, backing farther away from her.

"I could tell them all how small, quick, and unpleasant it was. What would your Penti girls think about ya then?" she taunted.

Shylo's back-peddling turned into what he did best when faced with a physical threat. What he'd always done when bullied in Florens. He ran from her. Shylo didn't understand how word had gotten out about his fib. The only reason he told Wilsall about it was to shut him up and get him to stop his teasing. He hadn't intended for his lie to be shared and discredit the Novi girl. Shylo didn't stop to change tunics or grab his cloak from his room. From his point of view, he'd completed the orders by returning supplies to House Didimo. As for the bracelet, he secured it onto his own wrist for safekeeping. It would give him a reason to have another encounter with the Senator the following day. Now he ran for the exit.

Skidding in the gravel before the green double doors, Shylo pulled open the right side. He chanced a glance back at the Novi quarters. The girl's door was closed. The villa seemed as quiet as it had been before and that's when he noticed it. The door on the Kai's second-story living quarters stood ajar. A blue light, bluer and brighter than that of the moon, shone through the crack. It was unlike any light he'd ever seen. The crack in the open door cast a thin ray of blue light onto the wooden deck overlooking the courtyard and the row of columns below. To confirm the oddity, Shylo glanced over the villa roof. The moon still lay below the Shield Mountains, having yet to rise and span the night sky. This blue light seemed entirely out of place. Shylo thought he should see what was caused it.

"Shylo?" he heard a feminine voice say from across the street.

Shylo stood in the villa entrance, halfway in, halfway out of its privacy walls. He turned to see the tall girl who'd captured most Penti trainees' attention, Ismay Ovando-Kai. He quickly closed the forest green door, fearing that if the Novi girl from House Didimo saw Shylo with a female, she would come running to spill the lies she'd threatened to spread about him.

"What are you doing this far north of Capitol Hill?" she asked, gathering up the extra fabric of her long gown and rushing across the gravel street.

"This is House Didimo," Shylo said, thumbing at the symbol painted on the exterior of the double doors, the three pine trees with long black trunks.

"Oh, of course. I forgot Senator Didimo-Kai was of the Third Noble Class like most in this neighborhood," Ismay said. She let her purple velvet gown fall past her ankles again.

Shylo hadn't seen Ismay wearing a formal Noble-woman's dress before. She always wore purple, as it displayed her wealth and was the primary color of House Ovando. Typically, she wore a long tunic, cropped to mid-shin in the front with a longer sort of train dropping to the ground in back. Tonight, though, she wore a full purple gown made of lightweight velvet. The angled neckline and waist belt were trimmed in a copper-colored stitching. From her chest to her navel, the front of the dress had an argyle pattern that included lighter shades of purple outlined with the same copper stitching. Her wavy black hair was similar in length to Shylo's, mid-neck, but where his hung naturally to each side with a part down the middle, one side of her hair was pinned back. Shylo thought it looked somewhat like the hairstyle Zethrillian people commonly wore, shaved on one side. Ismay's sleeves covered her arms, and she wore matching purple leather gloves. Her round face and the shallow V cut in her dress were all that exposed her skin.

"Walk with me," Ismay said, taking hold of his arm.

Shylo silently cursed himself for not offering the young Noble his arm before. The ways of a gentleman were not something Shylo grew up learning in the port town of Florens. Shylo attempted to make small talk, "I'm surprised to see you, Ismay. I thought you would be at the Canteen with Wilsall and the others by now."

"When we are in public, you will address me by my full name with the honorific title accompanying a Noble woman," she said, looking at a passing a carriage transporting a Senator and his much taller Zethrillian advisor.

"Sorry, Ismay Ovando-Kai," Shylo corrected. She was the only Noble in their cohort of Penti trainees, albeit a low ranking Fifth Class Noble.

"Penti Ovando-Kai is just fine, thank you," Ismay corrected him.

Shylo inhaled deeply, thinking the distinction was meaningless when the two of them were alone, walking up the hill toward the Canteen.

"Isn't Capitol Hill magnificent at night?" Ismay said.

"It truly is, Penti Ovando-Kai," Shylo said, staring ahead at the softly illuminated stone buildings crowning the highest point in the capital city. Most of the Imperial buildings had impressive facades lit by lumistones built into their decorative columns. Several, including the Senate Chamber at the base of the hill, were capped with massive domed roofs. From anywhere in the city, one could see the Imperial Palace perched at the top of the hill. The enormous white structure, with its granite foundation and limestone walls, glowed brightly. All four sides of the three-story rectangular palace were lit by the special illuminating columns and archways. The Imperial Palace represented the pinnacle of Rhydenar's political power. Simply being invited to the palace was a dream Shylo one day hoped to achieve.

Ismay squeezed Shylo's arm, "I say, isn't it magnificent!" she repeated.

Shylo frowned slightly. This was the major issue he took with Ismay's personality. She came from a very wealthy family of Perdigon Nobility and expected to be treated as such. By repeating the comment about Perdigon's iconic Capitol Hill, she was fishing for a compliment. "Only as beautiful as the up-and-coming Noblewoman who graces the glowing streets with her presence," he said, stealing most of the line from a work of fiction he'd recently finished reading.

"You're too kind, Eso," she said with a hint of scorn.

Frustrated by his bad luck, Shylo asked, "I've never seen you in this neighborhood before. Were you attending a party with the rest of House Ovando?"

"No. I don't like attending my father's functions. I was following his lead... Never mind."

"Your father's lead?" Shylo asked.

"It's nothing," she said.

"I only ask because usually after training or when you leave the Canteen you walk into the western villas, not north. And when I couldn't find anyone at the Didimo villa, I assumed there must be some important party underway nearby. I've never seen the villa so quiet," Shylo said, looking back over his shoulder at the sparsely populated street they'd walked down.

"I wouldn't know anything about what the Didimo household or any of its associated members are involved with," Ismay said defensively.

"If I offended you, Penti Ovando-Kai, I didn't mean to," Shylo said.

"Shylo, it's not your fault," she said in a remorseful tone. "I haven't been thinking straight since my father left on the overland supply mission with the Emperor's nephew, Benton Querci-Akai."

"But High Noble Benton hasn't returned. You said you were following your father's lead, I thought you were going to continue, but you trailed off," Shylo said.

"You're right, they are still beyond Perdigon's walls. Tonight was their expected arrival, but it seems they've been delayed." Ismay straightened as another carriage carrying a Senator's advisors and interns passed. She whispered, "I was following his lead, by acting on my own. That's why I'm alone on the north side. You see, our family owns several landholdings throughout Perdigon. With my father's delay, I was taking the initiative of a Kai and checking on the state of the villa that is in my name."

"Of course," Shylo said. As a Fifth Class Noble, she obviously owned a guard as well. He didn't know why she was out by herself and if she was checking on her villa, she should've been on the south side of the slopes surrounding Capitol Hill. It seemed like she was hiding something. At the very least, her explanation seemed wanting.

And why get so dressed up to check on something in person that a letter or servant could easily do for her? he wondered.

Shylo decided against pressing her on the matter. If he

wanted to have any chance at forming a more intimate relationship with Ismay, he shouldn't question her.

"What was it you said you father does?" Ismay asked, turning the conversation away from her affairs.

"He's a tanner, but he used to be in the army," Shylo said.

"So, your family has landholding?" Ismay asked.

"No. Both my parents are Eso. Mother was an accountant before she started bookkeeping for the tannery and, with my father unable to complete his service in the army, he didn't qualify for the landholding or the salary legionnaires receive after their twenty years," Shylo said.

"How was your father able to start a tannery without land?" Ismay asked.

"Legionnaires who are honorably discharged, as he was, are able to apply for a grant to start their own business. As he was still able to use his hands and seeing the need for another tanner in a port town like Florens, he received the grant, bought a building, and started the business," Shylo said.

"What simple lives you Esos lead. I sometimes envy not having to bear the weight of governing responsibilities," Ismay replied.

Shylo hesitated to form a response and did his best to continue talking cordially as they walked from the suburban villa neighborhood toward the increasingly crowded streets buffering Capitol Hill.

"Fresh shaves here. Get your scruff scraped and buffed for only a square piece," a stout muscular man called at them in a thick Agunzi accent. The southerner had reddish-orange skin, glowing orange eyes, and lacked any of the Agunzis' famously red hair on his rounded head. Ismay clung tighter to Shylo's arm as they passed the barbershop.

"I wouldn't let that wideback hold a razor to my neck. He might flex a finger and my head would end up on the floor," Shylo said to Ismay.

She chuckled at the remark. The Terra people from the south, though stout, were physically stronger than the Rhydarians of Old and New Rhydenar. Trusting one to perform the delicate business of a single-razor shave wasn't something Shylo would ever risk.

"Hot baths. Steam rooms. Clean your filthy bodies here," a New Rhydarian woman called from an archway leading to a dimly lit atrium.

The smell of sunstone-fried meat sizzling in spiced sauces drew Shylo's attention. The street vendor stood behind a wooden cart weighted down with the protective masonry required to keep the sunstone he cooked on from lighting the cart on fire. Fires were outlawed in the Empire as fires were what summoned the Volurem. Fire acted as a gateway for the enemy to use, transporting them out of Volourium and anywhere a flame took hold.

A tall man stood over the people crowding around the food stand. "Borca, done three ways," he shouted, his northern accent rising over the noisy street. The man pointed his long finger at Ismay and Shylo, "You two look hungry. Come buy this meat and add some muscle to those skinny bones. I have good lean protein right here, freshly harvested in the Shield Mountains."

Shylo slowed, his mouth salivating from the pungent aroma of freshly cooked red meat. Borca was a much smaller animal than the protein Shylo was raised on. He hadn't yet had the opportunity to try the mountain rodent. Animal protein was a staple in Shylo's diet but mongodo was more common than borca in Shylo's household, as mongodo hide was widely used in the empire.

Shylo's father, however, claimed borca offered a truer flavor of red meat than the rangeland animals he was raised on.

Ismay yanked on his arm, pulling Shylo away from the food cart. "You're not hungry?" he asked, skipping to keep up with her.

"I don't eat anything with fur," Ismay said.

Your under-tunic is made from a blend of borca wool and annoa cotton, and they don't ranch borca. Anything with their fur comes from those that are hunted, Shylo thought. He kept the notion to himself as he wanted to continue spending time with Ismay.

"Many Nobles are trying this diet. We mostly eat grains, root vegetables, tree nuts and fruits," she said. "I get my protein from the many varieties of fish caught in Brism Bay. But not anything with fur, especially borca. They're too cute, with those big eyes and little pink noses. Someday I'll have one as a pet."

Shylo tuned her out, thinking, *Most people in Perdigon eat what they can afford. Not many can afford to keep a potential meal as a pet.*

Rounding the street corner, Shylo and Ismay arrived at the Perdigon Hill Canteen. It was a long, low wooden building, two stories shorter than every other wood and brick structure below the east side of Capitol Hill. After moving to the capital, it didn't take Shylo long to learn the Perdigon Hill Canteen was the preferred drinking and eating establishment for any aspiring political trainee. Futures were made or destroyed by the connections one made during late nights at the Canteen. Shylo saw that the wide covered deck out front was swarming with Medi and Novi trainees, though he didn't see any of his Penti class-mates among the crowd. Usually when it was this busy, the

Penti trainees confined themselves to the tables near the back of the canteen.

Once they were within view of the Canteen, Ismay let go of Shylo's arm. She smiled at several older teens who wore black Novi belts around their short tunics. They created a gap for her to enter. Shylo hustled to stay in the narrow eddy created in her wake. The sounds of youthful shouting over one another filled Shylo's ears even before they entered the dimly lit building. The smell of sweat mixed with spilled sizzle, wine, and mead stung his nose. Across the packed room, Shylo saw his fellow Penti classmates at their usual table near the far wall. Normally, Shylo had to wind his way through the rowdy crowd to get through to his friends, but with Ismay, dressed as she was, the crowd parted for her. It was the first time Shylo made it the entire way through without having anyone spill a drop of liquid or a scrap of food on his tunic.

When they finally reached their friends, Shylo picked up on the vocal argument Wilsall was having with an older Novi. After realizing that the loudest of the shouting on this end of the canteen was coming from his friend and the older trainee, Shylo attempted to calm Wilsall.

"Will," Shylo said, planting himself directly in front of his classmate. Wilsall attempted to focus lazily on Shylo. He swayed, his mouth half open, ready to continue his shouting match with the trainee.

"And you can take that to the Treasury," Wilsall said, ignoring that Shylo was standing between them.

"Wilsall, what are you doing? He's a Novi," Shylo said.

"Shy-shy," Wilsall said, suddenly seeing him for what seemed like the first time. "I was just talking about you."

The scent of mead thick on his breath slapped Shylo's senses. "Scorched earth, how much drink have you had?"

"Only enough sizzle to stand up for my Penti brother. Go on Shy, tell this Novidiot that you bedded one of his Eso classmates," Wilsall said, loud enough for Ismay and everyone else around them to hear.

Shylo felt his heart sink deep within him at the same instant that he felt a firm hand grip his shoulder. He cringed as he turned to face the much stronger Novi. Shylo was in no position to argue with the older trainee. He glowered at Shylo; the Novi's dark face creased with hard lines as he waited for Shylo to say something. It was too crowded for Shylo to run. He'd have to speak, but he had a feeling that no matter what he said, he was going to feel knuckles striking his face soon.

The older trainee stood with his right arm cocked and ready to strike when Ismay put a gentle hand on the older boy's muscular arm. His eyes flickered, then he loosened his grip when he recognized who she was.

"Penti Ovando-Kai," he said, addressing her correctly.

Ismay smirked at Shylo, then gave her attention to the Novi trainee. "I'm sure whatever issue my fellow Penti classmates have raised is not of great concern to you."

"Pardon me, Ismay Ovando-Kai, this one is a liar," he said, pointing to Wilsall. "I want him and that one," he said, pointing at Shylo, "to apologize."

"I won't," Wilsall said, taunting the older boy.

The Novi flexed at Wilsall, forcing him to lean away from the potential hazard, but the older trainee did not strike. Ismay still gripped the Novi's left arm.

"Penti Sarapio-Ai is many things," Ismay started. "In some cases, he fits the description you just offered, but it is not his honor we're questioning. It is Penti Shylo Conserra's. If he says he bedded a Novi Eso, then you should be worried about your own reputation among the Novi trainees. It doesn't look good for an -Ai of any degree to be out-played by a Penti Eso."

"The Eso is lying. He's never even spoken with the girl he claims to have had sex with," the other teen said.

"Why don't we just clear this up for everyone?" Ismay said. "Shylo, did you lie to everyone about sleeping with the Eso girl as this Novi claims? Or are you really deserving of the attention the available Penti trainees will give you when they hear of it?"

Shylo studied her expression. He hadn't expected her response. She was smiling, and if he understood her correctly; she thought he was more desirable now after hearing he'd been with an older girl. He looked at the older teen, who ground his jaw, looking like he was ready to duel Shylo over the claim. "Well, the secret's out now, isn't it?" Shylo said. "I didn't lie about Jexsanna."

The Novi boy pulled his arm away from Shylo's shoulder. Before he could make his move, Ismay said, "I am a Fifth Class Noble of Perdigon and I forbid you, Novi-Ai, to commit an act of violence against my fellow Penti trainees when they have delivered the ugly truth."

The other Penti classmates who'd stopped their chatter to watch the argument's outcome erupted in cheers. Shylo saw that their disturbance had caused more than half of the canteen to notice their celebration. The Novi obeyed Ismay's command. It didn't matter that Ismay was a Penti, or younger and less experienced. She was a Fifth Class Noble; she outranked this Minor Noble.

As the older Novi disappeared into the crowd, Shylo felt a wave of guilt wash over him. Wilsall embraced him in a hug and forced a half-drunk bottle of sizzle into his hand. Shylo felt sick with himself, but he did not let them see, especially Ismay. He would not tell her the truth. Shylo pushed the worry to the back of his mind by drowning it out with the remaining mead. He continued mixing alcohols, bottle after bottle, late into the night.

Hours later, through his drunken haze, Shylo somehow found his way back to the Didimo villa. He didn't stop to wonder why the green doors were open, or about the puddle of dark liquid in the courtyard. Shylo only stopped when he saw the frizzy-haired Novi girl from House Didimo. He almost tripped over her lying on her side out in the courtyard, wearing only her smock. Shylo mumbled a greeting, thinking it odd that she was sleeping in the open between columns. He swayed over her as he stooped to shake the girl awake. She didn't move. Shylo looked left, down the rest of the courtyard and at the atrium. More motionless bodies dotted the gravel square, their blood spilled out in puddles, soaking into the ground. Shylo blinked, hoping he was caught up in a drunken nightmare. Lumistones illuminated all rooms in the villa. Shylo heard men's voices from somewhere inside. He looked down at the teen girl with a hauntingly sober realization. The puddle he had stepped in was her blood. She was dead, as were the others. Fear flooded Shylo as a distinctly hollow-sounding voice barked something indistinct. The shout was followed by a blood-curdling scream coming from Senator Didimo-Kai's living quarters. This shout of death was masked by bells tolling from the Palace at the top of the hill. The bells only sounded from the Palace when the Volurem attacked or when an Emperor died.

Shylo ran. He ran as fast as he could until that voice and the deathly scream that followed faded from his ears, but not the bells. The bells continued to ring.

THE NEW OBSERVER

THE DAY OF THE EMPEROR'S DEATH

The solid iron door of the narrow room creaked open, the sudden splash of afternoon sun momentarily blinding her.

"Number 2841," she heard one of the Masters calling her name from the observation deck as she blocked the direct sunlight with her hand.

Before she'd even stepped out into the arena, she over-heard another person say, "I think you're going to like this fighter even more, High Nobleman." She recognized the low voice as another of the Masters. Instantly, her guard was up. They rarely gathered on the training arena observation deck.

"I don't see how you could possibly top that last perfor-mance," a man's voice she had never heard before

43

responded. Number 2841 surmised this new observer was the reason for this surprise exhibition with the Volurem, those who were born of fire. Though she and the Masters had similar bone and muscle structure to the Volurem, Number 2841 did not burn like the Volurem. The Volurem were a people with charcoal skin, cracked with red magma that glowed from within. The Volurems' bodies sustained constant flame. Volurem could be summoned by flames and move in the fire. Number 2841 and the Masters were not of the fire. They did not emit flames like the Volurem. Number 2841 and the Masters could not be summoned over great distances when a new fire burned into existence. Here at the arena, Number 2841 did as she was trained to do, extinguish all Volurem.

She worked to quell her curiosity about the observer. If the Masters knew she had these thoughts, they would discipline her as they had her once-partner, Number 2759. She felt she could've done more to stop it. She had tried to warn her partner what would happen if he expressed any individuality. Just because they looked like the Masters, didn't mean they were the same as the Masters. However, he hadn't listened to her and the Masters hadn't hesitated in their punishment. After the Masters saw him disobey orders, her partner didn't return from live training. Number 2841 understood; he'd been culled from the group.

Number 2841 did not look up at the observation deck as she walked out of the staging area and into the fighting arena. The stone enclosure walled in a section of forested land to contain the Volurems' flames used in live training exercises. The charred stones near the base of the enclosure spoke to the many bouts they had faced in this place. She and the rest of those like her at the facility were elite fighters, trained specifically for one purpose, killing the Volurem. She stopped several strides away from the base of the wall. Though the question of why the newcomer was there took precedence over readying herself for the fight, Number 2841 knew that way of thinking was wrong. Adhering to the way of life the Masters instilled in her, Number 2841 obeyed and focused solely on the severity of the burnt vegetation before her. She instinctively began gauging which kind of Volurem soldiers were smoldering within the enclosed forest.

Based on the patchy areas where flare-ups scorched the underbrush within the arena, the previous fighter had faced his or her live exhibition round against Volurem foot soldiers. Number 2841 could see that several groupings of trees were blackened where the flame lengths from the Volurem soldiers doubled and tripled in size, crowning into the canopy. Having spent her life training in the arena instantly told her that fire from Volurem foot soldiers in a burn this small wouldn't crown into the canopy, not without high winds, of which there weren't that day. Volurem foot soldiers emitted a shallow, yellow and orange flame. They moved predictably as their behavior was driven by the wind and available fuels. Fire scorching into the canopy in an old-growth stand of trees like the one in this section of the arena indicated that magic had possessed the Volurem foot soldiers.

If there were Volurem soldiers within the confines of this sprawling arena that were possessed, a dragon's heart was the source that conjured the magic into them. All that Number 2841 had ever learned came from the Masters' teaching and previous experience fighting in the arena. Of all the Volurem she had faced, only one type could turn an average-sized flaming soldier into a hulking, blue-flamed goliath. When under the effect of the dragon's heart, these rare Volurem grew two- to three-times larger than the average Volurem foot soldier and didn't move as predictably. These possessed by the elemental magic attacked with pointed directive, manipulated by the dragon's heart. The Masters called the ones who controlled the possessed Volurem with a dragon's heart, Pyrignum.

Number 2841 had been in an arena with a Pyrignum before. She had seen its white flames extending high into the air above its grotesque molten scalp, but she hadn't had the opportunity to fight it. The Pyrignum was unique in that it was the only type of Volurem soldier that could channel magic from a dragon heart. The Masters warned her that the Pyrignum used the dragon heart to influence the surrounding Volurem soldiers' behavior. A Pyrignum protected itself near the heart of the inferno, using the dragon heart to turn average-sized foot soldiers into formidable enemies. Volurem soldiers that were possessed by a Pyrignum's magic were much less predictable and more difficult to kill.

Number 2841 had only defeated a handful of these Volurem soldiers possessed with magic in a live exhibition but had not had the chance to defeat the Volurem conjuring the magic. Based on the fire scarring she saw now, Number 2841 knew this was her chance to prove her worth to the Masters, to show them that she wasn't like her once-partner. She wanted to show them she wasn't a disappointment, as they had said she would be. She would show them that her infrequent disobedient thoughts were not a hinderance to her training or her abilities as they had been to her once-partner.

The sun beat down on the forested fighting arena. The

day's heat meant low humidity, prime conditions for the Volurem to thrive.

Number 2841 drew her willow-leaf saber and started toward the edge of the burn. As the wind picked up, she stopped to look past the treetops within the enclosure. The canopy arched toward the center where the forest was most dense; a likely place where a Pyrignum would hide. A less practiced soldier might not have noticed the sudden draw of wind that came next, but Number 2841 had trained her entire life to defeat the Volurem. Fighting the Volurem was all she knew. Suddenly the forbidden questions percolated into Number 2841's thoughts again. The Masters would kill her if they noticed any suggestion of free will. She knew that she had to follow her orders, and never seek validation from those on the observation deck. Yet, she wanted to show the new observer how well she could perform. That she was the best of those the Masters had molded through specialized training. That she was different. She was Number 2841.

There it is, she thought, espying the column of smoke rising above the canopy. She darted into the forest, prepared to face everything the Volurem fire touched.

"Though he assisted in creating vegetation suitable as the food source the lesser dragons needed to survive, Tourome didn't trust the lesser dragons in their clutch. They needed his and the other two Creators' help to continue living in this world they were creating. Tourome grew increasingly weary of them. And in the end, they paid the price with their blood." – The Dracolyth

THE LAST ORDER

The Day of the Emperor's Death

Standing safely atop the arena walls, they watched her reaction as she studied the burn scar from the preceding fight.

"It's just as you described," High Noble Benton said. "This one does appear quite unique. Not as strong looking as the other two though. Those slaves were much more muscle bound. I'll be eager to see if she's as good as you say."

"You will see, High Nobleman, that Number 2841 is not like the others here at the training facility. And it is not for her unique birthmarks," the arena master replied.

Number 2841's straight, ash-colored hair fell halfway

down her shoulder blades. While this white hair was the same color as the others being trained at the facility, Benton could see her unusual black skin was disrupted with blotchy red markings. "That's what those are? I assumed it was burn scarring," High Noble Benton said.

"You will find out soon, this one does not burn," the master replied.

Benton leaned forward in his chair, excited to hear confirmation of what he suspected. Other than her strange skin and straight white hair, she didn't look like anything he had expected. Like Benton and the masters at the training facility, Number 2841 fit within the range of average Rhydarian height, just over seventeen hands tall. Though she had the stature and build of a Rhydarian person, she didn't appear to look like either the New Rhydarians or Old Rhydarians.

She almost looks more like the Volurem, the High Noble noted after having seen what the Rhydarian Empire's enemy looked like up close for the first time.

After a brief hesitation upon walking out into the enclosure, she sprinted into the walled-in forest. The High Nobleman and his companions had witnessed only two live rounds before Number 2841 entered the secure training arena. The forest remained mostly intact. Benton, High Noble and nephew of the Emperor, had come to find out what his Imperial Majesty's coin and efforts cloaked in supreme secrecy had produced.

In a matter of moments, black plumes billowed from the heart of the arena as the Pyrignum used its dragon heart to fuel the fires of the Volurem, turning some of the burning foot soldiers into blue-flamed possessed Volurem. The High Noble felt a thrill course through his body at the sight of blue fire shooting skyward among the red-orange flames now alight in the green forest canopy. He waved aside a warning issued by the arena master and ran across the rampart, away from the observation deck where the two arena masters stood with his guard. Benton trusted his hired guardsmen to ensure that as a High Noble of Perdigon, he could leave the observation deck if he desired.

"High Noble," one of the masters called after him. Benton didn't want them to know his name in case he needed to deliver the last order. If it didn't go as he planned, Benton didn't want the rumor of him going behind the Emperor's back to reach Perdigon, the Rhydarian Empire's capital. "Do not leave the observation deck. I cannot ensure your safety. Please," the master pleaded loudly.

Benton paid no attention. He was the Emperor's nephew. He needed to see this mutant person, Number 2841, fighting in plain sight. Only then would he be able to make his decision about whether to issue *the last order*, as he thought of it. The masters claimed Number 2841 was the best fighter at their facility, regardless of the facts that her sparring partner had allegedly shown affection toward her and that she'd admitted to occasionally having disobedient thoughts.

From atop the thick granite wall trapping the fighters inside the arena, Benton followed Number 2841's movements. She ran with super-Terra speed, a pace faster than any Rhydarian; of that, he was sure. Number 2841 was just disappearing from Benton's line of sight when the rising column of smoke collapsed. The imploding column sent a roaring burst of wind in all directions, snapping off the tops of the trees and sending debris flying. Atop the towering ramparts, the gust nearly knocked the High Noble over. Benton braced himself against the stone. The brick wall vibrated from the intense force. Through the smoky haze below, Benton spotted dark-bodied figures. The Volurems' ember essence constantly shifted, their charcoal bodies glowing with bright reds as they shimmered in the flames. The Volurem soldiers oscillated between heights of sixteen to eighteen hands, their Terra-people-like figures maintained by the flames. But Benton understood these creatures were not people. They burned as they ran through the underbrush. Their fire ignited every living plant within reach. Their bodies, entirely immersed in or made up of fire, provided Benton with visual confirmation as to why his people called the Volurem infantry, the Engulfed. Though Benton had already watched the two previous fighters face Volurem, he had not been able to see the exhibition clearly through the thick foliage. Now, outside the safety of the observation deck, he could see them clearly. He could feel the heat rising from their wild fire, confirming every horrifying rumor Benton had ever heard about these demon fire people.

The forest floor glowed orange and yellow with ground fire as the Volurem advanced through the undergrowth. High Nobleman Benton Querci-Akai had never understood the Volurems' combat strategy. Being a distant third in line for the Emperor's throne of Rhydenar, Benton's Imperial tutors discouraged him from participating in the brutality of combat and instead encouraged him to learn how the Volurem fought. Benton did everything he could to skip his lessons. He was Akai, the honorific Rhydarians assigned to the members of the Imperial family. If he wanted to wage war, he could buy a legion like many of the Nobles and Senators of Perdigon did. Scholastic stimulation wasn't something that kept Benton's attention for long. He preferred more physical virtues. Regardless of his efforts to duck his Akai responsibilities, Benton had learned the Volurem were as predictable as the weather. Apart from the elements, only the possession by a Pyrignum conjuror could direct a Volurem army's course of attack. Seeing the Volurem from above now, Benton was sure they were as simple-minded as the commoners of the Empire and understood nothing of strategy. The Volurem didn't even don armor. They were as wild as their fire's behavior.

These Volurem are savage creatures. Animalistic in every aspect of their being. Subjected to the whim of which way the wind blows with little more thought preoccupying their minds than what they can burn next. Beasts indeed. These things are crude creatures and nothing more, Benton thought.

Smoke now obstructed his view, creating a grey haze that stung his eyes and drew unemotional tears. Benton felt the heat of the fire fight intensify as the smoke rose. He found himself sweating. As he swiped at his brow, Benton saw a naked figure dance among the flaming enemies. Her skin resembled the Volurem, black with red markings, but hers did not glow. Number 2841 moved through the fire as if she were wearing the dragon-scale armor the Rhydarians called 'brismil plate.' The fast-moving female soldier fell each Volurem foot soldier she met. She killed the enemy as though her saber was made of dragon bone and possessed an ancient dragon's magic. Benton could see, however, the glint of metal from the willow-leaf saber, which proved the blade was no brismil blade. The sword was well made steel, and she gained no advanced strength from brismil, yet she still cut the Volurem down and put out their flames as if they were made of Terra flesh. She swung the saber as though it was as light as a feather. With a bounding leap three times farther than a normal Rhydarian could jump, she dispatched a Volurem in one pass. Her blade hewed through the Volurem's thick charcoal neck, dropping his head to the burnt ground. It rolled to the base of the wall before the flames from the creature's face danced out, leaving behind a charred Volurem skull to turn to ash.

Benton longed for Number 2841 to look up at him and see the excitement on his face. He wanted her to know he was impressed, that she scared him with what she and the others like her could do. These mutant soldiers were the reason Benton had come to do what the Emperor couldn't and determine if these new Terra soldiers were a project gone wrong. A sudden increase in fire intensity blasted a jet of blue flames tipped in orange into the air, drawing Number 2841's attention. She faced the blaze as it crowned in the trees. A colossal Volurem soldier, possessed with magic, stood fifty hands tall, three times Number 2841's height and by Benton's estimate, a sixth of the total height of the arena walls. The giant Volurem's muscles flexed, cracking his charred skin, and exposing the molten red underneath. Blue flames flecked with orange rolled off his body and licked the sky over the treetops. He came at Number 2841 with a glossy black, two-handed great sword that was now over half his total size. She charged him with her single-handed, steel, willow-leaf blade. They collided with a flourish of sparks, twisting and folding just out of reach of one another's weapons.

Benton clutched the edge of the rampart with a white-knuckled grip. He saw the looming figure emerging. A second Volurem possessed with magic appeared through the burning timber. Wielding two inky black short swords as long as Number 2841's body, it joined the fighting. Benton thought Number 2841 had finally met her match. She proved him wrong.

The shower of sparks from the Volurem's blades crashing with Number 2841's saber ended in a flurry of twisting blue flames. Number 2841 emerged the victor in her encounter. She stood alive with two Volurem extinguished at her feet. Though Number 2841's body was marred with soot and ash, she was not burned.

Thin trails of smoke rose from the corpses of the defeated Volurem in the arena. The once-green forest ringed by granite walls appeared as a burnt skeleton. From within the scorched timber near the heart of the arena, a bright flame still burned. Benton could see clearly through the black and grey wasteland of the fighting ring. A white flame tipped with blue gave away the Pyrignum's hiding place. Number 2841 stalked through the standing black tree trunks. Hot ash rippled around her feet as she hunted the last Volurem.

Benton's breath caught in his throat as a wall of monstrous creatures made entirely of flame surged through the charred timber. Dragons formed of orange flames, growing larger than the scorched trees. The snarling beasts of fire bore down on Number 2841. The orange and yellow dragons snapped with exposed fangs of pure blue and white fire. While Benton flinched, Number 2841 held her ground. She did not defend herself. Instead, she charged through the flaming beasts, her attention fixed on the white flame of the Pyrignum beyond. The fire rushed over her in the form of gnashing, long-extinct creatures. Benton took a step back, bumping into the brismil-plated chest of his lead guard. The broad-chested man did not speak but pointed to the ashen arena. Every winged monster featured in the flames no longer burned through the black trees. The female fighter, Number 2841, slashed her blade through the orange and red neck of the final Volurem, the Pyrignum. Its white flame snuffed out. She bent down over the surprisingly small Volurem creature.

For something that can use a dragon's heart to possess and influence creatures of the flames, I would've thought it to be much bigger. And perhaps to have horns. Seeing it now, it doesn't seem that intimidating. It's about twice her height, but skinnier. Almost skeletal, Benton thought, feeling somewhat ashamed for having allowed this thing to have haunted his nightmares over a lifetime.

Benton flinched as Number 2841 ripped the glimmering dragon heart from the dead Pyrignum's chest. Number 2841 turned to look up at Benton and his guard for the first time. She raised the glowing opal gem of the dragon heart in her fist high above her head and grinned a gleaming white smile that brimmed with pride.

The test is complete, Benton thought, somewhat disappointed. Number 2841's final display confirmed Benton's suspicions. The mutant Terras bred in this facility had more than the skills necessary to become the Rhydarian Empire's most powerful weapon. *By showing her pride, Number 2841 has proven that she has free will. She hides it well from the arena masters, a little too well though,* he thought.

Benton realized Number 2841 wasn't like the others. She was proof that this new race of Terra people posed a threat to the Rhydarian Empire. She was different than the others and a vision of what they would become. Number 2841 had free will. Benton wouldn't allow it.

Benton Querci-Akai, High Noble of Perdigon and nephew to Emperor Jermanus, nodded to his entourage, signaling for his guard to carry out the last order. The one that would put an end to this secret training facility.

THE SCALED ONE

THE DAY OF THE EMPEROR'S DEATH

Number 2841 held the Pyrignum's source of magic in her hand. The dragon's heart, an opal-colored gem, sparkled, refracting light from the prism's sharp angles. Her chest heaved as she gulped the air, now clearing of smoke. The effort it took to fight more than one Volurem possessed with magic and withstand the Pyrignum's final blast of energy manipulation tired her. Her skin cooled in the ash falling around her. She looked away from the Masters' visitors; those who shared a similar

56

look to her guardians. Soot from her hands smeared across the glimmering dragon heart as she rotated it in her hands. Cooling much faster than her body, the magic gemstone's opal glow faded like the dying flames.

A subtle, short-lived humming drew her attention. A half a breath later she detected the sound of a blade cutting through flesh. Not the sound of a blade crackling through the thick charcoal skin of a Volurem soldier. This hewing slice sounded like the wet hack she heard when Number 2399 failed to defend herself in the last live training, when Number 2841's willow-leaf saber cut the other fighter's side open. She quickly looked up to the wall.

The Scaled One, she thought.

A man wearing the full body metallic gleam of brismil scale now stood among the strangers. Number 2841 had not seen him on the observation deck before.

The Scaled One charged the remaining Master. She couldn't see the other Masters on the rampart or the observation deck anymore. The Scaled One's blade met one of the Master's with the sound of metal striking stone. Then she saw it. The Scaled One now wielded a dragon blade. She knew this put the Master at a grave disadvantage. He didn't have the protection needed to withstand a dragon blade.

Number 2841 stood ankle-deep in ash waiting for one of the Masters to tell her how to react.

How will I obey them if they're dead? she wondered.

The dragon heart in her hand felt cold. She let it fall from her grip. It landed with a hollow thud against the ground, disappearing in the ash.

The Masters fought bravely. One of her Masters killed one of the strangers who attempted to team up with the Scaled One.

Call to me. Tell me to help you, she pled silently.

But the Master couldn't break his focus while trying to fend off the attack of this Scaled One and his white dragon-bone sword.

Suddenly the iron door under the observation deck opened. Another of the Masters appeared. The one who had explained what to do before today's live exhibition with Volurem. "Number 2841, come to me," he commanded.

She sheathed her blade and obeyed as she was trained to do.

When she crossed through the opening in the arena wall, closing the door behind her, the Master said, "Give me the dragon heart."

The dragon heart, no, I dropped it, she thought, just now feeling the absence of the gemstone from her hand. It was out in the ash. After being ripped from the Pyrignum's chest, it had gone cold and no longer felt of any value. Now that it was cold, the dragon heart would be indistinguishable from other stones.

"Number 2841. Give me the dragon heart," the Master repeated.

She showed him her empty palms, blackened from soot.

"To ash with you," he swore, flaring his nostrils.

Number 2841 met this Master's eyes and held his gaze. She sensed his discomfort but did not break eye contact first. She never did. *I can help with the fighting, just give me the order,* she shouted in her mind.

"Put away your weapon and go to your sleeping stall. Wait for a Master's orders," he commanded.

She hesitated, but obeyed, jogging through the dimly lit stone corridor toward the armory.

Why won't they let us help them? she wondered, slowing

as she heard the Master running up the stairs. The distant ring of his sword scraping free from his scabbard sounded before he released a battle cry. The clang of metal on metal rang out, echoing down the stairs and into the stone corridor. Metal-on-metal sword-fighting meant that more than just the Scaled One was attacking. How many, she could not know.

Do as you're ordered and live. Disobey and die, she told herself, repeating the Master's law. Number 2841 continued to follow orders, fighting the will to disobey and attack. As cries of death sounded through the stone corridors from the upper levels, she pinpointed the dull thud of a metal blade meeting the dragon blade. Number 2841 knew the Masters could not stop it. The Scaled One could weather their blows until they grew too tired to defend. He would cut them as easily as the dragon blade snuffed out the Volurem's fire. The dragon blade could, and likely would, kill the Masters with a single touch.

Whose orders do I follow then? she wondered.

Number 2841 faced the opening to the armory. Every weapon and every type of armor she had trained with during what felt like every single waking moment of her eighteen rotations rested in organized racks or hung from the walls. Only one item was currently missing. The one she'd always preferred over the bulky broadswords, the single-hand, willow-leaf saber. Another of the Master's voices let go a death cry.

The uncertainty drove Number 2841 to do something forbidden, something that she knew had resulted in her once-partner being culled from the arena. She decided of her own free will to keep the willow-leaf saber. She turned away from the armory and jogged toward her sleeping stall.

Once inside the rectangular room, she closed the door, locking herself in and the strangers out. She waited by the light of her palm-sized lumistone. The soft yellow light barely filled the stone room, but it was enough to see by. In case the Scaled One came inside.

After a time, the death screams stopped. Silence followed for an uncomfortably long time. Then she heard footsteps. A door creaked on its hinges and, again, she heard the faint wet slide of a blade slicing through flesh. The cadence repeated, this time slightly closer. As the intruders continued murdering the others like her in the training facility, Number 2841 understood it was going to happen to her too. She had no idea why these curly-haired, dark-skinned people were killing everyone. All she'd ever known was life within the walls of these training arenas.

As the door to the next stall squeaked on rusted hinges, she heard dragon-scale armor click on the granite floor.

Number 2842 hit the granite slab next to her sleeping stall. Number 2841 felt the vibrations of his thick corded muscles toppling lifeless to the cold stone floor. Now, dragon-scale armor clicked just outside the door to her stall. The latch twitched, then caught on the lock. She heard the Scaled One hum to himself. She sensed that he knew this was her stall, the one who killed the Pyrignum and looked up at the newcomers atop the walls. With a snap, the latch broke through the lock. The door swung in and banged into the wall. The Scaled One stood in the entrance with black blood dripping from his elongated ivory blade. The rapier guard on his dragon blade was made of a dragon's vertebra. The spine was magically crafted into the blade itself. A twisted collection of tail bones formed a cage-like guard around the pommel. The weapon was designed to kill unnatural beings.

The Scaled One must've seen the saber at her side as he hesitated to advance. When she remained perfectly still, he continued. He pulled back his enormous, single-hand dragon blade. She launched herself at the armored stranger. She hit him fast enough that he was too surprised to react and he dropped his dragon blade. If it hit the ground, she didn't hear it. All she heard was the sound of the Scaled One's body crushing the stranger standing directly behind him, the force from the blow smashing the man's body as the Scaled One collided with the corridor wall.

Number 2841 ran out of the room before the Scaled One could pry himself free from the blood-soaked depression in the wall. The rest of the strangers dotting the corridor stumbled back. Number 2841 saw the open stall doors beyond the strangers, black blood seeping into the hallway. She bolted into the open corridor, running for the nearest exit; not checking to see how close the Scaled One was behind her.

Number 2841 sprinted headlong into the iron gate separating the sleeping stalls from the room with food troughs. The brittle metal broke from the weight of her shoulder, leaving a shard embedded in her skin. She didn't let it slow her because she could hear the Scaled One crashing through the metal opening close on her heels. Number 2841 spotted the way out. The granite slab that sealed the exit to a world beyond the arena walls was open.

Did a Master flee without us? she wondered.

Number 2841 had never seen the opening exposed before. Beyond the thick wall, she saw a forest. It looked just like the forests she fought in during their training in the arenas.

Her keen ears picked up a light vibration that suddenly released within the room. It was the pulse of air sent out by an object as it appeared and hadn't been there a second ago. Without looking, she knew the dragon blade had been summoned into the Scaled One's grip. He was about to attack. Twisting with her saber, Number 2841 blocked a blow directed at her back from the stained dragon blade. The sudden change in momentum sent her stumbling to the side, and she careened uncontrollably through a row of empty wooden food troughs. The Scaled One took advantage of his position, passing up an opportunity to strike her and instead taking a position in front of the exit. His metallic bulk blocked the gap between Number 2841 and the world beyond the arena walls.

She regained her footing and attacked. She blinded the Scaled One with her blows, peppering his dragon blade so fast and hard that he could only defend. She moved through the single-grip sword forms, blending them in random combinations to keep the Scaled One from touching her with his dragon blade. She drove him back, landing several blows to the body. Her steel did not cut through the dragon-scale armor, despite her mutant strength and she knew it wouldn't. That's how it was the time she'd fought the Scaled One in the arena, when she lost. In an attempt to momentarily blind the Scaled One, she struck at his head. He bent to the side and the sharp edge of her steel blade came down on the neck. She felt her steel dig into the scaled armor.

How? she wondered, seeing a thin crack in the scales where her blade struck him.

The hit sent him tripping away from the applied pressure of her sword. The Scaled One stumbled to the side, touching his free hand to his armored neck. Number 2841 didn't hesitate; it wasn't anticipated, but it was the opening she needed.

She bolted through the hole in the wall, darting outside. Just as she now expected, the outside was a mirror image of the forested arena, only without walls. Pointed white peaks rose in the distance to her right and behind her. But the sky and the forest canopy before her extended without stone interruption for as far as her mutant eyes could see. In the far distance, before a strip of dark blue, she saw tiny, pointed structures ringed by stone.

Another facility, she thought. *The Masters there will give me orders.*

Number 2841 didn't let the sensory overload slow her. She spotted the harquice, four-legged short-haired animals that she'd been trained to ride. Only one of the lightly armored strangers stood with the equine animals. The rest of the strangers were still within the arena walls.

The soldier standing with the fifteen-hand-tall animals saw Number 2841 heading directly at him. She saw the broadsword belted to his waist. Luckily for him, the soldier decided against drawing his sword and ran. She grabbed a fist full of the harquice's light brown mane and hopped on. The leather seat strapped around the animal's back fit her build, but the large bags on its side would only slow the harquice in her escape. Number 2841 didn't have time to deal with them right there. She now spotted the Scaled One out of the corner of her eye as he emerged from the opening in the wall. As she encouraged the frenzied harquice to gallop at full speed into the forest, she studied the Scaled One. The color of his brismil plate, the make of his dragon blade, and the line of red blood trickling from the crack in his neck. The cut wasn't a mortal wound. The stranger under the magic armor would not die. He would give chase.

Number 2841 clung to the short-haired animal as it dodged low-hanging branches and jumped over fallen timber. She could feel the stumps where they'd cut away the harquice's wings rubbing against the inside of her legs.

A thought entered her mind, *Whose orders do I follow now that I'm in the outside?*

"As they thrived, the lesser dragons grew in numbers. They used the prime nesting grounds. Centuries passed and The Creators saw their superior magic becoming less important. The lesser dragons were self-sufficient now. With their independence came their greed." – The Dracolyth

A RUDE AWAKENING

S hylo awoke. His head throbbed from the night of excessive drinking. As instantly as the pain hit, so did the nightmare. Bodies littering the Didimo villa. A hollow voice barking an order followed by a penetrating scream from Senator Rembert Didimo-Kai's quarters. The faint voices of men inside the villa; and the bells.

Searching his immediate surroundings, Shylo was consumed with dread. He didn't know where in the city he was. Unfamiliar stucco walls trimmed with dark wood rose up on either side of the narrow gap between buildings where he'd apparently slept. He was on his side, stiff from a night spent on the ground in this alley. Spying through the crack between wooden supply crates that blocked his direct view of the street, Shylo saw the pitched roofline of the townhome opposite the alley. There was nothing but blue sky beyond. As Shylo sat up from the damp claystone foundation, he vaguely remembered positioning the bulky shipping crates to block the alley. He struggled now to remember where he'd gone after fleeing the Didimo villa, but nothing came to mind. The bells started ringing in his head, sending sharp pain into his temples with each toll. His typically quick thinking was bogged down from the alcohol's haze. Only death, the boxes, and darkness came clearly to mind. Seeing the pieces more clearly, Shylo understood what had happened to the people of House Didimo. It was as he first feared upon entering the courtyard before returning the supplies. House Didimo had become the latest victim of a Noble House war. He struggled to think what Didimo could've possibly done to deserve such horrific retaliation. So many more than the Kai had been slaughtered. Servants, the trainees, even slaves were victims of the violent attack. Overwhelming fear that Shylo was being targeted, being hunted for something he had no part in creating set his heart racing again. The Noble House responsible for this deadly invasion might still be hunting him.

Shylo tried to think of a reason that would warrant the bloodshed. The lies he'd told and then retold the night before about the Eso girl, Jexsanna, couldn't have been the motivation for such heinous violence. Shylo wondered if the -Ai, the Novi from the Canteen, had resources enough to commit an attack on a Noble House. Shylo was wearing Didimo colors when he'd lied at the Canteen. But no, someone in the Novi trainee cohort would know better. The repercussions of killing Shylo alone wouldn't be worth the punishment for the crime. The conflict Shylo created with the Minor Noble was personal. If that young man had wanted to act, he would've jumped Shylo on the walk back to the villa and made sure he was still breathing before he left. Besides, the palace bells had been ringing. The House Didimo slave who had collected Shylo off the docks the day he arrived in Perdigon had made it very clear to him that if he ever heard those bells ring, either the city was under attack or the Emperor was dead. Nothing else was important enough to warrant raising the city to its highest state of alarm.

Shylo stood, momentarily pressing into his head with both hands to keep the throbbing from bursting through his skull. When he could stand to open his eyes, he walked to the edge of the alley and stood on his tiptoes. He peered over the boxes at the street beyond. He almost hoped to smell smoke or see Perdigon in chaos, but that was not the case. Shylo didn't recognize the three- and four-story townhouses on this street, but the people were not rushing to arms. They were not fleeing to the port either.

Shylo studied a trio of working Esos. Their straight black hair and grey eyes told Shylo they were Old Rhydarian, two female and one male. They wore shortened, kneelength grey tunics and stockings. Their bloodshot eyes drooped with dark rings. Their slackened jaws and the continual shaking of their heads conveyed a sense of disbelief. The male was speaking vehemently while his gestures implied unanswerable questions. Shylo couldn't hear them, but instinctively knew what they were gossiping about. A Noble's entire villa, family, Senatorial trainees, working staff, and slaves had been slaughtered during the night. That, and the bells of Perdigon had rung.

Seeing that there was no immediate danger of the Volurem burning the capital, or the killers gutting him for wearing House Didimo colors, Shylo emerged from the alley. Judging by the angle of the sun, he was going to be late for his duties as a Penti trainee.

That's not right, though, he thought. Shylo wasn't sure if he could continue. His patron and his patron's entire staff were gone. *What does that mean for my future in the capital?*

Shylo's entire life goal of becoming a Senator's aide hinged on excelling in his Capitol Hill training. He had to go to the Hill and scramble to ensure that his future in the Penti class still existed. If he didn't, the hopes of Shylo's father would be realized. Part of Shylo thought the only reason his father had agreed to let his mother pay the Penti tuition was because he assumed Shylo would fail. After dropping out, the Legions would be waiting for him. Shylo had to seek temporary patronage through one of his friends. Wilsall or Ismay could help him through the rest of the rotation.

Finding new hope to push through his hangover, Shylo climbed over the crates blocking the alley and landed in the street. His sudden appearance from the narrow space between buildings caused some alarm among the trio of Old Rhydarians standing nearby. When they saw that he was just an Eso boy, dirty and stinking from a night at a canteen, they returned to gossiping. Shylo hoped to recognize some familiar sign or business on the street to help him identify where in the massive city he'd hidden. He found no such identifier. He turned right, hoping the uphill angle of the street would lead him closer to where he needed to be. Capitol Hill wasn't the only prominent hill in the city, but it was the tallest. He could gauge where he was by climbing to a decent vantage point.

As he passed the trio of Old Rhydarians, he overheard snippets of their conversation.

"It was a creature, a monstruous thing," he heard the man say.

"She told me it's been lurking on the roads outside the walls for weeks waiting to strike," one of the women said.

"Imagine it, a murderous monster within the walls," the third woman said.

A monster? Shylo wondered. The idea of a monster killing the members of House Didimo didn't sound right to him. He'd heard voices, Rhydarian voices, last night. But if there was a monster within the walls, perhaps it was reason enough to ring the palace bells.

Climbing to a cross section of streets, Shylo looked out through the gap in red tile rooftops. To his left the dirt avenue stair-stepped down the intersecting streets to the port. It was the familiar landmark Shylo needed. The port sat at the westernmost edge of Perdigon. Capitol Hill was northeast. He looked forward to finding a friendly face and someone to tell him what in the burning ash was going on.

Shylo observed the layer of grime covering the Didimo symbol on his chest. He didn't stop running but slowed to see if the brown blotch marring the symbol on his tunic was blood. The sludge seeped onto his finger and he smelled it. Recoiling, he discovered it wasn't blood and winced at the knowledge that he'd slept in an alley steeped with sewage. Shylo considered ripping the green tunic off but running through the streets of Perdigon, mostly naked, would surely result in his arrest by the Capitol Hill Guard immediately upon his arrival. At least with the dirty, stained tunic, he could prove that he wasn't just some poor Eso from down the slope. He was a Penti trainee. A victim from the horrors of the night.

After a while, Shylo began running into larger gatherings of people. As he neared the base of the Hill, the crowds became larger and more dense. The congestion in the dirt-packed streets was unavoidable. Everyone was moving in the same direction. Shifting through the crowd, Shylo overheard more conversations, each one differed about what had happened during the night. The one consistent theme: there'd been a violent attack. He heard many high-ranking Senators mentioned as the target. He heard names of the members on the Emperor's Advisory Council and even mention of the two next in line to the Throne of Rhydenar. Shylo heard one group say that the Emperor had been killed. Yet as he wove through the throngs, Shylo never heard that Senator Didimo-Kai or House Didimo had been targeted.

When the streets turned from hard-packed dirt to gravel, Shylo started searching for familiar buildings on the lower edges of Capitol Hill. He worked his way through the crowds, heading for the Senate Chambers. The limestone buildings creating a blocky X came into view. It was the library next to the Senate Chambers. The west crook of the X facing the Chambers was the Penti class gathering place where they met each morning before their training. Shylo hoped someone he knew would be there. While working his way across the street below the Chamber's massive stone facade, Shylo spotted a familiar face. Wilsall's short black curly hair bobbed atop his head as he moved through the mass of Perdigon citizens.

"Will!" Shylo called. "Wilsall!" he shouted over the noise of the crowd. Wilsall looked but didn't see who was calling. Shylo jumped up and down, waving over the mixed heights of the citizens surrounding him. His efforts drew Wilsall's attention, but the Minor Noble didn't seem to recognize Shylo at first. Shylo pushed his way through several more ranks of mixed Rhydarians to get closer to his friend.

"Shylo?" Wilsall finally said his name.

"Will, what in the blazes is going on?" Shylo asked in a panic.

"You don't know?" Wilsall asked.

"What happened last night?" Shylo asked. Even he could hear the panicked quiver in his voice. He checked his hands, they were shaking.

"Come here," Wilsall said, taking Shylo by the arm and dragging him across the flow of traffic. They tucked into an eddy forming around the multi-story, rectangular stone temple directly below the Senate Chambers.

Shylo's heart pulsed at a rate that felt like it would beat right out of his chest. He prepared himself for the reality of the situation, to hear it from someone else that his host Senator's entire house was murdered.

"You don't remember anything about what happened last night?" Wilsall asked. Shylo tried to look Wilsall in the eyes to see if he knew the same thing that Shylo did, but Wilsall's eyes bounced between Shylo's worry-stricken face and the crowded street beyond.

"I was at the Canteen with you and Ismay. We were drinking, a lot. Things with Ismay seemed like they were going smoothly. Then... I was at the Didimo villa. There were bodies lying in the courtyard. I heard this voice. It was hollow, like it was coming from the bottom of a well. Then, I heard a scream from the Didimo-Kai's chambers. Then the bells started ringing. And, and, I blacked out. I woke up in an alley, covered in filth and overheard these people talking about a monster or something. Will, I think Didimo-Kai was murdered by another Noble House. They might be looking for me. What do I do?"

"Shylo," Wilsall said, shaking him. He moved his round face to mirror Shylo's and said, "You're right. Senator Didimo-Kai was targeted and murdered last night."

"Holy ash, burning embers, this is bad," Shylo swore.

"The whole Didimo House was slaughtered," Wilsall said. As he explained the scene, his words sounded empty to Shylo, who could picture the horrid scene. "The slaves, too; everyone but you," he finished.

Shylo stared blankly at him, realizing his chances of continuing as a Penti trainee were falling apart before his eyes.

"And the bells were not ringing for some monster lurking in the forests beyond the city walls. They tolled because the Emperor was murdered. He and his two successors were assassinated at the Palace," Wilsall said.

"But what does that have to do with House Didimo?" Shylo stammered. He didn't understand why only House Didimo and the Akai were targeted in the attack. "No other Senators' villas were attacked?" he asked.

"You ask like you were expecting to hear more names on the death list," Wilsall said.

"I only ask because there's no connection between Didimo and the Emperor, or any of his successors."

"Not all of the successors died, you know. The assassins' attempt to wipe out the Imperial line of Akais was thwarted by poor planning," Wilsall said defensively.

"What do you mean?"

"Benton Querci-Akai wasn't in the Palace. He was outside Perdigon with High Commander Marxius Ovando-Kai and the guard. Ismay told me House Ovando's lead guard received a message telling of the High Noble and her father's new expected arrival time. The letter came to the Ovando villa early this morning," Wilsall said.

"You spoke to Ismay?" Shylo asked.

"She was the one who brought all this news to me. Ismay went to see your body when the lead Ovando guard told her what had happened. When you weren't among the dead, we feared..." Wilsall trailed off as something in the crowd beyond Shylo caught his attention.

"Wait here a moment, Shylo. I just saw my father in the crowd. I'll bring him over and we'll have you taken care of. Stay right here until I get back," Wilsall said.

Before Shylo could tell Wilsall that he didn't want to be left alone, his classmate disappeared into the crowded street. He almost couldn't believe what Wilsall had just told him.

The Emperor murdered? Both his heirs dead and gone in a single night? Shylo thought.

The Emperor and those who were next in line were dead and gone, just like Shylo's patron and the entire House Didimo. Everyone, including the trainees of House Didimo, were gone. That meant Shylo was the only person left in the trainee program associated with Senator Rembert Didimo-Kai. A Senator no more. Shylo saw his fate. There was no way he could continue to represent House Didimo as a Penti. He needed a sponsor to continue. Without one, he was just another Eso and he understood that the other Senators wouldn't pity him.

In the midst of the chaos on the streets, Shylo tried to figure out how he could fall in with another Senator's house. Wilsall didn't offer it but being brought in by House Sarapio was an option. If not Sarapio, then perhaps Ismay's sponsor would take him for the rest of the rotation? Now that such important members of the Rhydenar Empire were dead, most likely there would be replacements. At least one new Senator would need to be appointed or elected. Two, if the Magistrates decided to elect one of the members of the Senate as the next Emperor of Rhydenar. Between this demand for at least one new Senator and the help of his friends, Shylo hoped he might have a chance to continue his training at Capitol Hill. He understood it was a strange way to think in the middle of an attack of this magnitude, but he was consumed with his own survival and hanging onto his dream, his dream of rising to the pinnacle of an Eso's power and influence in Rhydarian government.

Shylo mentally prepared a pitch for Wilsall's father, a Fifth Class Noble and Senator. Yet Wilsall was nowhere in sight. He'd been gone far longer than it took to cross the street and return. Shylo noticed the crowd's movement had slowed to a shuffle. Talk among nearby pedestrians drew his attention.

"And only the Penti boy escaped," he heard one person say.

"He was plotting to assassinate the Emperor all along. Can you imagine the look on Rembert Didimo-Kai's face when the Palace Guard stormed his villa early this morning? I just hope they find the Penti weasel before he can escape to the wilds south of the Old Rhydarian border and into Agunzi territory."

"Yeah, and warn those wideback traitors that their connection with Didimo inside the capital has been severed for good," another said.

Shylo backed up against the limestone temple wall. He looked down at his stained tunic. He could still see House Didimo's symbol through the dried sewage. The lull in the crowd's migration up the hill ended and the two New Rhydarian men who were talking about Shylo passed by.

Searching for Wilsall in the crowd, Shylo's fear of being accused for something he had nothing to do with returned. He noticed two groups of Capitol Hill Guard forcing their way against the flow of traffic down the street. He saw them grab an Old Rhydarian teenager with light brown skin. His straight black hair was cut much shorter than Shylo's but there was no mistaking his ethnicity. Shylo crouched, sliding lower against the limestone wall at his back. Two of the men wearing Capitol Hill Guard leathers, armored with blue draco scales, questioned the lad while the others continued down the street. He watched as they targeted any Old Rhydarian male close to his age. They were looking for him!

The whole city seemed to think he was responsible for the assassination. He was just a Penti trainee, a lowly Eso. How could he possibly have done something of this magnitude? Such a plot would be difficult even for the Kai. But he also understood that there was no reasoning with an angry mob, or any group of guards who were following orders. He had to hide.

Shylo messed up his shaggy hair, pushing his bangs to hide his facial features. He crossed his arms and hunkered down, hoping to spot Wilsall and his father before the Capitol Hill Guard saw him.

Will knows what really happened, Shylo told himself. *Senator Sarapio-Kai will help me clear this mess up. House Sarapio wouldn't let me fall into the wrong hands, would they?*

Shylo stood up from his squatting position to search the nearby faces for Wilsall or his father. He didn't see them, and the Capitol Hill Guard continued to move down the street toward him.

Wilsall told me to stay put until he came back, Shylo thought.

The Capitol Hill Guard had already grabbed two more young men of Old Rhydarian ethnicity. When they found Shylo, they would take him. They would see the Didimo symbol and the color of his tunic. Shylo would be lucky to make it to a court. It would be easier for them to kill him on the spot. The Emperor was dead.

"The Creators became outnumbered by the offspring of the lesser dragons for whom they had expressly created Tarmigan. Tourome blamed his brothers, Pyrome and Brisrome, for crafting the downfall of The Creators. Being less aggressive than their Creator brother, Pyrome and Brisrome yielded to Tourome's advice." – The Dracolyth

FLUSHED

The Capitol Hill Guardsmen pushed their way closer to Shylo. And still no sign of Wilsall or his father.

They're not going to make it, Shylo thought.

His adrenaline spiked; he felt weak in the stomach. Like the gargous pheasant capable of hiding in the brush, remaining perfectly still until the last possible moment to escape, Shylo sprang from his hiding place and fled the guards. He kept low to the ground, moving quickly with short choppy steps, not risking exposing himself to the hunters by standing taller than anyone in the crowd. Crouching, Shylo forced his way against the flow of traffic.

The adrenaline helped clear his blistering headache, but

his weak stomach couldn't handle the added adrenaline. He keeled over, pitching what little remained in his stomach into the street. The surrounding people saw him stop, grab his stomach and wretch, moving out of his way in time. As Shylo coughed to clear his airway, he suddenly noticed the spectacle he was creating. Glancing back, he saw guards wearing the Imperial cobalt-blue scale surcoats. Draco scales were an expensive armor harvested off devolved dragons. The cobalt blue surcoats were a staple of the heavily armored Capitol Hill Guard. Standing on their toes, Shylo spotted one of the guards attempting to determine the cause of the commotion.

Seeing the faces of armed Rhydarians and knowing that they were now searching for him left him feeling as if every moment since leaving the Canteen had been a horrible nightmare. The bile burning his throat reminded Shylo that this was no nightmare. The Palace, Capitol Hill, and City Guard were trying to find him. The Emperor was dead, and Shylo was the last living representative of House Didimo in the city.

Keep moving, he told himself, pushing past the desire to explain his situation to the guards. They wouldn't listen. They would follow their orders as trained to do or kill him on the spot.

Faces in the crowd blurred as Shylo's mind raced in trying to locate a place to hide while also piecing together how House Didimo had come to be blamed for the assassinations. Each time Shylo thought he'd located an alcove where he could rest and collect himself, he saw armored guards pluck Old Rhydarians his age from the crowd.

Why? he shouted in his throbbing head. *How could anyone think I was capable of this level of deceit and treachery?*

Shylo knew that what he thought didn't matter. The Palace and the Noble class needed someone to blame. And the actual assassins were hiding behind this reasoning. It didn't matter that he wasn't there when it happened. Somehow, House Didimo was guilty and, by association, Shylo was too since he had survived.

While trying to reason this out, Shylo realized one certain fact: House Didimo had been delivered punishment *before* the Palace bells tolled. Those bells echoed in his patchy memory of the night before. The bells were not ringing before he returned to the villa. Shylo wondered if that meant a Noble House had reacted to accusations that a coup of some sort was in the works and House Didimo was involved. He knew that House Didimo was attacked before the bells rang. The first alarm from the Palace sounded just as Shylo was fleeing the villa. This scenario was the truth. The only rational explanation why every single person at House Didimo, including the slaves, was killed before the bells tolled was to cover something up. House Didimo had been set up.

Shylo considered returning to the Hill to tell someone in the Penti cohort of this realization. But there were the guards to contend with and he knew when the crowd heard an official announcement from the Palace, everyone would be looking for him. Who knows how many Old Rhydarian Eso boys his age would be killed this day? A wave of guilt washed over Shylo as he realized that the hate-fueled crowd would possibly murder innocent young men that had the same hairstyle, and the same skin and eye coloring as he had. He considered turning himself in.

What would that do? he asked himself. *Another innocent Eso dead while the real culprits escape?*

Though Shylo was not brave or strong enough to fight

an armed guard, he would continue to run. Fighting his yearning to find Wilsall or Ismay, Shylo pressed on. He lowered his head, hunching at times to avoid unwanted eyes. He wove his way through the streets, without a specific destination, simply trying to avoid all armored guards. The farther he went from Capitol Hill, the more the crowd thinned; so, too, did the Capitol Guard. He saw the light brown and grey shades of armored City Guard sprinkled throughout these surrounding neighborhoods. Shylo's determination to avoid capture led him to question what laws he'd be accused of breaking, not that his word against the Kai would sway the court.

In his Penti training, Shylo had observed that his attention to detail surpassed that of many other Penti trainees. They'd only recently started what promised to be a detailed review of law and order in the Empire. Shylo knew his knowledge on the subject was only general at this point, and with that knowledge, he calculated his chances of proving his innocence. His association with the House deemed responsible for the Emperor's murder was a certain death sentence. Testimonies from people like Ismay and Wilsall who were with him at the Canteen wouldn't be enough to absolve him from a charge of conspiracy with his House sponsor. Suddenly, he remembered the bracelet Senator Didimo-Kai gave him. Shylo saw in his mind's eye how the Kai would view his admission of being given a task by the Senator, how it was really meant to advance the assassination. He imagined the jury of Kai twisting his story of collecting supplies into helping sneak assassins into Capitol Hill. They'd say he was putting on a show for all the trainees at the Canteen that night. He was simply following a directive to divert any suspicion from House Didimo.

Shylo couldn't face trial, not while the emotions in the

capital were running so hot. When he had first emerged from the Perdigon Port Customs Barrier upon his arrival seven months earlier, he'd witnessed an enraged mob hang a man for stealing a harquice. Shylo shivered in imagining what the citizenry would do to someone believed to be responsible for the deaths of the Emperor and his successors.

The guard will continue to scour the capital until they find me, he thought.

Relying on the kindness of strangers in Perdigon wasn't an option. Hiding somewhere in the city wasn't an option. If he meant to survive, he had to leave the city. At least until the raw wound of losing the Emperor healed and perhaps more evidence became available. Then perhaps he could attempt to seek his friend's help.

Wilsall must've been detained, but all for the best, he told himself.

Remaining in the city was too risky, too dangerous. It might incriminate his classmates. Wilsall's offer to help him was selfless, but Shylo couldn't allow him to risk his future as well. As Shylo considered this, he realized that it was the first time Wilsall had done something that wasn't completely in his own best interest.

A good friend, Shylo thought, glimpsing Perdigon's towering walls through the gap in townhouse rooftops. He spotted the small dots that were City Guardsmen patrolling the ramparts.

"Ashes," he cursed under his breath.

Perdigon's thick granite wall ringed the entire city. It rose at least thirty levels, ten times taller than the Imperial Palace. Turrets spiked above the ramparts on every bend. Additional lookout stations rose over each of the mainland entrances. To ensure no Volurem could sneak through near the port, the wall extended into Brism Bay. Shylo couldn't leave through the gates. The City Guards were searching for an Old Rhydarian boy wearing a green tunic and yellow belt. Shylo still wore the Senator's bracelet, but he didn't want to give it up. Other than his pouch of coins, consisting of a few square pieces and one round coin, the copper bracelet was the most valuable item he had.

But I need to change clothes, Shylo thought.

He couldn't return to House Didimo. If guards weren't already stationed at the Didimo villa, they'd be there any moment.

Sneaking into the nearest alley, Shylo unbuckled his belt and slipped off his tunic. He considered leaving them both but seeing the sand-colored splotches on his body, he noticed they stood out more than the green Didimo Tunic. He slipped it back on but tossed the yellow belt. Clawing at his shirt front, he tried to erase or destroy the Didimo symbol.

"You there?" he heard someone say.

Shylo stopped trying to rip off the symbol and rolled out of the alley. Without looking back, he swiftly moved to an adjacent street.

The port, he decided. It provided his best chance to escape the city. He didn't have his legal documentation to get through customs, but usually the guards at the port were more concerned about who was entering the city than who was leaving.

Shylo slogged his way toward the west edge of Perdigon. Sticking to neighborhoods out of clear sight of the exterior wall, Shylo spent the hottest part of the day attempting to blend in while avoiding anyone wearing draco- or lazgron-scaled armor.

Fighting dehydration, he found a neighborhood well

among the Eso townhomes. After checking it was clear of any City Guard, Shylo drew a pail of fresh water. As he scooped handful after handful into his mouth, he studied what he could see of the nearby port. The wall at the Customs entrance, a thirty-hand-tall barrier stretching the length of Perdigon's beach, blocked his view of the docks. Shylo could see blue water beyond and dozens of ships anchored offshore. None of those he could see were actively sailing.

Having quenched his thirst, he again checked the empty corridor behind him. A glint, like sun reflecting off slate-colored armor, caught his attention. Up the hill, a rider on harquiceback headed down the dirt-packed avenue. Shylo scrambled away from the neighborhood well, tucking up against an adjacent wood-sided building. He looked farther down the narrow street. The little street was littered with crates and hand carts. Finding a secure place to hide, he crouched behind a wooden cart. He nearly cried out in surprise when a pair of window shutters opened directly overhead.

After flinching when the base of the shutter unexpectedly brushed wind through his hair, Shylo froze. He didn't dare look up to find a guard staring down at him. As his first breath passed without injury, Shylo pressed one shoulder back and cocked his head skyward. The six-story building continued uninterrupted, into the cloudless blue afternoon sky.

The tilted cart still blocked any view of his position from the avenue where the harquice rider could be heard descending. Shylo spun to face the wood building. Slowly, he rose until he could see inside through the window. He stopped, just in case. When a hand didn't swat him in the nose, he continued rising. The white stucco interior was lined with shelves crafted from driftwood. More driftwood shelving filled the room in rows. Below the open window was a sales counter. Directly left of the counter, a dark brown figure appeared. Shylo immediately dropped away from the window.

Luckily an angry Rhydarian shop owner didn't immediately vault through the open window after him. Shylo rose from a crouch again, this time faster. He felt a wave of relief when he saw that the dark brown figure was just a leather cloak hanging from a coatrack. Looking more carefully now, he didn't see anyone inside. Shylo noted a carving of a fish hanging just within view through the open shop door. The word, 'Supply,' was carved across the fish. The word triggered a thought. Shylo had never stolen anything, but now that his life was at stake, he eyed the brown cloak that hung within reach.

As soon as he decided to take the cloak, a man walked into the room. Shylo caught a glimpse of him before dropping out of view. The brawny New Rhydarian clutched a basket, walking with his head down. Shylo was fairly confident the shop worker hadn't seen him. Shylo heard something with sizable heft thump down on the counter. The man's footsteps settled near the window. Shylo held his breath, holding perfectly still.

Harquice hoofs sounded on the dirt-packed avenue, followed by the scuff of footfalls from the man inside the shop rushing toward the open door to witness the excitement outside.

Shylo recognized his opportunity. He shot up. The bald New Rhydarian's back was turned to Shylo as he craned his scarred neck to see up the street. The dark leather cloak was just out of reach as the hoofs pounded closer. Shylo hoisted himself onto the windowsill, pinching his stomach on the sharp angle of the sill. He grabbed the leather cloak and lifted it from the rack, carefully sliding it out the window. As he dropped out of view, he caught a glimpse of the harquice's wide nose through the open shop door.

Shylo crouched behind the cart with the worker's thick leather cloak in his hands. Taking it from a hard-working Rhydarian Eso didn't feel right. He wanted to at least pay for it, but he didn't have enough to supplement what a cloak like this was worth. Shylo recognized the leather.

Too smooth to be mongodo, he noted as felt it in his grip. *Ashes, this is descaled lazgron,* he realized in a fraction of a second. *I'll be strung up and beaten for stealing lizard leather,* he thought. Lazgron was the smaller cousin of the draco and, like the devolved dragon, it was commonly used for armor and among fighting men. *Even more expensive with the scales off,* he winced, but it was too late to be worried about being caught stealing at a time like this.

The harquice trotted past. Shylo attempted to mold himself into the wall when he saw the dimpled helmet of a City Guard turn his head to the side as he passed each intersection.

Blazing fire, Shylo cursed in his thoughts.

Reality sunk in again. The guard was most likely on his way to tell those at Customs to watch for the Didimo Penti trainee. The rest of the crowd would soon follow. Despite wanting to put the expensive cloak back, Shylo needed it. Stealing it was his only option. He had to have a new disguise. Shylo removed the copper bracelet and brought out the small pouch of coins from his trousers. Putting them in one hand and tucking the smooth leather under his arm, he sprang to his feet. Dropping the small compensation on the windowsill, he ran away from the shop.

While darting through side streets, he scanned for

somewhere new to hide. A sloshing sound echoed from the ground as though a decent amount of liquid was running through a hollow chamber near his feet. He slowed, following the noise to a stony opening. The smell was enough to explain the noise. Spending most of his time on Capitol Hill, Shylo had become used to the luxury of not having to think about where their waste washed away to.

It all runs downhill, he thought, never questioning where it ended. Now, looking at it anew, he remembered when he was younger reading a book about the history of Perdigon. It described how the capital city had converted ancient tunnels constructed by the area's first Terra tribes' people into sewer and aqueduct systems; far more sophisticated than what they had in Florens where he grew up.

Shylo wrapped himself in the thick leather cloak, pulling the hood over his head. He was surprised by the weight of the leather and wondered what it would be like with the scales on, like the armor the City Guard wore. Shylo noted the rounded arcs across the dirt-colored hide. He wondered how difficult it was to remove the scales and if it was anything like the series of soaking and scraping his father did to remove mongodo fur from the hide.

Feeling more confident in his appearance, Shylo continued slinking through the streets. More and more people appeared as he came within a block of the Customs barrier. The lazgron cloak was heavy and hot. Already he was sweating profusely. Shylo couldn't understand how Rhydarian soldiers could fight the Volurem in the peak of summer wearing thick leather like this. Soldiers also typically wore layers of borca wool to protect them from the flames. Even now, Shylo knew he wouldn't have done anything differently if he could. With his level of experience, serving on the fire lines in an Imperial Legion struck him as a more likely death sentence than what he faced now.

The strategy of getting past the Customs barrier without his documentation and stowing away on a ship appeared flimsier by the moment. From what he could see, the City Guard were locking down the capital from the inside as well. Even if he made it past the barrier, they'd be searching the ships for the next several days trying to find him. He needed a different way out of Perdigon. The sooner, the better.

Shylo reviewed his options. He couldn't endanger his classmates by going to them for help, at least right now. Escape through the city gates was too risky. They only opened for supply wagon trains, legions of soldiers, or at the reasonable demands of a Noble. All other access in and out of the city happened at the port. Unless he could find a wild harquice and fly over the wall or burrow like a borca underneath it, Shylo was trapped. Shylo wished he'd kept the book that described where he'd find the ancient Terra people's tunnels, though he doubted that would've proved useful. Any tunnels that weren't already in use would be blocked off or filled in by now. Otherwise, the Volurem could enter the city. If a fire started in the wood structures lining the hills of Perdigon, there was no telling the damage it would do. Close to a million people could go up in flames.

Turning himself in wouldn't do. Shylo wasn't guilty of anything heinous. He had to buy himself some time, a few days at least. There was one option he'd glazed over. Shylo cringed at the thought.

Burning ash, he thought, realizing it was his best option.

In no time, he retraced his steps to find the stone opening. Nearly gagging at the stench, Shylo waited until he couldn't see anyone in the street. He held his breath and crawled in headfirst.

Once inside the sewer, he couldn't help but wretch. Nothing but water and stinging bile came up. The methane stung his eyes and burned his throat. He crawled on his hands and knees into the dark slop. As he moved downslope into total darkness, the warmth of the waste chilled, and he grew cold. The lazgron cloak was the only thing keeping him from shivering.

At this point he slid on his stomach, giving up any hope of staying at least partially clean. The slick, angled stone allowed him to move faster on his stomach. Shylo headed down the underground tunnel until he heard a sloshing sound. He looked in vain into the dark behind him, hoping a tidal wave of waste from Capitol Hill wouldn't wash him away. The slop-slopping sound wasn't coming from behind him, though. It was up ahead. Slowly, careful not the lose his grip on the bricks and slide uncontrollably into the strange wetness, Shylo crawled until he saw a faint green glow. The light rippled across the stained tunnel walls. It was the water in Brism Bay lapping up into the tunnel.

Creeping as close as he dared before the final plummet into the water, Shylo tried to gauge whether the sewage tunnel was capped with a metal grate. He couldn't see the end of the submerged tunnel, only the water ebbing and flowing within the tunnel walls. Judging by the amount of light glowing through the murky water, the tunnel continued beneath the surface for at least several body lengths.

Shylo didn't pretend to know when high and low tides took place. He had no idea if waiting awhile would decrease the amount of time he would need to hold his breath. If the tunnel was capped with a metal grate, he'd have a difficult time trying to turn around, if he could turn around at all. And if this was how deep the water was at low tide, he didn't want to wait.

Filling his lungs with methane-rich air, Shylo launched himself headfirst into the water. With his arms stretched out in front of him to feel for the end of the tunnel, he kicked as hard as he could. As his chest started to burn for oxygen. Shylo felt his left hand hit metal as his right hand continued past. He opened his eyes. The salty ocean water stung his eyes worse than the sewer air had. Worse, he could see the end of the sewage tunnel was indeed capped with a rusted metal grate.

His right hand had slipped through one of the square holes in the grate. In a blink, Shylo could see that several squares appeared to be rusted through, leaving larger gaps. Shylo refused to return to the stench of the sewer. He grabbed hold of the rusted pieces and yanked. Chunks of metal broke free. Frantically, as his chest blazed from a lack of oxygen, Shylo ripped at the corroded grate until he'd created a sizable hole.

Fitting his arms through the rusted opening, he pulled his narrow frame through the gap. The lazgron cloak caught on a sharp edge of the broken metal. He pushed and kicked, swimming madly to break free to the surface. The snag gave in and Shylo clawed toward fresh air above. He didn't care that he might be seen by a City Guard. He needed to breathe.

Breaking through the surface, Shylo gasped, desperately treading water to keep his head above the surface despite the weight of the heavy waterlogged cloak. He quickly gained perspective on where he'd wound up. The sewer spat him straight out away from the wall. He was well beyond the shoreline as the walls of Perdigon extended out into the Bay, even at low tide. He didn't hear shouting from above, though the waves intermittently lapped into his ears.

The cloak was weighing him down. Shylo grew up in a coastal town and was a fair swimmer, but he couldn't last much longer without assistance. It seemed wrong to ditch the cloak after how he'd taken it. He wasn't going to discard such an expensive item. One glimpse at the forest beyond the wall and Shylo knew he would need it.

He swam sluggishly to the thick granite wall. The waves bounced him against the conglomerate of boulders. Though he continually lost his hold on the wet rock, Shylo managed to make his way around the width of the wall. He didn't take his eyes off the holds he was using to traverse the exterior of the wall until his leather sandals touched the white sand just offshore. As he worked his way through the chest-deep water, he realized he might make it to the vast wilderness beyond the walls. The only time he'd been outside the protection of a city wall before was when he sailed from Florens north to Perdigon.

Shylo waded through the water, looking past the canopy at the expanse of land beyond. The Apgar Forest spread like a thick beard on the snow-capped Shield Mountains. The only grassy opening in sight was a clear-cut between the walls of Perdigon and the edge of the wilderness. A sense of complete and utter loneliness fell over him. That fear, however, was cut short when Shylo heard shouting from the wall above. A City Guard had spotted him. Crossbow bolts would be raining down on him in a matter of moments. Shylo reached shore and ran. He ran across soft sand and onto the thick green grass beneath the wall. He ran faster still when the zinging of crossbow bolts whizzed down around him. Shylo didn't stop running until he was deep within the cover of the forest. It wasn't until that moment that he remembered seeing the column of smoke the day before. Shylo suddenly realized that at any moment, the Volurem could burn everything around him. The protection offered by the walls was gone. He was on his own.

THE YELLOW STONE

The Night of the Emperor's Death

A light glowing through the trees in the near distance drew her attention. Number 2841 stared at it, wondering if it was a Volurem, what it might do. The yellow glow did not move. She'd never seen Volurem burn that softly. She'd never seen one that didn't tear through the surrounding fuels.

She pulled on the rope, the one attached to the leather harness on the harquice's long-nosed face. The animal attempted to pull free. It bobbed its head back, but Number 2841 held the lead rope tightly in the hand not holding her sword.

Number 2841 tried to communicate with it again, but the mare hadn't responded to her earlier attempts other than with whinnies and neighing. This time, she jutted her

92

face forward, pointing her chin directly at the harquice's face. She flared her nostrils and bulged her eyes with a frown. If she had pointed ears like the harquice, she would've pinned them back as the mare was doing.

The harquice snorted her response and stamped backward slightly.

Number 2841 pulled on the rope and the harquice snapped its flat teeth at her. The snap would've seemed more aggressive had the harquice's saber fangs not been filed down flush with the rest of its top front teeth. Number 2841 mimicked the equine animal's movements, snapping her jaw at the animal.

The mare didn't seem impressed. It stared at Number 2841 with glossy brown eyes.

"Bah," she exclaimed, giving up her efforts to communicate with the domesticated mare. Number 2841 walked forward. The harquice followed with little prompting. The soft yellow glow remained in the same spot among the trees unlike any Volurem she'd ever encountered. The world outside the arena walls reminded her of the arena before any fighting with the Volurem could begin. Only now she saw no sign of Volurem anywhere. No two-legged or four-legged species like those who'd come to her residence within the arena grounds. She hadn't seen anyone since her fight with the Scaled One.

In case the glow belonged to an unsuspecting Volurem, Number 2841 chose her steps carefully. She led the harquice with one hand, so it couldn't spook and run off, and her willow-leaf saber in the other. Her bare feet probed the forest floor for dried sticks and pinecones that would give away her position and movement. The black night offered cover, especially given her black-and-rose skin. Her light hair was the only visual that might give her away.

As she and the harquice drew closer to the soft yellow light, it flickered. She stopped to study the glow. The light became obstructed. The flickering was an illusion. A dark figure on two legs glinted with the scaled body of an animal she'd fought before. The Masters called it a draco. The figure moved and the light became visible again. The person's arms shone dully, covered by chain mail; it looked like the kind the Masters wore. Examining her gently illuminated surroundings, Number 2841 now noticed more strangers. She edged closer, wary, in case she again needed to defend herself against the Scaled One.

She risked moving a couple of steps closer. Their low voices became louder, and she could see them more clearly by the light of the glowing stone, like the one that was in her sleeping stall. The strangers sat around the glowing rock; their gazes seemed transfixed on a black round item resting atop it. Number 2841 sniffed, smelling something she'd never smelled before. It seemed to be coming from the deep dish perched on the glowing rock. The scent made her mouth slick with saliva, and she had to stop herself from wandering into the crowd, blindly following her hunger. Fortunately, her training in the arena forced her to analyze the scene before running in, sword swinging.

Several strangers' faces appeared comparable to the Masters' and the outsiders who had come to the arena to kill the Masters. Their features were like Number 2841's as well: low hairline, upturned eyebrows, wide nose, and sharp and wide jawline. Two had dark brown skin, and short, tightly curled black hair. Their eyes sparkled with the same green as the Masters'. Among the five people surrounding the glowing rock, only these two resembled a familiar race. The others were of a likeness she'd never seen.

One of the other three, the only female among them,

had a tan complexion. Her nose wasn't as wide and stuck out noticeably compared to the curly-haired men. Her black hair hung straight, like Number 2841's. This feminine-looking one had softer features, arched eyebrows, and a more narrow, wide-lipped mouth. She wore the same green draco-scale armor as the other two similarly sized men. The female soldier stared with grey eyes that tapered to an oval shape in the corners.

The fourth soldier sat a full head and shoulders closer to the ground than the others. What the bulky man lacked in height he made up for in thickness. His skin and hair looked like the colors of fire. His shaggy, wavy hair burned redder than his reddish-orange face. His bones must've been twice the thickness as the three dark-haired soldiers. His head was much wider and his neck short and wide. He had a bulging Adam's Apple that she could see even in the dim light. Number 2841 noted that his thickness was all well-developed muscle. His round eyes burned a dark orange, the most similar in color among them to her red eyes. The man's brow bone protruded and was matted with thick eyebrows to match his hair. His strong nose bulged with a rounded ball on the tip. A thick red mustache covered his upper lip, drooping down over his wide mouth. The stout soldier wore slate grey armor of the same draco scale.

The fifth stranger dazzled Number 2841 with his extreme height. As he sat next to the more experienced-looking dark-haired soldier, the tall man's slender, narrow shoulders slouched forward at a height over the dark-haired man next to him. He wore no armor, only simple, lightweight, loose-fitting robes. His skin was a turquoise blue. His neck stretched more than twice the length of Number 2841's and the soft, rounded features of his head were as long as her harquice's forehead and nose combined. This man's eyes shone with the same yellow as the glowing stone before him. His purple hair hung wavey on one side down past his oval-shaped chin. On the other side of his head, the hair was shorter than the stout soldier's mustache. The tall man's wide nose was of the same shape as the dark-skinned soldiers', but it didn't stick out much past his high cheekbones. As she studied him, she realized that he took fewer than half as many breaths as the others.

The two male soldiers in green-scaled armor each wore a broadsword on their belts. The woman's blade had less reach than the males' but hers had more width. A weapon like the blade the Volurem foot soldiers used best in close-quarters fighting. The stout soldier with fiery hair had no blade. Behind him, leaning on the old-growth pine closest to their circle, rested a war scythe three times longer than the pikes Number 2841 trained with. The scythe's blade curved to a pointed tip and was a length between the broadswords and the short sword the other soldiers carried. The tall stranger had no weapon.

Though she didn't know if these strangers had any connection to those who'd attacked at the arena, Number 2841 couldn't stop her uncontrollable curiosity. The smell of the black metal dish was too tempting. No Master ordered her against showing herself.

She didn't have a person to watch her harquice like the strangers who'd attacked the Masters had. So, she did what she'd seen the Masters do while staging before training. She wrapped the lead rope around a tree and tucked the tail of the rope under itself. The animal dropped its head and began grazing on the green grass growing up through the forest duff.

This time, Number 2841 didn't tread so lightly as she

neared. She allowed her bare feet to break twigs until finally one crack gained the group's attention.

"What was that?" the woman asked.

"This is why our legion commander stopped allowing female graduates to join our ranks," one dark-haired soldier said. The weathered lines around his eyes and mouth told Number 2841 he was older than the other short-haired soldier.

"Quiet, I heard it too," the tall man said in a rumblingly low voice.

Number 2841 saw them clutching the hilts of their swords while the stout one rolled off his haunch to gather his long-bladed spear. The light from the glowing stone must've prevented them from seeing her because she did not hide behind a tree. She walked closer, the willow- leaf blade in her hand.

"Ashes," the older soldier said. "What in the blazes is that?" Number 2841 thought his change was odd. He'd spoken so calmly a moment ago.

"Halt," the red-haired man growled, lowering his pike to point at her bare chest from a few sword-lengths away.

Number 2841 did. She discerned these people were not the same as those who came to the arena. The Scaled One and the strangers had attacked her without question.

"Is she a Volurem?" the woman asked.

"Clearly she's not. She's not on fire," the older male soldier said.

"She has the same black and red markings," the tall man said.

Standing now, Number 2841 could see the tall one was roughly twenty-one hands tall. At least three hands taller than the older male soldier.

"She's dangerous, whatever she is," the red-haired man

said, his war scythe held as steady as the sound of his firm voice.

"Why is she naked?" the shorter of the male soldiers said in a slightly higher pitch than his companion.

"Lay down your sword and step into the light," the older male soldier ordered.

Number 2841 thought he sounded like one of the Masters. His voice was higher pitched, and scratchy. A quality similar to the Masters' after a day of barking orders during training. Number 2841 did what he commanded, not questioning if it was the right thing to do.

"Is she a Volurem slave, like the ones you said wander the burns after a fight?" the younger male soldier asked, his question directed at the tall man.

"I do not believe she is. Tarmigs have white hair like that, but their skin is slate-grey, like the lazgron lizard's scales," he said in a slow, deep voice.

Number 2841 didn't attempt to grab her saber as the female soldier walked behind her and collected it from the ground. The grey-eyed woman kept her short sword trained on Number 2841 as she carefully circled back to the glowing yellow stone.

"Sit down," the older soldier said.

Number 2841 did. She sat the same way she always did in her sleeping stall, with her knees bent, hugging them with her forearms.

The red-haired man allowed his spear to dip, nearly touching the ground.

The younger soldier looked away, his cheeks darkening slightly.

"Don't sit that way, hon," the straight-haired woman said. "We sit like this," she said, taking a seat and crossing her right leg over the top of her left, folding her palms over the short sword resting in her lap.

Number 2841 mirrored her actions. She wiggled her toes, excited to learn something new.

"I rather preferred the other way," the older male soldier said.

"You're such a mongodo, Helmer," the woman spat, her arched eyebrows pinching on her forehead and her thick lips pursed into a flat line. When the older shook his head, the female rose, leaving Number 2841's willow-leaf saber in the grass next to her. "I'll get her something to cover up with."

Helmer, the older soldier, met the stout man's gaze and rolled his eyes, taking a seat next to his companion. The one with the scythe remained standing, not allowing his spear tip to waver from its location hovering over the glowing yellow rock.

"Where did you come from?" the tall one asked.

Number 2841 pointed behind to the trees.

"There aren't any cities that way," Helmer grumbled.

"There are in New Rhydenar," the younger male soldier said. "Did you come from over the Shield Mountains?" he asked, his eyes sparkling in the stone's light.

"Don't get too comfortable with her, Petyr," the red-haired man said. "She stinks of smoke."

"That's what it smells like?" Petyr asked.

Number 2841 frowned. These men were heavily armed, like the soldiers she'd been told she would one day join. These people looked like her, some of them at least. Yet, the younger one, Petyr, looked only slightly younger than Number 2841 and he didn't know what smoke smelled like? The idea was as foreign as the strangers before her. Number 2841 had been smelling smoke her entire life.

"Here," the woman said, walking into view from behind the others. She threw a wool blanket across the ring of grey and black stones they were using to raise their glowing yellow stone off the ground. "Robson, put that war scythe down. She's not going to kill you. She's just a cold, lost slave."

Number 2841 wrapped her body in the grey and brown wool blanket, examining Robson.

He licked the ends of his furry red lip, then hesitantly lifted the war scythe away from where he'd been aiming at her chest.

"We'll keep a close eye on her until morning, then bring her along with us to meet back up with Commander Nolstram-Kai and the legion," Helmer said, laying the shiny steel broadsword across his lap. Leaning forward with his hands on his hips, he peered into the sizzling black metal dish. "Anyone want the rest of this, or should I pitch it?"

"I'm full," Robson said.

Petyr shook his head.

The tall one turned his nose away from the glowing yellow stone, looking toward the night sky.

"I'll throw it to the lazgrons, then," Helmer said.

"Don't waste it on those scavengers," the woman said. "She'll probably eat it. I bet she's starving," she said, nodding toward Number 2841.

Helmer, in his green-scaled surcoat, rocked back with an annoyed look on his face. "Fine," he said. "Are you hungry, slave girl?"

Number 2841 nodded. She didn't know what the word slave meant, but she knew the difference between boy and girl, man and woman. She didn't need the Masters to tell her.

"Go on, eat," the woman said, pointing to the black dish on the yellow stone.

Number 2841 studied it carefully. It smelled interesting, but this black sizzling dish wasn't like the food troughs at the arena. She looked at Petyr.

He nodded, motioning to the dish.

She stood, letting the wool blanket drop away, and hunched over the glowing yellow rock. The browned pieces of red meat and the small white grains around them smelled different from the food she ate at the arena. It smelled better. Her mouth started watering. Number 2841 bent down and picked up the yellow glowing rock with the black dish on top and held them in her bare hands.

"Whoa!" Helmer shouted. He wasn't the only shocked member of the group. Number 2841 could see the four soldiers were on their feet, backing away from her with horrified looks on their faces. The tall man's eyes bulged.

"Put it down before your hands melt off," Pyter said.

Number 2841 fed off their reaction, dropping the yellow glowing rock and the black dish.

"No!" the group shouted, but it was too late. Number 2841's confusion peaked just before the first spark took hold in the grass. All around where the yellow stone had hit the ground, Volurem sprouted in the tall grass. They started out small at first, but only remained a non-threatening size for the first moments as they grew with their fire. Number 2841 moved faster than the dark-haired soldiers. Only Robson reacted in sync with her.

Before she could skirt the fire and retrieve her weapon from the female soldier, a hand full of Volurem soldiers were on them. The tall man moved slower than the rest and didn't make it to his feet before a fast-moving Volurem caught hold of him. Without armor or a weapon, the tall man stood no chance. The Volurem sank its flaming hands into his flesh, burning his skin everywhere the Volurem soldier touched. In the blink of an eye, the Volurem stabbed a glossy black blade through the tall man's chest. He toppled to the ground, burning in the fire that spread through the grass, summoning soldiers in the spreading flames.

Helmer deflected the black blade of a Volurem that came stabbing at him while the younger soldier rushed to his side to help. His lack of experience showed as he engaged the Volurem without considering the entire scene. Two more Volurem soldiers were cropping up beside him where the tall man's body burned.

"Watch out," Robson said, stabbing with his scythe toward one of the Volurem soldiers, but the remaining Volurem reached Petyr uninhibited.

Number 2841 winced at the familiar sound of a blade sinking into flesh. The same wet sound the strangers' blades had made as they killed everyone at the arena.

She hurried over to the straight-haired woman and snatched her saber from the ground before she could be stopped. Number 2841 leapt into the flames. She danced with the Volurem, cutting them down with powerful strikes of her steel sword. Strength was a necessity when extinguishing a Volurem's fire with a steel blade. She saw Robson take on another while Helmer did everything possible to keep from being burned by the fire blazing off the Volurems' bodies.

Number 2841 ringed the edge of the spreading Volurem, cutting them down before they could grow to a number she could not handle. She didn't notice until she'd circled back to the other two soldiers that the woman was following her. She was the only one who stood inside the burn with Number 2841. Together they surrounded the remaining Volurem and Number 2841 extinguished their flames.

When the last Volurem's flame burned out, Robson pointed his scythe at her. "You!" he barked, charging at her with his war scythe aimed at her chest.

She attempted to dodge, but the short, muscular man moved as fast as she did. She blocked his spear, having to push his blade to the side with considerable effort. She'd never seen another person like her, other than those at the facility, who could move as she did.

"Stop, she didn't mean to," the woman said, but the other soldier joined his stout companion.

Number 2841 easily dodged and blocked Helmer's attacks. It was Robson she struggled to stay ahead of. To her, it seemed like the other woman did not want the men to kill her. And so, too, she did not want to kill this woman's companions. But they drove at her, time after time, until Robson drew blood from Number 2841's calf. The hit made her realize that they would kill her just as the Scaled One would have. She needed to end them.

The scythe drove at her again. This time she jumped at it. With her willow-leaf blade, Number 2841 swatted the long spear to the side and landed inside the stout man's reach. She slid the tip of her blade up into his massive chin, penetrating deep into his head. He dropped the scythe. Helmer came at her leading with his bludgeon of a broadsword. She pulled her saber free from the stout soldier's skull and spun. The older soldier whiffed a heavily weighted swing where her body had been. He stumbled directly into the revolving willow-leaf blade she held horizontally in her hand. It cut into his neck. Number 2841 caught the limp weight of his body. She heard a click to her right, like two stones clapping together, and the glow from the yellow cooking stone went out.

Number 2841 let the armored man's body fall from her grip. She stood in the darkness. All was silent. Number 2841 had a clear line of sight through the trees. The female soldier was running from the scene. Number 2841 had no idea why they'd reacted the way they had. She didn't mean to summon the Volurem. Had she known the stone was hot enough to burn, she wouldn't have dropped it. She wondered if there were more people like them out there. More who would try to kill her. Number 2841 looked down at the lifeless soldier at her feet. Something became clear. If she ever fought the Scaled One again, she was going to kill him. She was going to make sure nobody would try to kill her again.

A tearing sound, like ripped grass, came from the darkness behind her. Number 2841 swiveled, wondering if a Volurem spotted somewhere without her noticing. To her satisfaction, the harquice wandered into the mostly burnt grass opening. It trailed the lead rope, grazing near the edge of the burn.

Seeing the animal made her feel something inside. A warmth at the notion that the mare did not react as though she was strange. This feeling felt like the excitement she had when the female soldier had helped her sit in a new way. She wanted that feeling again. She wanted to find more people like the female soldier.

Number 2841 realized the men had acted strangely when they saw her without her fighting uniform. The uniform had burned off her body in the arena. She needed clothing to make her look more like them. She looked down at the dead soldier at her feet, noticing his body was about the same size as hers.

GALTERIUS-BREX

THE DAY BEFORE THE EMPEROR'S DEATH

"When will we see the military support your Emperor promised?" the Southern Warden asked, the deep red lines of his face appearing as rigid as his accented voice sounded.

"The Southern Division has currently been assigned to allocate its resources toward establishing strongholds along the Fringe while the weather holds," responded High Commander Galterius-Brex.

What the Southern Warden is asking for isn't beyond reason, Galterius thought. *When I was commanding the Hundred and Fifth Legion, I made similar demands to Emperor Jermanus. The difference then being that the*

Emperor was fighting right along with us. He saw the need for more support.

"I understand the fire fights we've seen this rotation are more intense than normal, but the Empire has decided —" he attempted to explain.

"To continue building the Wall," Warden Ulbris interrupted. "For the last ten rotations since my people's treaty with the Emperor, the Agunzi have sent our youth, our most gifted fighters, and our most brilliant minds to serve in your army. Where is the Division Emperor Jermanus promised our people?"

"In the peak of fire season, I direct the legions in my brigade to protect South Saypo," Galterius explained.

I would send all the Divisions in Old Rhydenar's four Imperial states if I could, Galterius wished he could tell his Agunzi counterpart. *My brigade is already in the south,* he thought. *And the rest of the Division still in Northern Saypo, but cruelly, I share the Division command with Marxius Ovando. High Commander Ovando-Kai would not commit any of his Divisions away from their current assignments to aid the Agunzi.*

"What of the Agunzi Division?" Ulbris asked. "The one we agreed to take charge of in our treaty."

And let them walk away from protecting the construction of the Fringe Barrier? Oh, these negotiations are taxing, Galterius fumed while rifling through some papers to provide cover for his hesitation to respond immediately. *The Agunzi infantry are the glue holding the Emperor's project together, whether he knows it or not. They fight the Volurem in the southern regions better than Rhydarians. Jermanus' cross-continent barrier through the Fringe wouldn't have made it as far as it has if it weren't for the treaty.*

No, Emperor Jermanus would never allow skilled Agunzi infantry forces to leave the Fringe Barrier to protect villages. Not when he could build a wall to keep the Volurem out of the Empire. But how to explain this to an Agunzi, this far north? Their minds aren't as quick to think in this region as they are closer to Volourium, Galterius considered.

"Once the Fringe Barrier is complete —" he began.

"Argh," Ulbris groaned, silencing Galterius with a wave of his widespread hand. "The Wall was supposed to be completed last rotation. It's not even halfway across Saypo and even that section is incomplete. The Volurem continue to scorch freely through the croplands to the east. Nandan's villages are flooding into Saypo as we speak."

"I understand your frustration but building a secure wall across northern Volourium is going to take more time and resources," Galterius said, truly realizing the Southern Warden's frustration. He'd grown up in the east, in the Imperial State of Choteau where, as an Eso, the Empire seemed a distant governing entity. It wasn't until he'd gained his first command in the 89th Legion that he started to see the Empire's influence on the Terra people of Tarmigan. Now, Galterius' New Rhydarian blood ran thick with his Imperial Loyalty. He knew the Empire's faults, the obstacles it presented for equality, and change. Galterius once thought he could help lead Rhydenar to a place where the Volurem were secondary to the systemic classism throughout the Empire. He spent decades forcing the Volurem deeper into Volourium, but they always came back the next fire season. Now that he'd left the battlefield and seen what it was like in Perdigon, at the heart of Rhydarian politics, Galterius questioned if he'd ever see the changes he'd hoped to help usher in for the Empire's next generation.

Galterius' effort to sympathize with the Agunzi Southern Warden fell short.

"There is no need for a wall when the fire brands can float over it, sparking and summoning the Volurem to blaze through our supply," Ulbris said, clenching his wide jaw and rolling his brawny shoulders forward.

Galterius kept his attention on the two southern fighters standing behind their warden. *It's good they agreed to leave their weapons outside the Capitol Building,* he thought. Galterius knew that wouldn't stop them from a fist fight though.

"If your army fails to send us the legions we need to protect our villages, the Agunzi people will not honor the treaty any longer," Ulbris said.

"You break the treaty, and you know what will happen," Galterius warned.

"Don't act as if this is a new concept. I've made our position very clear in the correspondence leading up to this meeting," he said flatly, the two Agunzi behind Ulbris balling their fists and glaring at Galterius.

Galterius tensed. *Don't test me,* he thought. A memory of his blade hewing through Agunzi soldiers in the South flashed through his mind's eye. In years past, just the way the three Agunzi were scowling at him, sitting with fists clenched and threatening postures, would've sent his New Rhydarian blood boiling. *Don't these southerners recognize the pink burn scars on my face? They should. Most do,* he thought, absentmindedly rubbing at the pink burn scar that marred the left side of his neck, extending up along the corner of his square jaw and melding his ear to the side of his head. Galterius' short black-and-grey beard would never fill in the disfigured mark. That side of his face and head would remain bald like his exposed forehead where his widow's peak inched his hairline farther back each year.

And if they don't recognize the story of this scar, the collection on my face, neck, and hands should be a warning to them, he thought. *Or will I have to expose the scars from the blades on my body to make my reputation known?* The only scar on Galterius' face not left by burns was the line across the bridge of his wide nose that continued over his left cheek. *An Agunzi gave me that one,* he thought. *Surely these Southerners would've heard of about that tale, even if they didn't recognize my name.* Galterius' adrenaline began to rise at the memory of that battle, but he took a subtle breath, forcing himself to think of the consequences. *A brawl in the palace would only increase the likelihood of secession from the Empire once they returned South,* he admitted silently.

Galterius felt a hand gently rest on his shoulder as a soft, low voice whispered into his ear, "This negotiation needs to end with an agreement."

Galterius glanced in frustration at his advisor. Isik's long Zethrillian face was close to his ear. Her words acted as a reminder to stay on course.

"You wouldn't want the Southern Warden to leave this negotiation and have him rallying the Agunzi break away from the Empire. What would the Senators say about you then? What would Marxius think, after leaving you in charge of the Division while he's on the overland supply mission with Benton?"

Galterius looked deep into Isik's large yellow eyes. *Ashes, she's right,* he told himself. *The Agunzi people are a proven and great asset to our infantry. I can't allow the Southern Warden to leave without an agreement.*

"For the Emperor," Galterius replied to Isik, though he

understood it was not for Emperor Jermanus that Galterius needed this negotiation to end positively. Though Emperor Jermanus' attention was focused on his floundering mine in the Shield Mountains, an Agunzi secession from the Empire would certainly draw his undivided attention, but not in a positive way.

If I want to separate myself from a shared command, and prove to everyone that I deserve my own Division, then I must find a way to ease the Southern Warden's mind.

Galterius-Brex slowly drew in another breath, a calming tactic he hadn't spent much time mastering during his often-violent career primarily spent conquering the southern reaches of Rhydenar with Emperor Jermanus. *I'm not that man anymore,* he told himself. *Leading a Brigade requires more politicking and less time in the field.*

Since coming to the capital three rotations ago, Galterius had replaced some of his muscle with fat. While dressed in his black lazgron surcoat, though, that change wasn't noticeable. He still appeared to have all of the hard-earned muscle he built up over many years of fighting in the South. Now in his fifty-first rotation, Galterius still stood the eighteen hands that he'd been in his thirties, having lost a half-a-hand in height to the effects of denser gravity in the south.

The Southern Warden, Ulbris, should at least know not to provoke me, Galterius continued in his conversation with himself. *I am the Rhydarian Commander who wields the black dragon fang. I am the man the Common Class calls the Eso King.*

"What supply did the Volurem burn?" Isik, Galterius' Zethrillian advisor asked the warden.

A frown ran across Ulbris' wide mouth, and he said, "You are taller than most Zethrillians I have seen in the capital. I have never been to Zethril though, as I'm sure you've never been any further south than Perdigon."

"I am a staggering twenty-seven hands tall, taller than most Zethrillians, just as you seem taller than most Agunzi. Despite the reputation my purple hair, elongated features, and aqua completion convey to your people, I would like to venture farther south and expand my way of thinking. You know the adage," she said, looking down her long nose at them.

"Our gravity would paralyze you, as it already makes your body sluggish here, near the New-Old Rhydarian border," one of the Agunzi men standing near Ulbris said.

"Yes, that's the very point I'm driving at here. Just like the effects on my body, there is one on my mind. As there is on yours," Isik replied.

The Agunzi stared blankly at them as if they hadn't understood Isik's mocking explanation.

Their blood flow has slowed here and the decreased oxygen isn't helping. It's making these Southerners more simple-minded than they would be at home, Galterius thought, knowing the opposite effect occurred with Isik and all Zethrillians who ventured south of Zethril. *Which is why the Agunzi fight, the Zethril advise, and the Rhydarians rule.*

"The gravity clearly has taken its toll on you as well," Isik said. "Though you may be stronger and faster here in Rhydenar, you are not thinking as clearly as I am. Just a moment ago you said that the Volurem can spot across the Fringe Barrier and burn up your supply."

"I am thinking just fine. I spoke of the supply your Emperor taxes from us each rotation," Ulbris said, craning his short meaty neck as best he could to look up at the towering woman across the table.

"If you're withholding from the Empire," she started, but Galterius touched his scarred hand to her elongated arm, signaling her to stop prodding.

"We realize the Fringe Barrier does not guarantee that the Volurem won't burn through the Empire, but it will dramatically decrease the chances of that happening," Galterius said, steering the conversation back toward an understanding and away from accusation.

The beefy Southerner shifted his gaze back to Galterius and said, "The ways of our people were working long before the Rhydenar Empire reached its hands into the South."

"We're trying to create a longer-term solution," Galterius responded. "One that will bring an end to the large-scale battles between us and the Volurem. The primitive structures work for the short term, one to three rotations, but then they require rebuilding. Our stone walls withstand the rotations better."

"Your wall is a farce," Ulbris said. "The Volurem's strength is increasing. If we are to survive them, we must be mobile."

Galterius' anger spiked. *I've spent my entire military career trying to make a more livable space for all Terra people.* "Have you forgotten why the Agunzi finally welcomed the Rhydarian Empire? Just because your blood flows more slowly here in Rhydenar and your need to think strategically demands more oxygen does not excuse you from —"

"I take offense!" the Southern Warden shouted, his slightly higher-pitched voice echoing around the room.

"High Commander Galterius-Brex is right," Isik said, her low voice adding to the tension at the table. "Because it is a stereotype does not make it untrue in this specific scenario. The greater good will come to your people by helping the Empire of Rhydenar complete the Fringe Barrier."

"My mind is working just fine, Zethrillian," Ulbris countered. "Need I remind you what I could do to that thin, wispy skeleton of yours."

"That's enough!" Galterius barked. "I will not allow my lapse in temperament to sour our negotiations and taint this relationship with violence."

Ulbris' deep orange eyes churned between Galterius and Isik, as he wisely sat back in the high-backed, wooden chair.

"I apologize for my offense to you, Warden Ulbris. That was not my intention. I was merely pointing out what brought our people to the terms of a treaty to begin with. The flames of the Volurem are powerful and our collaboration is paramount if we are to defeat them. The Empire needs Agunzi help," Galterius said.

The admission pained him, but with Emperor Jermanus' focus on delving into the depths of the Shield Mountains instead of completing construction of the Fringe Barrier, Galterius' view of the Emperor and his rule over the past three rotations had become tainted.

"Temporary protection that can be quickly rebuilt is more than we currently have. The crops we manage to defend are fewer each rotation, while the fruits of Northern Volourium are ripe for the taking," Ulbris said.

"You're suggesting the Empire expand farther south into Volourium?" Isik interrupted.

"Not to expand and live there. To strike and retreat, harvest the plentiful foods that grow there and bring them back behind the Fringe. The Volurem certainly don't need them," Ulbris said.

Galterius saw the other two stout Southerners nod eagerly at this idea.

"There is no evidence to support that this incredible risk is worth the minimal reward," Isik responded.

Galterius raised his hand to stop Isik but wanted to hear how they would respond, so he lowered it, allowing Isik to continue talking in his place.

"Based on my estimates, we would lose more Agunzi soldiers to the flames to do what exactly? Gain food that we can already grow in Rhydenar? Not only is it too dangerous, but when the Volurem scouts become wise to this proposed strategy, they will do as they have always done and burn the vegetation to charcoal and ash. It is a better use of our resources to focus on completing the Fringe Barrier and making sure our efforts to construct it are not overrun because the tribes in the South choose to disband from their contract of loyalty to the Empire and return to a devolved-style of warfare against the Volurem."

Galterius touched Isik's arm to stop her before tempers flared again. He realized it was difficult for her, considering, *for Isik to explain her elevated way of thinking to them must be like trying to explain politics to an adolescent.*

"Have you ever been to Volourium?" Ulbris asked.

"I have," Galterius answered.

"I'm asking the Zethrillian," Ulbris said, meeting Galterius' green and yellow eyes.

Isik folded her lengthy fingers across her lap. The tips of her winged sleeves hung loose at her sides, the fabric of her dark blue robe just slightly above the table where the five of them sat. The expensive folia linen that she wore proudly was a staple of Zethril. Isik licked her light blue-and-teal lips, and said, "No. I have not been to such a high field of gravity."

"Then you do not know how or where the food from the south grows," Ulbris stated flatly.

"I do," she replied with confidence, matching the warden's unblinking stare. "I don't need to have gone that far south to read the research. The scholarly works devoted to the subject are available and I have read most of them since coming to Perdigon."

"Croplands aside," Galterius said. "I asked you, Warden Ulbris, to meet with me to quell the tension that's arising between our peoples. I need to know that you, Ulbris, Southern Warden of the Empire, will honor the pledge of loyalty you made to Emperor Jermanus and continue fighting with us in the coming fire seasons."

"Because of your daughter's presence in Saypo, you've heard the rumors, that is why you called this meeting, High Commander?" Ulbris asked. "I can tell you this. I do not claim the title the Agunzi tribes are offering me, calling me the King of the South, but I am the Agunzi's voice. I came here to speak for all of us. The only thing that will keep the Agunzi tribes from going our own way in the fight with the Volurem is if you deliver the military support as promised. If you won't commit the twenty-five-thousand soldiers to help protect the Agunzi lands, then I need to see at least an increased effort in support. At least a Brigade's worth before spring's end," Ulbris said.

"That's three legions." Galterius said with a shake of his head. "Up to eighteen thousand soldiers. That will be difficult to bring together in such a short time. It would mean pulling hundreds of troops from contracted assignments. The Army Corps would need to form new contracts with —"

"Then draw them up," Ulbris demanded.

"Despite my reputation, I do not have that kind of

influence with the Senate. I can't guarantee a change in this rotation's current stationing, not for that many legions," Galterius said.

"You are a Brigade High Commander. Order the legions under your control to march to Saypo and Nandan," Ulbris said.

"I share the brigade command with another High Commander. As a Kai and Senator, he has more political power and outranks me. I have only one legion at my disposal, and they are already protecting construction efforts at the Fringe Barrier in South Saypo."

"If you can't convince the Senate to supply my people with the minimum legions necessary, then maybe you don't deserve to be called Eso King," Ulbris responded.

"I am not a king," Galterius growled through clenched teeth. He knew exactly what the Southern Warden was doing to provoke him. He drew in another deep breath and said, "As an Eso, I can't commit the legions you ask for. I will need to wait until High Commander Ovando-Kai returns to the capital. With his recommendation, we can seek authorization from the Senate to supply more legions to the South."

"Why can't you just order them now and ask for forgiveness later?" Ulbris asked. "The Volurem will not stop burning when they hit the Saypo-Nandan border. Already this season we have had to face them in great numbers. If the past three rotations are any indication of their strength and determination this fire season, the Volurem will burn deep into your Empire and beyond the Shield Mountains. This could be the rotation that they burn clear through to Zethril."

"If you think the Volurem are a threat to Zethril, you

do not know how elemental the Volurem's behavior is," Isik said.

"I'm aware of how the oxygen affects their intensity, but do you know how intense the Volurem can be? How could you? You're a Zethrillian," Ulbris said.

"That is correct. I am a Zethrillian, and as Galterius-Brex's advisor, I have researched Volurem behavior across all of Tarmigan's regions," Isik said.

"Then you must know how threatened my people are by this upcoming fire season," Ulbris mocked. "The fighting will be the most intense where the croplands are the most plentiful. What will Emperor Jermanus say when a third of the Empire's food supply burns because he spent all his time with his head in the dirt while his army spent its energy and resources trying to build a wall that the Volurem can spot over? It only takes one spark during the driest months to set the Empire ablaze."

Galterius couldn't ignore this harsh truth. This absence of leadership began when the Emperor turned his attention to mining for brismil. He would not be happy to learn that construction of the Fringe Barrier had led to a food short-age, given that the Empire had already run short over the last three rotations. He thought about what he would ask of Emperor Jermanus if he were in the Southern Warden's position, and said, "I can't promise that you will receive the number of troops and weapons that you have requested, but I will do what I can to secure you three legions. In the meantime, I can promise you six thousand of the best legionnaires in Rhydenar."

Ulbris stood abruptly, his square feet landing as wide as the war room table, "Deliver on your promise, Galterius-Brex. The fate of the Agunzi people is in your hands. If you don't, the whole of the Empire will suffer." With that final threat, the Agunzi warden left the palace war room.

Galterius shot a concerned look at the slender New Rhydarian man who madly scribbled his quill on parchment to document the meeting. Judging by the lack of any grey in his thick, curly black hair, the middle-aged man had recently graduated from Medi training.

Is he trustworthy enough to have been assigned to record this conversation with the Southern Warden? Galterius wondered. But that wasn't for Galterius to decide. He might live a wealthy lifestyle similar to a Noble and be recognized as enough of an asset to advise the Emperor in war, but he would never hold a Noble's political power. The best he could do was continue trying to impart what honor and integrity meant to him on to the Nobles of Perdigon.

"Taziana is not going to like that you've committed her legionnaires to fight with the Agunzi tribes," Isik said in a low whisper.

Galterius waited for the recorder to pack up his supplies and exit the Capitol meeting room in the north corridor before he responded. The moments dragged as the man worked his way around the table and across the oversized room. Once they were alone, Galterius replied to Isik's comment. "They are my soldiers. My daughter knows the chain of command better than most in the Rhydarian Army. She will not question a direct order from her High Commander."

"It's been three rotations since you last led your legion into battle. Who do you suppose they will feel more loyalty toward? The one bankrolling their efforts, or the one leading them in the heat of battle?" she said.

"Taz is an extension of my command. If they are loyal to

my daughter, then they are loyal to me," Galterius answered.

"Maybe it's time you reminded them who really leads the legion? Return south and fight with them again," Isik said.

I do prefer directing my legion on the field of a firefight to the political wrangling I've been forced to participate in at the Capitol these last three rotations, Galterius told himself. He longed to face the fires of the Volurem again but knew that his time in brismil plate was running thin. Galterius had already pushed his luck longer than most before Emperor Jermanus asked him to leave his family and serve as a secondary Division Commander in Perdigon. Every time he donned the dragon-scale armor, he again risked the cancerous disease caused from prolonged exposure, which would slowly and painfully end his life.

"I'll need Marxius' support if I'm going to convince the Senate to send more legions south," Galterius said.

"Realistically, I don't believe Marxius' influence will be enough," Isik said.

"Why not? He's been currying favor with Jermanus' nephew for an entire rotation. Benton being an Akai, he is not denied often. Maybe Marxius could influence him in some way," Galterius said.

"You've already pointed it out and still you don't see it?" Isik said. "If this fire season goes as projected, the Nobles of Perdigon will direct the legions to protect their interests. I wouldn't be surprised if they recalled their legions to Perdigon."

"We can't lose the Agunzi now. The strength and stamina of one well-trained wideback surpasses that of half the average Rhydarian troop."

"The Nobles don't care about the Agunzi. Their focus

is not on the functionality of the military, it's on their personal gains. We have too few well enough established cities between South Saypo and Perdigon to stop a large Volurem army from burning all the way through the Saypo Plains and Apgar Forest," Isik said.

"Which is exactly why we need to hold the Volurem at the Fringe," Galterius emphasized.

"What do you think Warden Ulbris meant with his closing threat?" Isik asked.

"Beyond his exact words, that's what I pay you to sniff out," Galterius said.

"Before the Agunzi tribes were absorbed into the southern Imperial states, they fiercely opposed the Rhydarian Empire. Almost as much as they oppose the Volurem," she said.

"You don't have to tell me that. But do you suspect they'll commit treason?" Galterius asked in a hushed voice.

"From what we've gathered, based on your daughter's reports, our alliance with the Agunzi is wearing dangerously thin. It's not a far stretch to think that Ulbris was lying when he denounced the name the tribes have given him. Would it be that hard for them to succeed and claim Ulbris as the King of the South?" Isik asked.

"You heard him; Warden Ulbris does not want to be a king. He wants to protect his people," Galterius said.

"Which is what a king does for his people. Whether he wants to be a king or not," Isik said.

Galterius mulled over this suggestion.

"Considering how this meeting went, I wouldn't be surprised to hear that the southern tribes are banding together in anticipation of the Empire's failure to deliver the legions they need and have requested. Even a warden with that much power is dangerous to the Empire. The

Agunzi are at the Fringe and control the front lines of our war with the Volurem. It's not complex strategic thinking to consider allowing hungry Volurem to rage through the Empire and weaken its armies for one season."

"What good would that do? Though they aid in battle, they have a fraction of our total military strength. If provoked, Rhydenar would beat them into submission as we did once before."

"After a rotation of large-scale burning across Rhydenar, the Agunzi could strike in the off season, when the Empire is weakened and scrambling just to feed the people," Isik responded.

"You think too much, Isik. The Agunzi wouldn't be that short-sighted. Emperor Jermanus would not allow them to get that close to overthrowing the Empire," Galterius said as he pondered these scenarios.

"Where you see Rhydenar as Tarmigan's largest empire, I see it spreading itself too thin. Our control at the Fringe is weak. The Agunzi have existed on Tarmigan as long as both of our peoples have."

"Rhydenar holds the power," Galterius said emphatically.

"For now," Isik replied calmly.

Galterius stood, smoothing out the wrinkles on the front of his black lazgron surcoat. His leather boots scrubbed along the wool rug several times before Isik took a step to catch up with him. After passing through the meeting room, Galterius led his Zethrillian advisor through the Great Rotunda and out the front entrance. Stopping on the steps to face the Port of Perdigon, he said, "Isik, before our next meeting, make sure Ulbris, the two men with him today, and the members of his Southern delegation don't do anything they might regret on their last night in the capital. I didn't like the way the Warden left our conversation."

The tall Zethrillian woman offered a polite nod before gracefully striding down the palace steps, passing through the statues and entering the streets of Capitol Hill. Zethrillians made for awful street spies. One thing Galterius had encouraged his advisor to do from the start was to cultivate as many snoops as would stay loyal to his bankroll. With Galterius' coin over the three rotations he'd employed Isik, they'd developed a network of Esos willing to watch the day-to-day happenings throughout Perdigon. Some Senators told Galterius to his face that trusting Esos was worthless. But the knowledge Isik supplied Galterius from their network of Esos was well worth his investment. If any conspiracies or coup attempts were building in the capital, Isik would know.

Somewhat comforted by his confidence in his network of Esos, Galterius focused on deciding which Nobles and Senators he could persuade to embrace and support this preventative battle strategy. He'd test the notion with a few Kai on the Defense Committee before leaving Capitol Hill for the day. If he could use Isik's reasoning to sway them, perhaps some with landholdings on the eastern edge of the Apgar Forest would support sending more legions to South Saypo and Nandan. Taking the reins of his harquice from a Capitol servant, Galterius mounted his mare with a new set of potential allies in mind. As he rode from the stone walkway, past the statues of early Rhydarian Emperors, he turned east onto the gravel streets. Galterius spotted a wisp of smoke rising in the east. It chuffed into the air, burning a small amount of fuel somewhere far beyond the walls of Perdigon before burning out. He slowed his mount, seeing that no one else had noted the brief fire near the base of the

Shield Mountains to the east. If an army of Volurem had made it that far north this early in the rotation, Galterius would've heard about it. The smoke spread like the beginning of a small dark rain cloud, trailing on the northern winds.

We have no legions there. The closest is several days to the south. How did that fire suddenly burn out at this time of day…?

Galterius shook his head. The Volurem could not be burning there. No cities, towns, villages, or pop-up settlements existed in that area. The thought that Benton and Marxius had run into a holdover Volurem from the last season entered his mind, but in the Shield Mountains? That was impossible. The mountains received too much snow in the off season. There shouldn't have been a fire there, yet he had witnessed it.

His thoughts drifted to one of Emperor Jermanus' possible mining operations somehow managing to defeat a small force of Volurem despite the miners' fears. But Galterius had no idea whether a brismil mine existed in that region. The Emperor kept those details close to his chest. The only proof of the mines' existence that Galterius knew of was the subversion of funds he saw in military reports that came through the Imperial Defense Committee, members of which he was on his way to speak with next.

And the Senators believe my network of Esos is a hollow investment, he almost smirked to himself.

Galterius spurred his harquice to ride down Capitol Hill to his next commitment at the Senate Chambers. He'd withhold the smoke sighting until he could determine if any of them were willing to send the Agunzi more support.

JERMANUS' FATE

THE NIGHT OF THE EMPEROR'S DEATH

Galterius led his harquice past the villa entrance and out into the dimly lit gravel street. Lumistones capped the ends of each hinge post, illuminating the symbols of Rhydenar's most distinguished upper class. Even at night and out among the sprawling estates surrounding Capitol Hill, Galterius felt cramped.

There was hardly anywhere in the city where he didn't feel claustrophobic. In the light of day, most of the city felt like an endless forest of high-rise buildings densely congested with all types of Terra peoples. Most Esos lived in the lower rolling hills that skirted the highest point in the city, Capitol Hill. Five- and six-level townhomes made of wood, sided in ash-stained stucco, and topped with clay-shingles spread from the surrounding Kai villas, competing for space right up to the massive granite stone walls of the city. The most successful Esos lived in stone-walled buildings tucked in with the Ai, under the expansive estates of Senators and Kai of Capitol Hill. Other low-ranking Nobles and wealthy Eso estates could be seen capping the smaller hills spread throughout the metropolitan area, but the Imperial Palace atop Capitol Hill overlooked them all. At the center of the city, the Palace gleamed like a jewel crowning the massive stone structures on Capitol Hill. Above the gated villas of the wealthy and the impressive government structures where politicians met to run the Rhydarian Empire, the Palace stood as a symbol of the Emperor's status over all of them. The whole place felt like a circus to Galterius.

Petting his harquice's long nose, he said, "Why can't anyone in this city listen to a reasonable argument? I'm not used to this type of defeat. On the battlefield I could use strength and strategic maneuvering to win. It isn't the same here in the capital. Not with these Senators and self-righteous Kai. Isik was right," he told his harquice. "They're too fearful to commit to protecting anything other than their home walls. Every Kai with a legion is too hesitant to send any soldiers south without first hearing Benton's supply report. None can see the bigger picture – that holding the Volurem at the Fringe Barrier is the key. Now I don't know what I'm going to do. The Agunzi will not be a part of our Empire for long if all we can do is send one legion in place of an entire Division. Ashes to Jermanus and his broken promises."

As Galterius led his mount around the corner to the

street where Emperor Jermanus had secured a villa for him, Galterius wondered what news the Emperor's nephew would report and how that would affect the legions of his Brigade stationed in Saypo. If the harvests really were down this season, that would draw resources away from construction of the Fringe Barrier again. Protecting the supply chains and moving large shipments to the closest ports would be the Empire's priority. Galterius didn't understand how the most historically productive croplands in the Empire could suddenly produce less each rotation. Though fighting had grown more intense since he left the field, the southern divisions had hardly lost any ground to the Volurem.

As he approached his lumistone-lit villa gate, he once again admired his symbol, the black dragon's fang, styled across the double-wide, copper-painted doors. Then he noticed Isik waiting for him. Her shoulders were flush with the top of his gate when she stepped into the gravel street to meet him.

"A letter for you, High Commander," she said in her deep Zethrillian accent.

Galterius frowned. Normally one of the Novi trainees delivered messages.

"Who's it from?" he asked, not wanting to take the letter if it were another from a magistrate summoning him to discuss the direction in which he was steering the Imperial Defense Committee.

"Look at the seal stamped into the wax," Isik suggested, handing it to Galterius.

Galterius saw the symbol; it was from his daughter. Aside from Galterius' wife, Taziana was the only other person who used his symbol, the one he designed when he was younger and still building his fame in the infantry. Esos who attained Noble-class wealth or fame, and they were few in Tarmigan, were not born into a Noble house with a family symbol. In this rare scenario when a commoner accumulated enough wealth to purchase land or gain command of a military legion, proper house identification was required. Galterius-Brex, who now had wealth and a legion of his own, used the symbol of his most cherished possession, his brismil sword. Though he owned a brismil scale, the magic sword came to him first. He earned the black dragon's fang more than the brismil scale he paid for. Keeping this ethos of earning one's station in life was how Galterius ran his legion. He wanted these values to reflect in his image. Galterius chose copper as his pop of color instead of the more popular gold or silver symbols of wealth. To the average Eso, copper was supreme; it would be the most expensive ore an Eso could afford in a lifetime. Galterius still felt the copper backdrop of his symbol kept him rooted in his simple beginnings.

"Any whispers of what the Agunzi delegation is doing tonight?" he asked Isik, taking the letter from Taziana.

"Gathering at the less reputable establishments down near the port," she said.

With no cause for concern, he broke the black wax seal imprinted with the dragon's fang. By the light of the lumis-tone, Galterius read the letter.

High Commander,

By the time this letter reaches you, our forces will have been tested in this year's first engagement with the Volurem. The fires are spreading closer to the Fringe, and we are about to face the first wave of Engulfed. Their intensity is low, but it's the earliest they've spread into the Fringe for as long as I can remember. Temperatures are slowly rising with each sunspan, though the relative humidity has held with the longer nightspans. When I look up, I can see the clouds changing, beginning to build to more than the flat wisps of the off-season. From the top of the wall, I saw a Volurem fire whirl in the far south. In the flats here, you can imagine how far one can see into the heart of Volourium, but it was the first fire whirl I have ever seen. You were wise to push me to let mother go north with the rest of the Brigade. Staying here in the south for the off-season has made a major difference in the way our legion holds their pikes and shields compared to the other legions who returned North. I should not have doubted you.

Rumors about the Agunzi tribes in South Saypo banding together continue to emerge. I suspect they're withholding fresh recruits as their numbers of enlisted widebacks are down more than a third from last rotation. The Empire's grip must remain firm on the Agunzi if the Southern Divisions are going to complete the Fringe Barrier. If the tribes don't stay united, control over the Fringe Barrier will waver and we may be forced to fight more than just the Volurem.

Send experienced soldiers with the messenger escorting the Hundred and First. We've heard reports from other legions along the Fringe Barrier of fire brands spotting beyond the wall.

Respectfully,
Commander Taziana-Brex

"Taz, what are you thinking?" Galterius said somewhat to himself as he lowered the letter.

"You can't micromanage her from here. Like I said before, return to the field or learn to play social politics; though, since you haven't learned the game here after three rotations, I don't see much hope for you," Isik said matter-of-factly.

Galterius tapped his leather sandal while waiting for an apology, but after several long moments of searching by

Isik's yellow eyes, Galterius said, "She's leading the legion from Saypo into the Fringe without clearance from the Senate. If it goes poorly, she could find other legions turning against her troops to save face with the Senate."

"She's a Brex. I have an inkling she'll come out of it unburnt," Isik said.

"If it goes too well, she might inspire less prepared legions to do the same. Taking unnecessary losses this early is not wise either," Galterius said.

"You would have them wait for Senate authorization before attacking a Volurem force approaching the unfinished Fringe Barrier?"

"Yes," Galterius said.

"To judge a call as minor as that in an active war zone? This is the Senate, a group of Nobles half of whom have never been within a league of a Volurem's fire? Why wait for their judgment?" Isik asked.

"If you lose Senate backing, the rest of the army could force you out. Then you're just six thousand soldiers without a war to fight and nothing to show for your service," Galterius replied.

"You believe the Senate holds that much power?" Isik asked.

Galterius measured her carefully with his gaze. "If not them, the Emperor himself," Galterius said.

"You obviously haven't read the War of the Burning Roses," Isik said.

"The only things I read that aren't about military tactics are the letters summoning me before the Defense Committee," Galterius growled.

"Speaking of the Palace," Isik said slowly.

"What do they want now?" Galterius asked, sensing the

letter from his daughter wasn't the only message Isik had to deliver.

"A commoner whispered something in my ear about a certain Emperor seen taking a meeting with a group of dirt-covered Rhydarians."

"The miners?" Galterius asked.

"Rumor has it they came in on a ship and left the palace with a chest too heavy to carry by hand. They had to buy a cart to carry it down to the port," Isik said.

Galterius tucked the letter from his daughter into the inside of his leather boot, opposite where he kept the steel knife in his stocking at all times. "That's it. I'm going to speak with Jermanus about this blazing mining operation."

"Without an invitation? Are you sure that is wise?" Isik said.

"Jermanus asked me to come to Perdigon and serve him on the Imperial Defense Committee. He picked me for a reason. I will not compromise my values by turning a blind eye to this reckless waste of wealth while our army needs resources to supply legion support to South Saypo and Nandan."

Galterius mounted his harquice. He instinctively felt at the leather pouch where his brismil scale was belted to his side. Not having his blade and matching scale armor still felt strange to him. Every time Galterius left his brismil blade at the villa and carried the scale armor with him, he felt an indescribable urgency of the brismil pulling at his consciousness. It was as if the matching set of blade and armor knew when they were separated and longed to be together. Ignoring the urge to collect his black dragon fang, Galterius heeled the harquice forward.

As he did, Isik said, "There's a reason honest Nobles don't exist in Perdigon."

Galterius called back over his shoulder, "Did you forget, Isik? I'm no Noble of Perdigon."

As the harquice's cloven hooves clattered through the hard-packed gravel streets, Galterius rode in earnest through the sprawling neighborhoods of the Kai. What he now planned to do was not acceptable in modern politics. The Senators he'd spent the evening trying to persuade to offer military support to the Agunzi would not appreciate Galterius' impatience. His intention to go directly to the Emperor was walking a very fine line and could be seen as double-dealing, something many Kai had failed to do successfully shortly before *retiring* to walled villas in northern New Rhydenar.

Passing through the brightly lit columns of the imperial stone buildings on Capitol Hill, Galterius climbed toward the crown of the city, the Palace. He slowed his harquice in the glow beneath the palace gate where four heavily armored guards stood. A guard stepped out, blocking the gated entrance to the palace courtyard. The light of the lumistone wall refracted off the Palace Guard's gold-colored draco-scale surcoat, shimmering like the lavish palace beyond.

"Palace is closed," he said bluntly, placing his steel-plated gauntlet to the scimitar hilt at his side.

Galterius checked the rank displayed on the guard's left shoulder. One black stripe. "Evening Corporal," he said, lifting his chin so the guard could better see him in the glowing light of the palace wall. Galterius wore his black leather surcoat. The silver dragon wing on each shoulder identified him as a High Commander.

The Corporal removed his hand from his side sword, saying, "High Commander Gal —"

"Come back tomorrow," another guard said, speaking over the Corporal.

Galterius' eyes shifted to the guard pushing off the corner edge of the glowing wall. While noting her Sergeant rank in the double black stripes, Galterius also recognized her wide, narrow-lipped smile. The Old Rhydarian youth had given Galterius some attitude before. Considering her rank, Galterius guessed she was likely an Ai, or possibly a Fifth Class Kai, who'd served as a legionnaire before securing a position with the Palace Guard. Based on how she sauntered forward, her shoulders slouched, and thumbs tucked loosely into the front of her sword belt, Galterius thought he knew her type. She looked to be the kind of entitled Noble Galterius refused to advance through the ranks of his own legion, based on their social status or personal connections.

"I'm here to speak to the Emperor in private," he said to the Sergeant.

"What for?"

"A personal matter," Galterius said.

"I don't believe his Imperial Majesty is receiving personal callers. It's late," she replied.

"It's of great importance," he said slowly and clearly, trying not to do something he might regret.

The Sergeant curled her lip, exposing crooked teeth, and said, "Like ash. Why would the Emperor want to hear an Eso's personal problem?"

"Not my personal problem, Sergeant," Galterius growled. He knew the only reason any junior officer might get away with speaking to him this way would be because of his Eso status, and, in this case, as a gatekeeper to the Imperial Palace despite being junior to him in rank. "The Emperor sent me a personal invitation. And unless you want to lose one of your black stripes, you will alert the Emperor to High Commander Galterius-Brex's presence."

The Sergeant snorted as if to dismiss the idea. But, after a moment's hesitation and several nervous glances between the Corporal and the other two Privates, the Sergeant gave her junior officer a nod. The Corporal opened the steel gate just enough to slip through. As he jogged along the well-lit paths that meandered through the courtyard garden, around a fountain, and to the palace steps, Galterius did not take his eyes off the Sergeant. She stared back at him with stormy grey eyes and ran her tongue through the jumble of her front teeth.

She was the first to break the stare down, her straight black bangs falling from behind her ear as she snapped to see the Corporal leading a palace servant back through the courtyard. Her relaxed shoulders sagged even more than they already had been.

"He will see you in his chambers, High Commander," the New Rhydarian Corporal said.

Galterius did not acknowledge the Sergeant as he rode his harquice through the palace gate. He gave a curt nod to the Corporal only.

The New Rhydarian palace servant took his harquice by the lead rope and led them to the palace steps. If it weren't for the massive rectangular stone palace, the courtyard at night would be the single place in Perdigon where Galterius didn't feel cramped. The lush gardens and open space could've held five villas. The Palace itself stretched as wide as the crest of Capitol Hill.

Stopping beneath the stairs and columns stacked with alternating lumistone and limestone blocks, Galterius dismounted. The servant curtsied, her ankle-length, light blue dress folding on the stone slab. Then she turned and led his mare away. Galterius faced the buttressing staircase that led to the towering double-wide palace doors. The gold trim sparkled in the light of the lumistone as he reached for the silver-plated handles. The doors opened just before he could touch them. Another servant dressed in a simple light-blue silk tunic pushed the door open, held it, and silently gestured for the High Commander to enter.

Galterius knew the route to the war room well. It was where he and the other Imperial Defense Committee members held their meetings and occasionally negotiated with allies. That room was to the left, through the West Gallery and then right.

"His Imperial Majesty awaits you in his chambers," the Old Rhydarian servant said, after closing the door behind him.

Galterius held his breath, trying to remember which direction Jermanus' chambers were once he reached the top of the staircase in front of him.

The old manservant understood Galterius' moment of hesitation and said, "Up the right staircase, turn right. First door on the left."

Standing outside Jermanus' chamber doors, Galterius paused to collect himself. He smoothed the sleeves of his surcoat and stared at the historical scenes carved into the wooden door panels. Measuring them, recalling each of the monumental moments throughout Rhydenar's history, his eyes fell to the last two panels on the bottom. The dark wood was bare of design. He wondered whose actions would be monumental enough to be carved into the final panels. Surely the completion of a barrier wide enough and tall enough to stretch the entire length of the Fringe and keep the fires of Volurem contained would be worthy. The wall that Galterius spent his career fighting to establish.

Being etched permanently into history in this way was a dream Galterius knew an Eso could not achieve. When the Fringe Barrier was complete, Emperor Jermanus would take the credit, not the men and women who fought to build it.

Taking a deep breath, Galterius gripped the golden handle to pull the door open. Before he weighted it, he thought he heard gurgling, that horrible, familiar choking sound when a Terra soldier's lungs flooded with blood. Galterius surged through the door, his heart pounding to the rhythm of battle. At the far end of the chamber directly across the suite, Jermanus clawed desperately at the blue and gold upholstered ottoman at the foot of his bed. Blood slicked the marbled floor, trailing onto the rug that surrounded the bed. Jermanus' hand slipped away from the leather ottoman. He slumped to his side at the foot of the bed.

"Help!" Galterius shouted. "The Emperor needs help!" he cried, running to Jermanus and dropping to his knees at the Emperor's side.

Jermanus' eyes rolled, searching the room for something but not focusing on anything. His face was stricken with horror. Galterius held the Emperor by the back of his head. His curly greying hair felt soft in Galterius' palm.

"Who did this to you?" he asked.

Screaming pierced the room from the open doorway as a servant entered. The Emperor's broad lips moved, attempting to speak, but his voice was absent. He flared his nostrils, trying to get a breath without drowning by his own viscous blood. He coughed, foamy bright red fluid slicking his lips and dribbling down his chin.

Galterius pictured how he saw the Emperor when he first came in. He saw Jermanus' white undershirt splotched red with half a dozen stab wounds on his ribs and chest.

The lacerations went straight in, ripping a three-finger-wide hole in the fabric and soaking the white shirt with too much blood.

"I'm listening," Galterius said, trying to prompt the Emperor to form words.

He felt the Emperor's head trying to turn, his eyes looking toward the open balcony window. Galterius had seen many Rhydarians die from less extensive wounds. There was nothing he could do to save the Emperor. He let the Emperor's head lay to rest on the rug. Galterius realized that other than himself, there was no one else in the room when he entered, and the balcony doors had been open.

He stood, turning to face the group of servants that had gathered in the entrance. There were no Palace Guard among them. "You," he said, pointing a New Rhydarian woman. "Get the Palace Guard."

They should be here already, he thought.

"And would somebody ring the bells," he barked at the handful of servants. "The Emperor has just been assassinated."

Galterius dashed for the balcony. *They couldn't have gone far,* Galterius thought, knowing he'd arrived moments after the assassination. He skidded out onto the balcony, searching the half-moon-shaped stone landing. The balcony faced away from the front gate and port and toward the Shield Mountains stretching to the east. *Three stories up,* Galterius noted, eliminating the possibility that the assassin could easily jump in escape. Just then, he caught sight of a hooded figure in a nondescript cloak and dark surcoat dropping out of sight over the edge of the stone railing. *Gotchya,* Galterius nearly called out but kept his thoughts silent. No guards were in sight and the hooded figure was looking directly down when Galterius saw him drop out of view.

He spotted the thick corded rope tied to the stone railing. The attacker hadn't seen him emerge onto the balcony.

Galterius pulled the short knife from his stocking and darted to the rope. Looking over the edge, he saw the hooded figure shimmying down the long rope. His attention was focused on the landing below. The drop might not kill the assassin, but it would injure him. He reached over and applied pressure to the thick rope with his small blade. The hooded figure felt Galterius on the rope because he instantly looked up. The hood shadowed the face, but Galterius could see the darkness of the skin. It was a New Rhydarian.

The stranger descended faster and, in the rush to cut the rope, Galterius' grip slipped. He dropped the knife. In an instant, Galterius made up his mind, *No time for this.* With no Palace Guard in sight, it was the only other option he had if he wanted to stop the murderer. He plunged his bare hand into the leather pouch on his belt, grabbing the brismil scale. The instant his bare skin touched the dragon scale, a dark metallic suit of scaled armor molded perfectly to his entire body. Galterius leapt over the balcony railing. His aim, to land on the assassin.

Air rushed through Galterius' ears as he rocketed toward where the New Rhydarian was now leaping off the rope. An instant before landing he realized he was going to hit the stone ground next to the assassin's landing place. Galterius tightened his grip on the brismil scale. He missed his mark, colliding with the stone slabs much harder than he expected. Pain bit his heels as his feet connected, sending a splintering sensation through his legs before he buckled under the force, knees bouncing into his chest and arms slapping the ground. He took the brunt of the fall through the brismil armor, its magic offering the strength to absorb the hit and prevent broken bones or damage to internal organs. When his hands slapped the stone though, Galterius lost hold of his scale. Usually, he locked it into the belt wrapped to his bare waist, but he hadn't had time when he grabbed it. *No,* he thought as the brismil scale bounced out of his hand and he instantly became exposed. His leather surcoat wasn't the protection he would need if the assassin turned a blade on him now.

Galterius' vision sparkled, swimming with white specks that warped the pinpricks in the darkness around him. He attempted to climb from the cracked depression in the slab and saw the cloaked assassin moving. The New Rhydarian beat him to his feet. Galterius fully expected the assassin to run from him, like most would have upon seeing the brismil scale, but the murderer did not. The hooded figure came at him, bloodied knife drawn and plunging toward Galterius.

Instinctively, Galterius reacted. He moved slower than he would've had he still been clad in his brismil-scale armor. Crossing his forearms, he blocked the descending assassin's arm, the long knife blade a hand's width from Galterius' throat. He sank backward, kicking his heel into the assassin's stomach. The stranger grunted as Galterius' heel connected with the soft spot and launched the cloaked figure into the empty space behind him. Galterius momentarily lost sight of the assassin as he half-flipped through the air, landing on his back. By the time Galterius rolled to his feet and faced the stranger, he was running away.

"Ash," Galterius cursed under his breath.

A glint of steel on the stone slab in front of him caught his attention. Galterius retrieved his broken handled knife and gave chase. As he did so, he scanned the immediate area for his brismil scale. Fear spiked in him. It was gone.

Suddenly, Galterius noticed the assassin veer sharply off his trajectory. Galterius saw the dark gloss of his brismil scale. The stranger was going to beat him to it.

"Ah!" he cried, hoping to distract the New Rhydarian. The assassin reached the dragon scale before Galterius could stab his short knife into the stranger's back. Galterius' blade glanced off the impervious brismil plate. He flexed in preparation to collide with the solid figure. It did nothing to soften the pain. Galterius slammed into the stranger's back, knocking them both to the ground. Galterius' whole side instantly went numb.

They rolled apart. Before Galterius could rise, he heard the clacking of his brismil-plate armor running away from him. He struggled to get to his feet, his entire right side refusing to cooperate. The click-clack of brismil on stone went silent as the assassin pocketed the scale in the cloak. With the dark hood hiding the New Rhydarian's identity, Galterius did not get a clear look at the assassin before he or she disappeared through the gardens. Despite his shouts of alarm, Galterius met no aid from the absent Palace Guard for far too long. When they finally found him, giving chase in the direction he pointed, Galterius knew he'd failed. He alone could've stopped the assassin from escaping. To make matters worse, the killer got away with his most valuable possession: his brismil plate. The dragon scale was worth twice the matching blade. He'd paid more for that single suit of armor than for his legion and his villa combined, and he had no replacement.

NOT ALONE

THE EVENING AFTER THE EMPEROR'S DEATH

Shylo hung his trousers on the lowest tree branch. Watching the sun drop, he hoped his tunic, trousers, and cloak would dry before nightfall. The rays of sun warming the grassy streambank provided a somewhat comfortable place to air-dry while the warmth lasted. If he was going to die by the blade of a City Guard, he was going to die as comfortably as he could. Shylo stretched his exposed body in the sunny patch of grass below the break in the forest canopy.

He closed his eyes and struggled to puzzle out all that had happened over the last two days. Where had everyone gone when he first returned from the Senate Chambers? The Novi girl had been alone in the Novi trainee quarters; in fact, she was the only one at the villa at that time as far as he could tell. That was until he'd seen the strange light, like the blue light of the moon, right before Ismay Ovando-Kai interrupted him. Or had he imagined that unusual glow? Shylo's head burned worse than the bile still stuck in his throat. He didn't understand why House Didimo had been viciously targeted with the false claims of assassinating the Emperor. Shylo hadn't noticed any hostility from other Penti trainees, no more than he was used to as an Eso. He hadn't heard any rumors about Senator Didimo-Kai feuding with fellow Nobles, though it wouldn't surprise Shylo if he had been purposefully left out of the loop. Shylo had barely proven his worth to justify wearing House Didimo colors, so it would be unlikely that he would be entrusted with any of the Senator's personal matters. None of these details changed the fact that the Emperor and his successors were dead.

Opening his eyes, Shylo stared at the blue sky through wide green leaves above. Something wasn't right. Suddenly, he had the overwhelming sense that he was being watched.

Why did I decide to stop running? Ashes, I should've known they'd come searching every inch of the forest this close to the city wall, he thought, regretting giving up so quickly after working his way around the wall. *They're going to kill me when they find me. I don't want to die,* he realized. Shylo sat up, his head still pulsing painfully.

He didn't see any draco- or lazgron-scaled guardsmen nearing. *No one's there. It's just because you're naked and paranoid,* he told himself.

Shylo contemplated how far he'd ventured into the forest. *I didn't go very far, did I? But I didn't want to go too far into the forest,* he told himself, fearful that he'd need to retreat into Brism Bay if Volurem spontaneously burst to life somewhere within the forest.

Leaves rustled to his immediate left, across the babbling

freshwater stream. He swallowed hard. *Lazgron?* he wondered. *What in the blazes could I possibly do if it were a lazgron? Or worse still, a draco.*

Shylo knew both predators inhabited the Apgar Forest. *Descended from the ancient dragons of Tarmigan,* Shylo cited from memory what he'd read about them. *Dracos devolved from their magical and much larger ancestors, the dragons of Tarmigan. But they don't fly, or spit fire,* Shylo told himself, knowing both lazgrons and dracos lacked any natural magical abilities. *Dracos are still extremely deadly, however. The deadliest predator to all animal life in Tarmigan.*

Shylo wondered how he could identify a draco from a lazgron. Lazgron was more likely, as they were more abundant in this part of Rhydenar. *A lazgron is similarly shaped to a draco, but with stunted legs and necks. Their tails, too,* he remembered. *Their tails are shorter. But I'll know it's a lazgron if it lacks wings. That's the easiest way to know for sure. It will be like the ones at the tracks in Florens,* he told himself.

The only lazgrons Shylo had ever seen in real life were at the racetrack in Florens. The memory seemed distant now. Shylo had only gone to the races because a younger boy in his neighborhood invited him in front of his father. When Shylo initially told the younger boy "No," Shylo's father pressured him to change his mind.

"You need to experience what a wild animal could do to a man if you're going to join the Legions," his father had said.

That was before mother advocated on my behalf to enter the Penti training program in Perdigon.

Yes, more likely a lazgron than a draco, he told himself,

focus returning to the noises in the forest. Shylo's imagination of what a lazgron could do to him in his current state sent a spike of fear through his body. The carnivorous lizards weren't as tall as harquice, but their bodies were twice as long. Shylo remembered seeing one take a bite out of another's hind leg during a race. After feeling the lazgron leather of his *new* cloak, Shylo now had an idea of how sharp their pointed 'teeth must be.

Hearing rustling in the trees, Shylo's vision of what might be in the forest got the better of him. He scrambled to his feet, preparing to abandon his clothing and run wild through the woods like the Tarmig nomads before they're captured by the Volurem and forced into slavery.

Shylo spotted the figure as it stepped out of the forest and gasped, "Ah!"

He was backing away from the streambank when his mind registered that the two-legged Terra person was not a giant lizard or a devolved dragon. It was a person, a female, though she was dressed in a man's army uniform. Shylo suddenly clapped his hands over his privates, "Ashing smoke —" he bit his tongue, remembering his modesty. Not that he had much at present.

The youthful-looking woman carefully edged her way into the sunlight on the opposite side of the stream. Shylo felt something sink in the pit of his stomach when he noticed her drawn saber. He should've continued to run from the capital. It was foolish to think he'd be safe by hiding far from the road, but still within a few hours' walk of the city walls.

This Terra person was unlike any person Shylo had ever seen. Her size, similar to Shylo's, indicated that she most likely came from somewhere in Rhydenar, but her skin was charcoal black, much darker than New Rhydarians. Her eyes burned an ember red, the same color of the splotchy pigmentation that broke through in seemingly random places across her exposed skin. These small patches of red, Shylo could see, weren't a result of burn scarring like other Rhydarians whose scars healed pink. Where her red pigmentation broke through the dark, it was smooth and healthy. She had unique ashen hair, too, a white-grey color. He'd never seen anyone as young looking with such white hair. She wore it down, naturally. It didn't curl like a New Rhydarian's or wave like Agunzi or Zethrillians'. Only Old Rhydarians, like Shylo, had straight hair. Without her feminine eyebrows, full lips, slightly softer face, and two perky mounds on her chest, Shylo would've mistaken her for a man given what she was wearing. Rhydarian and Agunzi women served in the military, but their armor surcoats had subtly different tailoring. She wore a chainmail-sleeved Imperial Army surcoat made of draco leather with dark green scales. She'd cinched the soldier's poorly fitting surcoat around her waist with a lazgron leather sword belt. The short tunic she wore underneath rose above the collar of the surcoat. Where the surcoat parted mid-thigh, he saw dark trousers tucked into mid-calf lazgron leather boots.

"Are you here to kill me?" Shylo asked, seeing that this armored fighter wasn't just out for a walk outside the walls.

She stared at him with unblinking ember eyes. She didn't speak as she measured him with her serious gaze.

Shylo felt a flush of color come to his cheeks as he realized she wasn't trying to hide the way she examined his bare body. "What are you looking at?" he asked defensively while moving for his damp cloak that hung on the thick tree branch to his right.

He froze when, faster than he thought possible, the female leapt across the stream and landed between Shylo and his clothing. Shylo stood, legs half a stride apart, his left hand at his side and right outstretched for the cloak. The slight curve of the woman's thin steel sword glinted in the late afternoon sun as it rested in the stranger's steady grip. The sharpened tip of her willow-leaf saber pointed at Shylo's bare chest just a hand's-width away.

Several breaths passed while he stared into her ember eyes. Shylo sensed a fiery rage smoldering within the young woman's pointed glare. It only lasted a moment, but when he remained still, she cocked her head obviously taking in his features once again. The way she looked at Shylo was the same way he looked at a Zethrillian advisor when he first saw the unique Terra person in the capital.

"What are you going to do to me?" Shylo asked.

She measured him with her gaze again.

Shockingly Shylo realized, *This is how I was looking at the Novi girl in her nightgown.*

He covered himself. "Are you going to kill me or..." he asked.

While holding her saber completely still, she swiveled to the side and tossed his tunic and trousers on the ground.

"Hey," he protested, stepping forward, but stopping when he felt the slight pressure of her cold steel touch his skin.

"Ow," he winced, reeling away, and brushing at his chest. The tip of her blade was so sharp it had pierced him with hardly any applied pressure. Red blood beaded up at the fingernail-long scratch in the middle of his sternum. "You cut me!" Shylo said.

The young woman, having finished tossing Shylo's wet

clothes onto the forest floor, sheathed her blade into a poor-fitting broadsword scabbard and took a step back. She crossed her arms, weighted one leg more than the other and watched Shylo as though he was some kind of attraction or object of amusement; only she didn't smile or laugh.

Shylo decided he didn't care that she was taking in his naked body with a quiet curiosity. She had pricked his skin, scratching his chest. "What are you thinking? You could've seriously hurt me," he whined, trying to remember what his father told him to do if he ever found himself in a position like this. None of those scenarios involved him being without clothing. When he reviewed the imaginary scenarios now, they all involved him already having a weapon, or being able to access one on the ground nearby.

Despite Shylo's comment about her endangering his life, she didn't seem to care, or if she did, she didn't show it.

Shylo moved around her, careful to keep his distance as he retrieved his clothes from the ground. He kept his back to her while brushing the grass and leafy debris from his green tunic, then shook out his black trousers. The inside of the lazgron leather cloak was already dry. The leather seemed to wick water easily and dried surprisingly quickly. Shylo wrapped the leather cloak around his waist, wearing it backwards. He tied the arms behind his back like an apron, letting the crease of the cloak parallel his backside.

With his clothing hung on the tree branch again, he addressed the stranger who continued to study him with a curious stare. "What do you want with me?" he asked. Shylo's initial thought was that she was some type of agent sent from the Palace to hunt him down. When she sheathed her blade and stepped back, however, he wasn't so sure that was the case. Shylo wasn't going to rule anything out until he could get a better read on the female soldier.

She kept her distance and continued to watch him in silence.

"Don't you speak?" he asked.

She didn't acknowledge his question.

Now that Shylo had a few moments to study her, he wasn't so sure that the young woman was from Rhydenar after all. He'd read about distant lands to the east, across the Touro Ocean, but didn't know of the races that lived there, if any. The only other known Terra people outside the Rhydarian Empire were across the Maelstrom Ocean. Based on the description from the few explorers who'd gone that far west and returned, the native people were similar in appearance to those within the Empire. No one, not even the Volurem as far as historians could tell, had been south of Volourium. The Ignis peoples' fire behavior grew with intensity the farther south one traveled toward the equator. No Terra person had made it as far south as the equator, in the heart of the land known as Volourium, and returned. The young woman was not a Tarmig either. Her size and coloring did not fit the descriptions Shylo had read in books about native Tarmigan nomads. Whatever mixture of races she was, she appeared to be older than Shylo, but not by much.

At least one rotation older than me, but no more than five, he thought. His estimate was based on her youthful skin and lively figure. *Either that, or gravity does not affect her as it does the men and women of Rhydenar.* Shylo had to admit that even dressed in a man's armor and with her unique hair and reddened skin, he found her attractive.

Before Shylo's mind drifted too far from the reality of where he was, he asked, "Do you understand anything I'm saying?"

She looked at him with the same blank stare.

"You don't speak Derian?" he asked. Derian was the standard dialect of the Rhydarian Empire. Though each culture in Tarmigan had its own local language, all civilized Terra people spoke Derian.

She blinked, shifted her weight to the other leg, the whole time studying him and nothing else.

Shylo didn't understand what she wanted if not to capture him or kill him. Surely, she didn't live beyond city walls. To Shylo's knowledge, there weren't established cities surrounding Perdigon to explain her wandering alone through this forest. The wilderness, in his opinion, was an ugly place. The land outside the protective walls of Rhydenar's cities or towns was busy with wild animals, many threatening. The increasingly rare Tarmig tribes' people could also be seen occasionally wandering through the ash fields behind the Volurem army, or so he'd heard from Wilsall. And, of course, there was the danger of encountering the unpredictable Volurem. As he searched his thoughts for an explanation as to what this female could possibly be doing out along this streambank alone, Shylo remembered the smoke column he'd seen to the east the day before. For some reason, the ill-fitting uniform the young woman wore reminded him of some Eso rumors he'd over-heard in the weeks before this disaster, of a monster outside the capital walls. Shylo first had to determine whether she was a threat to his life before pursuing any of these other details.

"You don't comprehend anything that I'm saying, do you?" he asked.

She measured him again but didn't respond.

"And you don't know who I am or where I'm from?"

She didn't acknowledge this question in any way.

"What about this? I'm considered dangerous and am a wanted citizen in Perdigon?" Shylo waited for her reaction. Now, she seemed confused but not threatened. "That doesn't get a reaction from you, not even a question?"

Without a word, the young woman pressed her hand to the pommel of her belted sword, lifted the tip away from the ground, and sat down cross-legged in the green grass. The corners of her supple lips turned up slightly. She was smiling with a closed mouth. Shylo couldn't believe her. She acted like Shylo was there to entertain her.

"You don't understand what I'm saying," Shylo stated again, more to himself.

She blinked, not betraying any indication of her objective or whether she understood what he'd said.

Despite her silence, Shylo was becoming increasingly confident that she hadn't been sent to bring him back to Perdigon. If that had been her intention, then the Nobles of Perdigon had gone to greater lengths than Shylo thought possible to catch a criminal. Shylo decided to test her further by telling someone who would be hunting him exactly what they would want to hear. "I'm wanted for conspiring with assassins," he confessed.

She hunched her shoulders, keeping her round, ember eyes locked on him as she plucked blades of grass from the edge of the stream, shredding them absentmindedly.

The confession, though it wasn't an admission to any guilt in the matter, released a sensation within Shylo that made him feel rational. He hadn't realized how much being blindsided by another Noble's house had left him feeling until now. Seeing the way this strange young woman peered up at him, seemingly clueless about what he'd told her, Shylo decided to run with the emotions the confession had pulled from him and speak bluntly. "I didn't kill the Emperor or his two heirs. I didn't even know it had happened until this morning," Shylo explained. The paranoia crawling through his veins thinned with each word. If she did understand, she showed no sign that she intended to take him captive. She sat quietly, appearing to study every detail about Shylo as if he were as unique in appearance as she was. Normally, Shylo would find the unwanted attention uncomfortable, but there was something in the way she looked at him. It made him feel like he wasn't totally alone.

Holding her attention, he continued to relate every detail that had happened to him since he first saw the column of smoke at the foot of the Senate Chambers. The freedom of speaking to a stranger who likely didn't understand him allowed Shylo to speak his mind. If she was waiting to apprehend him until he offered some admission of guilt in conspiring against the Empire, Shylo didn't allow her the opportunity. It was the first time since leaving Florens that Shylo could tell an entire story without feeling the need to warp details to impress his peers.

When he finished, he waited to see her reaction. He sat still and focused on the pile of torn grass. Her fingernails were stained by something dark. At first glance, he assumed the coloring was an aspect of her race, but looking closer, he noticed the same chalky residue smudged on her boots. Shylo opened his mouth to ask her about it but closed his lips when he noted a familiar scent. Suddenly he grew conscious of the wear on the sword handle in her hand and wondered exactly how she had come to be there outside the city walls, any city walls for that matter, alone, and wearing the uniform of an Imperial Legionnaire. He didn't know anything about this stranger. For all he knew, *she* could be the assassin. Shylo suddenly realized how vulnerable he'd made himself by letting his emotions take over. She could easily turn him in, get away, and he'd take the fall for everything.

HATCHING A PLAN

THE NIGHT AFTER THE EMPEROR'S DEATH

S hylo stiffened. The ringing of steel sang as the saber drew free from its sheath.

This is it, he thought. *This is how I die. I shouldn't have come with her.*

He stood, clenching his jaw, flexing his empty stomach, and waiting for the hewing swing to swish through the air behind him and bite into the back of his neck.

The killing stroke never came. Shylo finally moved when he heard her light footsteps jogging away into the forest.

"Wait, where are you —" he began, but she'd gone, her

silhouetted figure disappearing into the deepening shadows of night.

In a matter of moments, the dark forest became intensely quiet. The songbirds were sleeping. Not a single tree rat's high-pitched, repetitive call to be heard. The air turned chilly without a breath of wind. Shylo felt fear trickle down his neck as the sobering reality of being alone in the wilderness cycled through his brain. His thoughts turned to the potential dangers that could kill him out here. Volurem smoldering their way through the forest, creeping up behind him before burning him alive. A monster, something worse than a draco, rumored to be lurking outside Perdigon. Then Shylo's focus shifted to again seeing the bodies strewn throughout the House Didimo courtyard, dead before the Palace bells announced the Emperor's death.

Suddenly, a wet snort rustled the air behind him, the deep breath shattering the silence. Shylo jumped forward, spinning to face what was sure to be a horrible creature. Flinching again when he saw it, Shylo instantly felt the fool. A harquice, unsaddled but bridled and tethered to a tree. It pulled at its lead rope and stamped a front hoof as if pleading for freedom. The mare's wide eyes rolled as she tried to slip free in a panic.

"It's okay," Shylo said, wondering why his presence was causing the creature to react so negatively. Domestic harquice typically weren't afraid of Rhydarians. "There, there. Calm down, it's going to be okay. I'm not here to hurt you."

Approaching the long-faced, four-legged mount, Shylo admired the creature's rounded spurs. Like the nubs where its wings would've been as a wild animal, the spurs on its hind legs were cut and filed down. Most domestic harquice had their wings and spurs docked at birth, and later their two front fangs filed flush with the rest of their front teeth. Seeing a wild harquice, with its intimidating hand-length fangs, widespread leathery wings, and sharp defensive spurs, wasn't something Shylo had considered when leaving the capital. He considered the damage a wild harquice could inflict if it were in a panicked state like this domesticated one.

"That's right, it's okay. I'm no Volurem or anything spooky like that," Shylo said, stroking the harquice's brown, short-haired neck. The harquice's mane felt coarse in his hand as he attempted to calm the animal and untie it from the tree. The mare stopped stamping momentarily while Shylo appreciated the animal's comforting warmth.

"I'm kind of surprised the sound of my voice is working to calm you," Shylo said, attempting to distract the mare while freeing the lead rope with one hand. "I didn't grow up around harquice. With Florens on the Pryor River people travel by boat mostly. Even in the city there are few of your kind. But there are plenty of harquice in Perdigon, especially in the Kai villas. I have seen people speak openly to their harquice," Shylo said.

Suddenly the animal tossed her head. Shylo noticed her ears were now pinned flat against her arched neck. The seventeen-hand harquice reared. Shylo staggered away from her kicking front hooves. Narrowly avoiding a cloven hoof to his chest, Shylo tripped over a saddle on the ground that he hadn't seen in the dark. He fell onto the cold forest duff. Thundering stamps pounded the ground all around him as he rolled to avoid the animal's deadly stomps. Shylo spun blindly into a tree trunk, knocking his face on an exposed root. The hit to the bridge of his nose burned and his vision blurred as his eyes watered. The harquice's hooves clapped around him. Pinned between the tree trunk and the frenzied animal, Shylo curled into a ball and waited to be hit, but instead the harquice galloped past him and into the forest.

In the quiet that followed, Shylo popped up, and stood with his back against the tree. Breathing deeply while recovering from the sudden, violent outburst, Shylo waited to see if the mount would circle back. As the moments between breaths slowed, Shylo realized the animal likely had disappeared into the night for good. And for a reason. *It seemed to act out of fear*, Shylo thought. *A fear so intense that it caused a domesticated animal to attack him and escape into the forest the moment I freed it from the tree.*

Now he was alone again. *Was it my voice or my presence that caused such an intense reaction?* he wondered. Shylo felt a trickle running from his nostril and a warmth dripping from the tip. His hand trembled from the burst of adrenaline as he felt at the end of his nose. Knowing it was blood, he groaned and pinched his nostrils to stop the bleeding.

The strange young woman who'd led him to the harquice had not returned. *Why did she leave right when we got here?* Shylo asked himself. *Why am I angry that she left me?* he asked himself, realizing she could be going to get guards to turn him in.

Despite wanting to seek her out, Shylo saw no reason why he should risk his life by wandering through the wilderness at night. He knew he didn't have the skill set required to face the deadly animals that hunted there. Instead, Shylo sat down and wrapped himself tightly in his lazgron cloak for warmth. Suddenly the sounds of the forest became increasingly worrying. He heard everything more clearly now that he was paying attention; the buzzing, humming, and croaking of creatures in the night. Shylo hadn't realized how numb he'd grown to the tumult of urban nightlife in Perdigon.

Shylo sat huddled in his cloak against the harquice saddle when the woman returned alone. His clothes were still damp, but his body heat within the leather cloak was enough to keep him from shivering.

The young woman held a hen gargous pheasant firmly by the neck. She used the bird to gesture at the tree where the harquice should've been tethered.

"I don't know what happened," Shylo shrugged, not wanting to admit how he'd let her mount get away. He'd been through enough embarrassment, and the sight of the large fowl drew his full attention. Shylo hadn't eaten a scrap of food all day.

The woman tossed the pheasant on the ground near Shylo's feet and crouched next to him. She examined the ground around the saddle. Shylo didn't know what she was hoping to find in the darkness. After several uncomfortable moments, she made eye contact with Shylo and pointed in the direction of the harquice's escape.

"You can search for the mare in the morning," he said, reaching for the wild fowl. "We need to eat. I'm starving. How do you plan to cook..."

To Shylo's horror, the girl snatched the hen from his grip and took a large feathery bite from its neck.

"What in the flaming ash are you doing?" Shylo nearly yelled.

She chewed the mouthful of brown, red, and blue feathers, spitting most of them out and lapping her tongue like a hound.

"That's disgusting! I can't believe you did that. Don't you have something to cook with?" Shylo asked.

The young woman pulled the remaining feathers from

her mouth and swallowed the small amount of flesh she'd bitten free while looking at him as if he was the weird one.

"You're brutal. We need to cook this with a source of heat. A sunstone."

The young woman shook her head, making a whooshing noise and wiggling her fingers.

"No. Not with fire. That's how the Volurem are summoned. We need a sunstone. It's a rock that glows yellow with heat."

She shook her head angrily.

"What? Sunstones are perfectly safe. We just need to make sure we clear the ground down to bare soil, so it won't start a fire," Shylo said. Given the concerned look on her face, Shylo wondered if she had one but didn't know how to use it. Again, the memory of the smoke from the day before cropped up. Acting on a hunch, Shylo searched the saddlebag still attached to the saddle he'd been resting against.

The young woman shuffled toward him, but he found the cold smooth rock in her bags. Shylo pulled it out, holding it for her to see. She stopped when she saw him holding the smooth flat sunstone. Unlit, it was light grey. A nondescript stone just like any smooth river rock.

"See, it's safe to touch when it's not lit," he said.

She relaxed, taking a knee and helping Shylo clear a bare patch near the tree.

Shylo didn't think she was there to kill him. She acted innocent, more like a child than a young female soldier or a Noble's hired guard. He watched her as she helped clear the duff and grass. Shylo tried to imagine what she looked like without the military uniform. He felt a stirring sensation in stomach, like the one he felt when he was near Ismay. Shylo shook himself from this daydreaming. He didn't know anything about this stranger. Based on how she bit into the pheasant, there was a real possibility that she was feral. How she could survive outside a metropolis without a heat source for cooking, he didn't know.

Shylo placed the stone on the dirt. It was almost too dark to see the stone's faint yellow hue. Now that they were ready to use it, though, Shylo hesitated. He actually didn't know how to activate the stone so it would warm up. In Perdigon, House Didimo servants cooked for him, or he purchased street food. When he was younger, his parents hadn't allowed him to cook, as it was considered dangerous for children. By the time he was old enough to learn, he had refused to help in the kitchen. At the time, Shylo felt this small rebellion was a way for him to feel some control over his life. Looking at the cold sunstone now, he wished he'd made an effort to help with the meals.

"Do you know how to turn it on?" he asked her.

She balled her fist and hit it on the rock. It didn't light, and Shylo didn't know why he thought it might. She squeezed it with her hands for a moment, then put it down with the same result. Shylo wondered if it was conduction-dependent, like some tools used in smithing, so he tried placing the pheasant on the stone, but nothing happened. Seemingly out of frustration, the young woman drew her blade.

"What are you doing?" Shylo asked, hoping she wasn't about to turn on him.

To his surprise, she brought the pommel of her blade down on the stone, which created a familiar clicking noise. The stone flickered and then lit. Shylo broke into a satisfied laugh. He shared a smile with her that made him feel more like himself. That laughter quickly turned into worried gasps as a clump of forest duff he'd kicked into the dirt circle began to steam from the heat of the rock.

"Blazing Volurem," Shylo swore and grabbed the steaming leaves with his hand. "Ashes," he cursed again, dropping the steaming duff as it burned his palm.

Hurriedly, the young woman snatched up the leaves and rubbed them out between her palms.

Shylo was surprised that she showed no sign of discomfort when she touched the hot leaves. Together, they widened the ring of bare soil surrounding the lit sunstone, removing all debris with the potential to ignite.

Shylo returned to his seat, leaning against the harquice saddle, leaving space for his companion to lean on it too, if she wanted. She grabbed the pheasant from the dirt and plopped it directly on the sunstone, feathers and all. Shylo watched it for several breaths, seeing the feathers stick to the hot surface.

"I don't think that's the way to do it," Shylo said, wondering how she'd known to successfully hunt a pheasant yet not known how to properly eat it. "Shouldn't we take the feathers off first?"

When the warrioress didn't react, Shylo picked up the large pheasant. Using his cloak sleeve as a heat shield, he quickly rolled the rock over to create a clean cooking surface. He'd never eaten any type of bird cooked with its feathers. As he plucked the plumage, the young woman quietly observed.

"I can't believe you took a bite out of this thing raw, feathers and all," Shylo said after the uncomfortable silence ran long.

She shrugged.

"I guess we're both pretty hungry, but that's not how to eat a gargous," Shylo said.

She continued to stare at him, speechless.

The way she studied him, like she was as hesitant about trusting him as he was about trust her, made Shylo want to explain his predicament. "I'm not guilty, you know," Shylo said as he continued plucking. He didn't know what her intentions were, but if she planned to bring him to Perdigon in the morning, he wanted to make sure he'd done his due diligence in persuading her not to turn him in. "I need to prove my innocence."

She didn't acknowledge what he'd said. She leaned onto her side next to the sunstone while Shylo prepared the pheasant.

"Now that they've had a day to go over the evidence, they'll see that I wasn't capable of murdering the Emperor or his sons. Hopefully they'll find something that proves House Didimo was being framed. If not, the Kai will be hard-set on the idea that Didimo was behind it. None of them will want to risk their positions by digging into what really happened. If that's the case, it will be my word against theirs. That won't prove anything. I need to uncover more about it if I'm going to continue my training, but if I'm spotted near the gates, they might shoot me with a bolt."

The girl rested her black-rose cheek on her hand and stared at the glow of the sunstone. As her index finger on her left hand curled around her straight ash-white hair, Shylo almost let himself become entranced by her beauty, until he noticed the bloodstains. In the glow of the stone, he could see them on her right hand, too. Not the same shade as the pheasant blood. She had dark stains under her fingernails, too. They were blacker than dirt.

Shylo wondered if she'd run away from her legion, and that's why she was outside the city walls. Any explanation he could think of fell short when he again took in her one-of-a-kind skin tone and hair color. However she came to be there, she hadn't attacked him. More importantly, she didn't appear concerned about what Shylo was telling her. It was as though this soldier didn't know about the Emperor's death or didn't care.

He continued thinking through his plan out loud, "There's a chance that I'd be allowed to speak my side of the events to the Court, but only if I turn myself in. I really prefer to leave that as a last resort, though. If I'm going to prove that the entire Didimo household was murdered before the Emperor and his sons, I'll need help."

Shylo pulled the last of the feathers from the hen, all the while considering other options. *I can't return to the life I had been leading, I'm sure of that. But turning the popular opinion of the Kai, proving that my sponsor was framed for murdering the Akai, that would be something no Eso had ever done.* The possibility that he could discover which Noble House was behind the assassinations could open doors for Shylo. *Perhaps such a discovery and disclosure would allow me some way to remain involved in Perdigon politics and governance?*

"I could try to get a message to Wilsall or Ismay," he now said aloud. "But how? I don't have anything to write on or anyone to deliver the letter on my behalf. I guess I could stand on the road and hope someone would be kind enough to give me a piece of parchment. But typically, hunters and farmers don't read and write. The brutes guarding supply trains on the road probably don't have that level of sophistication either..."

Shylo now remembered the information he'd heard before he knew the Capitol Guard were hunting for him. "The Emperor's nephew and his entourage are returning to the capital soon," he said aloud with renewed enthusiasm.

The young woman looked from the glowing stone to Shylo, studying his sudden excitement.

"They were expected to arrive the other day, but Ismay had just received word that they were delayed. They'll most likely be traveling in on the road from Saypo. Ismay's father is with them. It's a long shot, but they might not have heard the news yet. They'll be at least a day or two behind the messenger, or else why would they have sent one. I could meet them outside the walls and give Ismay's father the message. Or better yet, I could explain my situation to them directly. They could take me back into the city. They would hear me out, especially without knowing that I'm an Eso. I still have the House Didimo tunic. They'll know I'm not lying when I say that I'm a Penti trainee with Ismay. They'd have to hear me out, right?" Shylo looked to the ember-eyed girl who stared at him with a concerned scowl. "What? Do you suddenly know about Marxius Ovando-Kai? Who am I kidding? Of course you don't. They'll take me in with them, I'm sure of it. I mean, look at me; a lost, down-on-his-luck Penti wandering about outside the walls. They'd have to take pity on me."

Satisfied with himself, Shylo laid the pheasant breast on the stone. The skin sizzled. As Shylo watched the bird cook, he mentally rehearsed a speech for Ismay's father. It was Shylo's best hope of returning to a life in Perdigon. If he failed to be convincing, or if they had already heard the news of what had happened in Perdigon, the returning Nobles would imprison him, or worse. If it didn't go to plan, the next day would be Shylo's last.

"As Pyrome and Brisrome predicted, worshipping spread, seeping deep into the culture of the two-legs, and The Creators' control grew. Through Tourome's efforts to cater to the needs of those who worshipped him, he gained a magical prowess that he had not believed possible." – The Dracolyth

OUTSIDE THE WALLS

"Hoo-ah!" a man's voice hollered, followed by a solid-sounding, heavily dealt, THWACK.

Shylo bolted upright. For an instant, his forested surroundings lit with a soft purple and orange glow offered comfort. As he struggled to wake fully, he realized that his dream of being safely welcomed back into House Didimo was a lie. The sound that woke him was not in his dream. Shylo sat rigidly on the ground next to the saddle, waiting for his senses to tell him where in the dense forest the noise had come from. Reality sank in like a lazgron's sharp teeth into a fresh kill. Shylo was still living a nightmare: wanted by the Palace, Capitol Hill, and City Guard for conspiring against the Emperor of Rhydenar.

"Ahhh! Ar-grhhll —" the male voice screamed, before

gurgling to a wet end.

Shylo's fear spiked, tripling his pulse as the thick brush rustled near the sound of the death cry. Small trees bent under the weight of something huge thrashing a stone's throw away from where he sat. In a panic, Shylo moved to wake the young woman only to realize she was not there. Shylo instantly conjured up a scene in which the rumored monster beyond the walls had killed her. A glossy flash in the thrashing brush drew his attention. Shylo saw a dark green tail as wide as a harquice's neck wiggling in the air behind a narrow-leafed lentri tree. The creature's tail was protected with scales similar in color to the surrounding forest foliage. The tail had knobby spikes along its spine. Dark-colored curved barbels wriggled like black-beaded reeds as they drooped off the bony knobs. Shylo's breath caught in his throat when he felt a firm grip on his shoulder from behind. An instant later a hand pressed firmly over his mouth, stifling his yelp.

The young woman pulled him to his feet and spun Shylo to face her, the entire time keeping her hand clasped over his mouth. When Shylo recognized her and the gesture she was making, he nodded. He crouched as she did and followed her away from the devolved dragon.

Hunched over and keeping his shoulders low to the ground, Shylo waddled behind her. She moved at a pace much faster than he was capable of. The hood of his lazgron cloak sagged over his head, blocking his vision. He could only see what was directly in front of his feet. Where she moved silently over the forest's obstacles, Shylo stumbled over roots and logs. He snapped sticks and broke branches, all while trying to keep up with his stealthy companion.

After a short time, Shylo lost sight of her backside and slowed. Stopping to kneel, he folded back his hood. The early morning glow provided enough light to see clearly through the trees, but Shylo couldn't find her.

She abandoned me, he thought. *She left me to be eaten by the draco that killed...* he realized the person being attacked by the devolved dragon wasn't with them. Shylo shivered at the realization that the only reasonable explanation for the scream was the last breath of a Perdigon guard who'd been looking to haul Shylo back for a crime he didn't commit. Shylo now found a suitable explanation for the harquice's fright the night before.

Had the draco been nearby and the harquice sensed it... he considered. *But why would a draco pass us by, unless she — but no, that's suicide?* Shylo speculated where the young woman had gone for so long when they arrived at her camp. He'd assumed it was to hunt after she returned with the pheasant, but perhaps that wasn't all she was doing.

A rock clacked against the trunk of the tree next to him. He twisted to see who or what had thrown it. She was standing there, her ash-white hair a complete mess, tangled with forest debris. Her face was speckled with a deep rust-colored mud. She waved for him to come.

As Shylo hurried to her, a brown animal moved through his peripheral vision. He dropped to the ground, not wanting to look, but forcing himself to. The monster he imagined wasn't there, but something more tangible and dangerous. Rhydarians, armored and mounted on harquice, rode through the gaps in the trees. They rode parallel to him, heading the opposite direction. Shylo saw the flash of steel swords and drawn bows as they charged the draco.

He felt a tug on the loose wrist of his leather cloak as the young woman pulled him to his feet and led him like a haltered animal through the undergrowth. Before he realized where she'd suddenly disappeared to, Shylo stepped away from the solid ground and somehow into open air. He dropped, hitting his chest on the edge of the hole in the earth. He grabbed a handful of leafy brush, but the roots ripped under his weight, and he continued to fall.

He landed almost as suddenly as he'd fallen into the hole. Sitting in the dank darkness, he struggled to take in his change in surroundings. His hind end felt cool and damp from the dirt. The musty scent reminded him of his parent's root cellar in Florens, not like the clay stone damp of the Didimo wine cellar. The only light came from the narrow hole above him. All of the noise above was silenced when the young woman crawled over Shylo and slid something bulky to block the opening.

In the absence of light, Shylo only had his other senses to tell him what was happening. He heard the young woman scurry down from the opening to ground level. He smelled something on her that instantly reminded him of the peak of summer. When the sky in Florens was hazy with smoke. Shylo scooted away from the opening, twisting to face her. All questions evaporated from his mind as he felt her gently, but firmly, push him onto his back and crawl on top of him. He couldn't help the natural reaction he experienced as she straddled his waist and started fidgeting with something near her hip.

Before he could embarrass himself by reciprocating the poorly timed show of affection, he heard a CRACK. The sound dissipated into the underground tunnel and a soft yellow light sprung to life in the older girl's hand. Shylo held his breath, all his previous feelings of arousal turning to paranoia, hoping she wasn't about to drop the sunstone on him. She resumed her crawling over him as Shylo could now see a tunnel that was crouching height and too narrow for two people to move through side-by-side.

"What is this, a flexis burrow?" he whispered. Shylo had only read about the hound-like predators but judging from their knee-high size, he knew this tunnel was much too large for such an animal. Shylo could sit upright comfortably, and the rounded sides were wide enough for him to turn around, about as much space as he'd had in the sewer. The memory of the sewer nearly caused him to lose some of the pheasant from last night's meal, but he forced it back down.

His companion had yet to answer a single question, but that didn't stop him from asking about where they were. She never spoke and remained consistent in that. She simply tossed the sunstone down the tunnel, illuminating its depths.

"Wait up," Shylo said, wondering how long it took a sunstone to heat. He had a decent idea based on how quickly the leaves from the night before began to steam. She didn't flinch as he had when she rubbed out the steaming duff. Even as she tossed the sunstone down the tunnel, she didn't make a sound.

Crawling by the light of the sunstone, Shylo noticed the smooth lines that shaped the earthen tunnel walls. "It looks like this tunnel was built by people, like a smooth tool carved it out," Shylo said, continuing this practice of thinking out loud while understanding that his companion most likely wouldn't reply. "I read a book about the Tarmigs. That's what they call the ancient Terra people who inhabited Rhydenar before we started building walls to protect ourselves against the Volurem. It's amazing to think they survived for so long without an army or city walls to protect them against the fires. And some still do, though most of those remaining are reportedly serving the Volurem as slaves. I don't understand how they can without burning to death. Maybe they're underground," he imagined. "Nomadic Tarmig tribes still exist, but none currently in Apgar. Any tribal people in this state were all enslaved before the Empire was formed." He paused, admiring the ancient craftsmanship.

"This tunnel has to be older than the Capital City itself," Shylo said, abruptly remembering what that meant about the tunnel's stability. Very few of those early tunnels remained. He tried not to focus on the idea of being buried alive. Right now, this tunnel was safer than roaming the surface.

"That thing back there," Shylo said, ducking his head to avoid a face full of dangling roots. "It was attacking a person. I heard someone screaming."

The young woman finally slowed her crawl and turned to look down her side at him.

The sunstone glowed directly beneath her. The dark rust splotches on her face that Shylo thought were mud now shone a deep red. Because of her frazzled hair, Shylo had assumed it was mud. Now, though, he could see clearly. Her face was splattered with blood. Those stains had not been there the night before.

"It was someone with the armored guard I saw. You knew they were in the forest this morning?" he asked.

She nodded, responding directly with understanding for the first time.

"They came for me," he said, not intending it as a question.

She answered with a shrug.

"Did you kill someone?" Shylo asked point-blank.

Her lips twitched as though she might speak, but after a moment she just stared at him.

Shylo thought of the polished draco-scale armor of

guardsmen riding through the forest toward the draco. "If you killed a Capitol Guardsman or a guardsman from a Noble house, there is absolutely no chance I will get the opportunity to present my innocence as an ignorant bystander," he said firmly.

She shook her head and drew the willow-leaf blade from her scabbard in the confined, earthy space. The young woman offered it hilt first to Shylo.

For a moment, Shylo considered using it against her. Only he wasn't being held prisoner by her. Shylo followed her willingly.

"I don't know what you want me to do with this?" Shylo said.

She pointed to the blade, running her fingertip along the clean flat of the blade.

"It's clean," he noted. "You didn't kill anyone?"

She waffled her hand and wrinkled her nose.

Shylo handed the saber back and said, "So you just maimed them, great."

She shook her head.

Shylo frowned.

She pointed to the clean blade again and shook her head.

"Are you suggesting you killed them with the draco?" Shylo asked.

She shrugged, the corners of her mouth just barely turning up with a light smile.

"But the blood on your face?" Shylo whispered. "You would've had to be close. Too close to survive."

She grunted as if he had just offended her. She snatched the saber back and continued crawling.

Shylo noticed she used her hand to roll the sunstone

along the tunnel and was about to ask her if that burned when she stopped. "What is it?" Shylo asked.

She pointed right at the tunnel wall.

Shylo sidled up next to her, hoping they weren't about to find a weak point in the wall that would suggest an imminent collapse. Clearing the tangled roots away, Shylo saw there was a wide stone that was chiseled smooth to match the curvature of the earthy tunnel wall. "Is that a painting?" Shylo asked, noting black markings on the stone.

The young woman nodded eagerly, pointing to the image of a dragon hovering above a globe.

Shylo recognized the image, only this was a more rudimentary version of the detailed painting on the cover of the religious text, The Dracolyth.

"It's a dragon," Shylo said.

The girl frowned, not understanding.

"A symbol of the old religion most prominent before the Empire. This is the scene drawn on the cover of their text, 'The Dracolyth.'"

She studied the pictograph carefully as though it was the first drawing she'd ever seen.

"I don't know much about the old religion. Only that the book, The Dracolyth, famously predicts the end of the world when the dragons return to Tarmigan."

She shook her head. She pointed to the camouflage color of the scales on her surcoat, then at the curved ceiling overhead.

"That thing back there was not a dragon. They have wings and look like a small dragon, but they are not dragons."

She shook her head, pointing at the scales, then at the pictograph of the dragon.

"Draco's devolved from their magical ancestors. Dracos

don't possess magic, they can't fly, and they can't breathe fire."

She shrugged, seeming satisfied with his answer, and continued rolling the sunstone down the tunnel.

As they made their way on hands and knees, Shylo considered all the opportunities this strange person had to turn him in or kill him. He didn't understand why she was helping him.

It wasn't until his knees were rubbed raw from crawling that she finally stopped. The filled-in tunnel before them revealed where the earth had finally caved in. Shylo heard the CLACK of the young woman's sword pommel punching the sunstone off. The pitch black exposed a thin circular glow of daylight overhead. The light expanded as the young woman lifted a rock away from the covered opening. She stood and spun around slowly looking in all directions before climbing to the surface. Shylo followed, stopping only to pick up the sunstone with his lazgron cloak and stuff it into the side pocket. The stone heated the leather, making him question how the young woman could roll it without burning her bare hands.

Back on the surface, he had to squint from the bright, mid-morning sun seeping through the canopy. The girl knelt by a large rock that had been covering the hole. Shylo took a double-take when she slid the heavy stone back over the hole with ease.

There was no sign of the devolved dragon or any armored guardsmen, so Shylo could focus on his mission once again. He needed to pass a message through the Noble to his daughter, Ismay, at the very least. If it seemed appropriate, he might attempt to get back inside the walls of Perdigon. He couldn't be sure if they'd heard the news yet, but if anyone would help Shylo now, it was his friends in the Penti cohort. Ismay's father was Shylo's best chance at getting through to them.

"We need to find the Saypo road," Shylo said, surprised to hear himself say *we* instead of *I*. The young woman wasn't his true friend, like Wilsall and Ismay, just friendly for some reason. And though he found himself comforted by his attraction to her, he had to keep in mind that he barely knew anything about her. He'd met her less than a day ago.

She waved him to follow her as she bounded through the brush toward an old-growth olackee tree.

Shylo questioned how she knew where she was going and grew even more puzzled when she stopped at the base of the tree and began to climb. "What are you doing?" he asked.

She hoisted herself into the crook of the lowest branch and sat on the wide stem, staring down at Shylo. She looked at Shylo with the same studious expression she had worn since their initial encounter.

Shylo relaxed his shoulders and approached the tree. He fell on his first attempt, his leather sandals sliding on the furrowed bark. On his second attempt, she helped him reach the first broad branch. Pausing only to pluck a finger-sized nut from the tree and eat it, he continued following her up through the branches. Shylo stopped midway, resting in a fork of the trunk and grazing on more of the lightly colored, soft-shell legumes. The young woman climbed the tree without fear, standing on branches that were far too thin for Shylo to trust. He might be wanted for his perceived affiliation with the Emperor's assassination, but he wasn't going to risk breaking a leg to reach the top of the tree. He called after the girl, "What are we doing in this tree?"

Shylo didn't expect a response. He hugged the larger of the main stems where he was sitting and looked out through the spacious branches. He saw no sign of guards, dracos, lazgron, or any other danger. Shylo felt the main trunk of the tree tremor and looked up. As nuts rained down, Shylo spotted the young woman pointing to his right. When she saw he was looking at her, she motioned for him to continue climbing up to where she stood.

"What do you see?" he asked, not wanting to continue climbing.

She pointed out over the canopy twice, before motioning for him to continue climbing.

"Why don't you speak," he muttered to himself as he attempted to climb higher. Shylo only made it a few more branches before the thought of falling outweighed his desire to know what the young woman was looking at. "Can you see the walls?" he asked.

She nodded with wide eyes.

"Okay, I'm heading down now," Shylo said.

As he shimmied down, he felt the tree vibrating again, only to look up to a hail of olackee nuts. "Stop that!" he insisted, missing his handhold on the next branch. Shylo slipped, falling away from the trunk. The rushing sensation of falling through open air came over him once again. This time, he knew it was a much longer fall than his entrance to the Tarmig tunnel. Remarkably, though, he stopped. Something pressed against his back, propping him up and rescuing him from falling all the way to the ground. Shylo quickly grabbed hold of the branch he'd originally missed. He turned to see that she had somehow moved from above him to the branch behind him and caught him before he'd fallen.

"How did you —" Shylo stammered. "But you were up

there and now you're..." No reply. Shylo was unnerved, and she remained calm, so he continued climbing down the tree with intense focus on his holds.

When he reached the ground, he faced the strange young woman. He studied her now, looking past his physical attraction toward her, attempting to see her through the same curious expression that she used to observe him. She wasn't any race of Terra people that Shylo knew of. He'd never seen her hair color either. For her to move from the top of tree and keep him from falling, she would've had to move three or four times faster than a normal Rhydarian. She'd moved the small boulders over the Tarmig tunnel with ease. It was as if she had the strength and speed of a Terra person who grew up in the south but looked nothing like the Agunzi people. Her body was the size of a Rhydarian, but she didn't have any of the racial markings identifying her as belonging to New or Old Rhydenar ethnicities. Even more curious was the suggestion that she'd been close enough to a feeding draco to get its victim's blood on her and yet she escaped unscathed. Shylo questioned, too, how she could touch the hot sunstone without burning her bare hands. If he were to tell anyone in the Penti cohort about her, they'd think he was lying. Yet, she was standing there in front of him, a new race of Terra.

I wish you would speak to me, he thought, but what he said out loud was, "What are you?" The question escaped him before he realized how rude it was. No matter how insensitive Shylo thought the question, the young woman didn't react negatively. She simply continued eyeing him with the same curiosity.

"The walls are that way?" he asked, pointing to the right of the tree.

She nodded.

Shylo took the lead, setting an angle toward the capital. He tried to focus on what he would say if they managed to find the road that cut through the Apgar Forest to Saypo and were lucky enough to cross paths with Ismay's father and the Emperor's nephew. Hopefully he'd catch them before they reached Perdigon. As he attempted to formulate his speech, Shylo wondered if she was still with him, how she'd fit into that explanation. His notion that she was a new breed of Rhydarian caused him to rethink the inexplicable feats she had performed.

After several hours of angling through the forest, Shylo eventually stumbled onto a road leading into Perdigon. There were only two main roads out of the city. He had a fifty-fifty chance that this was the road to Saypo, and no way of knowing if the Emperor's nephew and his guard had already passed by. The four-harquice-wide dirt path was littered with the last rotation's decaying leaves. Small trees and brush encroached on the infrequently used corridor through the forest. Some growth reached up to Shylo's waist, serving as a timeline of when the last large host of Imperial Legions had marched from Perdigon. Glancing at the sun, Shylo determined which direction the city lay. With nothing else to do but wait, Shylo searched for a comfortable place to sit near the road.

As the day lengthened with no sign of riders, Shylo desperately wished his companion could carry on a conversation. Each time he began to ask yet another question, Shylo stopped himself. Their ability to communicate had reached its potential. A one-sided conversation was something many of Shylo's Penti classmates performed with regularity, given the way they enjoyed talking over one another, but right now Shylo didn't see the point.

As the sun arched lower in the sky, Shylo's belly

growled. The pheasant and the handful of nuts were all he'd eaten since leaving Perdigon. The young woman straightening her back drew Shylo's attention; she was craning to see more clearly down the road. Shylo's pulse quickened when he saw the colorful surcoats of Nobles approaching in the distance. They were far enough away that Shylo couldn't make out their house symbols, but chances were extremely low that this group was any party other than the Emperor's nephew and his crew. Shylo knew this was his best and perhaps only opportunity to begin compiling the evidence that would prove him innocent.

"This is it," he said to his female companion. "It has to be them. Soon, I'll know my fate. Ashes, I hope they haven't already heard that House Didimo is to blame. I really want this wilderness experience to be over soon."

The young woman studied the approaching group with almost more interest than she'd given Shylo. She continually blocked his view of the road and wouldn't look away from them.

Fed up with her disregard for his need to verify whether it was the Emperor's nephew, Shylo stepped out from the small group of trees where they'd been sitting and headed toward the road. His hands trembled with nerves. He felt strange, almost wild with adrenaline. Shylo rehearsed the points of his prepared speech, starting with the proper way to address the High Noble. He said his whole name with the necessary honorific, Benton Querci-Akai. He could see them clearly now. The tallest Nobleman was Ismay's father, Marxius Ovando-Kai. He rode out in the lead. He was wearing full brismil-plate armor as he rode on the back of an eighteen-hand, black harquice. The High Noble and the rest of his guard followed.

Shylo's focus shattered into a thousand pieces as he was

struck from behind. The daylight flashed bright before he plunged chest-first into the thick brush surrounding the overgrown road. He did not know why this was happening to him, only that someone was pinning him to the forest floor. Strong hands held his mouth and stifled his shouts. The only thing he could see was a dark palm over his eyes. Despite his struggles to break free, he was overpowered. Whoever was holding him down made sure his arms were pinned behind his back and his legs were spread wide so he couldn't move them. He tried to call for help, to the young woman whose name he didn't even know, or to the group of Nobles passing by.

Though he failed to break free, Shylo heard a harquice stomp to a halt. The owner clicked his tongue and the harquice hooves resumed trotting. Shylo didn't stop trying to break free from whoever was holding him down until well after the sound of harquice hooves had faded into the distance. The unbelievably forceful grip holding him down and efficiently stifling his yells released him. Shylo scrambled free in a frenzy. He shouted for help, stumbling through the brush. When he looked back to see who was there, he saw only the young woman. That's when he realized it had to be her who had held him down.

"Why?" he gasped, trying to rationalize what she had done. "Why did you do that?!" he shouted.

She stepped forward, lips parting as if she wanted to speak.

"What in the blazes is wrong with you?!" Shylo felt a rage that he had never experienced boiling over. "Those people are my best hope in proving my innocence. I command you to tell me why the ash you stopped me," Shylo shouted like a crazed commander.

"They will not help you," she said simply.

Shylo gawked, blinking at her in disbelief. She spoke in well-formed and clear Derian. Her accent was one he didn't know, but she'd explained herself as he demanded. "What did you say to me?" Shylo asked.

"They will kill you like they killed the Masters," she said perfectly clearly.

Shylo chuckled with minor hysteria, "You could speak this whole time? What are you, insane? Didn't you understand what I've been telling you this whole time? That's my only way back," Shylo said, pointing in the direction of the Nobles. Without giving her the opportunity to explain herself, Shylo took off running down the road after the group. He didn't bother to look back to see if the young woman was following him. Shylo didn't care about her anymore.

He wasn't particularly fast for an Old Rhydarian, but it was what he knew to do in difficult situations. Shylo ran as fast as his legs would allow. He rounded a corner and saw a clear-cut in the timber between the edge of the forest and the city walls. The gate was open. Benton Querci-Akai and his entourage were riding through the entrance to the capital. Shylo watched his hopes of sussing out the Kai responsible for ending his dream to become a political advisor disappear. Within moments, High Noble Benton and Ismay's father, Marxius, would hear the news of the Emperor's murder. They would know that House Didimo's Eso Penti was wanted for conspiring to assassinate the Emperor and his two successors. Shylo slowed to a stop. He stood just within the protection of the forest. While the last of the guardsmen rode into the city, Shylo swore he could see two yellow eyes glaring back at him from among the group of Nobles.

"As time continued through the many cycles of the lesser dragons' lifespans, Tourome's superior magic over them was no longer satisfying. Tourome began to idolize what Tarmigan could become without lesser dragons overpopulating a world he'd created for himself." – The Dracolyth

BURNT HOPES

Two Days After the Emperor's Death

"To scorched earth with you!" Shylo shouted at the young woman. "Do you realize what you've done?" He was breathing heavier now in frustration than he had from his extended sprint. Shylo could not control his anger toward the warrioress. She had held him down by force. She'd prevented him from pleading his case to the only influential people who may not yet have been swayed by the lies about him. He was so angry that, if she were within striking distance, he might've hit her.

Bottling up this rage, Shylo turned away from the light-haired woman. Those yellow eyes continued to stare at him from the gate. Reacting without a thought for the consequences, Shylo darted out of the trees and to the very edge

179

of the buffer zone beneath the towering stone walls. He knew he could go no farther without risking taking a crossbow bolt. Frantically, Shylo waved his arms and shouted toward the gate, "Wait!" He was risking everything by exposing himself, but he didn't care. He had to get their attention and at least try to get someone to question the allegations against him before hearing the news. "Wait for me! Please help!"

Across the great distance between them, Shylo saw that the yellow eyes belonged to the man wearing brismil-plate armor. Ismay had the same yellow eyes. Shylo didn't understand how Ismay's father's eyes could be visible while wearing brismil plate. Normally, when a person touched a dragon scale, the plate formed to fit like a skin-sleeve over his body, his entire body. That's how the armor looked on the soldier Shylo and Wilsall had seen in the Senate Chambers. That man's eyes had taken on the metallic sheen of the supernatural armor.

"Marxius Ovando-Kai! I have a message for Ismay!" Shylo yelled to the Noble, hoping Ismay's father would be able to hear him with his enhanced senses while in brismil plate. Despite his efforts, the gates did not stop lowering.

"No," he gasped, realizing his defeat. Ismay's father, the Noble with New Rhydarian and Zethrillian blood, had seen him. Even though Shylo now knew that the party who rode past was the one he'd been searching for, they did not know him. Without a High Noble's invitation, Perdigon did not allow outsiders into the city without presenting their documents to the City Guard. The gate closed, dashing all of Shylo's hopes to reveal the party actually responsible for the coup that had taken place.

Shylo gambled everything in choosing to remain at the forest boundary, where the City Guard could spot him. He willed Marxius Ovando-Kai, to order that the gates be reopened. Shylo prayed that the Noble would ride out to greet him. As Shylo caught his breath, it became clear that the gates would not reopen.

He heard light footsteps approaching, her. He considered running out into the grassy clearing between the wall and the wilderness and ending his evasion of the law right then. He imagined stepping out into the road and turning himself in. Even as his pulse climbed at the thought, Shylo knew he wouldn't do it. He didn't trust the shooters on top of the wall. They would kill him; he couldn't give up his life like that, not yet. He wasn't guilty of anything. He couldn't give up when there was still a chance that Marxius Ovando-Kai had seen him and was readying a group of guardsmen to ride out. A plan like that could take time to assemble. Even if he'd heard the news of the assassination and had spotted Shylo calling after him, it could be a day or longer before Marxius could muster another search party to hunt for Shylo.

The footsteps behind him stopped and his thoughts returned to what this strange woman had cost him. He attempted to control his anger. He might be able to forgive her for thinking the men were from the hunting party sent to arrest Shylo, but the realization that she could speak set off his fuse. She'd played Shylo for a fool. This whole time they'd been together she had been able to speak and had chosen not to. The things Shylo told her, he said while confident that she could not repeat them. Shylo clenched his fists and turned to face her. His shoulders instinctively elevated, he hunched forward. It felt like he was flexing every muscle in his body to prevent himself from attacking her. Then he laid eyes on her. The girl with ash-white hair and burning eyes stood there, silent.

The fuse within Shylo burned to its end and he lost control. He had already reached the brink of what he considered rational behavior, but now he'd tipped the scale; he reacted with pure animal instinct. He stalked toward her with his head lowered and malice in his stormy grey eyes.

She did not try to calm him. She tilted her head to the side slightly, like she had done so many times before, and studied him with a puzzling expression.

This is how she responds to me? he thought. Her curious stare was beyond maddening. He broke into a hate-fueled charge and lunged at her with open arms, trying to tackle her to the ground as she had done to him.

She waited until he'd committed to the attack before dodging out of the way. Shylo stumbled past her, grabbing at the thin air where she had been an instant before. He released a frustrated roar, stumbled to a halt, and whirled to face her. Shylo saw her hand loosely gripping her sheathed sword. The pinching of her brow, flared nostrils, and parted lips remained on her puzzled face. Shylo could tell she did not want to draw her saber.

"I could blazing kill you," he said, spittle flying from his teeth like venom. Shylo had little fighting experience. He had no weapon, yet his blind anger drove him to attack again.

She easily dodged him. This time he fell to his hands and knees, sliding in the grass on the road.

"Why?" he demanded through gritted teeth.

She continued to silently study him.

Shylo discerned that he wouldn't catch her. Somehow, she moved too quickly. Even if he did catch her, she could control the fight and beat him. "I know you can speak. I know you can understand me," he said, remaining on his knees. "Tell me why? Tell me why you want me to die in the wilderness?"

She stood there, staring at him.

"I demand an answer from you," Shylo said with all the authority he could muster after throwing his immature tantrum.

To his surprise, she answered, "They would have killed you if you showed yourself."

Her voice was smooth, well-spoken but like her appearance, Shylo couldn't place from where in Tarmigan her accent originated.

"You don't know them. You don't know what they would've done to me," he said.

She brought her hand away from the single-handed hilt, her mouth parting and closing again as she seemed to not have an answer.

"One of those noblemen is my classmate's father. I could've gotten a message to her before he heard the news that I was wanted for treason. Even if he had heard it before getting here, his opinion might be swayed by his daughter. I need a fair trial to have a chance at life. I need help finding the evidence that would exonerate me. I won't get either out here, beyond the wall, and now, because they're already in the city, I'm as good as dead," Shylo said.

"You told me you have not met these noblemen. He would've killed you and tried to kill me. It was not the right time."

"What do you mean? I knew this was a gamble, but I didn't think the man who raised Ismay would kill a strange boy in the wilderness on sight. Not without asking questions. I've heard about the way he lobbies in the Senate Chambers. He isn't impulsive, like you," Shylo said, shifting into a cross-legged, seated position.

"The Scaled One killed The Masters," she said.

"What are you talking about? Ismay's father was on a supply mission. He went to check the inland suppliers and ensure they were going to meet their quotas for the rotation before the fire season makes inland trade routes too dangerous. He didn't kill the Masters, or whoever you were a slave to before you started bothering me."

"The Scaled One —"

"Give it up," Shylo interrupted her. "It doesn't matter. I'll just have to sit on the road and wait for someone to find me and hope they don't slit my throat before taking me to trial."

"Don't go back," she said.

"Thanks to you, I don't have any other choice. And I can't walk back or the City Guard will put a crossbow bolt through my chest," Shylo said.

"Don't give up. Out here is freedom," she said.

"Why am I even talking to you right now?" Shylo said. "I don't know who you are. I don't know where you came from. You showed up out of nowhere... I can't believe I thought I could trust you. I don't even know your name, yet you know almost everything about me."

"I can keep you safe. You are weak, but I can protect you," she said.

"Great, you can give backhanded compliments," Shylo said.

She made the same confused face that drove Shylo over the edge.

"You've done a great job protecting me so far," Shylo said sarcastically, while motioning toward the closed gates of Perdigon.

"Yes, you are alive because of me," she said.

"No, that's not what I —" *she doesn't understand*

sarcasm, he thought. "I don't know who you are. You don't know who I am. I don't understand why you want to protect me?"

"Because we are similar," she said.

Shylo tucked his chin with surprise, "What? We are nothing alike."

"You are alone, and I am alone. We are both here and —"

"Stop. Let me explain something to you, whoever you are."

"I am Number 2841," she said.

Shylo pinched the bridge of his nose with his fingers, attempting to gather himself before he launched off onto an angry tangent about how a number wasn't a name. "You and I are not at all alike. Nothing about us is even remotely close to similar. You are a girl, I'm a boy. Those are opposites. You are physically attractive, crazy strong, and way too fast for a normal Rhydarian. I don't mean to put myself down, but realistically, there's a reason why I'm sixteen and haven't had an intimate relationship with anyone; and it's not because I don't try. I've never been the strongest or fastest at anything. You're good at fighting, and unless you consider what we just had as one, I've never been in a real fight. Do you understand where I'm going with this?"

Number 2841 measured him with her gaze but did not respond.

"I'm not cut out to survive in the wilderness any longer. I don't rely on my physical strength to provide for myself, I rely on my mind. The only reason I came to Perdigon was to study hard and hopefully come as close as an Eso can get to being a politician. Being a Senator's advisor was my dream and the best I could hope to do in this world. It's either that or join the army and fight for success, and I think you can see how poorly I'd perform at that," Shylo said.

The young woman, Number 2841, shook her head. "I was not the biggest, the strongest, or the fastest when I started training. You can learn, you only lack experience. I can help you if you stay with me," she said.

"You didn't listen. I don't want to be a fighter or struggle to hunt and gather my food. I'd rather risk my chances with the uphill battle of defending myself in the Empire's courts than stay another night out here," Shylo said in defeat. Any other person Shylo had ever met would've read through the lines here, but Number 2841 wasn't like anyone he'd ever met. She didn't see what he was really trying to say.

"We are the same," she said again.

"No. We are not the same. Now please, for the love of the unburnt, leave me alone," Shylo pleaded. He spun on his rear to face away from her. Any Capitol Guard members out searching for him would return before nightfall. If nobody else came on the road, at least he knew he wouldn't have to remain in the wilderness another night.

Shylo could sense Number 2841 standing there, watching him. He stood, walked to a nearby tree on the side of the road and sat, leaning against the tree trunk, facing the forested road. He did his best to ignore Number 2841, but the young woman lingered within view, taking a stand within the forest. Almost every time a tree rat sounded, or a twig snapped, she darted into the thick understory. After more than an hour, Shylo couldn't take it anymore. She was acting like an annoying quadrel, the small furry felines some of his Penti classmates kept as pets.

When Number 2841 twitched to attention at the

sound of a nut dropping to the forest floor, Shylo said, "Please don't do that again."

She shot him an emotionless, blank stare.

Shylo knew she didn't know what he meant. "Number two hundred and whatever, if you go chasing after a nut one more time... Come over here and take a seat if you insist on staying near me," he said.

She looked longingly into the forest where the nut had clicked off the root before rolling to a stop in the leaves.

"Sit down," he said.

With some hesitation, she did, saying, "It's Number 2841."

"That's not a name," Shylo said, starting to regret inviting her to sit by him.

"It's what they called me," she said.

"Who are they?" he asked.

"The Masters," she said.

"And they're dead?" he asked.

She nodded.

"You believe Marxius did it?" he asked, pointing toward the city wall.

She nodded again.

Shylo didn't believe her. She probably hadn't seen very many Rhydarian and assumed anyone in a uniform or brismil plate was the same. He envisioned the young woman being brought over on a ship after the *Masters* found her tribe somewhere in the far western lands across the Maelstrom Ocean. The scenario he played out in his mind had her ship veering off course and landing somewhere in the Rhydarian Empire. Soldiers probably sought to claim her and others like her as their slaves. There was a skirmish and she escaped after stealing a soldier's uniform and harquice. After several long moments of silence, he said, "I would've given you a real name."

She perked up, dropping the blades of grass she complacently shredded.

"Because a number for a name isn't exactly a real name? It's more of an assignment or classification. Your masters probably didn't want you to have a real name because that would be too close to allowing a slave to know individuality. And independent thinking is not what they want from you."

"How did you know that?" she asked.

Shylo realized she really wanted to know how he'd come to that conclusion, so he said, "It's a common tool of oppression that the Nobles use. Beyond my observations, I've read about similar tactics used in politics to control conquered populations."

"Reading must be a powerful weapon. How does it work?" she asked.

"You don't know what reading is?" he asked.

She shook her head. "You can teach me?"

"I could if I had a book," he said, forgetting for a moment how he felt toward her betrayal.

"A book?" she asked.

Shylo considered how Number 2841 could know how to fight so well but didn't know what a book was. Abruptly, she flinched to attention, reaching for the blade. Shylo's first reaction was to check the city gate. Perhaps Marxius Ovando-Kai had seen him after all and was coming out to find the traitor. But when he glanced back, the gate was stationary.

"Hide," she said in a low voice, grabbing his cloak, and pulling him away from the road.

Shylo jerked his arm, yanking the leather out of her grip. "I'm staying here," he said.

"They're coming," she whispered.

"Good. Maybe one of them will think my side of the story is more believable and do some investigating for me while I sit in a cell. I told you, I'm going to take my chances with the guard and the court," Shylo said.

"They'll kill you," she said. "They were going to this morning before I —" she glanced up at the road. "Now. Go hide now."

Shylo rolled away from her, scrambling toward the edge of the road on his hands and knees. He heard her hiss with disapproval and when he glanced back, she was gone. Her warning, what she started to say about that morning gave him pause. He could hear trotting from around the bend. If he tried to run, they would see him through the trees. Something within him told him not to expose himself just yet. It didn't seem right. He slunk back to the tree and laid down in the tall grass surrounding trunk. Flipping the lazgron hood over his head, he lay perfectly still.

Judging by the rumbling Shylo felt through the wide-spread tree roots, the approaching group could be an army squadron. He hunkered low as they rode into view. Where he'd been willing to give himself up to the City Guard a moment ago, Shylo now hoped his hiding place was not too obvious. He waited as the Rhydarians started passing by without seeming to notice him. At first, the New Rhydarians were heavily armored in Capitol Guard draco-scale uniforms. As the troops continued toward the gate, the Capitol Guardsmen dwindled and Shylo saw a mixed variety of lightly and heavily armored Noble house guards. The colors of their scale armor and the uniforms they wore changed as frequently as the many house symbols and differing coats of arms they bore from past military service. Out of the two hundred-plus who rode past, all were dressed for battle. There wasn't a doubt in his mind now that Number 2841 was right. These men conveyed a mob mentality with their eyes and movements. Some wore torn uniforms, some had blood on their scaled armor and leather gloves. Shylo hoped it was draco or lazgron blood, and not from anyone they'd passed on the road.

As they rode by, Shylo remained perfectly still, knowing now that if he continued to stay motionless, he wouldn't likely be seen. The riders stretched so far back from the gate that by the time the first of the Capitol Guard had reached the gates, the last guards of the Noble houses bringing up the rear slowed right in front of Shylo. As they slowed, Shylo recognized one of the symbols, the familiar tri-colored circle featuring a spear-wielding warrior of House Sarapio. Wilsall's house was represented among the riders at the rear.

Shylo's pulse quickened with new hope, but he didn't bolt from his hiding place for fear that they would kill him before he could say anything. An opportunity began to present itself and Shylo saw a new plan unfolding before his eyes. The congestion at the gate caused the riders at the rear to congregate right where Shylo lay. Quickly searching the helmeted faces of the handful of men wearing House Sarapio's symbol, Shylo spotted Wilsall and Wilsall's father seated atop their harquice a few strides away. All of the guards were ahead. Now all Shylo needed to do was get Wilsall's attention without alerting the others. He prepared to rise from the grass but stopped when Wilsall dismounted. From the way he was dancing in his lightly armored tunic, Shylo surmised Wilsall had to relieve himself.

"I'll be right back," Wilsall told his father. The others in the rear slowly advanced out into the opening.

Will walked into the tall grass right in front of Shylo's hiding place and lifted his tunic.

"Will," Shylo whispered.

Wilsall pushed his tunic down and looked to either side.

"Wilsall, in front of you," Shylo said in a slightly louder whisper.

Wilsall leaned back as he spotted Shylo, then stepped forward as he recognized who he was. Wilsall glanced toward the armored men of his father's house as they chatted while waiting to enter the city. Shylo wondered why Wilsall wasn't more eager to come and talk to him. After checking the group, Wilsall high-stepped through the tall grass, stopping on the opposite side of the tree from Shylo.

"Shylo, what are you doing here?" Wilsall asked as he pulled up his tunic.

"I was trying to get a message to Ismay through Marxius Ovando-Kai, but I didn't make it in time," Shylo said.

"The Emperor to be is in the capital?" Wilsall asked.

Shylo didn't realize Benton was in the running to replace Jermanus. "I was hoping to explain my situation to someone who could help. But now that you're here, you can help me get back into the city with my head still attached, and after, you and Ismay can vouch for me. I'm going to have to find more evidence, though, if I'm going to prove my innocence."

"How did you get beyond the wall?" Wilsall asked.

"I..." Shylo began. "That's not important right now. I need to know that you will help me find out which of the Noble houses set House Didimo up."

"Yes," Wilsall said. "I can help you, but if these men see

me talking to you right now, they will come and deliver the mob's justice to you."

"They believe I killed the Emperor?"

"No matter what they thought before this morning, they know that you killed City Guardsmen in the forest," Wilsall said.

"I didn't kill anyone. A draco —"

"The draco only got to two of them before they killed it."

"There were more dead?" Shylo asked.

"A dozen, at least," Wilsall said seriously.

"Will. You know me. There's no way I could stand a chance against an armored guardsman. I don't even have a weapon."

"They tracked the harquice to your camp. They found the saddle and are blaming you for the harquice theft as well. They believe you're with the assassin who was behind the murders," Wilsall said.

"That's ridiculous. Anyone who knows me could tell that I'm not capable of killing anyone or masterminding an assassination. This is a huge misunderstanding. Clearly, I'm innocent," Shylo said.

"I know you are. And House Sarapio will help you prove it. Ismay and her father can help, too," Wilsall said.

"What should I do? I can wait here for you to come back with help?" Shylo said.

Wilsall started backing away from the tree and said, "Yes. Shylo, wait right here and I will return with help."

As Wilsall walked calmly back to the road where his harquice was grazing, Shylo felt a ray of hope. He was relieved to know that his fellow Penti classmate was going to help clear all this up for him. Even without House Didimo to back him, everyone in their Penti cohort of trainees would know that he, an Eso boy with no military training, was not capable of doing the things he was being accused of. All he had to do was wait right here by the trunk of the tree and they would come back with help.

Shylo glanced around the trunk of the tree to see the squadron of mixed guards' progress. House Sarapio's men leading the rear guard were near the open gate. Wilsall rode quickly to catch up with them. He saw Wilsall reach the rear of his house's grouping. Then House Sarapio's guards stopped abruptly while the rest of the guard continued on toward the gate. Shylo spied from the edge of the tree as they all looked back toward the forest. His heart dropped. He saw Wilsall point toward the tree. A moment later all of the House Sarapio guards spurred their harquice into a gallop. Shylo considered that they were just waiting for the rest of guardsmen to enter the city before coming to help, but when he saw the leading members of House Sarapio draw their broadswords as they headed in his direction, his hopes shattered. He understood now that his *friend* was not a friend anymore. Wilsall had turned him in, and likely not once, but twice.

*"The farther south we campaign, the more intense the
Volurem become. Their behavior is different from that of the
Engulfed Volurem we encountered in South Apgar. Their
influence seems to directly correlate with extreme weather
events. They fuel the storms equally as much as the wind feeds
their strength. They are more dangerous here than I ever
imagined." – Sunspan 352, The Book of Volteir*

NOBLE REASONING

The Morning After the Emperor's Death

"They've discovered the Noble House that is responsible," Isik said, her deep voice cutting through the steam of Galterius-Brex's bathhouse.

"They have?" Galterius asked, wading through the warm water toward where he heard her speaking.

Isik walked to the edge of the pool. She stood with her long arms hanging limp at her sides, a dark copper-colored robe loose around her gangly silhouette. "Members of the Senate are placing the blame on one of their own. They say they have proof that one of the Kai hosted the assassin and aided in the plot of the Akai murders."

"Who was it?" Galterius asked, emerging from the bath, wrapping a soft towel around his scarred body.

"A Third Class Noble, Senator Rembert Didimo-Kai," she said.

"Didimo," Galterius repeated, rubbing a section of the towel over his tightly curled greying hair. "Did they find the assassin?" Galterius asked. His hope of capturing Jermanus' and his sons' killer tore at his conscience. Though he wanted swift justice, losing his brismil plate also weighed heavily on his mind. It left him far more vulnerable.

Isik inhaled easily through her flat, narrow nostrils. Dark rings circled under her yellow, unblinking eyes. Her piercing gaze upon him, she said, "They have not found the individuals responsible for the deaths of the Emperor and his sons. Your dragon-scale is still missing."

"Ash," Galterius cursed, hesitating as her announcement struck him. "There was more than one assassin?"

"After listening to the statements of servants from throughout the Palace and then seeing Jermanus' heirs' chambers, I don't see how one Rhydarian could've killed all three Akai. The Imperial Highnesses were both seen alive and at opposite ends of the Palace while you waited for the Guard to admit you at the gate," Isik said.

Galterius scratched his trimmed beard. "There wouldn't have been time for the same assassin to kill each of Jermanus' sons and to be in the Emperor's chamber by the time I arrived," he confirmed as he considered the layout of the massive palace. Given Galterius' hesitation at the door to the Emperor's chambers and his awkward descent down the assassin's rope, he knew that a single Rhydarian could not have moved so quickly to have also killed the others. Besides, the assassin had stayed around long enough to steal his dragon scale. "And among the commoners, has your network of Esos heard or seen anything suspicious regarding my scale?" he asked.

"No," Isik said.

"Do they have any reason to lie to you?" Galterius asked.

"Not unless the killer gave them your scale to keep their mouths shut. In which case, we would've heard about an Eso suddenly acquiring brismil-plate armor."

"Blazes," he said under his breath as he turned away from Isik. Galterius had hoped the warm water would ease his discomfort over losing his brismil scale, but all the heat did was cause him to sweat more. "I need fresh air," he said, walking through the steamy room and into the brightly colored atrium.

"The Agunzi delegation set sail during the night tide," Isik said, moving to stand alongside him on the red and white tile. The mosaic included the previous owner's symbol on the atrium floor.

Staring through the open entrance to his peristyle, Galterius said, "I told you, the person I fought was Rhydarian, not Agunzi."

"That does not mean they weren't involved. Rhydarians are not immune to bribery," she said.

"A bribe alone wouldn't buy an Emperor and his successors' deaths. There are certainly more players pulling the strings than a few paid assassins," he said.

"Timely, don't you think? That this should come when a fracture in the South seems evident," she replied.

"Too timely," Galterius hummed. "I'm not sure I would ever suspect Senator Didimo-Kai capable of this either."

"How well did you really know the Senator?" Isik asked.

"Not well, but I like to think that given all my rotations of protecting the Emperor I'd know if someone were plotting to kill him right under my nose," Galterius growled.

"Sometimes the most docile-seeming people have the most to hide," Isik said.

Galterius considered what little he knew of Senator Didimo-Kai. He'd watched him lobby in the Senate Chamber Hall. He was well spoken, intelligent, but not devious. Galterius had met and briefly talked to Rembert at one of Galterius' parties. The Senator didn't seem the aggressive, overthrow-the-Emperor type.

"When did the Agunzi set sail?" he asked.

"Shortly after the ringing of the bells marking the assassination," Isik said.

"How can you be sure they departed *after* the assassination? The Customs offices at the port are closed at night," Galterius said.

"Several Agunzi were seen drinking with Warden Ulbris after our meeting. As I understand it, they were not easy to miss. They were drunk and making a scene. They were strongly encouraged to leave by the City Guard before Customs closed for the night. I was told they spoke openly about their dislike of Emperor Jermanus and how the Empire had abandoned their people in the war with the Volurem."

"That's nothing new. They've made their stand regarding the Emperor very clear. That doesn't mean they plotted his assassination," Galterius said.

"If they did, wouldn't they need to be close enough to the Capitol to oversee that their attempt went to plan? Wouldn't they intentionally hire a Rhydarian to kill the Emperor in case anyone saw them? And wouldn't they intentionally make a scene as far from the Palace as they could at the time of the killings, near the port, where they could slip away on a ship in the night?" Isik countered.

"You expect a wideback to hatch a complicated plan like that? Here in Rhydenar?" Galterius asked, somewhat rhetorically.

"They could have planned it in the South, during the off season. Used intel from anyone who had been to Perdigon to work out the details. Then all they would have had to do was write it down and stick to the plan when they came north."

"Isik, you're over-analyzing. There are more fractures within the Empire than our rift with the Agunzi. Only a few moments ago you told me that the Senate had uncovered the Rhydarian Noble House responsible. Does your mind run so fast that you forgot how House Didimo fits into this equation?" Galterius asked.

"They take the fall," Isik said.

"Only if they are responsible. The Capitol Guard will pry the truth of it from Senator Didimo-Kai's lips," Galterius said.

"They will not," Isik responded defiantly.

"How can you be sure?" Galterius asked.

"Because House Didimo was delivered the mob's justice. Every member in the villa was killed to answer for the Akais' murders," Isik said.

"They killed the entire Noble House?" Galterius asked, trying to comprehend why or how this could have happened so quickly. "How is that possible? The Emperor has only been dead for half a nightspan. It's mid-morning and the mob is still gathering outside the Palace walls, waiting to hear why the bells have tolled in the night."

"Nobles are not exempt from mob behavior. They cut

down every staff member, guard, and slave to the death," Isik said.

"How could they be so blinded by rage? Violence like that is extreme even for Noble House feuds," Galterius said. He knew acting so hatefully was possible. He'd been in a blood rage before, but this seemed irrational. "How could they have killed an entire house without saving one person to prosecute in a court of law? Are the Kai so short-sighted that they didn't think to keep the Senator or one his advisors alive?"

"They didn't kill everyone in House Didimo. There's still one member who has not been accounted for," Isik said.

"Who?" Galterius asked.

"It's an Eso from this rotation's Penti trainees. If the Guard or the mob find this young man, it's unlikely he'll be brought into the Palace dead or alive," Isik said.

"How was a Penti boy able to escape?" Galterius asked.

"He must not have been at the villa when it was attacked. I think it's likely he was at the Perdigon Hill Canteen. You know the one at the base of the Hill that the trainees frequent in the evenings," she said.

"I don't think a Penti would know if his Senator was harboring an assassination plan or an assassin. Especially if he's Eso," Galterius responded.

Isik shrugged, "That doesn't mean the Kai don't want to see him killed. He's probably innocent but now that he's escaped, he is a symbol of the House being blamed. They'll kill him when they find him.

"You're positive they haven't found him yet, and he's not already lying dead in an alley?" he asked.

Isik nodded. "I believe my sources would've heard about it by morning. And unless the City, Capitol Hill, or

Palace Guard recently found him, I haven't heard anything of his whereabouts."

"He'll go back to the Didimo villa, eventually. If we're going to get an answer out of the Penti Eso, I can't have him run through by a hot-headed City or Capitol Guard. If he does know something about Jermanus' killer, we must keep this Eso alive. This could be our best hope for finding the killers and bringing them to justice," Galterius said.

"I believe what you mean is this will be your best chance to find the Rhydarian who took your dragon scale," Isik said.

"This is bigger than finding my scale; surely you can see that," Galterius said.

"Of course. The Agunzi, or widebacks as you so lovingly call them, are at risk of burning. Or perhaps their allegiance is not as solid as it appeared," Isik said.

"I don't understand. You say the Nobles have already killed a Senator and his household for the crime, yet you continue to throw suspicion at the Southerners?"

"Precisely," Isik said. "I present it to you as I see it. A Senator's house to take the fall or the actions of an Agunzi insurrection."

"Accusations like that without proof will ensure the Agunzi fracture from our Empire," Galterius said.

"Which is why I agree with you that the Didimo Penti must be found alive," Isik said.

"It won't be easy if he chooses to walk into the Didimo villa, clueless that he's the center of a leaderless mob of Nobles," Galterius said.

"There is one Akai that the Nobles are already saying will take the throne. Benton Querci-Akai is the next in line to inherit the role of ruler over the Empire."

"The Emperor's nephew?" Galterius asked. "He

wouldn't take the role of leader. The brat has no desire for politics. The only reason Jermanus allowed him to live in the Palace at all was his obsession with Benton's mother. Once Jermanus' brother was killed in battle, the Emperor got what he wanted by having her all to himself, but her company came with the little Akai's baggage. Benton doesn't care about ruling the Empire and he never will. He busies himself with the pleasures that his family wealth buys him. The Magistrates will choose a Senator, a Kai with the experience needed to lead Rhydenar."

"I would not be so certain," Isik said. "The Emperor trusted the overland supply bid to his nephew. Without an accurate supply audit, Imperial states could go months in the summer without the provisions needed to sustain them if cut off by the Volurem. The Emperor does not trust that type of mission to just anyone. Even the Akai must earn that level of responsibility."

"It's not the only decision of Jermanus' that I questioned as of late. If they agree to crown Benton, our position with the Agunzi will be even more shaky. And before you accuse me, my concern is not for personal reasons against the Akai's disinterest in politics; it's the idea that he will move like a reed in the wind. He'll do what the Senate tells him to do, and we'll soon have more than one war on our hands.

"Isik, I saw the killer who took Jermanus' life. It seems the cracks in Rhydenar's control are deeper than I imagined."

"If I were you, I would be more worried about making sure the Nobles don't come after the Brex villa next. It wouldn't be hard for them to suggest that you killed the Emperor. They might try to use your family as leverage," Isik said.

"Which is why my wife and daughter are not permitted to live with me here. I'm just glad I sent Alexandria back to Saypo when I did. Had my wife stayed another month... Why come after me? The guards saw me. The servants saw me. They all know I had no rope or blade long enough to kill the Emperor."

"But you lied to them," Isik said.

"I did not. I told the Palace Guard the truth. A servant saw me grapple with the assassin from the balcony."

"You withheld the truth about your scale. You lied about it and in that lie the Nobles could find reason to suspect you," Isik said.

"Preposterous. Everyone knows my allegiance to the Emperor was true. I spent a lifetime serving Emperor Jermanus."

"What if a Noble realized the rushed actions against House Didimo imposed a premature sentence? And if the Penti Eso confirms the House was not responsible? The Nobles might turn the blame on you, an Eso who was known to be meeting with the Agunzi on the day of the assassination. They know you met with the representatives earlier in the day and that you were seen at the Palace just moments before Jermanus died," Isik said.

"Ah, ashes with you," Galterius said. "The new emperor will thank me for my attempt to catch one of the killers. The real fault is with the Palace Guard. They were the ones who failed, not me. I do not fail."

"This is war, Galterius. Not a war that you are used to, but one that is unfolding before you. You must prepare yourself for the next battle. You were right when you said you're not a Noble. With Jermanus gone, the Kai will come after you harder than they have before. Anticipating their moves will keep you alive in Perdigon. This is what you pay me for, my advice. Now take it. Which of all the Nobles in the Capitol wants to hurt you most by damaging your reputation or worse?"

As a Legion and Brigade High Commander, I must consider sage advice when it's given, even when I disagree at first, he told himself. *Isik's over-analytical mind is why I employ her. She is one of the few people in Perdigon I trust.*

After a moment's consideration, he said, "Marxius Ovando-Kai. He wants total control of the Saypo Division. He does not want to share command over the legions in the South..."

"Marxius is currently acting as personal guard to Benton on their overland supply mission. If Benton becomes emperor, you're right, Marxius will have put himself in a powerful position. And I don't think he's capable of the foresight. He has become close with Jermanus' nephew during the last rotation, closer than any other Noble in Perdigon, but with other aspirations in mind," Isik said.

"His gain, if any, would be by dumb luck. Marxius does not enjoy Benton. He complains about the Akai's attitude every time we meet to discuss Division strategy," Galterius said. "I don't know what he hoped to gain by getting closer to Benton. Regardless, he couldn't be responsible for the killings. Marxius has been on the road for too long and without swift communication," Galterius said.

"That kind of organization is beneath a Rhydarian, even if he has Zethrillian heritage. The amount of effort involved. It would take rotations of planning," Isik agreed.

Galterius paused, chewing on that idea.

"What?" Isik asked, reading him all too well.

"Marxius is part Zethrillian," he started.

"You can't be serious," Isik said.

"It's a stretch," Galterius admitted.

"Almost a further one than suggesting you committed the murders," Isik said. "Marxius' record of serving the Empire is almost as long as your own."

"You're right, but I don't believe this was the Agunzi's plot either," Galterius said.

"And the longer we spend talking in circles, the longer the party responsible has to escape," Isik said.

"All the more reason for me to get down to House Didimo and find that Penti Eso before the mob takes his life," Galterius said. He collected his tunic, pausing as he grabbed his belt and once again noted the brismil scale's absence.

Striding into the peristyle, Galterius took the first harquice and rode through his villa gate. He didn't need to inquire about House Didimo's symbol. Galterius was familiar with the three pine trees and green circle. It stuck in Galterius' mind as one of the humbler symbols among Perdigon's Senators. It didn't take him long to navigate into the neighborhood of sprawling Third Class Noble villas. As he neared the green gate, he found a heavily armored Capitol Hill Guard posted outside the Didimo villa privacy wall.

"Lieutenant, have you found the Penti Eso?" Galterius asked the New Rhydarian man, a Lieutenant Galterius determined by the three bars sewn to the shoulder of his surcoat.

The Capitol Lieutenant saluted Galterius, recognizing him without his uniform, and said, "No, High Commander. We have not yet located the Penti of House Didimo."

"At ease, Lieutenant. I need to access to this villa," Galterius said without dismounting his harquice.

"I'm not permitted to let anyone, including senior officers, inside this villa. The scene is… still active."

"I'm sure your Captain told you what happened at the Palace last night. I was there. I fought the Emperor's killer. If there is any evidence House Didimo is responsible, I need to see it. Now, I order you, as a High Commander and Imperial Defense Committee member, to grant me entrance to this villa," Galterius said.

The Lieutenant hesitated, then looked to either side of the gravel street. He shuffled to the gate, pulled the latch, and pushed in. Galterius rode into the courtyard and stiffened. Capitol Guard were hauling bodies into the center of the open peristyle, piling them in the courtyard. Dozens of bodies, blood-soaked from short swords and long knives, created a mound of stinking flesh. One guard looked up at Galterius as he sat atop his harquice. The guard, an officer with no mark on his left shoulder indicating his Private rank, dropped the young woman with curly dark hair and saluted him. The rest of the Capitol Guard ignored Galterius' presence.

Galterius rode to the guard who'd saluted, likely an Eso like himself. "You, there, Private. What are your orders?"

"Pile and burn the bodies for the crime of hiding known assassins, traitors against the Empire," the Private said.

"Were you here when the killing took place?" he asked, hoping to get an answer as to whether the Guard were given the order to kill or if the Nobles had carried it out in anger, as Isik told him.

The guard shook his head. "I wasn't here, High Commander. But when I got here, these bodies were already rock hard. They're proving to be extremely difficult to handle."

"How long have you been at this, Private?"

"All morning. I got here in the dark," he said.

Galterius gave the guard a soft nod, taking note of the information and allowing him to continue carrying out his orders. Galterius felt a sinking sensation that his and Isik's scenario of House Didimo taking the fall for a plot conjured by another party was likely true. For the bodies to have been found before dawn already stiff with rigor mortis meant the massacre had happened near the time of the assassination. With all of the confusion at the Palace, he didn't see how any one Senator or group of Nobles could've carried out this sickening act so quickly. House Didimo was not selected at random; he was sure of that. Whoever coordinated this assault wanted to make sure every person in House Didimo had died before any of them could be questioned about their responsibility for the assassinations. Only not all residents of House Didimo were in the villa at the time of attack. One remained alive, the Penti. And no matter who was behind the assassination, Galterius knew as long as the young man from Didimo lived, there was a chance that he could flush out the suspects. But Isik was right. He couldn't bully his way through this one. He needed to change his way of thinking if he was going to catch those responsible.

THE BAD MEN

Shylo ran. He had no choice. In a matter of moments, House Sarapio's armed guard would be on him. His classmate had betrayed him, again. Shylo saw things clearly now. Wilsall was never planning to return with his father to help Shylo the morning after the assassinations. He was gone for far too long. It was no wonder that after he left the Capitol Hill Guard concentrated their search on that street. Will set them on Shylo.

Why did I ever want to come to this place? he thought as he ran. *Why did I want so badly to serve these hateful Kai?* Kai who were rotten with corruption and willing to kill to gain more power.

And now this. Wilsall exposed Shylo, knowing his move could lead to Shylo's death. It could only mean one of two things. Either House Sarapio was making a play to curry favor in *capturing* those being blamed for what happened the night before last, or they were in on the coup. Shylo was an easy target. He lacked the strength and stamina to make much of a break in running for his life. He'd barely made it into the forest before the galloping hooves caught up with him.

He heard a 'SWOOSH' and half an instant later, he felt a blunt force crack him across the back. Shylo was lifted off his feet and sent sprawling onto all fours on the forest floor. The pain throbbed in a diagonal line from his kidney to his shoulder blade. The line burned from the flat face of the Sarapio guard's broadsword. Had the guard chosen to come down on him with the edge, Shylo would've suffered a killing blow.

"Surround him," Shylo heard one of them order.

Shylo struggled to stand.

"Don't use the edges of your blade. The Eso needs to be punished before the citizens see what a traitor to our Empire looks like," the man, Shylo recognized as Wilsall's father, commanded.

Shylo scrambled to his knees, saying, "I didn't do it," before he took another blunt hit from a broadsword, this one on the shoulder. The hit knocked him to the ground. He tried to crawl away, repeating his innocence but found his efforts of no use. He was surrounded by men thinking him less than Terra. Each time Shylo tried to climb to his feet and speak his truth, they delivered a punishing blow with the flat of their blades. The sharpened edges left cuts where they touched his skin, but none were deep enough to cause him to bleed out. Shylo doubled over as another guardsman slammed the pommel of his blade into Shylo's gut. He gagged, wishing they would just turn their weapons a quarter turn and end his suffering. Shylo struggled to catch a full breath as boots pounded his body.

Wilsall had to know he was innocent, but Shylo heard

no sympathy come from his *friend* as House Sarapio guards beat Shylo to a pulp. *And for what?* Shylo thought. *So Sarapio can move up a rung on the political ladder?*

The idea that Shylo had idolized people like this made him want to accept the blame. The Emperor, and all the others before him, created this system. They had to be more corrupt than the Kai that served them. Likely, Jermanus deserved what he had gotten. Shylo wanted to curse them all, but his will to escape was fading. He curled up on the ground to best protect himself. He suffered tunnel vision. The pain reached new heights.

"Do you want us to keep going?" he heard one guard ask.

He caught a glimpse of his Penti classmate, Wilsall Sarapio-Ai, son of a Fifth Class Nobleman, staring at him with a slight grin. Will nodded, giving the order to keep torturing Shylo to death.

Then he heard the wet slide of a sharp edge cutting through flesh. The beating stopped.

NUMBER 2841 HAD BEEN LURKING in the thick foliage of a nut tree. She peered through the gap in its bright green leaves to watch the last group of armed men still outside the open gates. She expected to see them carrying Shylo, slung over a harquice and tied up, but he wasn't there. Instead, she watched a youthful man in a bright red tunic rimmed in white. He had a tri-colored symbol on the breast of his light armor. Number 2841 could tell his thin armor was decorative, not the heavy draco-scale armor of a soldier. The young man's metal shoulder pads and helmet wouldn't protect him against the heat of the Volurem. To her surprise, the youthful man pointed back toward the wooded area where she and Shylo had been. A moment later, they took off at a gallop, drawing their weapons and heading directly toward Shylo's not-so-clever hiding place. Number 2841 quickly searched the canopy for smoke. She didn't see any; she sniffed and smelled nothing of the Volurem. She wondered what threat would make them charge with their weapons drawn.

Perhaps the monster Shylo spoke of, she thought.

Despite his stubborn determination to stay on the road and give himself up to the dangerous people hunting them, Number 2841 noted that Shylo hadn't gone with them into the city. If he had changed his mind, she would not abandon him. He was the only person who Number 2841 had met who spoke to her like she was a real person. Even more so than the female soldier she'd met the day she escaped the Scaled One. Number 2841 felt a responsibility to protect Shylo, even though he had said he didn't want her protection. She didn't know much about the world beyond the arena walls where she had trained, but it seemed that Shylo didn't know much more about the wildlands than she did. And he knew nothing of fighting or self-defense.

Number 2841 hopped down from the tree and drew her willow-leaf saber. She ran through the forest nearly silently, moving as fast as possible. All her years of training gave her confidence in confronting whatever threat faced Shylo or the men on harquice. She was not afraid of whatever danger those guards thought they faced. She slowed to hear the sound of steel blade hitting leather.

Number 2841 found the men in the red tunics and white cloaks. They'd dismounted and surrounded a round brown object. The strangers kicked the curled-up figure on the ground. Number 2841 didn't see Shylo, or the danger she thought these men had gone after. A weak gasp escaped the figure on the ground. At once, she recognized the lazgron cloak and Shylo's sandals. The armed men were beating Shylo.

Number 2841 didn't announce her presence while one of them sought orders from their Master. She moved stealthily and speedily to the nearest guards in the group. She struck with the ferocity that she brought to her live trainings. Two heads rolled off guards' shoulders before the rest realized she was there. Their sickeningly jovial shouts at beating Shylo turned to shouts of fear as they saw her white hair, black-rose complexion, and draco-scale surcoat moving faster than they could react. She stabbed another, piercing her saber through his forearm and gut as he reached for his sword. She pulled the blood-soaked blade from the man's body and turned it on another. He blocked her moves three times before the willow-leaf saber stabbed through his armpit and out the side of his neck. The three remaining guards were already retreating, scrambling to get back to their mounts before the two who were still mounted could give them orders. The young one of the two on harquice gawked at Number 2841 as if she were a night-mare. The older one, sharing a similar look to the younger one, positioned his harquice between Number 2841 and the younger man. She did not attack but stood protecting Shylo. The survivors galloped away as a tight group, fleeing for the massive stone wall, and yelling for aid. They were too far removed from the rest, from all those armored guards who'd kept riding unaware through the gate at the base of the massive wall.

Number 2841 crouched over Shylo, ready to protect him if any others showed up. She hissed at the fleeing men in red and white in the same way that an Engulfed Volurem soldier did when desperate. Shylo was under her protection now. He was innocent of the crimes they accused him of. Number 2841 would protect him in a way that she never could afford to do with any of the others like her at the arena. Shylo told her that he would've given her a real name and that was more than anyone had ever offered her as an individual. It was a way of thinking that she had not been allowed within the arena walls. And now she was going to give the orders.

The young man in red, the one who looked to be near Shylo and Number 2841's age, glanced over his shoulder once more as his harquice galloped closer to the wall, away from the dead guards splayed on the forest floor around her and Shylo. Number 2841 was undaunted by his gaze. Shylo needed her. He was wheezing with labored breathing. He was bruised and bleeding.

Just then she heard leaves rustling nearby and saw that the guardsman she'd pierced through the arm and gut was attempting to stand. Number 2841 lunged at him, sticking the tip of her blade to his neck and plunging it deep. It passed clean through, and a spout of warm red fluid flowed from him before he lay still.

The well-trained harquice from this troop had not run off in the frenzy of the quick skirmish. They waited, saddled, and ready to be ridden. Number 2841 grabbed a grey one by the lead rope and tied the rope to the back of the brown one's saddle. She expected that the full might of the two-hundred-and-fifty guardsmen who'd entered the city would come rushing back out through the hole in the wall within a matter of moments. Once the red-and-white armored guardsmen were able to relay what had happened, they'd be after them again. From the looks of things, she suspected Shylo wouldn't be able to run anytime soon. If they were going to get away from the bad men, they'd need to travel off the road. Number 2841 wished these harquice were like those she'd faced in the arena. Those harquice still had their wings. These less aggressive animals couldn't fly. She would have to use their head start to their advantage. She could find a place to hide in the forest like she had before.

Number 2841 heard shouts in the distance. The men she'd scared off had now reached the gate. They didn't have much time. Number 2841 went to Shylo's side. He kept his eyes closed, wincing with pain.

"Get up," she told him.

For once, he didn't answer. He just moaned and remained curled on the ground.

Shouts at the gate increased as the alarm was raised. Number 2841 picked Shylo up off the ground. He was lighter than she expected. He did not struggle, only murmured with discomfort. She draped him over the trailing harquice's saddle like a limp sack. He grunted but refused to move on his own. She rushed to get on the leading harquice, but stopped, realizing that as soon as they started moving, Shylo would fall off. She lifted him back off the saddle and hauled him under her arm to the lead mount. Pressing him against the animal's shoulder, Number 2841 climbed into position. She then hoisted the young man up onto the saddle, draping him over the neck of the dappled grey harquice. She realized the ride would cause Shylo more pain, but they had to move to survive.

Number 2841 spurred the harquice and they took off at a gallop down the road. She continually glanced over her shoulder, noting how their tracks stood out in contrast to the hundreds of tracks leading toward the city. They needed to disappear, to wash away their tracks. She remembered the creek where she'd first met Shylo. It wasn't far from where they'd come across the road. If the water could wash away her charcoal marking, it would wash away their animals' tracks.

Pulling hard on the reins, Number 2841 steered her mount away from the road and crashed into the forest. She had escaped a group of bad men before; she hoped now that she could do it again. Their lives depended on it.

*"The Pyrignum are difficult to gauge. They hunker, burning
as bright white flames within the heart of the Volurem force.
They seem to be able to influence the Volurem foot soldiers
they surround themselves with. At first, I thought as the
Commanders did, why don't the Pyrignum fight closer to the
front line? Now that I've seen how they use the Engulfed,
perhaps they can think independently from the storm and
there is more to their strategy than previously perceived." –
Sunspan 391, The Book of Volteir*

MARXIUS OVANDO-KAI

TWO DAYS AFTER THE EMPEROR'S DEATH

High Commander Marxius Ovando-Kai peered through Perdigon's gates, the wind brushing against his short, loosely curled black hair. In the moments that he obeyed the Akai's command to unclip the harness holding his fractured brismil scale together in one piece, Marxius thought he heard a voice. The scale still pressed against his skin, the brismil's fractured tip sprung ajar and hinged within its custom harness. As he went to remove the armor almost unconsciously, Marxius searched the perimeter of the clear-cut.

215

The dense forest sprung like a thicket of untamed wilderness in the distance. At the end of the grassy field, Marxius could not tell if he was seeing movement on the road or not. The sun, now directly overhead, broke through the scattered clouds, casting a dark shadow under the canopy where the dirt road disappeared into the woods.

"Ovando," Benton called out, commanding the Noble's attention while not honoring the Senator and High Commander with any honorific.

Marxius turned to face the Akai. He still wore the brismil-plate armor from his pronounced Adam's Apple down, while his face was now unprotected. He did not offer the Emperor's nephew any verbal response, not without being properly addressed here within Perdigon's walls.

"Why don't you wear your plate like this more often?" Benton asked.

"It dulls the heightened senses," Marxius replied, again looking out toward the forest. He felt at the buckle used to harness his brismil scale together. Unclipped, the strap failed to apply enough pressure to hold the two pieces of his chipped brismil scale tight. With the top piece of the scale not fitted tightly to the rest, Marxius' brismil armor failed to cover his entire body. It left his head exposed and so dulled the magical effects the brismil provided his senses.

"Don't," Benton said, dropping his voice.

Marxius could feel the High Noble's green-and-yellow eyes burning through him. Though it pained Marxius, he did as the young man commanded. He stilled his hand, letting it hover over the brismil scale, where it was belted tight to his bare skin at the open side flap in his tunic.

"I like the way this look suits you," Benton said. "The brismil gleaming, but you can still see the man underneath.

It's the striking image I want the people to see as we ride to the Palace."

Marxius thought he saw movement at the edge of the forest. The loose thread of that mutant girl who escaped into the wild nagged at him.

"Ovando, answer me," Benton said.

Marxius tightened his grip on the harquice's reins. Nothing would be more satisfying than to teach the cocky High Noble a lesson about addressing him properly in front of Esos, but he resisted this temptation. That kind of emotional outburst would only distance him from what Marxius really wanted. Accepting the role as Lead Guard for this mission had been Marxius' choice. He'd agreed to guide the Emperor's nephew on the dangerous overland mission on purpose. Though logging more time in his brismil scale was risky, having a good relationship with Benton was worth it. For some reason, Jermanus had a soft spot in his stony heart for the boy and agreed with most of his requests. Marxius would not throw away an off-season's worth of patience now that he was so close to having completed his mission with the High Noble.

As the gates closed, Marxius looked at the Akai with a closed-mouth smile, and said, "Whatever you desire, Benton Querci-Akai."

"Ride with me. I want you by my side when we reach Capitol Hill," Benton said, adjusting his long, wavy black hair. Like Marxius, the Emperor's nephew was a mix of two races, only instead of New Rhydarian and Zethrillian like Marxius, Benton was a mix of New Rhydarian and Old Rhydarian. He wore a stiff surcoat, like a soldier's uniform but made with descaled lazgron leather that was dyed dark blue and black to hide the stains from extended travel. Unlike the guards accompanying them, he wore no chainmail, leaving his sleeveless surcoat to expose his matching long-sleeved tunic. Benton readied his reins.

"Neihart, Sula, Angela, Sidney," Marxius called to four seasoned soldiers among their armored guard. "Take the lead until we're within unimpeded view of Capitol Hill."

Marxius allowed the four most experienced of the ten remaining guard to trot in two-by-two harquice formation. He had personally selected each of the eighteen guards. *Now ten returning*, he considered, steering his harquice into the middle of the group. With Benton at his side, Marxius rode with a clear view over those riding ahead. Having enough Zethrillian ancestry to have yellow eyes and a height a full two hands taller than the rest of the Rhydarians around him, Marxius knew he posed an impressive sight. *Probably the reason why Benton agreed to my proposition that I accompany him on his mission as his head guard. I'd be surprised if he'd known who I was before or why I was overqualified for the mission*, Marxius told himself.

"I was expecting more of a..." Benton started as they rode past the commoners, sparsely lining the streets and avenues near the South Gates. "More of a grateful crowd," he finished.

Marxius hummed in agreement as he noted the lack of any kind of reception. They had been delayed after their last order from the Akai, but he'd sent Lieutenant Sula as a messenger so those in the capital would know of their revised arrival. Sula's return was proof that their message had been received. In fact, Sula reported House Ovando's Lead Guard, Captain Bridger-Ai, who was charged with overseeing safety at the Ovando villa, was the recipient of that message. If it had failed to reach the right ears, Marxius was going to have a word with Bridger.

The Esos who gathered wore a mixture of emotions on

their faces. A horrible blend of joy and sorrow. Likely, the citizens heard the rumors of Volurem forces advancing much earlier than expected. The people's reaction or lack of reaction at seeing the Akai's safe return troubled him. As they drew closer to the base of Capitol Hill, the Eso crowds thinned.

"Where are the Nobles? Do they not desire to see their Akai's return?" Benton asked as they passed a group of young Ai and Fifth Class Nobles.

"I don't know. I was not expecting an underwhelming and somber welcome such as this," Marxius admitted. He hadn't expected the same return as he would've had they been an entire local legion returning after a long season of battling the Volurem, but their supply report surely deserved more than a minor Eso crowd and a few villa's-worth of Minor Nobles. Marxius wondered if someone could've found out about their detour. The one Benton insisted on taking, since his uncle's Treasury had funneled so much wealth into it. And yet he could find no record of value. Marxius absentmindedly felt at the cut on his neck where the fracture in his brismil plate left him exposed. He should've pressed Benton harder about following through with the escapee.

"They're acting as if they thought I wasn't going to return," Benton said, pointing at the brightening face of a young New Rhydarian Noblewoman who overenthusiastically started waving at the Akai.

"There's something wrong. There should be a stronger show of support to learn how the year's food supply will go," Marxius said.

"They don't understand the ray of hope I bring," Benton added.

Marxius whistled to the four guards, signaling them to

fall in behind the Akai now that they had crossed onto the gravel road beneath Capitol Hill.

Continuing up the avenue and past the unusually quiet streets, Marxius noticed Benton straighten in his saddle. The Palace gates crested into view. Marxius slowed, letting Benton take the lead. From his height advantage, Marxius spotted a group gathered within the Palace courtyard. At last, their Noble reception.

As they drew near, Marxius recognized the odd nature of the size and composition of the crowd waiting for them. Upper Class Nobles, Senators and their assistants packed the courtyard. Zethrillians stood out among the group, towering here and there over the remarkable crowd gathered in front of the Palace.

"Ha!" Benton said with tempered enthusiasm. "Now this is more the Noble reception I was expecting."

But why have they all gathered at the Palace? Marxius wondered. He'd never seen such a gathering of what appeared to be all three-hundred-and-sixty-eight of the other Senators and their aides, plus all of the important Nobles and their families.

The Palace Guard lined the lumistone wall, surrounding the Palace in their golden-scaled uniforms. The cobalt glow of the Capitol Hill Guard lined the last stretch of gravel road, mounted on harquice before the stone paths just inside the Palace's front gate.

Every guard member they passed was dressed in full draco-scale armor and armed with a spear, shield, and at least two blades. They were better equipped for action than the ten remaining members of Benton's overland guard. Suddenly, Marxius noticed Benton's serious silence. During their entire off-season traveling through wild terrain, he'd never seen the High Noble tight-lipped and speechless.

Even upon seeing the heavily armored force at the Palace and knowing what Benton had ordered Marxius to do at the secure facility, actions clearly outside the scope of their mission, Marxius still expected the young man to crack an insensitive joke.

Marxius' heartbeat quickened as he sensed something dire could happen to his family name for having followed the Akai's orders. Everything Marxius did was intended to preserve the prestige he'd built up for his daughter. Was following the Akai's order a grave mistake? He searched his thoughts for an argument to escape any potential accusations. What bothered him wasn't the idea that Marxius' position in Perdigon could be stripped from him. No, if he fell out of favor, his concern was that he'd be taking away the life he'd worked so hard to build for his daughter. Ismay's future could be at stake. At all costs, he had to make sure that she would be taken care of. That she could continue the legacy of House Ovando unburdened by his recent scornful act. His mind now swarmed with scenarios in which he would face disciplinary actions for having tampered with the Emperor's secret project, while Benton received only a minor slap on the wrist. Yet Marxius did not let his worries show. He held a steady gaze on the Palace steps as they rode through the judgmental looks of armored guards and a mass of Nobles within the Palace gate.

Marxius felt a chill up his spine upon noticing the abundance of black clothing on the Nobles. It was as if they'd been ordered to dress for a funeral. Marxius wasn't a religious man, but he prayed to the new god that his time on Tarmigan was not coming to a swift and bitter end.

Beyond the courtyard gardens and center fountain, Marxius saw an opening in the crowd at the base of the Palace steps. Among the Emperor's wife and Benton's mother, the two Magistrates, and the rest of the thirteen Imperial Advisors, Marxius recognized Galterius-Brex and his Zethrillian advisor. They stood next to the Commander of the Apgar Division, Major Commander Noestriff Landrich-Kai, an Old Rhydarian and head of one of Perdigon's Third Class Noble houses. His eye moved to a tall young woman shifting into view from behind the influential group at the Palace steps. He couldn't help but smile at the sight of his daughter, Ismay, watching him ride in with Benton. She did not smile back, but looked at him with sad, glossy yellow eyes.

Benton stopped in the middle of the opening, facing the Magistrates, the Imperial Advisors, and Emperor Jermanus' wife and mistress.

Marxius settled his harquice slightly behind Benton's, close enough now to notice the dark rings under the people's bloodshot eyes. Marxius observed the Emperor's absence.

"You're all ashen in the face. Tell me why," Benton said, seeming to think only of the joyful reception he'd been talking about since they left the Shield Mountains.

The Emperor's wife choked out a sob and the New Rhydarian advisor next to her wrapped his arms around her, pulling her in to a comforting embrace.

"Someone answer me," he now demanded, looking to the others standing in a half-circle around Benton.

"Didn't you receive our message?" Imperial Magistrate Inyez Bynum-Kai asked. The Noble wore black linen robes under his bright yellow magistrate cloak. Because he was the Imperial Magistrate on the Imperial Defense Committee, Marxius wasn't surprised to see him, but that both Imperial Magistrates were present for this reception at the Palace meant a Senate decision was required immediately. A decision that it seemed they'd gathered to decree right then and there, without the Emperor's intervention.

"There was no message," Benton said, repeating Marxius' thought but in a much more abrasive manner than the situation required.

"We have not gathered to honor your return. This reception is a necessity," Imperial Magistrate Lucerro Ventous-Kai said stiffly. Marxius had campaigned for this second, New Rhydarian Magistrate. Now Marxius read between the lines; he realized why Emperor Jermanus wasn't there. Why the Emperor's wife sobbed on the shoulder of an advisor. Why the entire Senate and the Noble class were present and dressed in black.

But he is not next in line, Marxius thought, realizing that neither of the Emperor's sons were present either.

"Does he know about this?" Benton asked, dismounting his harquice. "Where is he? Doesn't the Emperor care about the expected harvest for this rotation?"

"Your uncle was assassinated two nights ago," Magistrate Bynum-Kai said in a swift and low tone.

Marxius' jaw dropped at the words despite having deduced the horrible news on his own. *Emperor Jermanus Aquercia-Akai has been murdered.*

Benton did not skip a beat. The young man's sorrow lasted only a few seconds before he asked, "Who is Emperor now?"

Marxius thought of himself as desensitized to death after his many rotations in battle, but even he had reacted more than Benton. Jermanus' nephew acknowledged his uncle's death without emotion and failed to ask about his cousins' whereabouts. Benton normally showed his immaturity with backhanded compliments and insensitive jokes, but now, suddenly, he appeared to be all business.

"With the Empress renouncing the Throne, you have been chosen to serve as the next Emperor of Rhydenar," the Magistrates said in unison.

"You mean after my cousins?" Benton clarified.

Magistrates Bynum-Kai and Ventous-Kai shook their heads.

"Assassins murdered your cousins the same night as their father. You are the remaining Akai to inherit the Throne of Rhydenar," Ventous-Kai said.

Benton grinned, showing pleasure at the announcement. Marxius knew Jermanus had not invested the same level of effort in training his nephew, assuming that his direct heirs would be his successors, but the Emperor had shown more support for his nephew and sister-in-law than Marxius believed natural. They could've easily left Benton to fend for himself at a young age, yet Jermanus cared for his brother's wife and child. Still, Benton showed no empathy for the death of his uncle or older cousins.

"Is this gathering my coronation?" he asked.

"It is," Magistrate Bynum-Kai said.

"Is there a party planned?" Benton asked.

Marxius nearly dropped his reins at the question. He eyed the young man with a narrow glare, thinking, *This is who they've chosen to lead our great empire?*

Benton caught Marxius' unintentional glower of disapproval and turned to face him, saying, "What? I was told that the party for my uncle lasted three days. There were feasts, vats of wine, the fountain in the courtyard was filled with sizzle, and dozens of fights were held in his honor. If I am to be Emperor of Rhydenar, I expect nothing less."

"Your uncle drove the Volurem out of the South for ten rotations. He expanded the Empire's reach, taking control of the most fruitful lands the Empire has ever claimed," Marxius said, unable to hold his tongue.

"I have defeated my own enemies, or have you forgotten already?" Benton said, eyes widening.

Marxius stiffened in his saddle. Apparently ordering Marxius to kill the experimental soldiers one at a time, as they obeyed the command to stand still while Marxius drove his dragon's blade through them, was comparable in Benton's eyes.

"We have not had time to arrange such an event," Magistrate Bynum said, interrupting the terse exchange.

Benton folded his arms, scanning the crowd that awaited his next words. After an uncomfortable silence, he said, "The circumstances of my coronation are different from that of my uncle's... Very well, I accept."

A wave of relief seemed to wash over the audience. "But afterward, I will have my party," he said more quietly, so only Marxius and those standing in the half-moon circle near him could hear.

In his mind, Benton's callous response to the murders wasn't what stood out most to Marxius. It was how this turn of events greatly increased his control over the Senate. *All my years trying to outmaneuver and manipulate my way into a position of respect among the Senate and now this? It just drops into my lap?* he thought. *Serving as Benton's highest-ranking confidant couldn't have come at a better time.*

Marxius had been prepared to struggle to gain full control of the Saypo Division from Galterius-Brex, a mere Eso. Brex had been a thorn in his side. Now, this previous goal of controlling a Division seemed underrated. Given Benton's new position, Marxius needed to aim higher. *I just hope that putting up with the High Noble will be worth it.*

THE WAR ROOM

Galterius-Brex opened his sword case. The black dragon fang lay before him; a blade carved entirely of brismil bone from an ancient magical creature of Tarmigan. Within its inky stores remained traces of the dragon's magic. Capable of killing a Terra person and dousing a Volurem flame with little more than a scratch, a brismil blade did not belong in a city, locked away in a box. It belonged in the field. It belonged in battle.

Longer than a two-and-a-half-hand great sword and

three times the blade width, Galterius' hand-and-a-half brismil sword weighed less than a practice sword a fraction of its size. When the owner wore matching brismil plate, he or she did not need to wear the blade like a bronze, iron, or steel sword. If nearby, the wearer of the scale could summon the blade on command. Without a scale from the same dragon, the brismil blade could not be summoned while its scabbard was elsewhere. However, once the blade was drawn from its boney scabbard, a brismil blade would return to the sheath when its user let go of it. The brismil blade would vanish for the slightest of moments, reappearing in its scabbard even astonishing distances away. Brismil remains held a natural attraction to other remnants from the same dragon. The attraction would draw them to be whole.

Forging a dragon's bone fragment into a brismil blade was as much an art as a highly prized skill. Carving a sword from the rare dragon remains that qualified as brismil killed many a Rhydarian and Agunzi who attempted the apprenticeship. Any intrusive shaving, splinter, or nick to the maker's skin introduced a lethal poison that killed in a matter of moments. Keeping the trimmed carvings from reforming while continuing to separate the piece of bone that would become the blade proved the most difficult obstacle. Master brismil blade craftsmen and women needed to periodically insert the blade into a prefabricated sheath to allow the chipped and shaved bone fragments to collect around it. This process of letting the bone carvings collect around the mold, bonding together again, created the blade's scabbard.

Galterius carefully lifted his sheathed dragon fang sword from the case. In a smooth motion, he pulled the massive blade free from its rough black scabbard. Charcoal rings, like the innards of a tree, swirled along the length of the glossy black blade. Galterius moved through his sword formations, fulfilling his morning ritual. The ever-sharp edge of the blade hadn't cut him in all of his fifty-one rotations. It seemed to know its master's worth, guiding Galterius while he moved the black fang smoothly through the air. A new sensation came over Galterius, and he faltered. He felt a warmth from the blade, urging him to move out of his practiced motions and step toward the open window. Galterius tripped, dropping the blade as he caught himself on the windowsill. The blade vanished, returning to its scabbard on the tile floor. Checking for any scratch he might've caused in his skin, Galterius breathed rapidly. He hadn't felt the blade draw him toward something in that way since before he had gained ownership of its matching dragon scale. It was a sensation he'd been waiting to feel since the moment he lost the scale. Now, a week after the Emperor's death, he peered out the open window at the northern city walls and the Shield Mountains beyond. The draw he felt meant only one thing. The person who carried his matching scale had finally returned to the city.

Galterius grabbed his tunic and slipped into his sandals. He snatched the blade from the ground and jogged to the doorway.

"Galterius," he heard a deep, soothing voice roll through the portico.

"Not now, Isik," he said, slowing as he approached her in the hallway.

"The Emperor is requesting your expertise," she said.

"Benton wants me?" he asked, confused about what the newly appointed emperor could possibly want from him.

"It's about the skirmish outside the walls that happened

four days ago. The Emperor is calling the Imperial Defense Committee into an emergency session to decide on the method of pursuit," Isik said.

"What in the blazing fire has Benton been doing waiting to act on this for so long? I thought he'd decided this was a matter for the Noble Houses and City Guard," Galterius said.

In the days following Benton's return, he'd left the search for the white-haired assassin and the Didimo boy in the hands of the City Guard. Benton seemed less inclined to launch a full investigation as the suspected Noble responsible had already received the mob's justice. To satisfy the Kai's request for swift justice regarding the escaped assassin and the remaining member of House Didimo, Benton issued a statement inviting the Nobles do their part by aiding in the search beyond Perdigon's walls. In the meantime, the Emperor-elect had ordered the Senate to focus on a full review of the supply audit he'd helped to carry out.

Galterius was one of the many people living in the villas surrounding Capitol Hill that disapproved of how their new Emperor was handling the Akais' murders. By his estimation, Galterius was one of the few people who quietly suspected those truly responsible were still somewhere in the city walls. Waiting to feel the pull from his brismil blade was a tactic Galterius was beginning to regret, until now. He knew walking around the city with his brismil blade on hand would raise suspicion, driving the party responsible deeper into hiding. Therefore, Galterius had had to continue his normal routine, trying to avoid any notion that he suspected some of the Kai. Now that the scale was somewhere within his blade's natural draw, the risk was only worth the reward if the blade led him to the unsuspecting Rhydarian with his scale. Benton's sudden summons, however, wasn't something Galterius could bring a brismil blade to.

"Tell the Akai I can't make it to the committee meeting," Galterius said.

"And risk being replaced?" Isik said.

"There's something that is more important that I must do," Galterius countered.

"What could be more important than this? I thought you wanted to be a party to the decision regarding which house guard should take total control over this endeavor, since the assassins took something from you as well," Isik said.

"This will take up too much time. I need to..." Galterius hadn't told Isik about the blade's draw to the scale when in close proximity. He trusted Isik, but he didn't know if he should tell her yet about the sensation he felt from the sword. As far as he knew, the natural attraction between the bone and the scale from the same dragon was not common knowledge. He'd heard no one mention it and only discovered it for himself when his blade came close enough to the scale that Galterius couldn't ignore the drive to be near it.

"You should be more concerned with how quickly Benton is wanting to replace any Senators and advisors who do not follow his way of thinking. He's already ejected five Senators from the Assembly and a dozen of his uncle's advisors, and it's only been a few days. How do you think he'd react to an Eso who ignored his first defense meeting?" she asked.

Galterius hesitated in the doorway with his dragon fang in hand. The sensation he felt was the first sign that suggested the person with his scale was nearby. It could be his only chance to catch him, but as he considered his position, he wondered how likely it was that the person was just passing through. He was confident that the assailant he'd grappled with was a Rhydarian man. If this person was a Kai, then he'd be returning to the city, possibly thinking the time required to let things blow over had passed. Galterius couldn't afford to lose his position as a High Commander and Imperial Defense Committee member if he was going to confirm his credibility in capturing the party responsible for the murders. Just because a Kai had a dragon scale that he claimed was his didn't mean the Nobles would believe Galterius had caught the assassin. They believed the assassin was a white-haired monster that already escaped from the capital. Galterius' proof was something only he could confirm. He would need a confession, and that might take more time.

"Where are you going with that brismil blade?" Isik asked, just then seeming to realize that he was carrying it.

"I... had a feeling," he said.

"Whatever it is, it must wait. Do not give this fledgling Emperor a reason to distrust you; it could put everything you've worked for in jeopardy. I shouldn't need to point out that Marxius will use any means possible to drive a wedge between you and the Emperor. He wants to gain more control for himself."

"Marxius and I share command. Benton has put forth no hint that he intends to take charge of the military," Galterius said.

"Maybe while Jermanus was in control you could take comfort in that knowledge, but he is not anymore. Marxius has spent the entire off-season gaining favor with the new Emperor."

"Benton would be blind to deprive me of my role,"

Galterius said, focusing on proving his point rather than deciding if this risk to chase his *feeling* would be worth it. "The Akai should know that he would benefit by promoting me," Galterius added.

"Benton is young. He was not groomed for power, though his hunger for power is growing by the day. He will listen to the people he trusts the most and right now Marxius is high on that list. You would be wise to forget whatever it is you were about to do and go to the Palace," Isik said.

"Bah," Galterius rumbled, pacing back toward the main sleeping chamber. Once out of Isik's view, he pulled the blade from its sheath. He closed his eyes, hoping the guiding sensation would return. This time, he felt nothing from the blade. Galterius dropped it, letting the blade form into the scabbard again. Again, he pulled it, waiting to feel the attraction for his scale. He felt nothing, causing his frustration to mount. Because he had felt the sensation so briefly, the assassin must have traveled to the outer limits of what the blade could sense by now. Perhaps the assassin was still returning to the city, or a much less likely possibility, someone with a brismil fossil from the same dragon was near Perdigon.

Then a thought struck him: If his blade could draw him to the scale, could not the scale draw the assassin toward his blade? If the Rhydarian now in possession donned his scale armor and drew near enough, could this criminal summon his blade? In all the time he'd been fighting, Galterius had never heard of such an event.

Brismil-plated soldiers rarely fought against each other. Owning a matching brismil blade and scale set was incredibly rare. Among all of the skeletal remains of ancient dragons, very few of the scales and bones contained residual magic. Philosopher and historian Leadore Volteir theorized that single scales, teeth, claws, and spines contained magic because the dragons shed them or they were ripped out during battles while the dragons were still alive. What happened to the magic when the dragons died remained a mystery. Among all of the Nobles in Perdigon who owned brismil scale or blade, Marxius Ovando-Kai was the only other person who owned a matching pair. He'd been in Perdigon for multiple days while members of his house guard searched beyond the walls. Galterius' suspicion of Marxius' involvement in the plot to assassinate the Akai had gone with the absence of his scale's pull. Perhaps Marxius could give Galterius insight.

"Are you going to the Palace, or shall I tell the Emperor you 're unavailable?" Isik asked, interrupting these thoughts.

Galterius flinched, dropping the blade as if she'd caught him with contraband. "I'm coming," he said, returning the sheathed dragon fang to the locked box where he stored it.

"Be at the Palace in two hours," Isik said.

Galterius realized that he could've ridden to the South Gate and back by then, but without the sensation from the blade he'd only damage his effort to remain incognito.

Slipping on his High Commander surcoat and changing from sandals into black combat boots, Galterius dressed in formal military attire for the new Emperor. Patting several loose curls into place, he noted that he would need a trim soon to keep up the required appearance of a High Commander. Wiping the natural oils from his hair on the long tail of his lazgron surcoat, he saw the curly white hair that shed from his scalp. He swept it away, refusing to acknowledge what his wife, Alexandria, his daughter Taz, and the Captains of his legion had been implying even before he left them to serve on the Defense Committee. Galterius was getting older. He was like a tsuga fruit ripening past its prime, becoming wrinkled, its short hairs losing their rich pigment.

Galterius fought his desire to abandon his obligations to the new Emperor. Mounting the chocolate-brown harquice mare he preferred, Galterius rode speedily to the Palace. The guard, the Sergeant who'd given him a hard time twice before, did not question him. She opened the gate without hesitation. He dismounted, handing the mare to a servant at the Palace steps.

Passing through the massive front doors, he looked through the antechamber to the top of the grand staircase where he'd stood that night just moments before finding his leader and friend, Emperor Jermanus, stabbed and dying. As he was about to turn away from the corridor leading to the Emperor's bedchamber, Galterius noticed a man standing before the carved wooden door. He slowed, observing the guard who wore a House Guard uniform from one of the Noble houses. The purple cape hugging the broad shoulders of the New Rhydarian man did not give away specifically which house. House Ovando came to mind. Galterius then noticed Emperor Benton Querci-Akai and his green-and-yellow eyes that had been focused on the guard, now turning to the entrance where Galterius had paused.

Feeling that he'd seen something he shouldn't have, Galterius looked away, continuing through the West Gallery and to the War Room. As he entered, Isik's comment floated into his mind; he wondered if he'd just seen Marxius in a private audience with the Emperor before the meeting. Pushing through the door and into the high-ceilinged room, Galterius saw he was the last member of the thirteen to arrive. He silently cursed Isik for forgetting to consider the time they spent arguing when she told him when to arrive. Galterius spotted Marxius seated second to the right of the head of the table, moving up two seats closer to the Emperor and passing three senior-ranking Major Commanders. Marxius met Galterius' eyes. An exchange of unspoken tension passed between them as Galterius tried to gauge the situation; if Marxius was already in the War Room, then who had been speaking with the Emperor and why?

As people chatted while awaiting the Emperor's arrival, Galterius noted that he had been assigned a seat on the Emperor's left side, the less important side of the table. The seat was considered several steps below the station he'd held during Jermanus' meetings. Taking his place, he leaned forward to address the younger commander who shared his command over the Saypo Division. "Marxius Ovando-Kai, there's a matter I need to discuss with you," he said.

Marxius narrowed his oval yellow eyes at him from the other end of the table. In the days since Galterius had last seen Marxius, the High Commander had shaved the finger-length beard he'd grown over the off-season. His wavy dark hair was cut shorter than Galterius' and his clothing appeared freshly washed and steamed. Like Galterius' copper tunic, the stiff collar of Marxius' purple tunic stood up from the descaled lazgron surcoat, each side displaying the dragon wing of the High Commander rank. Seated, Marxius was a full hand-and-a-half taller than the rest of the Rhydarians on the committee. "Whatever it is, it will wait until the matter you handled so sloppily has been dealt with," Marxius said in his deep, authoritative voice.

Galterius' chest grew tight as he bottled up his desire to lash out at the comment. Before he could come up with a response, the door opened, and the Emperor entered. No guard followed him. The thirteen men and women on the Imperial Defense Committee hushed and stood, waiting for the Emperor to take his seat and begin the discussion.

Benton walked to the head of the table and demanded they take their seats. They were arranged six on either side. The Magistrate sat on the Emperor's right and the rest were seated in the descending order of their perceived importance. Galterius wondered what the Major Commanders thought of Marxius' sudden jump in the seating arrangement.

Wearing a dark purple tunic and matching toga dyed a shade of purple twice as rich as that of House Ovando's purple, the youthful Emperor took his place at the head of the table.

For several uncomfortable moments, his eyes wandered the room giving the impression that he didn't seem to understand his authority or how to start the meeting.

Magistrate Inyez cleared his throat, gaining the Emperor's attention, and said, "Would you like to begin?"

Benton waved at the group with a gesture. "This was your idea, not mine. What do I care if a few people who murdered my uncle and beloved cousins perish in the wilderness? Based on Sarapio's report, they fled with nothing. No supplies. If they don't come crawling back to the safety of Perdigon's walls, they'll starve," Benton said, glancing noticeably at Marxius. "That is if the dracos haven't already gotten to them," he finished.

"That was not my intention in recommending this meeting," the Magistrate said.

Benton shook his head. "Then why did I send an emergency summons to everyone on the committee? I'm in the midst of shuffling funds in the Imperial vault."

"Is that wise, considering you're waiting to hear the results of this years' supply audit, and considering how much money went to your uncle's mining operation?" the Magistrate now asked.

"I thought this was a defense committee, not a board of financial advisors," Benton responded, glaring daggers at Magistrate Inyez.

"Of course, your Imperial Majesty. Clearly, there's been an assault on the Empire that demands our full attention. I say the aggressors must be identified and dealt with. We need to prevent the idea that they, or any other group for that matter, can eliminate the top-most tier of our leadership and still live to escape the Imperial Justice System. Yes, that includes hunting down the assassins who killed House Sarapio guards, but it also means military action against whatever group hired them," Magistrate Inyez said.

"I thought we already did that," Benton said flatly. "Domino or something. The Noble house with the trees as their symbol."

"House Didimo," Marxius offered.

"Right, House Didimo. They're all dead, and the one that's out in the wilderness will die. I heard he was a Penti trainee. He probably hasn't spent a day beyond the wall. He'll die or come crawling back, like the assassin," Benton said.

"What makes you think they'll come crawling back?" Marxius now asked.

"They don't have anyone to give them shelter, protection, or food," Benton said, looking at Marxius. "No city or town in the Empire will let them within their walls now that I've sent out a decree."

"A single Noble's house would not have done this on its

own," the Magistrate said, diverting Benton's attention away from Marxius.

"Why not?" Benton asked. "House Ovando's guard uncovered the evidence. Apparently, there was an exchange of money and massive landholdings."

Galterius wondered if that was why he had seen an Ovando guard speaking in private with the Emperor.

"Forgive my candor, but I was very close to Senator Rembert Didimo-Kai. If he despised Jermanus enough to take matters into his own hands and assassinate him and his heirs, he hid his hatred extremely well," Major Commander Noestriff said.

"Senator Didimo-Kai often voted against Jermanus. Is it such a stretch to think he took matters into his own hands?" Marxius said.

"It is," Noestriff replied firmly. "I gambled with Senator Didimo on occasion. The man did not take risks."

"Or so he wanted you and everyone around him to believe to get away with political backstabbing," Marxius said.

The Major Commander reddened at the slight, no doubt irritated by the mischaracterization of his friend as well as the displacement in seating.

"What about the Southerners?" Benton asked. "They're continually rebelling against taxation. It could have been that Didimo sided with them, if he didn't take this action on his own."

"We can't blame an entire race without proof," Galterius said. Immediately, he felt the entire group's attention bearing down on him.

"You met with them on the day of the assassination," Senator Juventius Bodo-Kai, a retired Imperial Legion Commander, said.

Galterius addressed the Old Rhydarian Senator in the silver tunic and white toga, "The negotiations with Warden Ulbris involved discussion of the coming fire season defenses. The Southerners were frustrated but not hostile."

"How well can we trust the widebacks? They're constantly fracturing among themselves, despite our support and influence," Benton said. "I'd wager my money on them, if not all in on Didimo."

"If not the South, perhaps House Didimo isn't the only Noble responsible for plotting the assassination. It would take painstaking coordination to pull off what the assassins did, killing three people in different parts of the Palace without the Palace Guards noticing a thing," Senator Tamsin Sigune-Kai, a Third Class Kai, said.

Galterius considered bolstering her theory, pointing out what he'd learned the morning of Benton's arrival, that the Southern delegation had set sail before anyone had been killed.

"Enough speculation," Benton said. "This irks me to no end. I have more important matters to attend to."

"What would you like the Defense Committee to do about this; it can't go on much longer without action," Magistrate Inyez said.

"Find something that will prove Didimo was the sole perpetrator. If you can't, then find the proof that the Agunzi were behind it," Benton said.

"And if we can't find proof?" Marxius challenged.

"Then go and replace the floundering City Guard and disorganized Kai troops. If you don't believe they'll return to the city soon, then find the murderers that Galterius and the Sarapio guard let escape and kill them," Benton said, rising from his seat.

"I will volunteer to take over command of the group

that searches the wilderness outside the capital," Marxius said.

Galterius flushed. He couldn't allow Marxius to upstage him right after the new emperor had called him out on his failure.

"I will also volunteer my services as a proven military leader in hunting the assassins," Galterius said.

"Fine, just deal with it, and this time do not let them slip past you. It shouldn't be too difficult for you 'seasoned' High Commanders to come up with a better result than that conducted by the Noble houses and City Guard so far. The sooner it's done with, the better. I don't want to appear insensitive to the people by throwing a coronation party. I've already had to wait longer than I expected. I want it to be as noteworthy as my uncle's. That will be hard to do if I'm forced to wait until after the initial buzz of becoming Rhydenar's next emperor has worn off," Benton said.

The committee stood, curling their right hands into fists and holding them across their chests as a sign of respect for their Emperor.

Benton did not return the gesture, as was customary. He walked across the marble floor and out the door. As soon as the door had closed, the Magistrate said, "Everyone do their due diligence to find evidence of a responsible organization. It doesn't sit well with me to think the assassins and those pulling Senator Didimo's strings are walking away from this with confidence."

A jumbled response of nods and agreement sounded among the thirteen members.

"High Commanders Ovando-Kai, Brex, good luck beyond the walls," the Magistrate said with a nod to each of them. "This meeting is now adjourned."

Galterius hustled after Marxius, catching him in the

courtyard as he awaited the palace staff assigned to collect his harquice. "High Commander," Galterius said, standing on the stone slab beneath the steps.

"Galterius," Marxius replied, not dignifying him with any title other than his birth name.

"The matter I need to discuss with you is about the coming fire season," Galterius said.

"We can discuss our brigade tactics after we find the assassin and the Didimo Penti," Marxius said.

"It's about getting more legion support to the Agunzi tribes. That's what the Southern Warden wanted. I don't believe he would've allowed any of his tribes to retaliate before hearing our offer," Galterius said.

Marxius collected his harquice and began leading it toward the lumistone wall. Galterius followed, snapping his fingers impatiently at the staff to collect his mare as well.

"Why would we give more legion support to a fractured and undeserving region of Rhydenar?" Marxius responded. "The legions already have their assignments for the season. Jermanus' barrier is the priority this season. Besides, you heard what the Emperor said, it wouldn't take much for a confident wideback group to splinter off and influence a rebellious Senator."

"The Agunzi rally around Warden Ulbris. They would not go against his orders," Galterius said.

"How do you know? Is that what he told you in your meeting?" Marxius asked, reaching the open palace gate.

"He didn't have to. I've been hearing the same reports from multiple legions in South Saypo. They're calling Ulbris the King of the South," Galterius said, exiting the palace gate. He glanced back to see the servant hurrying his mare across the expansive green courtyard.

"This matter will have to wait," Marxius said, mounting his saddle.

"How many guards will you bring?" Galterius asked, switching the conversation to the hunt at hand.

"Two squads. We'll need to travel light," Marxius said.

"I'll do the same," Galterius said.

"Meet us at the South Gates. I have a hunch the Didimo boy didn't make it very far after the beating he got from Sarapio. If they're still together, they'll be within a day's ride for a few more days," Marxius said.

Galterius nodded, starting back to retrieve his harquice.

"And Gal," Marxius said, gathering his attention again. "Bring your scale. If we stay out past dark, you may need it."

Galterius swallowed hard, watching the High Commander ride down the street away from the Palace. Taking his mount, he rose into the saddle, and headed out toward his villa. As he passed through the gate, he saw the familiar shade of House Ovando purple worn by a tall Rhydarian girl with long, dark, wavy hair and yellow eyes. She spied from the edge of the street, watching Marxius gallop through Capitol Hill.

His daughter? Galterius wondered. *What is she doing out of training?*

With not a moment to waste, Galterius shifted his body into a riding posture and the harquice responded, taking off to pursue the answer to the larger question burning in his mind. *Once outside the walls, will I sense my scale? Or have I missed my opportunity?*

FINDING THE MESSENGER

Seven Days After the Emperor's Death

"**W**atch out!" Galterius called out. He drew his brismil blade from the dragon bone sheath and spurred his harquice forward. It was in times like these that Galterius wished his harquice still had wings.

The forest-green draco crashed through the timber. Galterius' hastily assembled guards rode close on his heels. These devolved dragons were still exceedingly dangerous, even without fire, wings, or the use of magic. Their scales were difficult to penetrate without the enhanced effects of brismil; their pointed teeth and claws sharp enough to cut through scales of their own kind. And though dracos had shrunk from the great sizes of their ancestors, dracos were still much larger than a Rhydarian mounted on a harquice. Galterius swiveled in his saddle to glimpse the attacking draco.

Thick branches popped under the weight of the

massive beast, the size of which equaled the span of Galterius' courtyard. The draco sped toward the line of guards on a trajectory that would narrowly miss Galterius' harquice. Expecting the creature's speed, Galterius swiped his dragon's fang over the heads of the two closest armored guards behind him, hoping to strike the draco as it launched from the trees. Where a normal steel blade would've only scratched the scales of a draco on a crossways blow, the brismil blade could easily cut through the layers of scale and hide. Galterius' blade was deadly even if it only caused a scratch. That's all it took for the residual preserved magic to take effect. All he had to do was nick the draco and it would eventually go down.

The draco emerged near where he expected. He felt the dragon's fang bite into the draco's neck, slicing through the scales and lopping off a section of barbels along its spine. As the two guardsmen behind Galterius ducked his swing, he watched the draco careen into three other guards behind them before its momentum carried it into the thicket of trees on the opposite side of the road.

Two of Galterius' guard lay on the side of the road, slashed open by the draco's powerful claws. The third and his harquice were missing, carried off by the draco's robust jaws.

"Form up, she's coming around!" Galterius heard the other High Commander, Marxius Ovando-Kai, shout.

In a practiced motion, Galterius dropped his dragon blade, letting it return to the hollow bone scabbard secured to his belt. When not wearing brismil plate, riding with an exposed brismil blade was dangerous. Galterius knew to use it sparingly, only when his life was in danger.

Returning his focus on controlling his frenzied harquice, Galterius slowed. He struggled to turn the mare until she could calm down after the draco attack. This wasn't the steady war harquice Galterius was used to riding into battle. This mount had spent little time outside the capital. Fourteen of Galterius' guard remained. They angled around with him, allowing the more experienced High Commander to take the lead in their return charge.

Galterius spotted Marxius emerging through his purple-capped guardsmen. He sat tall on his harquice, glistening in his brismil scale.

"Hold," Marxius shouted to the heavily armored men in his guard.

Galterius kept his gaze on the fast-moving green body as it again crashed through the trees, rounding on Marxius' group. Before Galterius could join them with the help of his brismil blade, the draco hurtled out of the trees and into full view.

The beast's black eyes lost sight of its target as it opened its deadly jaws. Its rows of dagger-length teeth threatened to gnash through several of the guards closest to Marxius. Its arms spread wide, three sharp claws sliced through the scaled armor of several House Ovando guardsmen, cutting them down as easily as a sickle hews wheat.

Marxius, protected and imbued with the magical advantages of his brismil scale, held his position. The draco's open jaws committed to colliding with him. Almost faster than Galterius could follow with his eyes, just as the creature's mouth bore down on Marxius, he shot his scale-clad arm up. Marxius caught the draco by the lower jaw, lifting it shut and holding on as the beast pulled him off his harquice. Marxius let it crash through his mount and the guard surrounding him, knocking half a dozen of them off their mounts as it passed.

Reaching the point of collision where the draco carried

Marxius away, Galterius urged his harquice to follow. It pulled away, refusing to go off the road. There wasn't time for Galterius to train the urbanized animal to charge after the predator. Biting off his frustration, Galterius leapt off the mare and darted beyond the road on foot. Following the tunnel of debris the draco had just created, Galterius watched Marxius' maneuvering. In a single motion, Marxius pulled himself up onto the draco's muzzle. The green creature thrashed its head up, trying to bite the scaled one. Marxius allowed the draco to launch him up into the air. While rising, Marxius held both hands over his head, summoning his massive two-handed dragon's claw. The ash-white blade, twice as thick as a great sword, formed in his hands with the tip pointed down. Marxius came down on the draco, skewering it through the neck, and pinning the devolved dragon to the forest floor.

The wriggling lizard-like head snapped several times, then slowed to a dead stop, lying motionless. Galterius ran into the scene with his dragon fang in hand. Marxius jumped from the draco's body, leaving his blade where it was, skewering the draco to the ground. The white brismil blade stayed in the creature's flesh for as long as it took Marxius to reach the ground. When he touched the forest floor, his dragon's claw disappeared, returning to the hollow bone scabbard strapped to his dying harquice. Not bothering to look back at the dead draco, Marxius unclipped the snap on his harness that held his fractured brismil scale together. The tip hinged slightly, and his bare head appeared. The brismil plate began at the center of his pronounced Adam's Apple and covered the rest of his body. As he drew closer, Galterius spotted a red line on Marxius' neck. A thin scab, right where the plate armor ended. Galterius hadn't noticed it during the meeting with

Benton because Marxius' surcoat, like Galterius', had a raised, rigid collar that, when buttoned, covered most of his neck. Now though, as Marxius needed to quickly access his brismil scale, he wore his surcoat open and unbuttoned on the front.

"Brave of you, High Commander," Marxius said, approaching Galterius.

Galterius frowned.

"To come out here and face a draco with no brismil plate," Marxius said.

"Enough time in that suit and you'll choose your opportunities to don it a little more wisely, Ovando-Kai," Galterius replied.

"The creature would have bitten me in half had I not had the suit," Marxius said, opening the flap on his tunic and loosening the belted-on harness that held the dragon scale against his bare skin. The metallic sheen of his brismil armor disappeared, exposing his dark skin. Marxius buttoned up the open flap on the side of his tunic.

"A risk you could've easily avoided by moving out of the draco's path before it was too late," Galterius responded. He heard the murmuring voices of his fractured guard approaching from the road. Galterius turned to them and ordered, "See to the High Commander's injured guard. Drusus," he said, singling out one of the New Rhydarians who Galterius knew had been tested in battle against the Volurem. Out of all his employed urban guardsmen, he could trust Drusus, a former legionnaire, to carry out the order. "Ride to the rest of the Ovando Guard and tell them we've killed the monster."

As Drusus sped away on his harquice, the rest of Galterius' guard acted as Galterius trained them, to help any others injured in a fight. While they moved to see to the injured Ovando Guard, Marxius commanded, "Hold on. Leave the Ovando Guard be. Do not help the injured."

Galterius shook his head at the High Commander and asked, "What are you doing? Those are members of your house guard."

"If they can't recover from that attack, they don't deserve to protect House Ovando," Marxius replied.

Galterius grimaced, saying in a hushed tone, "This is not the battlefield, Marxius. We have medical supplies and surgeons within the walls."

"Do not tell me how to run my house guard, Eso," Marxius growled. He led Galterius to the road where those too injured to walk called for help. Marxius pulled his dragon's blade from his dead harquice and said, "Is this what your few years away from the South have done to you? Perdigon's made you soft."

"If you cannot hear my words, you will not understand my wisdom, Ovando-Kai," Galterius said, quoting a sentiment that his wife, Alexandria-Brex, always told him when she needed Galterius to look beyond his stubbornness and see her point of view.

Marxius gave Galterius a nod, which Galterius initially took to be an acknowledgement that he was more than a Eso, he was his equal. That idea vanished when Marxius opened his mouth, and said, "Simply because you are old does not mean you are wise."

"The next time you are outnumbered and hurting for every last soldier, you will think of my wisdom. Even poor guards can become great soldiers," Galterius said.

Marxius laughed. "A guard from Perdigon becoming a great soldier? You have been away from the South for too long. None of these Rhydarians have been tested against the fires of the Volurem. They're Ai and Fifth Class Nobles. If they ever face the Volurem in battle, they will thank me for this experience."

Galterius held his tongue, locking eyes with Marxius' yellow-eyed glare.

"I was surprised the young Emperor listened to your advice and sent you with me to search for the Didimo boy. He knows of your name, because of your folly, but he probably didn't recognize your face as being the one who let Jermanus' assassin escape."

Galterius took a step forward. He and his guard outnumbered Marxius' at the moment, and they were outside the walls. If he were to ignore the rules of their ranking and social class, now was the time to do it.

"I'm curious why you volunteered. Was it because you failed to stop the assassin or is it because that Didimo boy took something from you as well?" Marxius said, patting at his side where the leather harness secured his chipped brismil scale.

Galterius put his hand to the hilt of his brismil blade. "You heard what those Nobles reported. The assassin killed the Sarapio Guards with ease. I might've let the killer escape my capture, but I defended myself well. We are not dealing with an ordinary Rhydarian."

"Or any Rhydarian at all," Marxius said. "You were hosting a delegation of Agunzi in the capital when the Emperor was assassinated, weren't you?"

"The day of, long before then. Besides, they set sail before the Emperor was killed. They could not have done it," Galterius said.

"I wonder how you know that, when the dock workers didn't know what time they left in the night," Marxius said.

"I said, the Agunzi could not have done it," Galterius said.

"And you couldn't have lost your scale," Marxius whispered, low enough for only the two of them to hear.

Galterius did not let his anger get the better of him, "I never said I was missing my brismil scale."

"I think I'll cut her open and see what's inside," Marxius said, pulling the sheath away from his blade as he no longer wore the matching plate.

Galterius saw Marxius' eyes trained on Galterius' empty pouch where a rock weighted the spot of his scale's harness. Having the bulge in the leather carrier where he could unbutton the flap of his tunic and press the scale's placeholder to his bare skin was intended to give the illusion that he still had his brismil scale. Galterius wasn't about to let the Kai expose him. He lifted the hilt of his brismil blade from his scabbard.

"The draco," Marxius said, almost teasingly. "I'll think I'll cut her open and see what she's been feeding on."

Galterius let go of the blade.

"House Sarapio, I believe it was, said a draco killed a handful of guards from the other Noble houses when they were beyond the wall that first day. Maybe the beast picked up our Didimo boy, and a scale as well?" Marxius marched back to the draco and slid his brismil blade along its underside. "Neihart," Marxius called to a guardsman who'd been knocked over by the draco but was back on his feet. "Come and cut this draco's stomach open so I can see who she's been eating."

Galterius stood with his guardsmen gathering around them. Marxius was fully capable of the act, but Galterius could see the pleasure he took in making his guard do the messy work. Neihart, a New Rhydarian guard of House Ovando used his steel dagger to cut a slit in the draco's exposed pink stomach. The stretched-out balloon sack of a stomach spilled half-digested Rhydarian remains onto the grass. Galterius heard one of his guards retch behind him.

"No sign of Southerners in here," Marxius said. He kicked aside an arm with a partially eaten wool sleeve that included a patch with the Imperial coat of arms: a white dragon skull. "There's our messenger who never delivered the news about Jermanus. That was the only Imperial Guard sent beyond the wall. The rest of those out searching have been City and Noble House Guards."

"Didimo house wears green. The house symbol is three trees," Galterius said.

Kicking through the chunks of partially digested flesh, Marxius said, "No one else and nothing else we're looking for in here."

"It's getting dark. We'll return to our search in the morning," Galterius said, signaling for his guard to mount their harquice.

"We will see what the Emperor has to say about it," Marxius said.

Once out of Marxius' view, Galterius lifted his blade from the dragon bone scabbard. He couldn't help checking for the sensation he felt in the blade before going back inside the city. He no longer felt the pull that he had earlier. Galterius thought he'd felt it again briefly when he was preparing his guard to go out beyond the walls with Marxius. Likely, the assassin with his scale was now too far away to feel the pull of the matching blade. It would be impossible to assume the Didimo boy had Galterius' scale. He wasn't New Rhydarian, like the assassin who made off with his scale. But the two could potentially be traveling together. House Sarapio described the person as having black skin, red burn scars, and with white hair, but they could've been mistaken. They weren't tested in battle and could've been so frightened by the assassin's skills that they mistook blood on the assassin's face for unique markings. The white hair could've been a lie, a detail said to impress the other Nobles. Wherever they were headed, on harquice or on foot, every village, town, and city would already have heard about the Emperor's death and the Didimo boy who was on the run. Banned from the protection of a walled fortress, the pair would not last long in the wilderness. The fire season was coming.

"Pyrome and Brisrome struggled to control their brother, Tourome. Eventually, after hundreds of lesser dragons had died by Tourome's blinding rage, The Creators stopped Tourome's rampage. The Creators knew their days of peace were over. Tourome's taste for blood only fueled his desire to rid his world of the lesser dragons." – The Dracolyth

THE TSUGA TREE

Ten Days After the Emperor's Death

Sensing the onset of a mild allergic reaction, Shylo tensed his torso. It did nothing to lessen the pain. He sneezed and an intense stabbing sensation spread from his sides to his core.

Out of all the Penti trainees, why did this have to happen to me? Shylo wondered while slowly drawing in a shallow breath. In the seven days since House Sarapio had beaten him, Shylo's condition had only slightly improved. The biggest gains over the recent spans: his current ability to push through the pain in his sides and walk alongside the mare Number 2841 had stolen for him.

"Why do you make that noise? When you do, it's painful, I can tell," Number 2841 said.

Shylo hesitated in bringing the ripe tsuga fruit to his lips. He eyed the young woman in much the same way that she often looked at him. Shylo didn't understand how someone so skilled with a blade and so stealthy in the wilderness could be so ignorant. "It's not like I want to sneeze. I can't help doing it. It's because of all the trees and grasses."

"The trees and grasses did nothing to you. Why blame them for your loud flinching?" she asked.

"No," Shylo sighed, the deep exhale hurting slightly. "I'm not blaming them for hurting me. It's their pollen."

She shook her head.

"Forget it," Shylo said, massaging the corners of his jaw. It was still tender. Shylo needed to focus on finishing his fruit. They faced another long day of wading through the thick underbrush in the wilderness. Not knowing where they were or where they were going weighed heavily on Shylo. As he studied her, he couldn't discern why Number 2841 stayed with him. While she seemed to thrive in the wilderness, Shylo could not ignore his inability to adapt. In a matter of days, Shylo had gone from using the knowledge he'd been accumulating for years, putting it into practice as a Penti, to having to rely completely on a person he barely knew.

He dropped his gaze, staring absentmindedly at his weathered clothing and thinking, *I should've paid closer attention to my father's lessons. Lessons on becoming a man,* as Shylo's father put it. The training he tried repeatedly to get Shylo to take seriously in order to prepare him for the legions; a station in life Shylo never planned to take.

Looking down, Shylo noticed his black leggings were more torn up than whole. His sandals were not the right footgear; consequently, the tops of his feet were all scratched up. Fiddling with the hem on his tunic, it was apparent the House Didimo tunic was not holding up so well either. The stitching where Shylo had removed his Didimo patch was hardly noticeable beneath the smattering of stains. The dark stains and many holes left Shylo feeling more like the refugee he'd become and less like the aspiring Penti trainee he'd been. Only the lazgron cloak proved useful in the wilderness.

Shylo shifted on the ground, feeling the full discomfort of his bruised body. That he was moving on his own, Shylo hoped was a sign he could fully recover. During most of the days since the House Sarapio attack, Shylo's stillness gave him ample time to rehash events that had taken place after leaving the Senate Chamber. He shivered thinking about his inability to see the bigger picture.

His mother's warning cycled repeatedly through his thoughts, "Don't trust anyone above your social rank, even an Eso will push others down to get ahead."

Why didn't I see it? he cursed himself for being so foolish to believe that even an Ai, a minor Noble within the Penti trainee program, could be his friend. Shylo had forgotten his place. He was an Eso and always would be. While he considered the events from a more removed vantage point, he could not reconcile why so many Kai wanted to catch him. If it was clear to him that a lowly Eso Penti trainee could not possibly have assassinated three royals in the Palace, surely all of his superiors knew this as well. And it was ludicrous to think that Senator Rembert Didimo-Kai would have taken Shylo in confidence had the Third Class Noble even orchestrated or participated in such a scheme, Shylo mused.

That just goes to show their way of thinking, he told himself. But betrayal of Esos by Nobles was commonplace.

I should've known better than to trust one. In the darkest corners of his thoughts, Shylo almost wished he had stepped out from the edge of the forest and into full view of the walls. At least then, he would've remained ignorant of Wilsall's betrayal.

Shylo understood that Wilsall used him to position his family name with a more accomplished group of Nobles. Shylo had read of such maneuvers before arriving in Perdigon. By catching the escaped Penti, Sarapio would've been rewarded by the Akai. Wilsall might've hoped to buy himself a villa and small guard with the earnings, making him Kai.

Why didn't I see how Wilsall only ever put me down, made fun of me in front of Ismay, and manipulated me for answers during training? If I wasn't smart enough to see how one of my closest peers was treating me, how could I have ever thought I'd be an effective advisor one day? Shylo thought. But he knew that door had closed before he'd even escaped the city. *I will never be an advisor to any Senator.*

To disrupt these circular thoughts, Shylo shucked more of the thick tsuga husk to expose the light blue melon. He bit into the fruit. Sweet, tangy juice gushed into his mouth. His teeth passed easily through the not too soft, yet not too hard fruit, a relief for his aching jaw. Shylo's grey eyes widened, juice weeping from his dry lips. "Where did you find this?" he asked.

"From the tsuga tree," Number 2841 said through a mouthful.

Shylo shook his head. "No, I've tasted tsuga a thousand times before. This one is different. It's not hard or sour like the others."

"This is the same fruit. It came from the same type of tree. Before, you called it, tsuga?"

"Ashes," Shylo cursed, his frustration stemming from her limited understanding. He held the melon out, "Yes, this is tsuga fruit. It's one of the most common fruits grown in many city gardens throughout Rhydenar. I've never tasted one so ripe. Usually, they're sour and have a firm crunch. The best tsuga I had was harvested somewhere in the South, near the Fringe. They used to come through Florens sometimes when the Volurem blocked other southern trade routes. I remember seeing them piled high on these massive wooden shipping barges and wondered what kind of events must've led them to haul that much fruit north to the Pryor River. But none of those tsuga were this ripe. This one is sweet and juicy. Where did you find it?"

"Not far from here. Come, I'll show you the clearing," she said, hopping to her feet and extending a sticky palm to Shylo.

Shylo set down his fruit, making to take her hand, then paused. Something about feeling this excited didn't sit right with him. They were still being hunted by guards and Shylo didn't know how far away from Perdigon they were. "Is it safe? We've been moving around more the last few days. You told me you'd seen guards in the forest," Shylo said.

"They're past us now. Only one has doubled back and that man didn't return. They won't hurt you as long as you're by my side," she said, instantly wagging her hand in his face, trying to get him to take it.

Reluctantly, Shylo braced for the pain that would come from standing. He took her hand, flexing while Number 2841 pulled him to his feet. He exhaled a slow and ragged breath then took a moment to gather himself and slowly began following her. As they walked, Shylo couldn't help but admire this strange person he'd stumbled across. She knew so little about typical everyday life in Rhydenar, yet she had a wealth of knowledge about survival. She'd found tsuga fruit that tasted better than any he'd had. Thinking about her willingness to help him led him to wonder why, among all the people he'd known in Florens and Perdigon, no one had acted the way she did toward him.

While trying to puzzle out how she could trust him so easily Shylo almost walked into Number 2841's back. She'd stopped at the edge of an opening in the forest. The foliage in the roughly shaped oval had been stripped from the few dark trees still standing. The skeleton trees nearly glowed with a shine that reflected off burnt trunks and limbs. All underbrush was gone, torched by Volurem flames. Black logs littered the clearing and chunks of sleek charcoal sparkled in the new grass. Among the tumble of old and new near the clearing, Shylo noticed half of a skull. It clearly didn't belong to a Terra person but did look strikingly similar to a Terra person's skull. The difference was where the finger-long protrusions sprouted like tines, occurring sporadically across the top of the skull. And in the raised bumps that arched down from a prominent brow, curling around the eye socket.

"Get down," Shylo snapped. He struggled to crouch, feebly dropping to one knee, and leaning against a living tree.

"What are you doing?" Number 2841 asked, still standing in full view of the charred opening.

"That's a fire scar. The ashen Volurem have been here. There's one's skull right there," Shylo swore.

He'd been so preoccupied thinking about Number 2841, with her unique skill set and knowledge, that he nearly forgot about the dangers of being outside a walled city. He immediately thought of seeing the smoke from the

Capitol steps with Senator Didimo-Kai the day the disasters began to unfold. He quickly considered the cause, remembering something he had read about how fires could spark to life outside the walls during storms at the height of fire season, though it was still too early in the season for this burned area to have been started by a storm. Shylo hadn't seen a storm in this rotation that reached this far north in Rhydenar. Yet this could be a recent fire scar. If he and Number 2841 were caught in the wilderness with Volurem now, they would have no way to protect themselves from the flames.

"Get up. The fire is gone. They've been gone for a long time," Number 2841 said.

"How do you know?" Shylo asked, ignoring the ache of his clenched jaw.

"Look," she said, taking a few steps closer to the clearing.

"Stop. You could be in danger," Shylo hissed.

"See, the embers are all out. This is where I got the fruit. No fire people came for me," she said with certainty.

Shylo examined the opening from the base of the tree where he knelt. The clearing, though previously burned, was now thick with green vegetation sprouting through charred earth.

"Even if there was an Engulfed Volurem, you are safe with me," she said, ignoring Shylo's skepticism and striding confidently into the opening.

Shylo didn't dare move from his hiding place, not because of pain, but because he still didn't believe it was safe. He decided to wait and see what happened to the young woman before standing. He expected to see a flame sprout from one of the downed logs, catching fire around Number 2841. Once she crossed the length of the opening unharmed, Shylo acknowledged that he saw no sign of active Volurem.

Stiffly, he rose to his feet. He made his way the short distance to the edge of the clearing. Number 2841 cawed loudly, drawing his attention away from the recent growth in the clearing. The young woman pointed to a tree at the far edge. He spotted the tsuga tree. Its trunk appeared twice the thickness of Shylo's narrow frame. Arching branches bowed close to the ground, laden with ripe fruit. To Shylo's surprise, though the tree appeared charred around its base and its lower branches drooped leafless and dead, somehow the tree was covered with more fruit than any tsuga tree Shylo had seen in a city garden.

Number 2841 scrambled up into the tree to gather more of the sweet fruit. As she did, Shylo heard a high-pitched chirp. The noise seemed to come from a log directly in front of him. He scanned the downed trees. He was positive it came from somewhere only a few strides in front of him.

The chirp sounded again, and Shylo pinpointed its origin. He saw a grey, furry critter scamper across a black log and stop. It perched on its rounded hind end, balancing with its stumpy legs. The rodent's fluffy front paws hung limp above its rounded white belly as it sat perfectly still. The instant Shylo saw that it wasn't a Volurem sparking to life, he thought of how to catch it. In his eyes, the three-hand-tall rodent would be enough food to keep him and his companion going for days. They hadn't eaten meat since the gargous on that first night out of Perdigon. Shylo's stomach growled and his mouth watered. The four-legged creature was similar in size to a rooster pheasant. Its grey fur was flecked with black from its rounded ears to its fluffy ball tail. The only bare skin on the critter was its snubbed pink nose. It held something green in its front paws, nibbling at it in short, vigorous bursts.

"Caw!" Shylo shouted, poorly mimicking Number 2841's bird-like sound to get her attention.

The grey rodent's short ears now flattened to the back of its head. It held itself perfectly still. Shylo realized his mistake. After several uncomfortable moments of holding as still as the furry critter, Shylo recognized that he didn't have a good chance of catching it. Better not to chase it, making it hide from whatever burrow it came from. He'd watch and wait for his companion to return.

As he leaned back against a blackened tree trunk, Shylo spotted movement in the undergrowth at the edge of the clearing. At first, the way it moved, crouched, advancing slowly, and stopping for several breaths before continuing, didn't raise any alarms. That was how Number 2841 moved through the forest sometimes, when they weren't marching aimlessly. But when he saw the young woman drop from the tsuga tree, her coat stuffed with fruit, Shylo's paranoia took over. He wanted to yell at her, to warn her about the thing creeping through the forest, but he couldn't without giving himself away too.

Several horrible ideas came to mind about what lurked in the underbrush. A killer, hired to hunt Shylo and bring him back to the capital, seemed most likely. But the way it moved brought flashbacks of the draco that devoured an armored guard. Shylo tried to get Number 2841's attention by waving his arms. She was bent over, picking up downed tsuga fruit. Shylo tried to get a better sense of what was stalking through the trees. Maybe he didn't need to be worried if it were something less dangerous, like a lost mongodo. That idea quickly faded as he realized the large range animal wouldn't survive long in the forests of Apgar.

They roamed the grassy plains of Saypo and relied on herd size to survive predator attacks. A lost mongodo would be too big a meal for a lazgron, but a prime target for a draco.

The color of the figure matched the underbrush it crawled through. Shylo kept losing track of it, only to find it again when it moved because then he could see its slightly reflective glossy coat. Shylo then spotted a fist-sized black eye and a row of white teeth. The same teeth he'd seen on lazgron at the tracks in Florens. The lazgron's wide head was flat like a shovel and had the shape of a snake head, tapering to a rounded nose with two slits for nostrils. It stood lower to the ground than a harquice, but with its tail, the lazgron was almost twice as long. Its scaled body swayed as it waddled closer to the edge of the clearing where Number 2841 walked. She was heading back toward him now, focused on carrying the tsuga fruit. She acted as if the creature wasn't there.

Shylo cupped his hands to call to her but hesitated when he saw the furry rodent still perched on the log, small round ears pinned back and pink nose sniffing the air. The furry meal had its back turned to Number 2841. *Ashes, but I want to eat a full meal. She would too. I don't want to spook it.*

In his moment of hesitation, the lazgron emerged from the trees. It moved quickly, remaining low to the ground, using the dead logs to hide its advancing position. Shylo knew there was no chance now that Number 2841 would have time to catch the furry critter. The lazgron was nearly on her. Shylo felt an overwhelming need to call out a warning. As he inhaled to shout, the furry animal barked an astonishingly shrill chirp. The sudden alarm caused Shylo's warning to die in his throat. The chirp triggered Number 2841 to let go of her surcoat and allow the fruit to fall away as she reached for her blade. Her saber was pulled free from its scabbard and held in a ready position before the last tsuga husk hit the ground. Shylo struggled to track her movements as Number 2841 brandished the steel blade, turned toward the lazgron, and defended herself.

No, I waited too long! Shylo thought, consumed with guilt. He'd hesitated and again found himself selfishly allowing others to defend him at their expense. He'd let the fear of what might happen prevent him from doing the honorable thing for the last time. This time he wouldn't run. Shylo had to do something.

Pushing through his soreness, he rushed out into the opening. Breaking off a dead branch from a downed tree, Shylo held it up over his shoulder, trying to mimic Number 2841's attack form.

The massive lizard pulled away from the young woman and stood broadside between them. Shylo instantly saw that the lizard's glossy camouflage scales were smeared with a line of black blood oozing out of a deep gash. The animal was wounded. All the pent-up aggression Shylo felt poured out. Shylo released a foolhardy battle cry. In response to his shrill cry of frustration, the lazgron reared its head, and faced him. Shylo swallowed hard, now seeing its razor-sharp teeth dripping with saliva. The jet-black eyes focused on him.

The lazgron snapped its tail and launched itself at him. He staggered back, clutching tightly to the stick as he clumsily fell over a downed tree. The lazgron roared a deadly howl. Shylo closed his eyes, holding the stick and hoping it would somehow protect him. The creature's bite didn't come. A couple of heartbeats later, he cracked his eyes open at the sound of the beast angling to his side. Shylo propped himself up on his elbows to see what had turned the creature away. There he saw Number 2841 straddling the lazgron. She wrapped her legs tightly around its girth, somehow pinning the large lizard to the ground. A moment later, Shylo heard bone give way as Number 2841 drove the tip of her saber through the back of its skull. The large lizard crumpled in the green grass. All its intensity, the fierceness with which the animal attacked, was gone the instant the willow-leaf saber entered its skull.

Shylo leaned on his elbows, his sides burning, but he could not take his eyes off the unusual Terra person. He didn't know if he should fear her or what she would do to him if he ever failed to remain in her good graces. She'd saved him again; he owed her his gratitude, if not his life.

"The Creators could not die, so Pyrome and Brisrome came to an agreement with their last living clutch mate. They divided the planet to allow each of The Creators to rule over lesser dragons however they wished within their respective territories. Tourome agreed but only after his brothers deferred to him in allowing him to choose his section of the world first." – The Dracolyth

JEXSANNA

TEN DAYS AFTER THE EMPEROR'S DEATH

S hylo lay in new grass, his elbows propping him up on a bed of charcoal duff. He stared as Number 2841 pulled the saber from the lazgron's wide head. Shylo squeezed his grip on the dead branch. His entire body stung.

Number 2841 wiped her sword clean in the grass and looked over at Shylo. "You didn't drop the stick."

Shylo took another look at the dead tree branch in his hand. Months of suffering through his father's 'training to become a man' flashed through his memory. Shylo always dropped the practice sword whenever he fell. Lying in the clearing now, he attempted to understand how it was that he still held the stick. It couldn't have been from muscle memory. The pain then, he surmised, or the mixed feelings he had about Number 2841. Shylo knew he should be thanking her for saving his life, but he found himself holding back. He felt a fear bubbling under the surface, like the fear he felt when those from House Sarapio were chasing him down in the forest. He didn't know how Number 2841 would react if she knew that Shylo had hesitated to sound a warning. Her comment caught him off guard. Shylo expected her to accuse him of something. He thought of how Ismay would've reacted and continued to hold the stick.

"And now I know something about you that you do not," she said, sheathing her sword.

Shylo relaxed his grip but waited for an accusation.

"If you can run out to face a lazgron, you are not as weak as you say you are. I think soon you can ride the harquice. Now, get up," she demanded, extending her hand.

Shylo accepted her grip, letting her pull him to his feet. After one last tight squeeze on the stick, he dropped it. "That thing could've killed you," Shylo said.

She nodded, her face expressionless.

"And the first thing you think to say to me is, you didn't drop the stick?" he asked.

She cracked a smile, "Those are good instincts. You never let the sword go in a fight."

"This isn't some kind of training exercise. You could've died, and I was... I didn't do anything about it."

"I know. I saw you. You were hunting that furry animal," she said.

"But we don't need it. You had already collected enough fruit from the tsuga tree. Catching that meal shouldn't have been my priority. I should've warned you about the lazgron," Shylo said.

"I did not need you to tell me the lazgron was there," she said.

"If that rodent hadn't boarked," he said, misspeaking because of his tender jaw.

"Boark? I don't know that word," she said.

"Is that what that was," he asked, more to himself after hearing the word. "A borca? Aside from the blended wool fabrics, I've only seen the small cuts of meat before."

"I could tell there was a predator nearby. That furry thing, what did you call it?" she said.

"I think it was a borca," Shylo confirmed.

"The borca's behavior and alarming boark were more than enough of a sign to alert me of the danger in the forest," she said.

"It barked," Shylo corrected out of habit, then said, "Wait, you could tell it was behind you? But you were acting as though you were ignorant of its proximity."

"Ignorant?" she asked.

"It means you didn't know."

"I knew. I could smell its musk. The wind is blowing," she said, motioning in the direction where the lazgron first emerged.

"Who are you?" Shylo asked in admiration, the previous fear of her still lingering in the back of his mind. A fear that he only now recognized was no longer necessary. He'd never met anybody quite like this woman, her selfless acts to help him mystified him and her physical appearance seemed to be a Terra subspecies but none that he knew of. Her devotion to protecting him was unlike anything Shylo had experienced.

She answered, "I'm Number —"

"No," Shylo stopped her. "I refuse to keep calling you that, as if you're a slave and that's the number your masters assigned you. Don't you think it's demeaning?"

"What? Why? That is my name. The Masters assigned it to me like all the others."

"If we're going to keep traveling together, you need a Rhydarian name. What name, not number, do you want me to call you?" Shylo asked.

She chewed at the inside of her lip and quietly started gathering the spilled tsuga fruit. After a time, she said, "How did you decide your name?"

"I didn't choose my name. My parents gave it to me," he said.

"Your parents?" she asked.

"You know, the adults who raised you. Your mother and father. We all have parents," Shylo said.

Number 2841 shrugged, "I don't think we did."

"You were born. If you were born, then you had to have parents. That's how it works," Shylo said. He really hoped she wasn't going to press him on the subject, as he didn't know her well enough to explain the intimate details of sex without feeling embarrassed. For all his lying back in Perdigon, Shylo hadn't done it yet. He knew how making a baby worked, and that there were other ways to achieve pleasure depending on a person's sexual preference. But Shylo had not experienced what it was like with a partner.

"I know I was born, but I don't know by who. Being with another person in that way was something The Masters made very clear wasn't allowed. But I never saw or heard of the others like me having parents. There were only The Masters, but they did not look like us."

"How?"

"They weren't the same skin color. Their bone structure was slightly different. They didn't have straight hair, or the same color as ours. They were similar, but not the same," she said.

"They were Rhydarians?" Shylo asked.

"Like you, yes, but curly hair and green eyes."

"New Rhydarian?" Shylo asked.

She shrugged.

"Did they have names?" Shylo asked.

"Master," she said.

"Not them. The others like you?"

"Number 2843, Number 2684 —"

"Those aren't names," Shylo interrupted. "Those are assignments; they're different from a name. Didn't any of the others like you know their parents? Surely you had a family before?"

"Number 2759 was my once-mate. He spoke to me more than the others. We did not know anyone before The Masters. They are all I've ever known. Everything I can remember from before is them," she said.

"Your once-mate?" Shylo asked, wondering if that meant what he assumed it did.

She looked away from him and Shylo sensed pain. He heard it in her voice as she said, "He was, different. Like me."

Shylo saw the glisten in her eyes and knew she was withholding a sensitive piece of her past. He could only imagine what it was like to have a mate, a person you cared for emotionally, and somehow be separated from them. He understood the potential emotional baggage that could come from a hardship and decided to stop asking about her past life. With an armful of fruit, he steered the conversation forward. "What about the name, Rosey?" he asked. "I could call you that, because you have some red pigment in your skin."

She scowled, stuffing the last of the fruit in with the others.

"Not Rosey? Okay, maybe something a little stronger. What about Ninfa?" he asked.

Number 2841 pursed her lower lip as she stepped over a downed log and started back toward their small camp.

"Wait, aren't we going to... do something with that thing?" he said, pointing to the dead lazgron that was already losing its camouflage coloring and fading to a slate grey.

"Like what?" she asked.

"I don't know, maybe we should eat it or something? It's fresh meat, right?" he said.

She spit toward the creature, and said, "That predator is not for eating."

"Why not? We're starving and need the food."

"It makes you sick. Bad sick and then you die," she said.

Shylo instantly took a step away from the body. He supposed they could use the skin for another cloak or two, but Number 2841 already had a draco-scale surcoat, and Shylo's cloak was holding up fine. Hurrying to catch up with her, Shylo switched back to suggesting a name, "How about Carmine?"

She harrumphed through her wide-set nostrils.

"That's a fine name. It's my mother's, actually," Shylo said.

"Ugh," she grunted in disapproval.

"What? My mother is a pleasant person," he said, then muttered to himself, "unlike you sometimes."

Number 2841 sneered at him.

The aggressive pose made Shylo flinch, and he winced.

He was about to apologize when a high-pitched chirp sounded next to him. The sound startled him less than Number 2841's scowl. The noise gave him an idea, and he said, "Maybe I could call you Chirp?"

She shushed him, motioning for him to stay put as she started trudging toward the log where the furry grey rodent perched.

After seeing how fast the borca had run when the lazgron emerged from the woods, Shylo had little faith that Number 2841 could catch the critter.

She was getting surprisingly close to the animal when he thought, *She might really have a chance.*

The borca chirped, then bolted down the log. Number 2841 let go of the fruit a second time and vaulted after the critter. She stretched out, hand extended as she and the borca dove. She folded as she crossed over the black, charred log. Shylo couldn't see if she caught it. He stepped closer, eager to learn if she was successful. She rolled over the log and showed him an empty palm. Shylo accepted the loss, thinking the animal deserved to live after warning Number 2841 about the lazgron before Shylo could. He turned his back on her, and she let out a gleeful snicker. Shylo swiveled to see the borca in her other hand. She gripped it around the middle as it let out chirp after chirp.

Shylo rushed to where she stood among her spilled fruits. "I can't believe you got it?" he said.

She stuffed the chirping borca into her front pocket and buttoned it closed.

"Wait, you're not going to kill it?" he asked. Once inside the coat, the borca stopped chirping, and Shylo said, "It might escape."

She pulled a handful of grass from the ground and

stuffed it into the surcoat front pocket. "Better fresh," she said.

Shylo watched as Number 2841 pulled several olackee nuts from the opposite pocket and dropped them into the one with the borca. "Are you feeding it?" he asked.

She nodded.

"Why?"

"He's hungry," she said, as if it were obvious.

Shylo wondered how she knew it was a male when she didn't know its common name a few moments ago. Her knowledge about the world was so different from his. It was like she was from a different world altogether.

"Hey," Shylo said. "Just so we are clear, that is not your pet. We're going to eat it. Don't go giving it a name or anything."

Shylo took her silence as an agreement. They were starving and he couldn't afford to let either of them get attached to the fury animal. The quicker they killed it, the better.

When they returned to where they'd made camp, Number 2841 said, "I think his name is Chirp."

"Blazing fire. Why did you go and say that?" Shylo growled. He dropped the fruit on the ground, saying, "You can't give him a name."

"Why not? You want to give me a name. I want to give Chirp a name," she said.

"Because we aren't going to kill you. How am I supposed to wring Chirp's neck and cook him over the sunstone now?" he asked.

Number 2841 opened her pocket, pulled Chirp out and stroked her thumb over his palm-sized head. "Easy. I could do it like this —"

"No!" Shylo said, lunging for her with his arms

outstretched and moving too fast for his healing bruises. "Ouch," he winced, doubling over before he could take Chirp.

"Shylo. I did not do it," she said, showing him the grey furry creature.

Seeing the fluffy rodent and its bright pink nose brought him a strange sense of relief. He knew that emotion wasn't the one he wanted to feel. It wasn't the emotion his father, a proud Eso, would've felt. He straightened, rising despite the aches in his sides.

"We can't get attached to Chirp. I mean it, we can't get attached to him, or it, rather. We're going to eat it and that's that." Shylo forced himself to look away from the wide-eyed borca. It chirped a high-pitched bark. "If it's going to keep making that noise, we'll have to cook him before nightfall," he said.

"You mean, cook it," Number 2841 corrected.

Shylo glanced at her, seeing the fuzzy rodent held in her hand. He nodded and moved to prepare his harquice saddle. He had run after a lazgron with a stick. And though this attempt was foolhardy, he'd proven to himself that he might be ready to handle sitting on a moving harquice. After several failed attempts to lift the saddle past the base of his rib cage, Number 2841 helped him. She fitted his saddle onto the harquice mare while Shylo packed their saddlebags with fruit. With all the excitement of the lazgron attack, Shylo realized he hadn't taken the time to consider the burn scar in the woods.

"I can't believe there was so much fresh growth in that fire scar," Shylo said, while gathering up the last of their sparse belongings.

"And the ripe tsuga," she added.

"Yeah. It can't have been growing like that without

someone planting and tending to it. Every Rhydarian knows our crops can't survive the fires," Shylo said.

"They can't?" she asked.

"No, the fires burn them up. Why do you think the Empire is building a barrier across the Fringe?" Shylo said, unsure if Number 2841 knew the extent to which the Empire went in suppressing the Volurem.

"Do all your cities do this?" she asked.

"Yes, they all have walls," Shylo said.

"I mean, do they all try to grow food in the wilderness?" she asked.

"Cities don't try it anymore. It's too risky if a fire does come through. Maybe a village would," Shylo said, and only then realized what she was suggesting. "Ashes, that's what more than a week of starvation will do to your brain," he muttered to himself.

"What?" she asked.

"You just suggested it. There must be a village nearby. That's the only thing that makes sense," Shylo said.

"Oh," she replied, looking down at her feet and becoming noticeably quiet.

"What's wrong? This is good. We can go inside the walls, eat a proper meal, and sleep in a warm bed," he said.

"You want me to come with you? Into a village?" she asked, leaning away from him slightly.

"Yes. Of course. Why wouldn't I want you to come with me?" The corners of her mouth didn't turn up into a smile, as he expected. She pulled at her harquice's mane, avoiding eye contact with Shylo. "It's not going to be like the last time," Shylo said.

She raised her glistening eyes to look at him with all the innocence of a child.

Shylo's heart melted like a ball of winter snow before a

sunstone. "Trust me," he said, almost pleading with her. He would understand if she didn't.

She looked away from him, seeming to contemplate whether he was worth the risk.

Shylo put himself in her shoes for a moment. In the short time he'd known her, almost every chance he'd had to give her a reason to trust him, Shylo had acted selfishly first. He'd been acting as a Noble of Perdigon, not as an independent Eso with a simple goal. His behavior toward her made his skin crawl, and he said out of desperation, "I won't get mad at you this time. I promise."

Number 2841 folded her arms across her chest, weighted her left leg, and said, "Give me a name."

"I tried. You didn't like the ones I suggested," Shylo said.

"If we are going into the walls of one of your cities, I want a name, one like yours," she said.

Shylo considered it. "Osanna," he said, using the first name that came to mind. It was the name of an Ai in his Penti trainee class.

She thought on it for a moment, then shook her head.

Shylo flared his nostrils, trying to keep his cool. If she wanted a name, then she would need to accept one that he suggested. But because she'd thought longer on Osanna than any of the others he'd suggested thus far, Shylo began searching his memory for people he knew with similar sounding names. "Boswanna," he said.

She shook her head.

"Keyanna," he said.

She shook her head.

Despite how hard he tried to avoid saying the name, one kept creeping into his head. It was the name of the older girl who Shylo lied about having had sex with to impress his peers. Every time he tried to think of a new name, he kept circling back to hers, like a little bug that wouldn't go away. He decided to say it aloud to get it out of his system, and his mind. "Jexsanna."

She raised her eyebrows. She took several strides, pacing lightly in a small semi-circle near the harquice. "Jexsanna," she said.

"Jexsanna," she said again.

"Please tell me you don't like it," Shylo said.

"I like it. My name will be Jexsanna," she said.

Shylo sank. "Of course," he muttered.

"Jexsanna," she said again.

"Ash, you're almost as annoying as Chirp," Shylo said. He cringed at his absentmindedness. "Burnt trees, first you have me calling the ashing borca, Chirp, and now you want to have the name of the girl that I..."

"That you what?"

"Never mind. We need to prove that the clearing was planted. If there's a village or town nearby, you will see it from the top of the trees," Shylo said. He winced as he sat on the ground, trying to find a comfortable resting position. Becoming completely comfortable proved difficult with the young woman quietly saying, "Jexsanna," repeatedly to herself as she climbed a nearby tree.

TOTAL CONTROL

Ten Days After the Emperor's Death

Marxius Ovando-Kai walked through the Palace entrance, passing by the off-branching East and West galleries, and into the antechamber before the Great Hall. Servants hustled in and out of corridors on either side. Marxius scanned the antechamber to determine the cause of the activity. He looked to the tops of either staircase. To the right, the Emperor's chambers, guard rooms and subsequent chamber rooms, and to the left, where the rest of the Akai's chambers were. Servants passed in and out of sight, carrying bed sheets and tray tables. A noisy rabble from servants arose in the Great Hall, echoing through the vast opening as Marxius spotted the staff carrying barrels of wine, sizzle, and mead in from the kitchens. Marxius realized the cause of the busyness. They were preparing for the Emperor's party. He'd assumed Benton would at least wait until the white-haired assassin and the Didimo boy had been dealt with or found dead.

Angling left to the corridor behind the stairs, Marxius headed to the Council Room. He entered, seeing that they had already served food and drinks before their Imperial Advisors' meeting, something the Imperial Defense Committee did not enjoy. Eleven Senators, two Zethrillian advisors, and both magistrates were all present, chatting in three- and four-person clusters of men and women that made up the cliques within the advisor group. Among them, Marxius saw an unwelcome guest, Eso and High Commander Galterius-Brex.

Striding across the Council Room toward the advisors' table, Marxius drew the attention of most Advisory Council members. Magistrate Inyez spoke over the others' conversations, asking Marxius, "Where is Emperor Benton Querci-Akai?"

"Am I his chaperone, too?" Marxius replied snidely, only remembering who had asked him after the biting words had left his mouth. He forced himself to take his eyes off the elephant in the room, Galterius, and said, "Sorry, Magistrate, I meant to say, I do not know where the Emperor is."

"I understand your frustration," Inyez replied. "You mustn't be discouraged after your loss of guardsmen in this week's event."

"You heard about the draco, did you?" Marxius said.

He'd last been in the company of the Imperial Advisory Council in the days before he and Galterius took over the hunt for the white-haired assassin and the Didimo boy. Leaving control of his villa and his daughter's protection to the Lead Guard in House Ovando, Marxius had spent very little time in the company of those on Capitol Hill as of late. He was preoccupied with finishing the task he'd let slip through his fingers a week prior, when he let Number 2841 escape the arena. Marxius forced himself to keep his gaze on Galterius as he spoke. The Eso was clearly not supposed to be there, and it bothered him to no end when a person acted outside his station.

"I wouldn't break the news to his Imperial Majesty if Captain Bridger-Ai was among the dead," Magistrate Inyez said.

Marxius straightened at the mention of his Lead Guard. "Captain Bridger-Ai was not on the excursion. He's been seeing to my villa's security while I've been beyond the walls. Why would the Emperor care if the Minor Noble had died?"

"You didn't see him deep in a private audience with the Emperor before the Defense Committee meeting?" Inyez asked.

"I did not realize Emperor Benton was so familiar with the senior ranking officer within my house guard," Marxius responded.

"It was probably something to do with the... party," Inyez said, awkwardly looking away.

Quick to change the subject from what was sure to be the top rumor spreading among all Nobles by the following morning, Marxius asked, "What is he doing here?" He nodded toward the New Rhydarian High Commander.

"His Imperial Majesty requested that the High

Commander deliver his report from today's outing but then he got sidetracked by the planning and, well, told him to wait in here," Inyez explained.

"I already gave Benton the details of today's report. Esos aren't permitted to be in an Imperial advisory meeting," Marxius said, not caring if Galterius overheard his complaint. It was true that Marxius left the search early to get ready for this meeting but seeing Galterius there was the last straw. It was bad enough that he had to share command of a Division with the Eso, he, too, shared the responsibility of the search for Number 2841 and the Didimo Penti.

"We tried explaining the rule to the Emperor, but he insisted that it wasn't 'anything his uncle wouldn't have done.' We all know how Jermanus felt about an Eso's place in government," Inyez said.

Marxius wondered which rumor would be more cherished in the gossip among the Kai and Ai. An Eso's presence at an Imperial Council meeting, or the fact that Marxius did not know his most trusted house guard had held a meeting in private with the new Emperor. He was beginning to see markers that reminded him of the way his relationship with his ex-wife had crumbled. The same markers that he sensed forming in his relationship with their daughter, Ismay. But there was a clear difference with the Captain. Marxius was Bridger's employer, not his partner, and Captain Bridger was loyal to Marxius' bankroll. "I will have a word with Galterius about his being here," Marxius said to all present, as he moved to kick Galterius out of the council room.

Only two steps into his advance on the Eso, the door opened. A blast of noise from bustling servants flooded the entrance as the Emperor casually strolled in. He wore a bright white toga and carried a golden chalice in his hand.

"Let's make this quick. I'm already overlapping on important tasks," he stopped partway to the table as the sixteen advisors moved to their seats. Benton took a large swig, emptying the liquid inside, staining his upper lip dark red. When he swallowed, he seemed to notice Galterius standing awkwardly near the table without a seat. "Ah, yes. The High Commander. We'll start with you."

"It is not wise to invite an Eso into our company, never mind having his report overlap into our meeting," Magistrate Lucerro Ventous-Kai said from his seat second to the right of the Emperor's.

Marxius took his seat next to the magistrates, Benton joining at the head of the table.

"Magistrate Lucerro, I take it that you are in charge, or did I misunderstand what rank I hold as Emperor?" Benton asked tartly, while placing his empty chalice on an open scroll and staining the white pulp with dribbles of wine.

The Magistrate uncomfortably adjusted the gold chain fastener on his yellow cloak. After a moment, Inyez spoke up in place of his counterpart, and said, "None of us at this table are here to lead except for you, your Imperial Majesty. We are gathered here to give you sound advice and offer suggestions."

Benton pursed his lips, taking a moment to calculate the elder Magistrate's response. Marxius wondered if the impulsive young man would demand a Magistrate be removed from his office and elect a replacement on the spot. He'd already done it to several dozen Senators and the advisors serving under them. The hatred building in the Emperor's eyes fizzled when Galterius cleared his throat from the far end of the table where he stood, drawing everyone's focus away from the growing tension.

"As you're pressed for time, your Imperial Majesty, I will give my report as you have requested," Galterius said.

Marxius hoped the Emperor would continue acting without thinking in his intoxicated state of mind and discipline the Eso for speaking out of turn. It could allow Marxius even more of a reason to influence a transfer or demotion for the aging High Commander. He didn't know how much longer he could stand to share command with someone so far beneath his Noble rank.

"Yes, I'm interested to hear what you discovered beyond the wall, particularly what happened the other day. I've already heard from Ovando-Kai, but I'd like to hear what happened from someone not basking in the glory of slaying a draco," Benton said.

Marxius set his jaw, forcing himself to remain silent. Benton's choice to divert their attention to something other than the state of his rule, was poorly timed. The Emperor was acting more obnoxious than normal. Benton's unprofessional approach was far more irritating to Marxius than anything he'd faced since becoming closer with the Akai. Even more so than how his daughter, Ismay, blatantly chose to do the opposite of whatever Marxius asked of her. He'd noticed her following him around the city after his return from the supply mission. He knew she'd only continue distancing herself emotionally if he pressed her about it. Losing Ismay to his ex-, driving her away from him was the last thing he wanted. Despite her teenage rebellious streak, he still loved her more than anything. Which is why Marxius wasn't willing to be the one to point out how irrational Benton was behaving. He did not understand why Benton insisted on wasting valuable time. Whatever Galterius had to say about the outing that happened three days ago, it would not differ from Marxius' take on the events of the day.

"The draco incident," Galterius nodded, continuing with some hesitation. It seemed he too didn't understand why the Emperor wanted his account of the event. "We did not locate the Penti from House Didimo, or his accomplice," Galterius said.

"And you can confirm that the remains inside the draco were not those of the assassin?" Benton asked.

"I... Cannot," Galterius said. "We discovered some undigested remains from more than one New Rhydarian. It's possible the draco killed the assassin and the Didimo boy escaped."

"Precisely what I wanted to hear. Proof that the draco got to the assassin, which probably explains why they haven't come back to the walls. The wilderness will have killed the Penti from House Didimo by now," Benton said.

Marxius realized what Benton was trying to do. He wanted to hear a reason, any reason, why Number 2841 hadn't come back to Perdigon or been found. Benton thought she would, but Marxius knew better. He knew the white-haired mutant was still out there.

"And if he does happen to last longer in the wild, the fire season will rid the world of his betrayal," Magistrate Lucerro chimed in.

Marxius shot a glare at him, thinking, *Coward.* The Magistrate was just trying to save face with the intoxicated young Emperor.

"Good. Now that that's settled," Benton said, rubbing his hands together.

"I haven't given my report of the day," Galterius said.

"There's no need. You are free to go," Benton waved dismissively at him.

Marxius studied Galterius' scarred face. He had a determined stiffness to him. He wasn't leaving. Marxius felt a sickening in his gut, knowing that the Eso was going to open his mouth again, continuing to waste the Kai's time.

"There was more than one assassin," Galterius said.

Marxius watched Benton's jaw hinge ajar. Marxius could hardly believe it himself. It was as if the High Commander were trying to lose his good graces with the new emperor.

"What did you say?" Benton demanded, anger returning.

"More than one assassin killed your Akai family members, your Majesty. Though the draco remains from earlier in the week were not conclusive, we know that at least one skilled killer slew the Sarapio Guards and escaped with the Didimo boy. I believe the accounts from Senator Sarapio-Kai and his son about the white-haired soldier should be taken seriously. They do, however, differ from the description of the assassin I faced outside the Palace. That suggests the people who wielded the knives, killing your family, are still alive. Based on the evidence and how they've managed to disappear without a trace, I do not believe we're dealing with normal Rhydarians," Galterius explained.

Marxius awaited Benton's response. He was expecting the Akai to unleash a major disciplinary action for Galterius' unprovoked statement. And when he was inhaling to speak, Senator Mustaf-Kai, a Second Class Old Rhydarian Noble serving on the advisory council, said, "Because the assassins are not from Rhydenar."

"I know what I saw," Galterius said defensively. "The person who killed Jermanus was Rhydarian. There's no mistaking it."

"The one who wielded the knife, maybe, but this

betrayal has Agunzi written all over it. Everyone here knows they were angry with the Empire for shifting resources away from the Saypo and Nandan portions of the Fringe Barrier," Hassyth, one of the Zethrillian advisors, said in a deep voice.

"We can't ignore that a rebellion from the South has been a long time coming. We've neglected our pact with them for too many rotations," Major Commander Noestriff Landrich-Kai said.

A squabble broke out among the fifteen advisors and Benton quickly ended their self-provoked arguing by shouting, "Quiet!"

The advisors grew silent, waiting to hear what the Emperor would say.

"This is not a matter that is up for debate. I don't have time to listen to your arguing. You are supposed to advise me on these matters, not waste my time arguing among yourselves," Benton said, speaking to those in the Council.

"We can't keep searching the wilderness with no result in sight. We must take action on this matter. How we react to the murder of the Akais must be swift. The whole of the Empire is watching us," Magistrate Inyez said.

"With what proof are we to direct this action?" Benton barked, his anger from Galterius' interruption now aimed at the senior member of the Council. "If I'm not mistaken, we already took action on one of our own Senators, killing the Kai responsible for allowing assassins into the capital. With eyewitnesses such as the Eso High Commander and Captain Bridger-Ai confirming the murders were carried out by Rhydarians, drawing this matter out into a lengthy war with the Agunzi isn't serving us any justice. I say justice was served to the plotters of this assassination when House Didimo came to its violent end. That is the only action that matters. The plot to kill Jermanus was hatched within the walls of Perdigon. It was carried out by a Rhydarian Senator. You speak of keeping the Empire under control. To preserve the power of this empire, we must control the Nobles before they turn on Senators, Councilors, and other members of the government. You all know, though you don't speak openly of it, the cutthroat game you Nobles play for control over one another. It's easy to see that one of them took this play for power too far; they turned the tactics on the pinnacle of our government. You can chase after those who held the knives all you want, but make no mistake, there would be no knife without the Noble Kai," Benton said, spittle flying from his stained lips.

"The Southerners want to —"

"I don't give a burning ember what the widebacks want. They do not hold any control over us in Rhydenar. But if blaming them is what it takes for this government to move on to more important matters, fine. You want me to punish the Agunzi? Let them keep their minor contributions. Let them think they've gained their independence. Cut them off from our military protection; that will be their punishment. They can face the fires of the summer alone. Then we'll see how badly they want us to finish building that wall."

"That is not a wise course of action," Galterius said.

Benton spun, stiffening with rage when he saw Galterius. "Why are you still here?" he spat.

To Marxius' and everyone else's surprise, Galterius said, "Because if you do what they want, putting the blame for these murders on the Agunzi, knowing it was Kai —"

"Stop," Benton ordered, silencing Galterius. A sense of calm seemed to wash over the Emperor, as though he'd suddenly entered the eye of a storm. His cheeks creased with a devious smile and, he said, "And what makes you, the Eso and High Commander my uncle trusted so thoroughly, think that you can voice your opinion on this matter?"

"I did not mean to speak out of turn, but I have spent more time among the southern people than anyone here, including the Major Commanders in this room."

Galterius' comment sparked an idea that delighted Marxius, one that he could use to his advantage.

"Leave, Eso, before I change my mind about what I should do to you," Benton said.

Galterius placed his right fist over his heart before turning to leave.

"Your Imperial Majesty," Marxius said, standing from his seat.

"Out with it, this meeting has already been derailed and turned into a colossal waste of my time," Benton said.

Marxius swiftly walked to Benton's side and leaned down to speak so the others wouldn't hear. "I think the Eso can serve a purpose for you."

Marxius saw Benton's green-and-yellow eyes shift to Galterius' cloak as he walked across the room.

"If you entertain him a while longer, I can make sure he takes the weight of this need of the council to find the *assassins* off your shoulders," Marxius whispered.

Galterius placed his hand on the door to open it and Benton said, "Wait, Eso. It's come to my attention that you may yet prove useful on this topic."

Marxius continued whispering in the Emperor's ear, "They believe the blonde mutant is one of the assassins. In my estimation, based on what I've seen in searching beyond the walls, she still has the Didimo boy. If Galterius catches up with them, he'll have them executed in your name. It would be prudent to keep the pressure on. If she were to fall into the wrong hands... If you keep Galterius on her trail, you'll have an experienced military mind tracking her. In the worst-case scenario, Galterius loses poorly trained guards that are easily replaced, and the old Eso dies by the mutant's sword. The Nobles already believe she is Didimo's hired assassin. She wouldn't last the season. This is your chance to finish what we started in the Shield Mountains and respond to the public demand for retribution in the name of Jermanus' assassination, all in one act," Marxius whispered.

Benton motioned for Marxius to take his seat as the Eso High Commander cautiously returned to the table.

"Tell me, High Commander Brex, how would you handle the assassination and the threat of fracture in the South if you were in my position?" Benton asked, his tone puzzling.

Galterius straightened as he glanced around at the bewildered faces of those at the table, and said, "I would lead an Imperial delegation to the South and personally discuss the terms of the treaty with those among the Agunzi tribes wanting independence. I would devote a battalion's worth of soldiers to track down and find the assassins and the Didimo Penti trainee. Once I had them in custody, I would pressure them for the truth and uncover the plot behind the late Emperor's assassination. I would also pressure the Noble houses who slaughtered House Didimo —"

"Stop," Benton said, again.

Marxius knew that tone: Benton's sigh-ridden tone that meant he would hear no more on a subject. If Marxius was going to ensure that Galterius left the capital, then Marxius needed to steer Benton and the council in that direction.

"I agree with what the High Commander said. We

should commit more resources to finding the assassins. If the killers make it through the fire season while also conjuring more deceptive strikes on the Palace, we'll lose the control Jermanus secured for Rhydenar in his term," Marxius said.

"We already discussed this in the Defense Committee. I can't commit military support to tracking a few murderers. We have already given the legions their assignments for the rotation and if the smoke reports are reliable predictors of how the forests in Apgar are to fare this season, we need Commander so-and-so with the Hundred and First where he is, patrolling the routes between cities. Unless someone is willing to fund the mission as a private endeavor, I won't commit Imperial support," Benton said.

"Why did you talk the Emperor into letting the Eso voice his opinion?" Magistrate Lucerro asked Marxius.

"Because Galterius and the Emperor are both right. The Empire needs to see that we still command control, despite the horrors that occurred. Yet, we do not have the flexibility in the military to allow a battalion to abandon its post. Therefore, I believe Galterius is our answer. It is no secret that he has the finances to fund and supply the pursuit of the assassin or assassins, as he claims. I'm sure that many of the Noble houses will be willing to contribute a handful of their guards for a regular crew to form under Galterius' leadership. I will offer up a dozen of my guard for you, Galterius. Captain Bridger-Ai will make a fine second in your command."

"I object to this," Galterius said. "I am needed here on the Imperial Defense Committee and serving as co-command for the Saypo Division."

"Isn't that why we have thirteen members on the Defense Committee?" Marxius asked. "To allow room for members' absence in the face of important matters such as this?"

"This mission is of the utmost importance to the Empire," Benton said, glancing at Marxius.

"I think it's a wise choice," Major Commander Noestriff said. "If Galterius did uncover an Agunzi group collaborating with House Didimo, then he can lead a disciplinary action without returning to the capital for a guide. The Eso knows the routes through the South and, with the battalion's force of arms, he will be a threat to any one of the Agunzi tribes."

"And if needed, his legion wouldn't be too far away and could be summoned to aid him," Marxius reasoned.

"I agree with High Commander Ovando-Kai," Magistrate Inyez said. "Galterius was the one who let the assassin escape the Palace. Therefore, he should accept the responsibility of putting an end to this chase. I vote that Galterius be the one to take on this matter and relieve the Emperor so he can attend to more stately matters."

Marxius grinned as the others around the table voiced their agreement to send Galterius beyond the walls. At first, he thought Benton's intoxication would hinder this meeting. Now though, Marxius almost wanted to thank the young man for his loose-mouthed approach. He set up a perfect scenario and opportunity to finally be rid of the thorn in Marxius' side. The High Commander didn't have his brismil plate, Marxius was sure of it. He wouldn't last much longer than the Didimo boy in the wilderness. And if he did accomplish his goal and caught the mutant girl everyone falsely believed was the escaped assassin, then Galterius would execute her with his brismil blade. In the meantime, Marxius could lead the Division in the way he saw fit and focus more of his own efforts on uncovering the truth of how the assassins were able to escape the Palace without detection. Marxius suspected that Didimo was not the only Noble house involved.

"Then it's settled," Emperor Benton said. "High Commander Brex will use his vast wealth to lead and supply a company of guards to track down the assassins and their House Didimo accomplice." Benton stood up and turned to leave the table.

"Emperor, where are you going?" Magistrate Inyez said.

Benton motioned at them with his empty chalice and said, "We are done here. The matter was settled."

The Magistrate and several other Senators stirred in their seats. "We have a host of issues we need to discuss, your Imperial Majesty," Magistrate Lucerro chimed in.

"What issues?" Benton asked.

"A review of the supply audits, the shipping tariffs, and the arrangement with the Zethril, to name a few. Not to mention how we plan to get the resources needed for continuing the Fringe Barrier inland. Given how this season has started, it will be more taxing than the previous rotations," the Magistrate explained.

Benton chewed at the inside of his lip, then said, "Ovando, you will take my place in these meetings."

The advisors around the table, including Marxius, choked, several coughing and having to clear their throats from the shock of the announcement. "Your Imperial Majesty, that is not wise. There is no position within our government structure that allows for one military Commander or Senator to take on such an important, over-arching role," Magistrate Inyez said.

"Of course, you'll need my approval before action," Benton said. "But I see no reason why these meetings can't be held without me. I trust Marxius to be able to condense the results and provide me the details. Yes?"

"But the structure?" the Magistrate said, shaking his head.

"I am the Emperor and this is how I am going to rule. I think you'll find that I'm able to streamline some of the ridiculous procedures that my uncle continued to implement. Times are changing Magistrate, we need a modern way of rule for a modern ruler," Benton said. He tipped the golden chalice toward Marxius and said, "Don't wage war unless you clear it with me, okay, Ovando?"

Marxius nodded.

"From this point forward, Ovando-Kai will act as my voice in all Imperial meetings unless I decide otherwise. Ovando, you'll report back to me after each meeting. Do not disappoint me," Benton said, pointedly looking at the members of the Council, waiting to see their show of respect before leaving the Council Room. Marxius was the first to put his fist over his heart as the others jumped to stand and salute at this dramatic exit.

Once the door closed behind him, the most senior officers on the Council squirmed in their chairs as they looked wide-eyed at Marxius.

"I won't stand for this corruption," Lucerro said. "We shouldn't allow one of us to have this much control."

Rumblings of agreement spread among the council members and before the others in the room aimed their sights on deposing Marxius, he said, "I agree with the Magistrate and despite what the Emperor just said, I will not act as his voice at these meetings."

Marxius saw the hesitancy in their expressions as he spoke. "The Emperor is young, new to having this much control. Give him time to warm up to his position. In the meantime, I vote that we should continue these meetings. We can collectively write down what the Emperor needs to hear. If proceeding in this way, fairly and equally giving input on the report I deliver is the best way to get the Emperor's attention on these matters, then we should continue," Marxius said.

As he offered this temporary solution, he realized just how much control the Emperor had bestowed on him. If the Council believed him, trusted Marxius that he would be honest in his delivery of the report, then he would be the only person among them to know if what the Council wanted Benton to hear made it to his attention. "Who is for continuing with this notion until the Emperor can be swayed to return to these meetings?" he asked.

Looking around the room, Marxius could feel unspoken resentment and spite from some of the members.

"I will not cast my vote as we are now sixteen members. This discission is up to you," Marxius said. "All in favor?" The others started casting their opinions, voicing 'aye.' With Magistrate Inyez's vote, those in favor polled at nine, a majority. There was no need to ask for those not in favor. "Then we shall proceed."

"For the next order of discussion," the Magistrate began.

While they droned on, Marxius wished even more deeply that Galterius would perish along with everyone responsible for Jermanus' murder. He never dreamed he would climb so fast within the Empire hierarchy. Almost giddy, Marxius felt that if he ever learned who had assassinated Jermanus, he should thank them for improving his life and the life of his family. He had to work to make his face appear serious while his thoughts wandered. All he had ever wanted in this world was to secure the best position for his daughter. He would do anything to ensure that Ismay's future had the best trajectory for success. Suddenly, he lost interest in uncovering the truth about the Emperor's assassination. Jermanus' death was the best thing that had happened to House Ovando. Marxius' legacy was everything to him and if preserving this new status meant letting the truth die with the last Didimo member, then Marxius would carry on as Benton had done.

Marxius now saw how some of the Council members leaned in to listen to him. A majority didn't want to ruffle his feathers, or perhaps they had their own plans to manipulate his report. It seemed, in that moment, that the Empire's control was resting in their hands.

DIFFERENT LIVES

*J*exsanna, she thought, repeating the name again in her head as she scanned the forest. She agreed with Shylo that it sounded much better than her old name. The one The Masters gave her, Number 2841.

A clatter in the distance drew her attention. To her right, Shylo winced as he climbed down from the harquice.

"I hate to —"

She dipped over to Shylo and cupped her hand over his mouth, silencing him. Jexsanna pursed her full lips, staring directly into Shylo's oval, storm-grey eyes. "Shhh."

Shylo wrinkled his face, creasing where the dark bruises were fading into shades of yellow. Seeing his confusion, Jexsanna wondered why his long-distance hearing was so much worse than his short-distance hearing. Perhaps his ears were damaged and would heal with time.

"Stay here," she whispered.

"Wait," Shylo said, grabbing her wrist before she could leave him. "Where are you going?"

"A harquice is coming. Stay still. Be quiet," she said, then darted away. Moisture wicked off the foliage, slicking her draco-scale surcoat as she approached the sound. The clacking cloven hooves now slopped through mud. Jexsanna noted the absence of crashing through brush.

A path is nearby, she thought. It should be the same one that she expected their pursuers would be taking. The path led to the town she'd spotted from the top of the tree.

Jexsanna crouched, still moving through the damp brush. At a wide tree, she hunkered behind the thick trunk where she could see the narrow clearing along a path through the trees. The harquice, the one she could hear, was almost there. A tall figure, with tight-curled black hair and purple cloak flapping behind him, galloped into view. His silvery draco-scale armor glistened from the day's rain. He gripped the harquice reins with stucco, mud-covered hands, a shade of brown much lighter than his natural complexion. Jexsanna didn't hear or see anyone with the lone rider. He sped past.

She waited for the heavy nostril chuffing from the harquice to fade before stepping out of the forest to examine the path. The two-harquice-wide dirt path was saturated and puddled after the recent rain. Only one set of tracks was evident.

A scout? Jexsanna wondered. She'd learned the tactics a legion used when she was a child in the arena. She remembered spending days being drilled about formations and their movements. Scouts often led a military unit, but from what she'd been taught, scouts rarely traveled alone. She didn't know if they rode that fast or why this one was washed clean from the rain, except for his muddy hands. *How could scouts observe every potential threat if they rode so vigorously? And why the mud with no blood?*

Jexsanna's uncertainty of the world she'd stepped into again bubbled to the surface. Without walls, she felt she needed to consider so many more constantly changing elements. Keeping it all straight was tough enough, never mind the new ideas and words Shylo offered every day.

She returned to him and their two harquice so silently that she startled Shylo when she emerged from the brush.

"Ashes," he cursed. "You need to announce yourself if you're going to do that."

"Jexsanna," she said, trying to do what he said. He had so many rules, it was hard to keep them all straight. *Back in the arena, The Masters had rules, but they were simple. Easy to follow and remember because of the consequences.* Shylo's rules, it seemed to her, weren't consistent and had no repercussions.

"You do it like this. Shylo, I'm coming back now. Don't act a complete fool and fall over yourself."

"Maybe you will hear me coming when your ears heal," she said.

"What? My ears aren't damaged, they're working just fine," Shylo said. "Speaking of which, did you hear anything more? I take it the harquice you heard was a false alarm?"

She shook her head. "There was a man. He's far gone now."

"Did you kill him?" Shylo asked.

"No. He was riding too fast to be a threat. But his arms were muddy."

"There's a road?" he asked, not acknowledging her mention of the strange mud.

She nodded.

"It will lead to the town. We should follow it," Shylo said.

"Not yet. The man could've been a scout."

"That means we're ahead of them. Shouldn't we get a move on? I'm moving a little faster now. I'm sure I could ride for longer," he said.

"We're moving slow for a reason. I want to get behind whoever is searching for us. Then we can keep them within our sight. That is how the predator hunts," she said.

"What? I thought we wanted to escape them?" Shylo said.

"Yes," Jexsanna agreed.

"Then why not go now?" he asked.

She shook her head. "They could be too close now. The scout in front had fresh mud on his hands. It's not a wise maneuver to go now, especially with your handicap."

"Why is the mud important to you? It proves nothing. And I'm not crippled. I'm getting less sore every day," he said, stretching to the side and wincing after bending part of the way through his lean. "Ouch."

"Not your bruises. Your senses are too poor. You can't hear someone coming unless they are right on top of you," she said.

"I can hear just fine for your information. We're not all super Terra people like you," Shylo said.

"I don't understand?" she said.

"I know. I'm just frustrated that I'm slowing us down. You're probably planning on leaving me like you should've already if you wanted to stay alive," Shylo said.

"We are alive, because of me. Yes, you are slow," she agreed.

Shylo's posture slouched forward. He dipped his head slightly.

"You're not a soldier," she said, trying to clarify that she meant she wasn't going to leave him because he was slow. She liked him more for not being like a soldier. He was not like The Masters or the others like her at the arena, not entirely.

"Yeah. I know I'm not a soldier," he said. "So, what do you think I'm capable of doing in this situation?"

"We find a place to hide. And wait," she said.

"Get pounded nearly to death, hauled around the woods, too weak to move, then when I can finally do something, it's sit and wait. The stuff of legends, huh," he mumbled.

She didn't know what he meant or was talking about. Jexsanna did what she had done when Shylo wasn't being himself. She left him to his thoughts. That's what Jexsanna liked when she needed to ponder something. She didn't want any voices distracting her. She wanted silence, so she gave it to him.

Remembering where she saw one of the marked boulders, Jexsanna led Shylo and their harquice back the way they'd come until she located it. The mark reminded Jexsanna of the draco claw her once-partner, Number 2759, had given her. She remembered how she felt when he handed it to her wrapped in a hide cloth. It was the first time anyone but The Masters had given her something.

Etched into the boulder, and turned a dark black from weathering, the claw marked the rocks that covered the tunnels in the forest. Since they first discovered the one outside the large walled city, Jexsanna had yet to find one that wasn't ancient looking. They'd once been a home for people, as Shylo told her. She pushed the boulder, rocking it side to side to waddle it away from the round opening in the ground.

"I wonder what the Senators would say if they knew about these tunnels," Shylo asked.

Jexsanna leashed the harquice to a tree, wondering why Shylo asked her questions that she didn't know the answer to. "We can hide in here. I'll check the path if I hear anything. Once we're sure the bad people are gone, then we can move on," she said.

"Maybe this one has a warm bed and some food," Shylo said in a tone that she now understood meant he wasn't being serious.

"What is it like?" she asked, gathering the sunstone, some nuts and annoa fruit from the saddlebags.

"What do you mean?" Shylo asked, entering the Tarmig tunnel first.

"Where you came from. You sometimes talk about the people who are hunting you, but you don't talk about what it was like before me," she said.

"I've told you what happened. Somebody set me up and I don't know why. They're trying to find me still, but I don't know anything," Shylo said.

"I know all that. But when you're with me, you don't need to worry about them. I can protect you from them. They've never stopped coming for me. Even within the walls of where I am from, they came repeatedly. The Masters encouraged them to come and test us. There are always more of them to fight. So don't worry about them now. When we are behind them, we can leave for a new place where this group won't be," she said.

"How do you know they won't come to where we go next?" Shylo asked.

"Without walls to trap me, I can go as far as I want. This world is too big for them to find me," Jexsanna said.

"And if it's smaller than you think?" he asked.

Jexsanna sparked the sunstone and placed it in front of them. Chirp popped his head out of her surcoat pocket and crawled out into the dank tunnel to wander. *It's already bigger than I could've imagined,* she thought. "What is it like?" she asked.

"The world? They mapped the known world. There's Zethril to the north, Volourium to the —"

"Tell me what it's like for you, where you came from. What did you do before you left?" she asked.

"I didn't leave by choice," Shylo started.

Jexsanna frowned at him.

"Fine. It's like nothing you can find out here in the woods. There're towering buildings, roads and streets without a single sprouting bush poking through because there are so many people traveling on them. There's food being cooked on almost every corner. The smells. The smells from a medley of pan-fried vegetables, baked buns, sweet rolls, flowering gardens, and steaming water baths," Shylo said.

"What is that?" she asked.

"A hot bath? You've had to have a hot bath, with sunstone in water?" Shylo asked in surprise.

She shook her head. "Cold water only."

"Oh, the warm water baths and steam houses are a major luxury for people where I'm from. Back in the villa, that's the Senator's estate where I was training, they had a vast pool of warm water and a steam room for the Nobles. One time, after I came home from the day's lessons, I took off my sandals and dipped my toes in while nobody was watching. The warmth. It climbed my leg, sparked a desire within me to earn that level of comfort someday. As an advisor to a Senator, I might've had a villa of my own."

"The villa, it's big?" she asked.

"It's huge! You walk in from the street through a gate because large walls surround each villa."

"Your people like to build walls," she said.

"Yes, they do," he chuckled. "After the privacy wall, you walk into the courtyard. It's a large space, almost as big as that clearing we were in with the lazgron the other day. This courtyard is gravel, but also includes gardens where the cooks grow vegetables and herbs for our meals. Lining the courtyard are covered paths with stone columns. There are rooms for the servants and trainees. At the back end, the main house with its steaming pool, the entertaining and dining area, and a kitchen in the way back. Above it, the Senator and his family's rooms and living area. And behind that, the latrines, and slave living quarters."

"You have slaves?" Jexsanna asked. She understood from her few experiences in hearing the word that it wasn't a good station.

"Not me. I was only living there at the Senator's villa."

"What did you do for this Senator?" she asked, wondering what people did in a city where they didn't have to train for fighting.

"I was as a Penti trainee. I was there training to advise a Senator on political matters," he said.

"I don't know what any of that means," Jexsanna admitted. She'd heard him say those things before but hadn't understood, only that Shylo spoke passionately about them.

"Maybe it would be easier to tell you what my average day was like," Shylo said.

"Yes," she nodded.

"In the morning, I'd go to the dining area where the Senator's servants had prepared breakfast for us trainees."

"Like how I and the others like me would go to the troughs and eat before our training," she said.

"Exactly. Wait, you ate out of a trough?"

"Yes, didn't you?" she asked.

"No, but some of our animals eat out of troughs. We ate portioned meals on plates. The people who prepared the meal brought them out to the table where we sat, like we are now."

"Sounds like your Senator is like The Masters?" she asked.

"In a way, yes," he said.

"And the villa, is like the arena I fought in," she said.

"Maybe? I don't know. It sounds like there might be a difference in living conditions on that one. But regardless, I would leave breakfast and go to meet the rest of my Penti classmates for training."

"Penti, is a class. Like a group of similarly skilled sparring partners?" she asked.

"Kind of, but instead of sparring, we learned about the legislature, the executive branch, and the judicial system," Shylo responded.

Jexsanna leaned away from him as if he'd insulted her.

"Those are what make up a government," Shylo said.

She frowned, not understanding.

"A state of power that rules the people, in our case, an Empire. You know, a group of people who all live by a set of rules. Those people who make the rules and administer them is what a government is," Shylo said.

Jexsanna nodded slowly, remembering the rules The Masters used to train her. If that was what government was, she didn't think she liked it.

"I'd meet the other Pentis outside the Senate Library," Shylo continued. "A library is a place filled with books of all kinds. The books in the Senate Library offer a wide scope of knowledge. In a book, you can learn what other people have experienced, what they've learned or studied. Whether it's an event in history, a world belief, or a story created from their imagination, there's always something to be learned from a book. That's what I've always liked about books, it's probably because of my abstract way of thinking."

"Abstract?" she asked.

"Yeah, like a thought or an idea. It's different from how you think. You're more strategic-minded. That's why you've kept me alive so long," he said.

"And you went to this place of books and ideas every day?" Jexsanna asked.

"Not every day. We just met outside it because of the convenient location. Once our class began, we'd spend the first part of the day reviewing lessons taught by an instructor. We had several mentors who taught us, most of whom were retired Senators or advisors. Then we'd break for lunch. I usually went with Wilsall and his friends..."

"We had a break once. It was when one of The Masters died unexpectedly. They gave us a break from our training for a short time until we got a replacement Master," Jexsanna said.

"We led very different lives," Shylo said. "Anyway, we'd return after lunch and spend the rest of the afternoon shadowing either an advisor or a Medi. Medis are a more advanced cohort of trainees. Then I'd usually head to the Canteen with Wilsall and we'd drink until it got late. I'd walk home and sleep in my chambers until morning. Then do it all over again."

"I hydrated during my sparring lessons. Not all at once after," Jexsanna said.

Shylo scowled, then shook his head. "That's not what I, never mind."

"What?"

"It's not important. What about you? What was the average day like for you, before you escaped when the bad men came?" he asked.

"I told you," Jexsanna said, feeling the fear she felt when the Scaled One came into her sleeping stall. The memory of what he did to everyone, all the others like her, stabbed at her heart like a dagger.

"When did you tell me?" Shylo asked.

"Just now. I ate at the troughs with all the others. I fought, trained, and hydrated. I went to the hall and ate again. Then I slept in my stall," she said.

"That's it?"

She nodded.

"Did you ever get to do anything else?" he asked.

"Did you?" she replied, trying to avoid thinking about the Scaled One and the mixed emotions she felt about hiding from him right before Shylo was beaten. If she saw him again, she wouldn't run. She would fight.

"Yes, I did other things. Once I moved to Perdigon, I could do whatever I wanted in my free time," Shylo said.

"You moved from one city to another?" she asked.

"That's what moving is, yes," he said. "I've mentioned Florens before. It was the other city I lived in. The one I was raised in. My father always made me work when I wasn't in school. I tried to hide from him in the library, but he'd send my mother or one of my younger sisters to find me. My mother would sometimes let me stay and read. She'd tell my father she couldn't find me. But once I moved away from them, I didn't have parents nearby to tell me what to do," he said.

"But the Senator was your Master?" she said.

"He wasn't my master. I was his student, his mentee. I was paying him to let me study there," Shylo said.

"I don't understand," Jexsanna said. Their conversation was getting too strange for her liking. The things he was talking about, being able to do what he wanted when he wanted, was like the dreams her once-partner spoke of. What she was doing now, in a way. But Shylo spoke about it like it was commonplace. Like it wasn't a privilege or a goal.

"It's okay. I can show you what it was like when we get into the town," Shylo said.

The thought of such a different life suddenly overwhelmed her. She felt as if the walls of the tunnel were closing in around her. "I think I heard something," she said.

"Really?" Shylo asked. "But we were just out there and you said it was safe here."

"Stay here," she said and crawled past Chirp to exit the tunnel. Climbing out into a fresh downpour, Jexsanna distanced herself from the tunnel. She didn't mind getting wet; she'd needed to get out. She didn't know what had come over her. She hadn't thought about her once-partner in that way for a long time. It bothered her some that Shylo reminded her of him. It made her think about the short time she'd shared with him.

Jexsanna stood in the rain, wondering if it was a good idea for her to go into the town with Shylo. Thinking about it made her uneasy, like the feeling she got when Shylo talked about how he wanted to find a way to prove his innocence. She didn't understand why they couldn't just disappear somewhere together. She thought she'd like to live in a part of the world where the people couldn't find them, like they had been. Where the Scaled One couldn't hurt them. It was what she wanted. It was what she thought Shylo needed. And if anyone tried to get in the way of what she wanted, like the Scaled One, then she was going to finish the mess the Scaled One had started. She wasn't going to be vulnerable like that again. She vowed to protect Shylo and would, no matter what. He was good to her. Better to her than anyone had been, even her once-partner. Shylo had given her a name. A real name.

The pounding of many hooves sounded in the distance. Jexsanna slid her sword from her sheath and went to see what kind of enemy was out there this time.

"Though he agreed to remain peacefully within the center troposphere, Tourome had no plans to stay true to his word. He got to work, plotting the best way to rid Tarmigan of the infestation that was the lesser dragons. Pyrome and Brisrome proved the major obstacle, but Tourome created a solution."—
The Dracolyth

YAAK

"Hold still. I need to cover this red splotch on your cheek a little more," Shylo said. He smeared a glob of the light brown stucco mud onto her face.

She wiggled away from his muddy hand before he could finish.

"Jexsanna," Shylo groaned in frustration. He regretted that he'd suggested the name four days prior. "You knew this was coming. If you didn't want to don a disguise, then we should've stayed out in front of the four-hundred guards you saw march by the other day."

"We need to stay behind them," Jexsanna replied.

"I don't know which is worse right now, trying to keep

308

tabs on where they're searching next, or trying to get you to cooperate," Shylo sighed. Crossing through the forest to the town walls wasn't more than a hard day's ride, but they had purposely advanced slowly. As Jexsanna explained it to him, they wanted to keep their position behind the battalion of guards to better anticipate where to hide.

Jexsanna stayed Shylo's hand as he moved to finish covering her red and white facial markings. "You are the one they're hunting, not me. Why don't you have to cover your face and hands with mud?"

"They are looking for both of us. Remember how you killed those men? They saw you too. Besides, I don't need the mud disguise because I can blend in better than you," Shylo said.

She wrinkled her muddy nose at him and said, "I still think we should wait a few more days to make sure."

"We've been camped outside this town for a few days now. It's been raining so hard that we can only see tracks that are so fresh you probably would've heard them by now. You told me how quickly they were moving. They're done with this area. Why would they come back? Don't you want to eat real food and sleep in a dry bed?" Shylo said.

"Our tunnel is dry," Jexsanna said.

"It's puddled with water. We haven't seen anyone since that first night."

"That's because we've been hiding," she responded.

"We're out of food and we haven't turned up much of anything in our scavenging."

Jexsanna didn't raise the issue about Chirp still being alive. Shylo sensed that she'd grown more attached to the critter than he had.

"Once you've experienced what a town has to offer, you'll know that I wasn't making any of it up. You'll thank me. Now, hold still while I finish," Shylo said, smearing more mud onto his thumb.

She curled her upper lip at him.

"I wasn't the one who slaughtered those Sarapio guards," Shylo said. "You don't look like other Rhydarians," he added after a few moments. "The color of your hair and the red in your skin will give both of us away," Shylo said, as he plastered more of the stucco mud on Jexsanna's face.

As he thickened the light brown mud, he noticed she was looking at him again. He didn't think it as strange as when he first encountered her. When she looked at him like that, he ignored it, but she usually did it from a greater distance, studying him with those ember eyes. He stared into back them, wondering if they were truly the color of an ember. Shylo hadn't seen a fire up close, only the smoke columns from far-away battles. Now, he stared deeply into her eyes. He let his hand fall to the base of her neck, gently resting on her soft skin. He looked at her lips, full and slightly parted. He'd never known anyone like her and a part of him feared how close they'd become in their short time together. At times, he didn't need to hear her say anything, almost like he could sense what she was thinking. Before he realized what he was doing, Shylo felt himself leaning in toward her for a kiss. It wasn't until he was a breath away from pressing his lips against hers that he stopped himself. They stared into each other's eyes, but he couldn't tell what she was thinking. She hadn't stopped him or pulled away. Jexsanna held Shylo's gaze.

"Chirp!" the borca squawked from Jexsanna's surcoat pocket.

Shylo stepped back, blinking to clear away his lapse in judgement. Straightening, he said, "Okay, now we need to swap our outward look. Your soldier's garb for my cloak"

Jexsanna recoiled, falling into a defensive stance and protecting her sword with one hand and the borca with the other.

"I don't want your sword," Shylo said.

Jexsanna moved her hand, so both were protecting the pocket where the borca rested.

"I know there aren't pockets to hold Chirp in that cloak," Shylo said, ignoring the smirk on Jexsanna's muddy face when he called the borca by name. The borca that Shylo still told himself would be dinner one of these nights.

"If someone sees a young man around my age that is of Old Rhydarian ancestry with a face like mine, still healing from the last of my bruises, and I'm not wearing a soldier's uniform, we're done for. It's been two weeks since the Emperor met his fate. I know exactly how fast word spreads. I should. I was a Penti trainee for burning sake. There is no way that a town this close to Perdigon hasn't already heard the news, especially considering that a battalion of guards passed through a few days ago. I wouldn't be surprised to see signs posted with rough sketches of us and a reward to encourage people to be on the lookout for anyone with white hair or wearing a House Didimo symbol.

"Will the people here think it's strange that a soldier is traveling with no one else but a cloaked stranger?" Jexsanna asked.

"No, it's not too far-fetched to assume you're a mercenary and I'm a soldier recently discharged from service. With these yellow bruises on my face, I shouldn't have a problem convincing anyone of that. I'll make up a story and say my legion commander punished me and discharged me from service without honors," Shylo said.

Shylo started taking off his cloak. Jexsanna measured him with her curious expression again.

"It's not polite to stare," Shylo said, thinking back to the day they first met when she watched him in the nude. Since then, he'd learned about Jexsanna's once-mate and his death. It was hard to imagine that she had experienced love and loss at her age. She only looked a rotation or two older than him at the most. Though Shylo hadn't had sex with anyone before, he'd seen both Rhydarian sexes in the nude, even before he went to live in Perdigon.

Shylo offered her the lazgron cloak, saying, "Come on, let's trade."

Jexsanna hesitated, then unbuckled her belt and dropped the willow-leaf saber to the forest floor. In one motion she pulled Chirp from her surcoat pocket, bent down to place him on the ground, then slipped the surcoat off without unbuttoning it.

Shylo hesitated, which he should go for, Chirp or the surcoat. He could hardly believe Jexsanna had set Chirp down like that. The furry rodent could easily scurry away. To his surprise Chirp walked to Jexsanna's feet and sat, staring up at her. Shylo followed Chirp's gaze, noticing Jexsanna was standing in front of him without any decent clothing. He still wore his dirty tunic and tattered trousers. He hadn't known what to expect when Jexsanna took off the surcoat with chainmail sleeves, but he didn't think she would remove the grey and black wool tunic with it. Her leggings ended just above her knees, and Shylo could see right through the thin undergarment that draped over her body. It was all that separated Shylo's gaze from her bare skin.

The loose-fitting undergarment may have been an ivory white at one point. It was a unisex length; like a short tunic, it reached to mid-thigh. Shylo thought it was made of silk at first but was most likely the less expensive blend of hemp and cotton. It reminded him of a similar garment he'd seen hanging below Ismay's tunic one day. Shylo admired Jexsanna's athletic body and the curvature of her hips. Remembering his manners, Shylo lifted his gaze. Shylo noticed Jexsanna joining his upturned gaze, searching the tops of the trees.

"What is it?" she asked, missing the point of why he looked away.

Shylo handed her the cloak. "You're practically naked," he said, having to look toward her to find the surcoat she was offering him. When he did, he saw her again, this time from a side angle view. His gaze lingered a little too long, yet he found it difficult to look away.

"Is this what staring is?" she asked.

How can she be so skilled at some things, like fighting and survival, yet she doesn't know the simplest social cues? Shylo wondered. It was like she'd never spent a day in her life doing anything other than fighting and surviving. Before he forced his eyes away from her body, Shylo was surprised to see the black and red marbling blended more evenly on the hidden parts of her body. Her face was mostly dark, with smears of red and streaks of white, but below her neck, the red and white coloring became more pronounced. "Yes, that is staring," he said, accepting the surcoat from her, only then noticing the black stain on her shoulder that appeared to have a healing scab under it. "What's that?" he asked.

Surprisingly, Jexsanna pulled away from him, acting flustered for the first time since he'd met her. She used her hand to cover the dark scab.

"I'm sorry," Shylo said, not sure if he should ask more about it and what had caused it. He separated the tunic from the surcoat. Handing it back to her, he said, "I don't need this. You can put the tunic back on."

In a hurry, Jexsanna took the tunic and slipped it over her top, seeming to relax once her shoulder was covered. Shylo wondered why she felt more embarrassed about him seeing her scab than she did about him seeing the rest of her body.

Rather than unbuckling the entire front of the surcoat, Shylo slipped it over his head. The scaled surcoat felt much heavier than his descaled lazgron leather cloak. The draco scales and chainmail sleeves held a weight similar to his cloak when it was waterlogged. Shylo wondered how Jexsanna was able to move so swiftly while wearing it. Especially because she looked to have no Agunzi in her as the Agunzi were inherently stronger and much faster-moving than Rhydarians.

Wearing the short grey-and-black tunic and the hooded lazgron cloak, all that showed of Jexsanna's skin were her mud-smeared hands and face.

"Now it's time for your hair," Shylo said. Jexsanna's ash-white hair was visible, even when she pulled up the hood on the cloak. Shylo helped her coat her hair in mud and wrap it into a bun on the top of her head. Through all of these adjustments, Shylo was surprised by how Chirp remained at Jexsanna's side, quietly staring at her, and not letting her get more than a few steps away.

Shylo helped Jexsanna fit the deep hood over her head. He stepped back, studied her, and chuckled to himself, "As long as you keep that hood on, you'll pass for New Rhydarian." Shylo could tell that she was still hesitant to go into the town since she didn't smile. "How do I look?" he asked, splaying his arms, and turning for her.

"The same," she said.

"I know I still look like me, but what I mean is, do you think I will pass as not me," he asked.

She stood still for a long time, taking longer to form a response than anyone Shylo knew of. With the hood covering much of her face, Shylo couldn't tell what she was thinking. He noted the willow-leaf saber flaring the back of the cloak on her left side. He realized how threatening she appeared and wondered if it was a good idea to have switched clothing. The more he critiqued her intimidating appearance, the more Shylo thought it might not be a bad thing. If keeping any strangers from asking questions was their objective, then it would help. The people within the town walls wouldn't pester them. They might assume Shylo and Jexsanna were following the guards in hopes of scoring the generous bounty for their capture.

"Come on, Chirp, you're coming with me," Shylo said, trying to grab the borca near Jexsanna's feet.

Chirp scrambled out of reach, hiding behind Jexsanna's leg.

Shylo attempted to grab him again, but the furry rodent again rushed around to Jexsanna's opposite leg.

"This is why I was worried about you setting him down," Shylo said in frustration.

"You need to gain Chirp's trust," she said. Holding her hand to the ground, the borca scrambled into her palm.

Shylo shook his head. "How can you be wise enough to gain an animal's trust, yet have no idea what it's like for me to see you undressed?"

Jexsanna placed Chirp into Shylo's front coat pocket. When she let go, the animal started chirping repeatedly, his volume escalating with each high-pitched bark.

"He's going to attract another lazgron going on like

that," Shylo said as they parted the underbrush in search of the path that led toward town.

"Give Chirp some of these," she said, gathering a handful of nuts off the ground. "Oh, and this," she said, stripping a handful of purple berries from a bush.

Shylo stuffed them into the pocket where the borca was squirming. As soon as he did, Chirp settled down quietly. Shylo pulled a fat handful of the drupes from the bush, saying, "Better get enough to keep him quiet until we can find a place to host us."

Chirp remained silent as Shylo and Jexsanna retrieved their harquice and led them a short distance through the brush, emerging onto the path. Following it toward the walled town, Shylo noticed a fresh set of carriage tracks in the mud.

Jexsanna pointed them out a moment later, stopping and scanning the forest.

"It's only one set, Jexsanna," Shylo said. "They're probably from whoever is tending to the clearing in the wilderness. See, they come from that direction, and, with the rain, it would be a good time to go check on them."

Jexsanna slowly and silently followed a few steps behind Shylo as he continued on the narrow path. He noticed that something had flattened the plants growing in the path. Shylo hoped it was the lack of canopy protecting the small plants along the road from the hard rains over the previous two days.

"Entering Yaak," Shylo read on the wooden sign hanging from a stack of stones before the town walls. The sandstone walls were not nearly as thick or high as those encircling Perdigon. In comparison, Shylo thought they were much smaller even than the walls surrounding Florens where he grew up.

By Shylo's estimate, Yaak's walls were double the height of a draco. He imagined they weren't tall enough to serve as much of a defense against a Volurem blaze.

"Halt!" he heard a man call from a stone turret overlooking the town's gated entrance.

Shylo and Jexsanna stopped, their two harquice trailing by lead rope. The watchman studied them for several long breaths, then said, "Do you have any weapons?"

Shylo didn't have any on him, though he was dressed as a soldier. Jexsanna did, but when she pulled back the handle of her saber, it didn't stick out so much and was hardly noticeable under the cloak. Shylo knew she wouldn't part with it even if they admitted to having it. "No," he said, spinning with his arms splayed in the same way he did for Jexsanna after putting on the surcoat. "We come unarmed."

"Leave your harquice inside near the gate with the others," the watchman said as he opened the entrance.

Shylo swelled a little in his chest, looking at Jexsanna's hooded features, and whispered, "Well, that was easier than I expected. They must be desperate for trade or some traveler's income." As he said it, Shylo realized he didn't have any coin. The only other item of wealth, Senator Didimo-Kai's bracelet, he'd left as compensation for the lazgron cloak. Shylo felt a moment of panic when he realized he hadn't thought through this plan very thoroughly, but he was forced to swallow his fear when the stone gate opened.

As Shylo and Jexsanna passed through the wall, Shylo reflected that the only part of their plan that seemed to be going to schedule was Jexsanna's idea that they wait to attempt their entrance at dusk. In the dim light, the lumistones were not as efficient.

They stood in an inner portico softly lit by the sparsely spaced lumistones. The watchman, wearing a descaled lazgron surcoat and no chainmail, appeared as he descended a set of wooden stairs angling down from the turret. His black New Rhydarian hair was long and dreaded, and in the dim light Shylo made out the striped coloring of his face. His jaw was set, forming a boxy chin. Shylo could smell the swill on him from several arms-lengths away.

"The others are already at The Dirty Shame," the watchman said in a slurred voice.

Before Shylo could ask what he was talking about, the man held out two palm-sized wooden discs. Shylo accepted them, and the watchman said, "These are your meal tokens. You can present them to the saloon for your supper, but if you want to sleep within the walls that costs extra."

Shylo nodded, handing one of the wooden tokens to Jexsanna.

The intoxicated watchman suddenly seemed to be looking at Shylo more closely than before. He swayed slightly, then said, "What'd you do to get a beating like that?"

"Couldn't hold my drink," he said, giving a vague answer and hoping the town watchman wouldn't question him anymore.

"Yeah, I've been in your shoes. It'll heal up. It's already to the yellowing phase. Believe me, things get better," he said, blinking frequently as he spoke. "Dirty Shame is on the second block. You can't miss it."

Shylo thanked the guard.

"I'll take your mounts and put them in with the others," he said, hiccupping on the last word.

Shylo handed off their harquice to the stranger and quietly started down the dirt street toward the saloon. He didn't say anything to Jexsanna, whose deep hood masked her face well in the dusk. The mud on her face and hands had hardly been necessary.

Only a moment after leaving the city entrance, Shylo heard noise from the crowded saloon. Whatever event was underway, the watchman clearly thought they were a part of it. Shylo's growing fear that it was a group of Perdigon guards out hunting for them became a reality when he saw a man in draco-scale surcoat emerge from The Dirty Shame. His tightly trimmed greying hair was just how Shylo remembered seeing it two weeks earlier when Shylo had first seen the famous New Rhydarian commander back in the Senate Chambers. Galterius-Brex now walked into the street, facing Shylo and Jexsanna only a short jog away.

Shylo nearly stumbled to a stop. If Galterius-Brex was in Yaak, that meant he was leading a well-supplied guard, probably the battalion of men out looking for them. Shylo had no doubt that the wealthy Eso was in Yaak searching for him. With nowhere to hide, Shylo stopped dead in his tracks. If Galterius-Brex recognized him, he and Jexsanna would be executed as all traitors of the Empire were. Every instinct in his body told him to run, but he couldn't. He stood still, petrified with fear.

THE DIRTY SHAME

Fourteen Days After the Emperor's Death

Shylo held still, too petrified to move. The open dirt street left him completely exposed with nowhere to hide. He faced Galterius-Brex as the High Commander walked between the row of buildings where storefronts transitioned to two-story townhouses. Though it was evening, Galterius' broad-shouldered figure, dark surcoat, and copper cloak immediately gave away the famous Eso's identity. Shylo hoped that the low light of dusk combined with the overcast sky was enough to conceal his own identity. Small lumistones framed into stucco-sided townhouses on both sides of the six-harquice-wide street glowed brighter as night fell. Soft yellow rays filtering through the cracks of closed wooden shutters and doorways added to the light on Yaak's main street. Shylo's heart pounded faster as Galterius approached. A wooden staircase to their left and a covered wagon to their right were the only possible cover Shylo and Jexsanna could jump behind.

Jexsanna continued walking past Shylo, further closing the gap between them and the famous Commander. Shylo flexed, a dull pain from his beating still ever-present along his sides.

What is she doing? he wondered. Jexsanna's awareness of her surroundings surpassed his own. Shylo remembered when he'd been following Jexsanna while a draco devoured Perdigon guards beyond the walls. The deep hood acted as blinders for him, the same as they did on a harquice pulling a carriage. He realized Jexsanna hadn't noticed that he'd stopped.

Galterius continued walking without pause. He held his head high, shoulders rolled back, moving with the poise of a seasoned leader. Galterius hadn't made him out yet. And with Jexsanna's deep hood, he had a few moments to think. *Keep moving,* were his first thoughts. The longer he waited, the more cause for attention he'd attract. Shylo eyed the weathered canvas stretched over the wagon to his right. The door flap was slightly open and inviting. He could divert from his path, continue walking to the wagon. But Jexsanna was continuing past it, still failing to notice that he'd stopped.

Shylo entertained the idea of hiding while Jexsanna continued walking down the street. Her disguise was much less likely to attract a closer look from Galterius. She could calmly walk past him without risking capture. Shylo on the other hand, knew his *disguise* was much more revealing. All he did to mask his identity was don an Imperial Legionnaire's uniform. He still looked himself, the Old Rhydarian young man they were searching for. By hiding in the wagon, they would almost surely avoid capture altogether. Shylo saw the door to this opportunity closing. A part of him wanted to take the easy route, and selfishly make this call for both their fates. The Penti trainee in him, the Eso who had felt a need to prove that he belonged among the Ai and Kai training with him, wanted to save himself.

If I do this, I run the risk of separating from Jexsanna permanently. Shylo felt that his breath had been forced out of him at the thought. *I mean, c'mon. I must know our paths will part someday, right? She doesn't expect we're going to be at each other's side forever, does she?* As the notion settled, he thought how it was a miracle they hadn't separated already after more than a week spent in the woods, avoiding capture. Shylo wondered what it meant to him that Jexsanna had come into the town with him, despite her reluctance. The wagon offered safety, but only for one.

In the moment he'd taken to consider all of this, Shylo saw Galterius glance toward Jexsanna. Before the High Commander's attention shifted to Shylo, Shylo's adrenaline kicked in and he began to move; the wagon was still open. Out of the corner of his eye, he noticed Jexsanna slowing. Her hood turned to the right and left, searching for him. He glanced at the covered wagon.

I can't just abandon her after all we've been through, he thought, a weight sinking in his stomach for even having considered leaving her. He couldn't part with her like that. *That's something Wilsall would do, and I am nothing like him,* he told himself. Shylo would rather run the risk of being in Galterius' presence than leave Jexsanna alone.

She spun, looking for him. The motion seemed to pique Galterius' interest in them, no longer looking as poised as before. The opportunity that the wagon offered had closed. Shylo felt his run from the Empire coming to an end. If his disguise failed to keep their cover, his quest to prove his innocence, or escape the watchful eye of the Rhydarian government altogether, would end.

Shylo lowered his head and angled quickly to the right side of the street, walking as close to the two-story townhouses as he could. Jexsanna waited for him near the intersection still the better part of a block away from Galterius. Shylo motioned for her to join him as he turned right onto the intersecting street. He chanced a glance toward Galterius as they rounded the turn. Galterius had slowed and was watching with mild interest.

Even with the draco-scale uniform, Shylo's straight black hair was a dead giveaway to his Old Rhydarian ethnicity. With the soldier's chainmail and surcoat, Shylo originally thought he wouldn't generate many questions. He had planned to interact with civilians only.

I shouldn't have pushed so hard for us to come here, he thought, feeling deep regret about choosing to enter Yaak. After seeing the way Galterius eyed him, Shylo understood that any military official who saw a single soldier traveling with a cloaked individual nowhere near any issued assignment was likely to have questions. Shylo held his breath as they distanced themselves from the High Commander, waiting to hear his voice barking the order to halt.

At a sudden sound, Shylo nearly bolted into a run before he recognized it as the saloon doors opening. A collective wave of voices spilled into the otherwise quiet street. A voice too deep to be Rhydarian called after Galterius-Brex.

"High Commander, if you would?" the distinctly rich tone of a Zethrillian said.

Shylo didn't check to see if Galterius was following them. Instead, he quickened his pace toward the next intersecting street. Sensing a new path of escape, Shylo cut left around the nearest corner. Leaning against the wall, tucked into the shadows of the townhouse on the corner, Shylo peered around the wooden trim to see if Galterius-Brex was following them. The High Commander faced their direction but waited for the Zethrillian.

"What are you doing?" Jexsanna asked, the close sound of her voice causing Shylo to jump.

"We're hiding," Shylo whispered.

"From what?" she asked, looking into the empty street before them.

"From him," Shylo hushed, thumbing toward the intersection they'd come from. Shylo suddenly realized he had been so preoccupied with avoiding Galterius that he hadn't thought to check for other guards lurking within view. He hastily glanced around in all directions, yet saw no threat of Imperial soldiers or Perdigon guardsmen.

"Do you know him?" she asked.

"*Of* him, yes. I recognize him. He's a well-known Imperial Commander," Shylo said, again checking on Galterius' position.

In the intersection, Galterius stood dwarfed in comparison to the towering woman from Zethril. Though Galterius' stature showed the wear of years spent fighting in the South, he still stood sixteen-and-a-half-hands tall. His frame still held its thick musculature, despite spending the last three years in the capital. Where Galterius' short greying hair and dark features faded into the nightfall, the Zethrillian with him appeared to glow in comparison. Her turquoise figure glistened like a pool of tidal water in the light of the lumistones. Her purple hair had been shaved to stubble on the left side of her head. The rest was braided, folded along the back of her head, down her neck and past her shoulders.

The two were speaking quietly now; Shylo couldn't hear them. Straining to make out a single word, he noticed Galterius staring down the street, looking directly at their hiding place. Shylo reacted on instinct, bumping into Jexsanna before steadying himself. "We need to move, now," he said.

They passed several glowing windows of occupied townhouses, only slowing when the long shadows cast by closed storefronts provided some sense of cover. Fear burned into Shylo's thoughts like a Volurem ember taking hold in dry grass.

If Galterius was the commander assigned by the new Emperor to capture us, then I've underestimated the lengths the Empire will go to track us down, he realized. *The battalion of guardsmen we saw pass several days earlier,* Shylo remembered, *I assumed it was a mob of enraged Noble houses. Jexsanna said they were wearing a mixture of uniforms, a wide range of color and with varying symbols. Ashes,* he cursed.

Having avoided capture for well over a week had led Shylo to mistakenly believe that the large group of guards weren't traveling on an official campaign. He assumed they were on a mission led by a handful of Senators, not under the leadership of an Imperial High Commander. Shylo remembered what he'd read about Galterius, *the High Commander served the Empire directly. Galterius-Brex isn't the type of man to leave his station for personal vengeance. His presence means our capture was deemed more significant.*

Through the recognition of this fear, Shylo saw how his time with Jexsanna had created a false sense of security.

She'd kept him from being hauled back into the capital. Now, finding Galterius in Yaak, within a few days of seeing the armored guard, Shylo didn't know if they'd make it out of town.

Following Jexsanna through the corner and stopping under the two-story wooden building on their left, Shylo searched the main street with wide eyes. One building across from them glowed brighter with lumistone light than any other in their immediate surroundings. The saloon stretched three times wider than the other storefronts along the main street and a rabble of noisy, enthusiastic voices swelled from within the rustic log building. There was no sign, but Shylo recognized it as the place where Galterius had just departed, The Dirty Shame.

Spying down the main street to the intersection where Galterius had been, Shylo now spotted the Zethrillian. She passed from view, walking in the opposite direction. Galterius wasn't in sight. "I think we lost him," Shylo whispered.

"He might not suspect it if we circle back to where we started. That is how predators behave. We must not be the hunted. We will be the hunters," Jexsanna said.

"Jexsanna, we need to leave," Shylo said.

"What about the meal, the warm bed? I've never seen a place like this," she said, looking around at the tightly packed townhouses and buildings.

"No, you were right before. We shouldn't have come here," Shylo said.

"I don't want to leave this place because of one man. I'm not afraid of him. You told me the meal was worth this risk," Jexsanna said, taking a deep breath though her nose. "And it smells like the yellow stone, but so much... more."

"What yellow stone? No, never mind, I don't care. To ashes with the meal. We can't eat if we're dead," he said.

"This place, I've never seen anything like it. It's so different from the arena," she said.

Shylo felt the borca squirm in his surcoat pocket and said, "This place is a dump. It's a popup town, unknown and off the maps. We don't need the meal, we can eat Chirp if we need to," Shylo said, absentmindedly transferring several of the berries from one pocket into the other to settle the rodent.

"Listen to the voices coming from that place," she said, pointing to The Dirty Shame. "Don't you want to see if anyone can provide you with the information you seek? The meal was not our only objective."

"I just got all the information we needed. The only reason I wanted to find out what kind of search party was out here was to determine how we should proceed. Clearly by sending one of the Empire's most experienced military leaders to capture us, the Emperor and his council have not forgotten about us. We need to get as far from here as possible."

"That is not true, Shylo. You talk constantly about how the Noble people set you up. I believe you. Maybe there is someone in there who can help," Jexsanna said.

"It's not worth the risk. Galterius could recognize me."

"He is not in there. We saw him leave," Jexsanna said.

"But there could be more highly trained guards in there," Shylo argued.

"After all your talking me into this, you want to leave this place, wasting the tokens that would give us what smells like more than you promised from the meal. I don't like this side of you, Shylo," Jexsanna said.

"I don't know why the watchman gave us these meal

tokens. He probably thought we were with Galterius' guards and just arriving late," Shylo surmised.

"Then our disguises worked, and we should go inside," Jexsanna said, pulling on the lazgron cloak flaps. "The watchman did not come after us. Even that commander you recognized and the tall one let us walk away from them. I am now convinced it is as you said, and the food is worth the risk. I won't leave without the meal you promised."

Shylo sighed, realizing he wasn't going to talk Jexsanna out of this.

"The food will give us the strength we need to go far from here," Jexsanna said.

Shylo's stomach growled, and he felt warmth from Chirp in his pocket. If they ate a large meal here, it meant at least another few days before having to go through with killing the borca.

"Fine," Shylo said, trying to convince himself to ignore his instincts. "I guess, just because we saw Galterius-Brex doesn't mean there's a search party. I mean, we did only see a few fresh tracks in the road. Maybe they were from him. He does have the armor and skill that would allow him to travel in limited company. It's possible that he's on an unrelated mission and those meal tokens are how Yaak gets newcomers to tie one on at The Dirty Shame and spend more than they otherwise would."

Shylo's half-hearted reasoning didn't breathe confidence into his choice to follow Jexsanna. Galterius could be in Yaak for another reason. Shylo remembered the conversation he'd overheard in the Senate Chambers. The senior advisors were discussing what to do to address the increasing fire danger while also facing a disagreement with the Agunzi people.

"Perhaps the new Emperor has satisfied the South's

request for more supplies and Galterius is on his way to oversee the operations?" Shylo said.

"Yes," Jexsanna nodded.

"But if that were the case, they'd be sailing, not crossing overland. It's too dangerous now that fire season is starting. The Emperor's nephew was already causing alarm by delaying his return to Perdigon before the assassination," Shylo said.

"With the rain, no fires are starting on their own," Jexsanna said.

"I guess Galterius has a matching brismil scale and blade for his own protection. Otherwise, why would a Zethrillian be with him?" Shylo asked rhetorically. "A High Commander wouldn't take his most valued advisor outside Perdigon unless he was moving house for an extended period of time." He chewed on the idea for a moment longer, saying, "A big meal would be nice. And it's free... This goes against everything my mind is telling me to do, but let's try it."

"I go in before you and make sure it's safe," she said.

Shylo experienced a mild wave of relief. He knew she was prone to a violent reckoning if provoked, but Shylo didn't want to be the one to test the crowd in the saloon. "I agree," he said. "Why don't you go in first and see if people act strange? If not, then I'll come inside and join you."

"And if they attack, I will meet you at the harquice," she said with confidence.

Shylo imagined a room full of Rhydarians facing Jexsanna in a brawl. Even with her dazzling fighting skills and steel saber, if confronted by a large group of guards or soldiers, Shylo didn't expect that she would escape. She proved capable of fighting off a handful of Sarapio guards, but they had been focused on beating Shylo. If it came down to it, Shylo believed a swarm of people could subdue Jexsanna.

"Okay, but remember your disguise and try to be inconspicuous," he said.

"Inconspicuous?" she asked.

"Don't give anyone a reason to suspect that you don't belong," Shylo said, unable to tell from her hidden expression if she understood.

Jexsanna led Shylo out into the main street, now fully lit by lumistone. Casually, he separated from her and walked to the side of the saloon, hiding in the shadow cast by the balcony overhead. Several closed windows spanned the side of the saloon. Shylo attempted to peek through the narrow slats but couldn't see clearly enough to observe what was happening inside. Frustrated, he looked for a better way to watch Jexsanna's progress and instantly became aware of how alone he was. The darkest thoughts he'd had since leaving Perdigon returned. Like a primal instinct, the idea to walk away and disappear into the night nagged at him. Shylo squeezed his eyes shut, forcing the thought from his mind. The sudden sensation felt akin to a time when Shylo's father brought him atop the Florens City wall. They stood three times taller than the highest trees in the forest. While facing the impressive coastal vista, all Shylo could think about was what it would feel like to jump. He knew the thought was wrong, and he would never act on it. But even now, as Shylo slunk in the shadows of The Dirty Shame, the same tingling sensation in his hands and feet returned, the same feelings he experienced when peering over the edge of the Florens wall.

As he stared through the gap between the log exterior of The Dirty Shame and the balcony stairs leading to the now-empty main street, a glorious scent filled his nostrils. The shifting wind carried the distraction his mind desperately needed. All the aromas from the tavern kitchen hit him. He pinpointed the pungent smells of seared meat, vegetables sauteed in a medley of spices, and nuts roasting in a sunstone oven. The full realization that he hadn't had a decent meal since the night before leaving Perdigon consumed him. Shylo couldn't leave Yaak without at least tasting some of the food that now had him drooling at the windowsill.

Jexsanna hadn't emerged from The Dirty Shame. Shylo didn't hear any sounds of fighting from inside either, so he carefully cracked open one of the wooden shutters. Many voices, each one seeming to talk over the other, flowed out through the open window. Shylo waited a few moments longer to see if anyone would pull the shutters closed again. When nobody did and he couldn't stand to remain unaware of the goings-on inside, he stepped forward.

The lumistone-lit tavern brimmed with a mixture of armored Rhydarians, all of whom wore a medley of colored cloaks wrapped over lazgron leather surcoats. None bore weapons and only a dozen of the men and women wore armor with scale-on. Fewer still with draco-scale surcoats like the one Shylo wore. The symbols among them suggested they were guards employed by the Nobles of Perdigon. Of those Shylo could see, he didn't recognize any from the predominant Senators. They didn't have the rigid, militant look that members of Galterius' guard should have had. Sprinkled in with the guards were what appeared to be Yaak locals. The locals wore fur-crafted vests and jackets, and different variations of tanned leather clothing. None of the Rhydarians Shylo saw appeared to be with a well-trained Imperial campaign. Shylo couldn't decide if they were associated with Galterius, or even a part of the same search party.

I wonder if the Palace has set a reward for our capture, Shylo thought. He didn't see the symbols of any houses that he recognized. The crowd was a mix of Rhydarian men and women. It appeared that all but a few of the two dozen or more round tables were full, each seating six to eight people. The tree slab bar top extended out of view to his right. All stools were occupied.

It only took him a few minutes to spot Jexsanna's hooded figure. She was seated at a table in the opposite corner, near the front door. Had it not been one of the few nearly empty tables, Shylo assumed she would've picked one near the exit, anyway. There was one New Rhydarian man at the table. He wore a slate-grey lazgron-scale surcoat with a purple tunic beneath his chainmail sleeves. He held a mug in his grip, but was slouching in his chair, his chin resting on his sternum. Shylo could see his eyes were closed and facial expression slack as he breathed slowly. The man was asleep.

Jexsanna sat in a chair next to the taller stranger who slouched at the table. She had her back to the corner. Shylo could see her scanning the crowd from within her deep hood. A full plate of nearly untouched food sat in front of her tablemate. Shylo's mouth watered as he watched Jexsanna snatch handfuls of roasted nuts and seasoned vegetables from the man's plate. Shylo wanted the food, too. He wanted it more desperately than he wanted to disappear at the moment. Taking a deep breath, he walked to the saloon entrance and pushed through the swinging doors.

He stood still for a moment, briefly expecting people inside to stop their chatter and stare at him all at once.

When only one person looked up and then went right back to enjoying a meal, Shylo skirted the inside wall to where Jexsanna was just finishing up eating all of the food on the stranger's plate. Shylo took the seat facing the wall so he could still see most of the room if he looked right, but only allowing any possible observers to see a side profile of his face. However, Shylo's focus was no longer on the strangers drinking and shouting over each other. It was on the last scraps of mongodo steak that Jexsanna was stuffing into her mouth.

Before Shylo could say anything to her, a firm voice from behind said, "You two better have tokens, or it's back outside the walls with ya."

Shylo glanced to his right to see a stout woman, dark-faced with reddish hair. She stared at them with her thick hands on her sturdy hips, her stance spread as wide as her shoulders. Shylo noticed that she was tapping a cudgel tucked into her belt.

Shylo nodded while he fumbled for the wooden token the watchman had given them. He and Jexsanna each handed the woman one.

Shaking them in her hand, the bouncer said, "Get your meal and drink from the bar. Don't ask about staying the night. Every spare bed's spoken for. You'll have to go back and sleep in the encampment with the other regulars."

When she sauntered away from the table, Shylo pieced together what she meant by 'the other regulars.' This was the irregular battalion of mixed guards, as he had suspected. Suddenly, Shylo felt more eyes from the crowd lingering on them. People were taking notice. Shylo hoped they had not overheard what she told them. Clearly, the others seemed to know Shylo and Jexsanna weren't with their party. He hoped the dim lighting was enough to mask their identity.

"Can you get me a dish of food and a drink?" Shylo quietly asked Jexsanna.

She stood without hesitation, excitedly working her way around the table.

He watched her while trying to keep most of his face hidden by his right shoulder and raised coat collar. He noticed Jexsanna drawing many lasting stares and several people pointing at the blade that caused her lazgron cloak to flair out behind her. Though she gathered unwanted attention, Shylo was grateful to see nobody confronting her.

As Shylo returned his gaze to the sleeping man at their table, he noticed another burly brute of a man staring directly at him. The stranger was wearing a dark red, draco-scale surcoat with a dark brown cloak pinned around his shoulders. His hood was up, resting on the top of his head so his broad face showed through. His loose curly hair was a mix of black and red, as was his short beard. His neck had pink scarring, not like scars from a blade. They were like the ones Galterius bore, marked by fire. The man stared at Shylo with round, orange eyes. Without saying a word to the others, he got up, showing that his broad figure was slightly shorter than an average Rhydarian at fifteen hands. He strolled over to Shylo as he squirmed nervously in his chair.

Shylo tried to look away, acting like he didn't notice the burly man eyeing him. Still, the wide-chested gent pulled out a chair, spun it around and sat down, folding his muscular forearms on the seatback. Shylo continued to ignore him, hoping he wouldn't start talking to him. The man said nothing but continued to study him like Jexsanna often did.

"You took a hell of a beating, boy," he said in a serious tone.

Shylo nodded.

"The Imperials did that to you?" he asked, his gruff voice sounding hard enough to break leather.

Shylo met the man's orange eyes for a moment, then looked away at the crowd behind them, hoping to see Jexsanna returning. He spotted her still waiting near the kitchen.

"What did you do? Resist Galterius-Brex's orders?" he asked.

Shylo frowned, instinctively responding, "Sorry?"

The man groaned, creating a sound like a boulder shifting on the mountainside. "Haven't met many soldiers who apologize for anything," he said. "It's true, then, the Imperials north of the Fringe have gone soft."

Shylo breathed a sigh of relief when Jexsanna joined them at the table. She slid a plate of mongodo steak with pan-fried vegetables and roasted nuts toward Shylo and handed him a pint of dark liquid. Shylo didn't explain his situation to the man or wait for Jexsanna to take a seat. Instead, he grabbed the steaming mongodo steak with both hands, and took a healthy bite. Red juice dripped down his hands and chin as he chewed.

Beside him, the stout stranger chuckled, "They might've gone soft in the North, but you still eat like this is your last meal."

"Hello," Jexsanna said to the man.

Shylo wanted to scream at her. He tried to convey his warning through wide eyes and pursed lips. But like all social cues, Jexsanna did not get the message. She continued with her introductions.

"My name is Jexsanna," she said proudly.

"Jexsanna, eh?" the man said. "And what's a young thing like you doing with this rag-tag bunch of Perdigon regulars?"

"Oh, we're not with these people," she said through mouthfuls of red meat.

Shylo's mind told him to slap his hand over her mouth and tell her to be quiet, but he didn't want to cause a bigger scene. His mouth was too full to override her comments. While trying to chew and swallow faster, Shylo noticed the stout man peering more closely at Jexsanna, trying to get a better look under her hood.

"Why are you all covered in stucco mud?" he asked.

Before Shylo could swallow, she said innocently, "It was his idea."

"Really?" he said.

She nodded just as Shylo found his voice. Yet, Jexsanna's words had already done too much damage.

"Tell me, *friend*, why would you want to cover up your partner's face with mud and hide her in that deep hood?"

From the man's tone, Shylo expected that he already knew the answer, but wanted to hear Shylo's response. This stranger was enjoying toying with them, like a lazgron with a wounded animal. Shylo scooted his rear end to the edge of the chair, preparing to bolt at a moment's notice.

"Friends, are we? I should ask your name then, to know exactly what kind of friend you are."

"Sandor," he said flatly. "You wouldn't have heard of me in these parts."

"Us either."

"The mud?" Sandor asked.

"Would you believe it? She took a worse beating than I did. I'd heard that the stucco mud has healing properties." Shylo said, trying to sound convincing.

Sandor burst out laughing, releasing three booming guffaws that rose over all the chatter around them. His reaction drew a lot of attention, but Shylo noticed nobody wanted to stare at the man for long. "That's good," he chuckled. "You're a cleaver grunt, aren't you?"

"Clearly, if we managed to get food tokens without being in the group of regulars," Shylo replied, deciding in that moment their best chance at a peaceful departure from the table was to appeal to the stranger's crude sense of humor.

Sandor straightened his smile into a steely, flat-lipped expression. "I've been hearing a lot of rumors coming from the capital."

As he spoke, Shylo attempted to make a telepathic suggestion to Jexsanna. He ate as much as he could quickly while trying to avoid answering any more questions. He wanted Jexsanna to read his mind that it was time for them to go.

Sandor seemed to be waiting for a response from Shylo, but Shylo now focused on Jexsanna who had turned her attention to the door behind Shylo. He saw the whites around her black and red eyes show. Immediately, Shylo wondered who could get such a reaction out of her. Jexsanna didn't know anyone except for her masters, whoever they were.

"Mind if I join your table?" Galterius-Brex said over Shylo's shoulder.

Shylo's heart skipped a beat as Jexsanna reached to her side. Shylo did not want it to go down this way. He didn't want to be captured like this.

Surprisingly, Sandor spoke in an equally powerful voice, responding to Galterius, "Yes, I do mind, actually. Blaze off, old-timer."

Shylo confirmed his suspicions then that Sandor was not associated with the group of regulars either. A disgruntled soldier might speak down about a superior behind his or her back, but nobody serving under Galterius-Brex would speak to their superior officer in that way.

"Son," Galterius said, placing a hand on Sandor's thick shoulder. "Do you have any idea who you're talking to?"

Sandor backhanded Galterius' hand off his shoulder and shot up from his chair onto his feet. He stood shorter than Galterius but was thicker-boned, and at a decade or more younger, appeared the stronger. The previously imagined hush Shylo expected to hear when he first entered The Dirty Shame had arrived. All laughter died away and the chattering voices went silent as Sandor stood chest-to-chest with the famous Eso, High Commander Galterius-Brex.

Chirp squirmed in Shylo's pocket, and that's when Shylo first smelled the smoke.

SMOKE

Galterius stood in the intersection down the street from the Dirty Shame, peering into the dim corridor. As the lumistone light gradually increased among the townhouses, he saw clearly through three intersections. Since Isik distracted him, Galterius could no longer see the solo Imperial legionnaire and his hooded companion. Galterius felt unsettled seeing the

339

young man in the dark green draco-scale armor, the more he pondered it. He didn't have a single legionnaire in his command. Among the few guards in this cobbled-together battalion who had served in the Army, none still wore Imperial armor.

"I didn't see anyone who matched your description of the white-haired assassin. Perhaps the Rhydarian who has your scale is continuing south as you insisted three spans ago, or maybe it's back north, like you said five spans ago," Isik said.

"No, the scale is here, somewhere," Galterius said, keeping his gaze trained on the street that the young man and his cloaked companion had scurried down.

"How am I supposed to advise you when you're acting like this?" Isik said.

Galterius frowned, tuning out her voice to further focus his mind's eye. He hadn't gotten a good look at soldier's face but noticed his hair was straight. The only members of his regular troops with straight hair were Old Rhydarian, only one an ex-legionnaire. Along with the straight hair, the draco-scale armor stood out as an oddity more than anything. Most of the guard selected for the mission by Marxius Ovando-Kai were Ai or low-class Kai. Few had military-grade surcoats.

Movement at the corner of his eye gained his full attention. Galterius immediately turned away from Isik and stared at the townhouse where he noticed it. He wasn't sure what he'd seen, but it appeared to be at the edge of the first intersection. It was getting dark, and Galterius couldn't determine if what he saw was of any consequence. He cursed the night. His vision wasn't what it used to be.

"Gal, are you listening to me?" Isik asked.

"Use my full name when we're in public, Isik," Galterius ordered.

"Galterius-Brex, what do you suggest we do? We can't stage in Yaak for much longer. Ovando-Kai's pressuring us for results," she said.

"Is that what Captain Bridger said? The Ai is worse than I thought," Galterius muttered.

"It's Captain Bridger-Kai now," Isik said.

"That's what he's been doing this whole time? I gathered he was the selfish type, but leveraging this promotion so he could secure landholdings and a small guard before leaving Perdigon? I expected more of a sense of duty from Ovando's lead guard."

"I can't say for certain. I don't have my network of Esos at my disposal," Isik replied.

"He used the Emperor's attention to his advantage. He's supposed to be my second in command. Bridger hasn't spent more than a day with the battalion since we left," Galterius fumed.

"You saw the messenger's palace uniform, and the seal on the letter. Bridger didn't make up the excuse to leave," Isik said.

"And suddenly he returns as a Kai? He's shirking his responsibilities. This would never have happened if I had control over who was assigned to this campaign," Galterius said.

"The Captain is still in the saloon if you wish to have this conversation with him directly," Isik said.

"I know where he is," Galterius snorted. "He's too intoxicated to think straight. I'll have words with him in the morning."

"My advice is what you pay me for; if you don't like it, that is not my problem. Unless you have another issue you want to ignore my counsel on, I'm going to return to our room," Isik said.

"Isik, what would you do if you were in my position?" Galterius asked.

"For starters, I would decide on which direction we should go in our search," she replied.

"I explained to you why I hesitated."

"We need more to go on than your gut feeling," Isik said.

"I told you. This isn't a gut feeling. It's... something else," he said.

"When did you last have this, more-than-just-a-feeling?" Isik asked.

"Today. It was strongest as we neared Yaak," he said. Galterius hadn't yet shared with her the force he felt from his sword that pulled him here, to Yaak. Galterius was now regretting honoring the town's statute to submit all weapons at the gate. Had he not been setting an example for the others in his command and representing the Empire, Galterius would have kept the blade. Spending hours with no luck in his search, however, had him leaving The Dirty Shame with the intention of collecting the dragon fang and using it to suss out the culprit.

"Did you consider that your presence in Yaak might've forced them to leave? If I were the assassins and I saw an Imperial High Commander and his guard coming to town, I would leave," she said.

"Jermanus' murderer, the New Rhydarian who stole my brismil scale, was near here when we arrived. There's only one way out of this town and the watchmen will do their duty," he said, hoping to keep his doubts about the watchmen's capabilities, let alone their sobriety, out of his tone.

"Yaak's walls are hardly the fortress that surrounds Perdigon. Anyone with a good rope or tall enough ladder could easily bypass the gate," Isik said.

"The watchmen can see the entire town. The Emperor's small contribution to our cause ran out in paying for the battalion's meals, so I kicked in a little extra to reward the watchmen to stay vigilant," Galterius said.

"So, you're suggesting that if anyone had departed without using the front gate, these watchmen would've seen the perpetrators and made a fuss," Isik said.

"That's their job," he said dryly.

"The front gate watchman on duty was already tipsy when we arrived. How long do you think his services will be of value? Until he can't remember?"

"He'd have to be drinking hard and fast for that to happen in that short of a time span," Galterius replied.

"Unfortunately, not everyone shares your sense of duty," Isik said.

"It is a value I expect from anyone under my employ," he barked.

"I'll go ask him then, point blank," she threatened. "It's not any more of a hinderance to me as I've already sacrificed my comfort enough."

Galterius frowned, unsure what she meant.

"By having to sleep in one of your Rhydarian-sized beds. Never mind, the Creator only knows how much you'll complain about what could've been if we don't get this resolved," Isik said.

"Isik, you're right. Of course, you are. You have a knack for knowing what I might do in these situations," Galterius said.

"Which is why I'm going to go talk to the watchman at the front gate," Isik said, taking a long stride back toward the intersection, then slowing. "Why did you change your attitude so quickly? What are you really up to?"

"Did you happen to get a good look at the pair that entered the town before you distracted me?" he asked.

"No, they appeared as generic as any of these other Rhydarian guards. Why?" Isik said.

"It will become clear in a moment. Can you resist the urge to speak with the watchman and stay here for me? Keep a lookout on the saloon?" he asked.

"You suspect them? Those two?" she said, motioning to the darkened side street.

"I didn't recognize them."

"We've only been gone from the capital for four days and in that time we have already doubled back because of this, your gut feeling. You're still confusing the names of those who take your direct orders. How do you expect to know if there's a pair of guards you haven't met?" she said.

"I know it's late and you're tired, physically, but try to see this from a fresh point of view," Galterius said.

"Okay," Isik said, straightening. "They came into Yaak through the only entrance. They were well behind the rest of the troops assigned to take their meal in Yaak today. Maybe there was a pair that decided not to wait as instructed and came today instead of tomorrow. These aren't the soldiers you're used to training. These are Kai and Ai guards from Perdigon. Do you expect them to act like your legionnaires and obey when you tell them only half can come into Yaak for meals while the other half are left to twiddle their thumbs at camp?" Isik said.

"If the assassins strike, or there's a Volurem attack —"

"With this rain? I cannot see the excuse for fire danger," Isik said.

"You've never been south of Perdigon. You don't know

how fast the Volurem can scorch dry fuels. Yes, we've received significant moisture, but that can change in less than a sunspan given how dry it's been this off-season," Galterius said.

"You can't expect the guards of Perdigon to act like your soldiers," Isik added.

"What were they thinking assigning me two-hundred-and-fifty people with minimal training? Most of these guards haven't been tested in battle. Those who have, gained the experience so long ago that today they couldn't tell the difference between an Engulfed Volurem and an Agunzi. Marxius and Benton intentionally set me up for failure."

"They did, at least Marxius did. He wants you to fail. There's no other reason for sending you out with inexperienced guards," Isik said.

"I take my direction from the Emperor. Emperor Benton gave me this order. I'm not about to abandon the Empire because I didn't get my way," Galterius countered.

"Benton did not select the members of your battalion," Isik said.

"He did make the final decision. The Emperor approved Marxius' choices," Galterius said.

"I wonder if they think by sending you on this ill-fated mission that they'll be rid of you permanently or cause you to defect from the Empire entirely?" Isik said.

"I will not turn my back on the Rhydarian Empire. I disagree with Emperor Benton's behavior since he was elected to his position, but an Empire is and must be more than a single leader. There are checks and balances in place. I must have faith in the system."

"Even if the Magistrates are corruptible?" Isik asked.

"They know the military is the true power and the

Legions decide who will become Magistrates," Galterius said.

"For now," Isik said.

Galterius grunted, signaling that he was done with their conversation. "Watch the saloon doors, or don't, if you think this mission is a failure already. I'll keep searching for answers," he said stubbornly.

Leading with his chest, Galterius stalked toward the gate. He could see the long-haired guard milling near the harquice corral. As he neared the gate, Galterius felt the brismil blade's dull attraction pulling at the back of his mind. Galterius worked to avoid the distraction. He found the watchman standing on the second step of the stairs leading up to the top of the wall. The dark-haired man was taking a pull off a wineskin. Galterius cleared his throat to announce his presence and give the watchman a chance to hide his drink.

The New Rhydarian lowered and clutched the wineskin to his chest, glancing over his shoulder. Galterius tried to act ignorant as the watchman choked on his swill and hurried to cork his flask. Tucking it away into his surcoat, he dried his lips on his sleeve. "High Commander, I wasn't expecting to see you."

Galterius straightened, standing with his hands clasped together behind the small of his back. He waited for the watchman to salute as most trained officers would, but this man didn't. Galterius couldn't help feeling disappointment after his lifetime of service. Since the man was Eso, like him, Galterius chose to look past it. In his mind, he chalked it up to poor training. Simply because he was one of the town's watchmen didn't mean he'd served in the military.

With the silence between them growing awkward, the

guard said, "Do you wish to leave, High Commander? I can ready your harquice."

"No," Galterius said, recoiling from the strong whiff of alcohol on the man's breath. "I want to know if anyone has left Yaak since I arrived."

"You mean after the majority of your guard skirted the walls to go back to your camp?" he asked.

"I want to know if you let anyone other than my troop members leave," Galterius said.

The watchman swayed slightly as he tried to work out what he was being asked to remember. "Like I said, other than your guards, nobody's left Yaak since you showed up."

To check his accuracy, Galterius asked, "Have you let anyone in?"

The man nodded, his long dreads falling over his shoulders. "Just let two more of your people in. Sent them to The Dirty Shame like you asked," he said somewhat proudly.

"Did you get their names?" Galterius asked.

"No names, that's not usually what I ask folk. He was wearing a soldier's surcoat, though. Locals don't have the coin to have draco scales of any kind. If we did, I'd have one. Peace of mind against the lazgrons," he said.

"The legionnaire, was he New or Old Rhydarian?" Galterius asked.

"Ol'. There's no mistaking with that hair, though his face was awful dark, but I think that was from the beating. The bruises were yellowing. Must have been somewhere near a week ago he got them, give or take based on the severity. I wouldn't want to know what he did to deserve it, but how you run your outfit is none of my business," the watchman said, leaning in and giving Galterius a wink.

Galterius denied nothing. "And the young soldier's companion. Did you get a look at him?"

The watchmen nodded again, this time rising on his toes as he bobbed excitedly. "Yep. Saw right under that hood. He was New Rhydarian, muddy too. He had a ball of long hair knotted up in that lazgron hood. Looked more of the grime from the type we see in these parts of the forest, if you know what I mean."

"And you sent them to The Dirty Shame?" Galterius asked, sensing he needed to speak with these two before writing them off. They matched the ethnicity of the pair he was looking for.

"Just like you said to, High Commander. I saw that young man's grey eyes light up when I handed him those meal tokens. They were hungry, by golly. I bet they're diving into their meals right now," he said.

Galterius turned to see the glowing lights seeping through the closed windows of The Dirty Shame. He now suspected that they hadn't gone directly to the saloon because they saw him. He hadn't paid any attention to them until the young man stopped and the cloaked companion turned to face the soldier. Galterius thanked the watchman with a nod, saying, "I'm not leaving Yaak, but I would like to take a moment to see my harquice."

"I can show you to the mare," the watchman said.

"That won't be necessary. I can find her in the corral just fine," Galterius said.

The watchman dismissed himself, failing again to salute before stumbling up the stairs to his perch.

Galterius entered the corral. Sifting through the many harquice, it didn't take him long to find the mare with his saddle. The dragon blade led him directly to her. The blade seemed to call for him, longing for him to hold it again.

Galterius' excitement in having the sword in hand after only hours of going without it sent his heart racing. His mouth salivated as he gripped the hilt. A warmth soaked his body, like sinking into a warm pool of water. He unbuckled the scabbard from the harquice and strapped the belt around his middle. He snugged it slightly higher than normal, so the scabbard wouldn't drag on the ground when he walked. Galterius pulled the blade free, admiring the tree ring-like lines on its inky face. The feeling came back to him. Galterius sensed the dragon fang urging him on. He followed its guidance, leading him out of the corral and back down the dirt street. He was sure the magnetism drawing the blade closer to its scale match was what was urging him toward the corner of the saloon. His scale was in The Dirty Shame.

Isik emerged from the building across the street where she'd been standing watch over the saloon. "What did the watchman say?" she asked, her soft facial features screwed up with worry.

"No one has left the town. The person who has the other half of my brismil collection is in that saloon, on the left side, near the wall. They are there right now."

"Do you intend to run in with your brismil blade drawn like that?" Isik asked.

"I will not let them get away, again," he said.

"Give me the sword, Galterius," Isik said.

He frowned at her again.

"There are over a hundred armed guards in that saloon. You don't need the blade," Isik said.

"Have you ever seen what a Rhydarian in brismil plate can do?" Galterius asked.

She hesitated to respond, dark blue lips thinly parted.

"The scale gives you power. It enhances strength, speed,

awareness. When it's a part of you, the scale imparts its remnant magic. Do you know what would happen to those men and women if a trained assassin put my scale on?" Galterius asked.

"We need to apprehend the suspect. How will we know the truth if they are dead before you can speak to them?" Isik said.

"The blade is a last resort," Galterius said.

"I don't understand your confidence. How can you be sure they have your scale?" she asked again.

"Not they, he. A New Rhydarian man has it," Galterius said.

"What if the scale traded hands? You can't be sure it's with the same person after all this time," Isik said.

"I don't need to be sure. I can feel it," he said.

"I saw those two Rhydarians enter the saloon," Isik said.

Galterius nodded, feeling the attraction through his brismil blade.

"The one in the hooded cloak went first. The other, in draco-scale surcoat crouched by those stairs for a short time," she said, pointing across the street to the exterior staircase on the side of The Dirty Shame. "He went in next. I have not seen them leave."

"Be prepared to raise an alarm if I need the watchman to lock down Yaak," Galterius said, dropping his brismil blade and letting it vanish into its scabbard.

"Galterius, do you need to do it this way?" Isik said.

"Someone has my brismil scale. If he puts it on before I can apprehend him, we'll need the watchmen to do their best to keep him within the walls."

"You'd face a skilled assassin with a brismil scale knowing you don't have the same protection? You should order your guard to capture him. Go back to the camp and get the rest of the troops if need be. Surround the saloon and make sure he can't leave," Isik said.

"That will take too much time. I could lose him by then. I have to do this now," Galterius said.

"Why then did you bring the guards?" she asked.

Galterius couldn't explain it further. The connection he felt between the blade and the scale, it was the strongest it had been since the assassin stole it.

"I recommend you come up with a different plan," Isik suggested. "We know what they look like now. We know where they are, and we can get the rest of the battalion to surround The Dirty Shame. Even with brismil plate, they wouldn't overcome those odds. Not if the guards followed orders."

"Normally, I'd say you were right, Isik. You know the likelihood of what the outcome will be. I can't make the precise calculation, but with this... I have a feeling. I must go with my instincts."

"Look where your instincts have gotten you," Isik said.

"Exactly," he said. "Go. Warn the watchmen," he told Isik and headed for the saloon doors.

Galterius entered The Dirty Shame. The dull lumistones weren't much brighter than before, but he didn't need to scan the crowd. His brismil blade was pulling his attention to the left. At the round table in the corner, where the hooded Rhydarian and his straight-haired Old Rhydarian accomplice sat. They were speaking with a brawny man with red-streaked hair and orange eyes. He wore dark red draco-scale armor and appeared to be overly interested in the duo. Galterius sensed it was them, the assassin and the Didimo boy. The only other person Galterius saw at the table was the drunk Captain of House Ovando, and he was passed out from celebrating his new status as a Kai. Galterius pieced it together. The Didimo boy and the assassin had come to Yaak to meet with a Rhydarian Southerner. He cursed himself for not listening to Isik's hunch right away. What they had failed to plan for, though, was the effect that the dragon fang had on Galterius. He knew one of them at the table had his brismil scale.

He walked over to them. "Mind if I join your table?"

"Yes, I do mind actually," the man said harshly. The stranger did not realize who he was speaking to. His next words solidified that fact for Galterius. "Blaze off, old-timer."

Without thinking, Galterius' demand for respect overcame him. He'd been able to shrug off disdain when it came from Nobles in the capital. He could rise above most insults with several moments of deep breathing, but when it came from a traitor, Galterius wouldn't let it stand. Galterius would let him know exactly who he was before he ripped the brismil scale from the brute's cold, dead hands.

"Son," Galterius said, placing a firm grip on the man's draco-scaled shoulder. Galterius wasn't intimidated by the man's strength advantage. Galterius had the brismil blade. "Do you have any idea who you're talking to?" he asked, hoping the man would soon recognize him as the High Commander who fought with the assassin on the night of Jermanus' murder.

To Galterius' surprise, the thick-chested man swatted away his grip with a backhanded strike. As he shot up from his chair, anyone who hadn't already been watching gasped and looked on in awed anticipation. The stranger stood chest-to-chest with Galterius. Instantly, Galterius realized the brute was a full hand shorter than he was and struggled to remember the height of the assassin. The exchange happened quickly; they had never stood side-by-side like this. Galterius couldn't back down now, though. He met the man's orange-eyed glare, staring down at the stout aggressor.

"I know exactly who I'm talking to," the man said plainly, with a slight Agunzi accent. "A has-been Eso King."

Galterius' moment of doubting that this was the person he was hunting for fled. The dragon's fang sang in his mind, shouting that the brismil scale was right there at that table. Galterius had heard more than enough. This man was the one who betrayed the Empire. Galterius whipped his forehead down with all the might he could muster over such a short distance. His head cracked into the shorter man's, but not directly at his intended target. Instead of smashing the bridge of the man's prominent wide nose, Galterius' forehead glanced off the man's cheekbone. The pain struck him as he realized his first hit was off the mark. This stranger moved much faster than Galterius expected, and he had the presence of mind to avoid a direct headbutt from close quarters.

Galterius felt a punishing blow to the side of his body. The man landed a body hit before stumbling away to check his face for injury. Galterius staggered against the table at his side, generating disgruntled complaints from the guards before they realized that it was their High Commander who was in this physical altercation.

Galterius prepared for the man to put on the brismil scale and attack. He thought of drawing the brismil blade but didn't since his opponent produced no scale. He instead balled his fists, preparing for the next exchange in their fight. Galterius hadn't expected the brute would want to bludgeon him rather than resolving their conflict by more advanced means. He expected the stout man or one of the other two to don the brismil scale. He glanced at the table. The two companions had turned toward the window, noses up; they were sniffing the air.

Meanwhile, the man came at Galterius, punishing him with a flurry of punches. Galterius blocked them as fast as he could, but the powerful strikes drove him back.

Galterius finally ducked a combination of punches from the brute, catching short breaths between strikes. He used his height advantage, rolling to the side and pummeling the attacker with jabs. Galterius landed three solid hits on the man's blocky chin. They didn't knock him off his course and only seemed to anger him further. The only thing that seemed to stop his opponent from unleashing his unbridled rage was the one word everyone in The Dirty Shame was now shouting.

"Fire!"

Almost as if he were regaining his senses, Galterius heard the dinging of the watchman's warning bell. He felt his nose dripping blood. He'd been focused on the fight, but through the smell of metallic blood he caught a faint whiff of smoke. As the stranger abandoned their fight to flee the saloon with the others, Galterius followed. He did not care how or where the Volurem had been summoned. Galterius would not let his brismil scale escape again.

BRISMIL SCALE

Fourteen Days After the Emperor's Death

Shylo's back tensed up and he stiffened in his seat.

Is that? he wondered, catching a whiff of the familiar scent of peak fire season.

Shylo's instincts distracted him from the tense standoff between Galterius-Brex and the man, someone in the crowd had called 'Sandor.'

"Smoke," he said hollowly. The fear of that word numbed his body. The potential destruction of the Volurem made this argument at his table seem trivial.

Jexsanna's rapid movement interrupted Shylo's blank stare. She flung open the nearest shutters, allowing the overwhelming smell to penetrate the room and succeeded, for the moment, in distracting others in The Dirty Shame from the fight.

"Fire!" someone shouted, sending the crowd inside the saloon scrambling.

Yaak locals and Perdigon guards swarmed the exit, clogging the space between Shylo's table and the saloon doors. Shylo followed Jexsanna through the open window. As he crawled through the frame, Shylo felt a firm pair of hands hit him in the back. He fell through the opening, sprawling toward the wooden decking outside. Without thinking of how badly the landing would hurt his healing bruises, Shylo did his best to avoid landing with his full weight on the surcoat pocket. Somehow, he successfully protected Chirp from the fall by shouldering the initial hit and suffering a blow to the side of his face. Through his pain, Shylo preserved his presence of mind to shift his hips, crashing down on the side opposite from the borca's hiding place.

Feeling a sudden rush of anger at whoever almost made him squish Chirp, Shylo rolled onto his back, shouting from the deck, "Hey, what the ash?" Shylo's objection was drown out by the crowd and the ringing of Yaak's warning bells.

Shylo didn't know what he expected to happen in voicing his objection; an altercation or an apology from whoever pushed him possibly. He hesitated when he saw who was crawling through the window behind him. The New Rhydarian man who had been passed out at their table, sleeping through their conversation and the confrontation with Galterius. The suddenly alert man now moved across the deck with total agility. Almost as quickly as Shylo comprehended his sobriety, the man disappeared into the gathering crowd, never once offering so much as a glance back at the place where Shylo had fallen.

Jexsanna's cloaked figure settled into his line of sight. "Get up," she commanded.

He winced, more from the fresh blow than from the pain in his sides as she helped him to his feet. "Did you see that?" Shylo asked. He'd lost sight of the faux drunkard in the gathering crowd. An uneasy sensation come over Shylo knowing that this stranger likely overheard everything said at the table.

"The Volurem are close. We need to attack," Jexsanna said.

"Are you insane? I'm not leaving this town," Shylo replied.

"The walls are too small. It will burn when they come. We are safer in the black," she said.

"I don't understand. It just rained. How is this happening?" Shylo said.

"If the Volurem took hold after the rain, it's not good. They must be well established with a large force if they are burning now. We must get into the black," Jexsanna insisted.

Shylo had never heard anyone refer to the wilderness at night as *the black*, but Jexsanna clearly had not been raised in the same culture as he had. "We're not safe out there. We need the walls," Shylo warned.

Jexsanna's hood directed toward the entrance of The Dirty Shame. Before Shylo could see what spooked her, Jexsanna grabbed his arm and pulled him. Shylo struggled to keep his footing as she dragged him deeper into the crowded street.

Near the end of the block, Shylo's discomfort became too much to bear. Through the pain racking his sides, he said, "Jexsanna, stop."

She let go. Given the shadows of her hooded cloak and the evening light, it was difficult for Shylo to read her reaction.

"I'm not going beyond the walls. I don't care how good of a fighter you think you are. There's a wildfire out there. You said it yourself; we'd need an army to stop the Volurem."

"I will fight our way through to safety," Jexsanna said matter-of-factly.

"You can't," Shylo said. "You don't have a brismil scale and that's not a brismil blade. That borca wool tunic and lazgron leather might protect you from the radiant heat of small flames. Ashes, the legions don't even send their soldiers into battle without thick wool layering and draco-scale armor, and they can't go up against a flaming front alone."

"Maybe this is true for you, but it's not for me," she replied.

"You don't understand. That fire is burning through the forest even after days of rain. The Creator only knows what kind of Volurem they are, savage enough to burn through this humidity. Maybe you think you could outrun the flames, but not me. And even if you can miraculously escape, I can't. Not if I leave these walls. I can't fight fire or outrun it," Shylo said.

"I can stop them," Jexsanna said.

"If you go, I will not follow you," Shylo said.

Though Jexsanna's face was concealed in shadows, Shylo could still envision the disapproving look she was likely giving him. In place of her response, however, a familiar voice sounded over the commotion.

"Stop!" the High Commander called.

Shylo snapped to attention, spotting an inky blade sprouting over the heads of the people gathering in the street. The sword was three times as thick as a broadsword and longer than any great sword Shylo had seen. Galterius held it firmly in his grip. The brismil blade's flat face was lined with ash-white tracings that resembled the wood grain of a sawn log. Galterius held his famous dragon fang over his head, eyes searching the faces among the crowd. Shylo didn't know the High Commander, but swore he recognized the expression, the way his scarred face curved downward, his head tilted slightly forward and eyes burned with frustration. Suddenly the brismil blade in his hand appeared threatening instead of awe-inspiring. Almost as if Galterius could read Shylo's mind, the High Commander dropped the blade, making it disappear back into its scabbard under his surcoat. His scarred features remained serious, but Shylo noticed something about the way he carried himself changed in that moment. Galterius rolled his shoulders back, he stood taller, and folded his arms behind the small of his back, taking on the commanding presence Shylo expected of a High Commander. He addressed the crowd now that he'd attracted their undivided attention.

"All Imperial guards under my command, go to the main gate and await your orders. Isik, and any troop captains or squad bosses will accompany me to top of the wall. Regulars of Perdigon, be prepared to ride into battle," Galterius said, his bold voice carrying throughout the crowd.

Given Galterius' order, Shylo confirmed what he'd already surmised, that these people were not the High Commander's legionnaires. Shylo didn't know what kind of training it took to become a guard at a Noble's villa in Perdigon, but the look of terror settling on their pale faces suggested being tested against the Volurem wasn't a prereq-uisite. Shylo had witnessed guards like these prevent thefts and minor skirmishes between Noble houses with confidence. But confronting Volurem left the entire group looking apprehensive.

"Townspeople of Yaak," Galterius bellowed. "The walls of this town may withstand the flames, but firebrands will float over them. They can catch in anything flammable, and if allowed to run wild, will burn this town to the ground. Go to your homes, cover anything flammable with leather if you can. Watch for any embers drifting in and stamp them out before they can spark to life. As a last resort, be prepared to flee Yaak on harquice. Do not go beyond the walls unless I command it. Anyone of fighting age or anyone with fighting experience, I ask you to join my guard at the gate. Metal weapons of any kind can kill Engulfed Volurem if directed at their weak points. In this hour, not only does your town need you, but your Empire is counting on you."

Shylo felt Jexsanna tug at his chainmail sleeve. He could tell what she wanted to say. She wanted to join Galterius and fight the fire.

"Jexsanna," he said. "That is the authority figure the Empire sent out here to hunt us down. There's no other reason that a High Commander would travel beyond the walls of Perdigon with a large force of guards instead of soldiers. They are here to track us down and bring us back to the palace. Galterius and his troops will force us into custody. Didn't you see what was about to happen back there?"

Jexsanna shook her head.

"Of course you didn't," Shylo said under his breath.

"He's coming this way," Jexsanna said.

Based on his estimation, more than a hundred of Galterius' Rhydarians and a quarter as many locals had left the comfort of The Dirty Shame. Adding in Yaak citizens continuing to emerge from their homes, Shylo placed the crowd's size to be nearing two hundred Rhydarians. Though the High Commander took charge of the scene, Shylo sensed that Galterius had not stopped looking for him and Jexsanna. Galterius scrutinized each person's face as he started toward the gate.

Shylo broke away from the group. Jexsanna hustled with him to observe the scene from a safe distance. Galterius and his Zethrillian advisor led a half dozen of the guards up the stairs near the gate to the top of the wall. In the night sky beyond, the Volurem's glow reflected off clouds overhead. Shylo had never been close enough to the Volurem to see the hue produced by their flames. Despite his lifelong fear of the Volurem, something about seeing the pulsing reds, oranges, and yellows painting the smoky haze piqued Shylo's interest.

Fascinating, Shylo thought. *I've only seen Terra people up until this point in my life. Most of whom were Rhydarian until I came to the capital. Now that I see the glow of the Volurem, I can't help but want to get a closer look. I wonder what kind of Ignis people are out there. The Engulfed Volurem are most common, the Ignis people's foot soldiers. Engulfed Volurem vary in intensity based on the natural elements of their surroundings. And if there are any Possessed Volurem, then we are doomed. Possessed Volurem mean a Pyrignum is controlling them with the magic of its dragon heart.*

Whether it was bravery that had been released during the act of temporarily escaping the famous High Commander or an academic desire to see his first Ignis person in the wild, something within Shylo urged him to climb to the top of the wall.

While searching for a way up that wouldn't disclose his

location to the High Commander, Shylo spotted a ladder. He didn't remember it being there when they arrived. Two watchmen stood atop the wall to the left of it, distracted by the creatures burning in the forest.

Shylo almost said something to Jexsanna but closed his mouth. He imagined her seeing the flames and leaping off the wall to fight the Volurem alone. If he could just sneak a peek before Galterius' guard marched out, he imagined Jexsanna would still be there. Without a second thought, Shylo backed away from her. Jexsanna's deep hood played to his advantage and Shylo separated from her, staying out of sight.

While climbing the ladder, the thought of what would happen if Shylo was on the wall when Galterius gave the order. *Will Jexsanna leave without me? What if she had the same dark thoughts I did earlier, but acted on them? Without her, I'd be on my own...*

Shylo wondered what it would be like. If the town didn't burn to the ground, he might find a new life for himself in Yaak. He shook the thought from his head. If Shylo were on his own, he'd be caught by Galterius within a few days. Jexsanna was the one keeping them from being imprisoned. Being jailed wasn't a pleasant thought, but without Jexsanna, Shylo wondered if his sentencing would be any lighter. Galterius hadn't confirmed who Shylo was yet. The High Commander didn't get a chance to confront him at The Dirty Shame. He might be able to claim that he was already in Yaak when Galterius and his troops arrived. And yet, he needed to face the facts. There'd been a coup. Shylo saw the members of House Didimo dead while the bells were tolling, which meant they were killed before or during the coup, targeted by the Noble house or houses truly responsible. The fact that Galterius and a battalion of guards were still hunting for him told Shylo they feared what his being alive meant. He could expose the culprits. But Shylo didn't have any proof. Why couldn't anyone see that his not being present during the attack at the Didimo villa was simply an accident? He didn't know who the killers were or why they'd come after House Didimo in the first place.

Shylo approached the top of the ladder. He checked to make sure Jexsanna was still focused on Galterius. She wasn't at the corner anymore. He found her looking up at him as she took the first steps onto the ladder below.

When Shylo crested the wall, he expected to hear an angry order from the watchmen to get down. They saw him, taking note, then returned to focus on the fire.

From atop the two-and-a-half-story stone barrier, Shylo could not see out across the forest to the flames. The surrounding treetops still blocked his view. The Volurem's glow shone the brightest straight out from the gate. The orangish haze drifting through gaps in the trees seemed to envelope the sky in its soft glow. This limited view left it nearly impossible to gauge the exact distance to the Volurem. Anxiously searching the gloom, Shylo spotted individual flare-ups splashing brighter orange light that reflected in the low-hanging clouds. Then, a jet of brilliant yellow and orange flames shot up into the night sky before turning to thick black smoke.

Shylo attempted to gauge the reaction of anyone else who may have seen the flare-up. Galterius stood down the wall to the right amidst a group of officers. The Zethrillian woman towered over all of them, but Shylo's gaze fixed on the famous Eso. He held his brismil blade and was again studying the faces in the crowd rather than the fire activity.

Something bumped him. Jexsanna was standing beside

him now, her hood pulled back exposing the dried mud on her hair and face. Her eyes were the color of the embers in the distance. Shylo sensed a stoic energy surrounding Jexsanna. Unlike Galterius, Jexsanna didn't appear concerned about and or fearful of the Volurem's growing size in the distance.

A harsh voice cut through their silence as Sandor spoke from somewhere nearby, "Thought you could get away from me?"

Shylo turned, surprised to see the man in red draco-scale armor stepping off the ladder onto the wall. Though he didn't have a weapon in hand, he was more than capable of apprehending Shylo. Jexsanna was all that separated Shylo from the brawny man. Her presence gave Shylo a moment to scan the wall for another way down. He spotted the Zethrillian advisor. She stood next to Galterius, part way down the stairs, grasping at his copper-colored cloak, no doubt trying desperately to stop the Commander from leading his guard beyond the wall. Galterius, though, paid her no mind. Instead, he held his brismil blade, pointing it at the crowd. Cheers erupted below. Shylo hoped the gates would open. If they did, and they made a break for it, he and Jexsanna could use the commotion to their advantage and escape.

"There's no use trying to run. You won't get around me. You make for the gate and Galterius will have his guard put you two into custody before you make it off this wall," Sandor said.

Shylo saw the guard and armed citizens of Yaak pushing up against one another, preparing to rush out and attack. With their harquice champing at the bit, Shylo knew the order to charge was coming. He needed it to come, now, but the people at the gate were penned in while Galterius seemed to be arguing with the Zethrillian advisor. In the tightly packed crowd surrounding the gate, Shylo spotted someone hunkering down among the mounted guard at the front of the pack. This person was the only one in the front few rows on foot rather than harquice. Shylo recognized him. It was the man who'd shoved him through the window.

"I knew that mud was covering more than met the eye," Sandor said, breaking Shylo's gaze. "There's a pretty price on your head. And yours, too," he added, pointing at Shylo.

"What's a pretty price?" Jexsanna asked, almost sounding threatening, though Shylo knew her question was more likely honest than mocking.

The brute laughed, "Rumor has it the assassins who killed Jermanus and his heirs have a magical gift unlike the magic found in the remains given to us by the Creator. You two have cultivated quite the reputation."

"What if it's not," Shylo said, bluffing to buy them more time.

Sandor's grin faded.

"We have something more powerful than brismil," he lied.

"We do?" Jexsanna asked.

Sandor's hesitation eroded as quickly as the question left her lips.

"We didn't do anything," Shylo said, honestly. As he spoke, he heard Galterius' voice addressing the crowd.

"When you assassinate the Emperor, many people offer a reward for your capture, dead or alive," Sandor said.

"Jexsanna had nothing to do with the assassination. She wasn't even in the capital when it happened," Shylo said.

"Likely story from an accomplice," Sandor replied.

Shylo felt the weight of everything closing in on them.

Galterius and his guard within clear view, a host of Volurem burning outside the town, and now this formidable Sandor person.

"Fine, I admit it. I was in the capital at the time of the assassinations. If you think I'm the Didimo Penti everyone's looking for, you're right. I am the Eso from House Didimo that everyone seems to think orchestrated the assassinations, but I was not anywhere near the Palace when the Emperor and his heirs were murdered. I don't understand how an entire house could've kept the coup a secret or why people think they'd all participate, even the lowly servants? None of them were guilty, they were set up. Everyone was killed before the warning bells tolled from the Palace," Shylo said.

Suddenly, a roar erupted below. The gates opened. Shylo saw Galterius' brismil blade drop from his hand and disappear as a look of horror crossed his face. Harquice moved through the gate as the High Commander's shouts to stop were swallowed by the people's battle cries. To Shylo's surprise, Galterius cursed someone named Captain Bridger as he leapt off the landing, hitting the ground hard. He fell to his side as the bulk of the guard continued moving forward without their High Commander in the lead. Shylo leaned over the edge to see the proceedings. He spotted the man on foot who had been hiding. The stranger who pushed Shylo out the window veered to the left, away from group.

"Don't get any bright ideas, Didimo boy," Sandor said. "I'll see the price on your head is honored whether you're dead or alive."

"I'm not going to try anything," Shylo said. The commotion from the guard leaving Yaak was dying down. Between Galterius' leap and the man from the saloon hiding, Shylo was more distracted than both Sandor and Jexsanna. "I think that man is up to something," Shylo said, pointing with a truthful sense of curiosity.

"Nah, nah, nah. Don't try to distract me with that old trick," Sandor said.

"No, really. See that guy right there, hiding in the trees? He was the same Rhydarian who pretended to be drunk at our table. He pushed me out the window and jogged away into the crowd, sober as a bird. I think he was listening to our conversation the whole time," Shylo said, emphatically jabbing his finger toward the thicket of trees still visible in the light of the lumistone.

Jexsanna studied the spot with intensity, causing Sandor to take a brief glance away from them. Shylo tried getting Jexsanna's attention, but her gaze was fixed on the trees.

"Just because that man's in the brush doesn't mean anything. It could be anyone. You know a small battalion is camped out there," Sandor said.

Shylo finally caught her gaze. He met her eyes, holding them for a moment and silently trying to convey his urgency to act on Sandor.

"It looks like the same one," Jexsanna said.

"No, that bloke? There's no way he walked out of that place sober. You're both mistaken," Sandor said.

"It's him," Shylo insisted. As he spoke, the tall Zethrillian ran out of the gate among the last of the guard. Shylo had never seen a Zethrillian run before. He didn't understand why she was leaving Yaak. A Zethrillian was more helpless than Shylo would be in a fight. While Galterius and his harquice sped through the gate, past his advisor and shouted for a Captain Bridger to halt among the guard, Shylo recognized this was his and Jexsanna's chance to surprise Sandor. Yet Jexsanna stood calmly next to him and Shylo failed to take the lead. Jexsanna said she would protect him and, once again, he found himself counting on her to act first.

As the High Commander sped past the man in the trees, Shylo saw the stranger step out from his hiding place. He dipped his bare hand into his pocket and instantly transformed his skin into a gleaming metallic suit of scale armor. The instantaneous transformation was still registering in Shylo's mind when the stranger took off after the High Commander at a dead sprint.

"A scale," Shylo whispered. He checked Jexsanna to make sure she'd seen it, too.

"It is him," Shylo heard her say. He nearly screamed as Jexsanna leapt off the wall.

"Don't," Sandor barked at her, but his threat was of little use.

Jexsanna landed firmly on her feet, absorbing the sizable drop easily by crouching in the grass. In a flash, she drew her willow-leaf saber and took off in pursuit.

Shylo blinked, not knowing whether he should follow her or stay within the walls of Yaak. Sandor stepped toward Shylo as he realized Jexsanna had abandoned him. She left him when he needed her protection. Within the pocket of his surcoat, Shylo felt movement. Movement from a piece of Jexsanna that she'd left in his charge. It wasn't her blade, or her skill, but it was something Shylo could use. As Sandor moved to grab him, Shylo squeezed his pocket, producing an ear-piercing, "Chirp!" Sandor flinched, giving Shylo a final opening. He couldn't jump off the wall without crippling himself, so he did the only thing he could do. What he did best in dangerous or difficult situations; he ran.

OPPOSING FORCES

Fourteen Days After the Emperor's Death

Shylo sprinted across the narrow rampart, his flight spurred by disgruntled grunts from his pursuer, drawing nearer with each step. Taking hold of the wooden banister, Shylo gripped the top pole of the watchmen's staircase. He hoped his spur-of-the-moment calculation was correct. Using his momentum, he swung around the banister, vaulting himself down the stairs in a last-second change in direction. An instant later, Shylo heard the sound he was hoping for. The wooden banister popped, breaking free under the added weight from Sandor. Shylo understood that in a straight sprint there was no contest for a Rhydarian racing an Agunzi.

Since Tarmigan's gravity density increased the closer to Volourium and the equatorial region one traveled, anyone

369

born or living in the South gained the advantage of speed and strength, Shylo surmised. *The farther north they go, the faster and stronger they seem in comparison to natives of the other regions.*

Based on the red in Sandor's hair, his shorter stature, and his orange eyes, Shylo was counting on applying these natural limitations to escape Sandor and make it off the wall. He guessed at the holding capacity of the railing and Sandor's muscular weight. Shylo guessed right. It didn't hold.

Skipping off the landing onto the ground, Shylo chanced a glance at the top of the wall. Sandor was already climbing to his feet while the watchmen around him took notice.

"Hold the gate!" Shylo yelled, seeing the last two harquice leaving Yaak by lead rope.

A watchman released the chains, letting the front gate remain open.

"No, he's not a soldier. Stop him!" Sandor shouted as he thundered down the stairs.

Before the confused watchman could block Shylo's exit, he darted past the lightly armored townsman and beyond the wall. Instantly, the gravity of what he'd done slammed him in the chest. He now faced being in a forest alive with active Volurem and guards sent to capture him.

On the path before him, Shylo's noticed the tall figure leading two harquice. Her Zethrillian form stood out, silhouetted against the darkness. The advisor didn't see him as Shylo overcame her. He knew that what he was doing was selfish, but Sandor was on his heels and the Zethrillian woman only needed one mount. Shylo held onto the mane and saddle of the harquice he'd grabbed as both animals spooked. Settling into the saddle, he spied over his shoulder.

The advisor disappeared from the path, dragged off into the brush by the startled mare. In the remaining light cast through the closing gap of the gate, Shylo spotted Sandor's red draco-scale armor passing through. An instant later, the soft lumistone light from Yaak disappeared. He sensed that the gate would not open again.

He tried to get his bearings in the dark. A black corridor swallowed him as he galloped down the path. He was alone. Shylo saw no sign of Jexsanna. Galterius and the rest of the Perdigon regulars were nowhere in sight. The only assurance of any type of life was the orange glow reflecting off the clouds overhead. He knew Rhydarians would be there wherever the fires spotted. The orange glow grew brighter with each stride.

"What have I done?" Shylo wondered, his lungs tightening in the dense smoke.

He pulled up on the reins, panicked now that he was riding alone and unarmed into a blazing fire fight. The harquice snapped its muzzle forward, yanking the reins free in its frenzy. Shylo had suddenly lost control of everything. His eyes stung, tears welling from the smoke.

Get it together, Shylo, he thought, urging himself to come up with a plan.

Snapping up the reins, he pulled in on one side, calling, "Whoa!" He forced the mare in ever tighter circles until it settled, each circle having restored a bit of his confidence.

Stopped on the path, Shylo attempted to analyze his options. Sandor pursued from behind. A Volurem blaze burned in the trees before him. And Jexsanna was... he felt an overwhelming need to find her. Searching the darkness for *the black,* as she called it, Shylo struggled to put himself in her frame of mind.

Why did she leave me like that? he thought. *She said, it's him. She said it right when that man from the saloon, the one Galterius called Bridger, donned the brismil plate,* Shylo realized. Something that Jexsanna had said to Shylo came to light. *The Scaled One,* he remembered her saying when Marxius Ovando-Kai rode past them outside Perdigon's southern gate.

But she knows that not every soldier in brismil armor is the same person, right? he wondered. Jexsanna knew so much about combat and strategy. It was only logical that she would know this simple fact. *Unless the Masters kept this knowledge from her.* Another piece to Jexsanna's puzzle fell into place as Shylo considered all she'd said. She didn't like to talk about how the bad men slaughtered everyone at the place where she was trained, but the fact that she began wandering in the wilderness around the same time that the Akai were killed, and her conviction that someone in brismil-scale armor had tried to kill her, too, couldn't be a coincidence.

Shylo now remembered Ismay's comment that her father had been delayed the night of the Emperor's death. Shylo could hardly believe what this revelation suggested. *Was Ismay a part of this coup as well?* he wondered. Cursing silently at the Kai, *Ashing cowards and backstabbing fire scars. I should've heeded my mother's advice and been more wary. I might've seen it coming...*

The harquice stamped its feet in discomfort as a hot blast rushed past them. Bright yellow and orange flames burned into view through gaps in the forest. Shylo froze as he watched a single Engulfed Volurem soldier run across the path before him, shrinking as it sprinted through the forest. The creature dwindled and disappeared. Shylo saw it clearly before it faded. He was surprised to see its silhouette, eerily similar to that of his own people. The Engulfed Volurem was like a Rhydarian when he first saw it, only with charcoal black skin that was cracked and glowed with brilliant red magma. Flames danced from its skin. In its wake, the single Engulfed Volurem left a trail of smoldering flames, slowly dancing into the undergrowth. Alone, the flaming person was unable to maintain its fire, shrinking in size as the humidity of the forest quelled the flames. Shylo remembered reading about this type of Ignis behavior. The Volurem was a *spotter*, one that was acting apart from the main fire, but still within the natural behavior of the Engulfed. It ran alone, spotting and spreading the size of the Volurem force. How more Engulfed Volurem could be summoned into life was something that had always puzzled Shylo. This aspect of their existence remained the greatest mystery.

Knowing that Jexsanna was somewhere out here in the forest forced him to go against his instinct. He loosed the reins, heeling the harquice toward the smoldering flames that flickered in the path. Glancing down at the dark footprints where the single Volurem had run through, he saw little hints of Volurem smoldering in the foliage as they struggled to sprout. His heart raced as he galloped through, committing to his fate.

Breathing harder now, Shylo felt his chest grow tighter the more he sucked in the smoke. He blinked rapidly, his eyes watering. The smoke thickened and the glow of the Volurem grew brighter. Rounding a corner, Shylo reined in on his mount. A wall of flames burned in front of him. This was his first bona fide glimpse of a battle with the Volurem. Disorganized guards scrambled through thick undergrowth on either side of the path. Volurem foot soldiers, the Engulfed, burned and stabbed their way through the troops on the right as they struggled to form a cohesive front line.

Among the thudding clash of steel on Ignis blades, Shylo discerned an unexpected sound. The clang of metal ringing against metal came from several individuals between Shylo and the flames, centered in the path.

Galterius-Brex's deep, commanding voice rose over the crackling flames and the yelling of the guards, "Bridger, enough! If you want to keep your life, you will stand down."

Galterius stood on the right edge of the path, black brismil blade in hand. The man from the saloon squared off from the opposite edge of the path. He still wore the full brismil-plate armor and wielded a broadsword. Between them, Jexsanna crouched in a fighting stance. She wore no armor, only the lazgron cloak and grey tunic. She brandished her willow-leaf saber.

"Call off your dog," Bridger shouted, charging Jexsanna.

Shylo coughed with a sudden inhalation. He tried calling out, but the smoke choked him, stifling his attempt.

The metallic figure moved so fast, Shylo struggled to keep track of him. The dragon scale gifted the Rhydarian man with unnatural speed. Only the ringing of steel on steel told Shylo that Jexsanna was matching his attacks. Shylo struggled to comprehend Jexsanna's speed and fighting ability. Bridger drove her toward Galterius.

"Give up the scale," Galterius replied, bobbing with his dragon fang unsheathed and waiting for the right moment to strike.

Shylo watched nervously as Jexsanna appeared to be overpowered by the brismil scale's advantage.

"For the right price, Galterius," Bridger said.

"Your life is not high enough?" Galterius replied.

Jexsanna broke the series of blocks during this distraction. She drove at the man in the brismil armor, somehow outpacing him. Shylo saw Jexsanna's blade spark against the dragon scale. She landed hits to his arms, legs, and sides. She drove him away from Galterius, almost as if she was protecting him.

"Let me take him," Galterius shouted, charging in after them.

Jexsanna kicked Bridger, pushing him away before spinning to face the advancing High Commander.

What are you doing? Shylo thought, watching helplessly as the Engulfed Volurem continued to chew through the leaderless Perdigon guard nearby.

"Move," Galterius yelled, bringing his dragon fang swooping down at Jexsanna.

"No," Shylo coughed.

Jexsanna's speed carried the advantage against the High Commander, and she blocked his swing, forcing it to the side.

"Why are you defending me from him?" Galterius snapped. "If you won't let this man try to make this brismil whole again, I will deliver Imperial justice on you first, traitor."

"You don't have that authority anymore, Galterius. Only your wealth can save you now. My offer still stands. Continue to refuse and face the consequences of a higher bidder," Bridger said.

Galterius spat at the newly promoted Captain and charged. Bridger rolled to the right, launching a counterattack at Galterius. Galterius readied his dragon fang, but Jexsanna beat him to the punch. She defended the famous Eso again. Shylo couldn't understand why. This man,

Bridger, could solve their problem. If Jexsanna let them kill each other, they'd be rid of their captors. But she didn't know that Bridger couldn't have been the one who murdered the others like her. Shylo had to tell her.

Harquice hooves pounded the ground behind Shylo, forcing him to momentarily avert his attention. Sandor entered the fray, unskillfully attempting to control his mount with one hand while wielding a great sword in the other. The stout man gripped the massive sword as if it were a single-handed saber. His face glowed in the light of the flaming front. His orange eyes locked onto the continuing struggle among Jexsanna, Bridger, and Galterius.

Shylo couldn't run now. Not while Jexsanna remained engaged between two opposing forces.

"You've pushed me too far," Galterius said, this time directing his attack at Jexsanna's back.

Out of the corner of his eye, Shylo noticed Sandor dismount and rush him, but Shylo didn't care. Jexsanna was under attack from both sides now. Galterius pointed the tip of his dragon fang at her, attempting to run both Jexsanna and Bridger through with one stabbing motion. Shylo assumed she would move. Like the lazgron, she had a keen sense for approaching danger. But as Galterius led with the tip of his brismil sword, Jexsanna showed no sign of acknowledging the strike.

"Jexsanna, behind you!" Shylo shouted. Miraculously, over the roar of the flames and cries of the guard, Jexsanna reacted to Shylo's warning.

She stabbed Bridger in the neck, the tip of her saber not breaking through but forcing the Captain to stumble back. In a blur, she spun, slapping the tip of Galterius' brismil blade to the side as he stabbed it into open air.

Having saved Jexsanna from being run through, Shylo

dug his heels into the harquice to move away from Sandor. He felt his harquice sidestepping instead of riding forward, only to notice Sandor held both lead ropes firmly in one hand. Sandor pulled the animal back in to his side, never once looking away from the fight.

While Jexsanna regained her stance, Shylo noticed the Volurem making a run through the trees. He shifted in his saddle, feeling the heat from the Engulfed radiating through the forest. The Engulfed Volurem appeared unhindered by the remaining guards, their fire roaring up through the canopy. Black smoke spewed into the dark sky.

Shylo stared wide-eyed at the Engulfed. The Rhydarian-like figures ran through the flames that burned along the open corridor. Their skin cracked, glowing a molten red to match the glowing of their eyes. Yellow and orange flames left their bodies and spread into the forest. They now moved as a group, feeding off each other's energy. Each held a glossy black blade that they used to slash through the guardsmen. Unlike the solo Engulfed that faded into the green vegetation, when these Volurem at the front showed signs of dwindling, they circled back into the fire, letting more intensely heated Engulfed take their place.

With the extreme heat of Volurem leaving those in the clearing sweating, Shylo felt tempted to flee, but Jexsanna stubbornly remained between the Captain and the High Commander. Shylo pulled on his harquice's lead rope, attempting to rip it from Sandor's hands. He didn't want to dismount and run at the fire on foot. He couldn't outrun the Volurem without a harquice, but it seemed he didn't have any other choice. Shylo had to make it out with Jexsanna. He closed his eyes and readied himself to jump down off the mare.

"Commander Ambrose led his legion to sweep up the wandering Engulfed. I followed from a distance. I think the Volurem are more intelligent than we've perceived. I have seen what I believe are Tarmig people wandering the ash-fall in the wake of this battle. I can't communicate with them as they speak a native dialect, but I believe they are being enslaved by Volurem. How they have survived the fires, I do not know. Perhaps they are blessed by the higher power that is present here." – Sunspan 408, The Book of Volteir

VOLUREM BURNING

Fourteen Days After the Emperor's Death

Galterius blocked the woman's saber. The heat rolling off the approaching Volurem fried his exposed skin, stinging his cheeks and neck. He backed away from the woman, failing to comprehend how she moved so quickly without a dragon scale. She should've buckled under the force of his brismil blade, too, yet she continued to defend herself as if Galterius' blade were a practice sword and Captain Bridger lacked the scale he wore.

Even more confusing to Galterius was why this mud-covered woman had stopped the Captain from stabbing Galterius in the back. It was clear to Galterius now which assailant in The Dirty Shame had stolen his brismil scale. The others at the table clearly were accomplices to the crime but Captain Bridger-Kai of House Ovando, who had feigned drunkenness, was Jermanus' murderer. The other three here weren't Galterius concern right now. He understood the pulling sensations now. Bridger was wearing Galterius' dragon scale.

Bridger didn't know how I was tracking the scale so accurately. The sensations match perfectly with Bridger's absence from our campaign, Galterius realized. *Bridger was trying to retrieve the scale before answering the Emperor's summons. It's been Ovando's man the whole time.*

As for the roles of this woman who moved with unnatural speed, the man from the saloon, and the Didimo boy, Galterius would force a confession from the Captain once the poison from his dragon fang leached through the plate armor and into Bridger's bloodstream. He just needed to land a crucial blow while the muddy woman distracted the Captain.

To his right, Galterius noticed the Engulfed slowing in their advance. The Volurem in the lead had now circled back to intensify their flames. Pretty soon the fire would be of a size that would allow the Volurem to rotate more intense Engulfed Volurem soldiers to the front at a faster pace. The damp foliage was drying out quickly in the hot wind and wouldn't slow them much longer. Had Galterius' guard not rushed out of the gate without him, they might've had a decent chance of stopping the Volurem. Now, Galterius needed to return to camp if possible and lead what was left of his regulars, if any, to the back of the fire, starting in at the heel and fighting their way up the flanks. But first, he needed his scale. Galterius couldn't leave without it. Still, if the Volurem intensified much more, none of them would outrun the flaming front.

Galterius could not keep up with the fighting pace of the Kai and the muddy female. He needed his scale but couldn't find a smoke-free breath to revitalize his efforts. Movement nearby distracted him. The Agunzi- Rhydarian from the saloon held onto two saddled harquice with his left hand. The House Didimo Penti jumped down from one and attempted to run at them. Almost as quickly as he did this, the Didimo boy was yanked off his feet. The Agunzi dropped the lead rope and hauled the young man in by his surcoat collar with one hand, throwing him to the ground. Behind them, Galterius saw a tall figure step into the light, her blue-and-green face sparkling with sweat.

"Isik?" he said, wondering why she followed him beyond the walls.

Galterius prepared to cut around the cloaked woman and land a strike on Bridger. The dragon fang's longing to become whole again acted as an accelerant to his desire for revenge. It was the only thing that Galterius saw that could redeem his standing in the Empire. The Volurem had already burned or scared off half of his battalion because he had chosen to focus on the scale. Reclaiming his brismil scale and revealing Captain Bridger-Kai's betrayal would allow Galterius to further pursue his future as a military leader and advisor to the Emperor.

But is that what I truly want? he considered.

Emperor Benton would likely remove him from his co-command of the Saypo Division if he returned defeated and empty-handed.

Now that Jermanus is dead, is continuing to climb the ranks in Perdigon what I want?

Several Volurem Engulfed broke free from the front of the fire and ran directly at them. The rest of the Engulfed looked to be preparing for another big run as well. If their intensity increased, it would be too strong for his borca wool tunic and draco-scale surcoat. To withstand the flames, he needed his scale. As Galterius attempted his next attack, the cloaked woman kicked Bridger back and blocked his path.

"Why are you doing this?" Galterius demanded through gasps as he tried to hack her out of his way.

She didn't respond, holding her blade at Galterius and checking on Bridger's position.

In a mocking gesture, Bridger pointed his finger at Galterius, curling it in a summons to come after him. Before Galterius could make another attempt, Bridger swiveled to face the Volurem front and ran headlong at them.

"No!" Galterius shouted, taking a few steps toward the flames, swinging his brismil blade at the heat. It did nothing to dampen its effect on him. His face burned to where he felt it would blister.

"No!" he shouted again in frustration as he watched the man wearing his brismil scale hack his way through the flaming Volurem front and disappear into the fire.

Galterius reluctantly dropped his brismil blade before it led him into the fire in pursuit of the scale. He'd seen too many fire fights to know that draco scale didn't hold up for long against a force of Engulfed this size. The dragon fang would clear a path for him, but without brismil plate, he would die from the radiant heat before making it through the second line.

Back-peddling away from the heat, Galterius noticed the strange woman holding her ground. She wore less protection than he did with only a thin wool tunic and lazgron cloak. Yet she moved aggressively toward the flames. Galterius heard the young man behind him crying out, fearful for what Galterius knew was going to happen if the Rhydarian stepped into the flaming front without protection. Despite common sense and the pleas of her companion, she ran after Bridger, jumping through the gap, and into the most intense of the Volurem's heat. He expected to see her fall to her knees and become fuel for the Engulfed, but she didn't. She disappeared into the flames, saber swinging.

"Isik," Galterius called, running from the red-eyed Volurem.

To his surprise, the Agunzi and the Didimo boy had gone. Isik was already leading a harquice back down the road when he caught up to the towering woman. She hunched over, coughing uncontrollably as she struggled to keep a swift pace.

"Isik, you have to get to Yaak," Galterius said, pulling the lead rope from her grip.

She shook her head, coughing too much to speak.

"You're too exposed out here," he said, urging her to sit on the harquice.

"The assassin..." she coughed, reluctantly pulling herself up onto the saddle. Once seated, her feet still grazed the ground as they headed back along the road to town. Though she was tall, her Zethrillian bones and thin figure weighed the same as a bulky Rhydarian.

"I will deal with Bridger," Galterius said.

"Captain Bridger-Kai?" she said, her face creased with worry.

"He has my scale. I'll handle him if he survives the

Engulfed. Right now, you need to ride to Yaak and wait for me there," Galterius commanded.

"The boy, he's —"

"I see them," Galterius said, spotting the other harquice trotting down the dimly lit corridor of trees. "Beat them to the gate and I'll deal with them next," he said.

Isik nearly fell backward as the harquice took off in the opposite direction of the Volurem. Her cursing faded in the growing roar of the Volurem behind Galterius.

He ran, putting some distance between himself and the advancing fire. It didn't take long before he caught up with the stout man. To his surprise, the Didimo boy was sitting on the harquice and willingly being led. Just a few moments ago, he had been struggling to break free, but now he seemed to have given up. Galterius replayed in his head the image of the woman leaping into the Volurem fire. He recalled the young man's pleas for her to stop. They all knew it; there was no way she had survived.

As Galterius approached the pair, the Agunzi pulled the harquice sharply to the left and took off into the forest. Galterius slowed, not sure why they weren't returning to the protection of the town wall, such as it was. If they thought they could get around the Volurem on foot, they were mistaken. The Engulfed were on the brink of blowing up the surrounding forest. The Didimo boy would burn like his companion. He didn't know what the Agunzi had up his sleeve, but if he got away, too, Galterius would have nothing to show for this folly. Galterius had to catch them.

Choosing his path by the glow of the Volurem, Galterius waded into the undergrowth. He ran, his energy quickly fading. He wasn't used to fighting and maneuvering around the Volurem without his brismil scale. If he was this tired now, he knew he would not last in attempting to capture the Didimo boy *and* continuing to circle around to reach the rest of his battalion at their camp. Galterius had little choice but to brandish his dragon fang. The blade's magic gave him strength, but nowhere near as much as the scale did. Again, he needed to catch them, all of them.

Feeling a boost, Galterius sprinted through the brush, cutting down thick bushes to increase his speed. Angling around some, Galterius blocked the Agunzi leading the harquice. In his most commanding voice, he said, "Hold it right there or I swear I'll run this blade through your thick skull."

"Not until we're well out of range of that fire," the Agunzi retorted.

"Neither of you is leaving my sight. You're both under arrest for aiding in the assassination of Emperor Jermanus and his Akai heirs," Galterius said.

"You need to check yourself, old timer," the man replied, unphased.

"The name's High Commander Galterius-Brex," he growled.

"And mine is Sandor Hydemar. You can ask around if we survive this. I have reliable witnesses who will place me outside the capital on the night of those murders. And unless you can pull this Didimo boy from my grip, I'll be the one taking him in for the reward."

Galterius felt that he'd heard the name Sandor Hydemar before but couldn't place the context. No matter who Sandor thought he was, Galterius would not let him get away with the Didimo boy. "Over my dead body," Galterius said, lifting the point of his brismil blade at the man.

"It won't matter whose dead body this is over because

in a few minutes, we'll all be burnt to a crisp," the young man said matter-of-factly, obviously exhausted.

"The Didimo boy's right. I need to move if we're going to escape the blaze of this fire," Sandor said.

"For burning sake, my name is Shylo. Now can we please put our differences aside until we've cleared the Volurem front," Shylo said in frustration.

"Ashes, he's right. Come on," Sandor said, glancing at the flames in the nearby trees.

Galterius held firm, his brismil blade pointed at Sandor's chest.

"Don't make me break my promise," Sandor said. "I told the boy,"

"It's Shylo," he corrected.

With a crossways glare, Sandor continued, "I told Shylo that I'd agree to get us out of this mess if he stopped resisting. Now if you go and make me kill you, that will slow us up to where the Volurem will burn us all. Either hop on the harquice and we'll settle this later or get out of my way."

"Blazes," Galterius swore, dropping his blade, allowing it to vanish back into its scabbard. He knew they were right. Fighting each other was a death sentence, and he couldn't stand to live with himself if he let them escape. In a stride, he hopped onto the harquice, sitting right behind Shylo in the saddle.

Sandor started running. It surprised Galterius how quickly a man his size could run. He must've spent most of his time in the South to have the strength and stamina to move through the forest faster than a harquice could trot. They paralleled Yaak trying to get around the Volurem front. He was just thinking that they might move fast enough to escape the Volurem when Galterius noticed the orange glow through the trees directly in front of them.

"Ashes of Volourium," Galterius swore, realizing the seriousness of the danger. Sandor slowed. "We can't keep heading in this direction."

"I say we can," Sandor countered.

"Galterius is right," Shylo said. "There are Volurem ahead if we continue in this direction."

"A spot must've summoned a flanking force. We might be able to get to Yaak's walls if we angle through the green," Galterius said, noticing Shylo perk up at the idea.

"You saw how fast the Engulfed made that last run, and now there're no Imperials to tangle them up. It's too late to turn back. We need to go forward," Sandor said.

"We'll run into the same problem if we head directly into that spot fire," Galterius said.

"We'll be safe in the black," Shylo muttered.

A chirping noise sounded from somewhere on the harquice.

"What was that, a borca?" Sandor asked.

"Wait, Didimo boy, what did you just say?" Galterius asked.

"The Creator be damned, my name is not Didimo boy," Shylo barked. "I barely knew the blazing Senator. It was my first term as a Penti trainee. I was the newest person in the Didimo House, the least affiliated with the house, for ashing sake. My name is Shylo. I'm an Eso from Florens, and what I was saying is, we'll be safe in the black."

"We don't care who you think you are, keep your thoughts to yourself, young'un," Sandor said.

"There's no outrunning the Volurem if we continue into the darkness. Their fire needs the unburnt fuel. They're too well established now to beat them back with anything but a well-trained legion or a few days of heavy rain," Galterius said.

"I didn't say we should continue running into the night," Shylo said. "I noticed it when I passed the Volurem spotter's tracks. And the way Sandor was able to kill the sprouting Volurem before they grew."

"That was before the wind picked up," Sandor interrupted.

"Not a wind, a Pyrignum," Galterius corrected.

"There's no Pyrignum with this burn," Sandor said.

"Like ash," Galterius argued. "How else do you explain the Engulfed establishing so quickly this far north, in a forest that's seen two days' rain?"

"I don't care how they got started," Sandor said. "I know there isn't a Pyrignum in this bunch."

"How?" Galterius demanded.

"Call it a gut instinct, a sixth sense, magic, whatever you want but I know there's no Pyrignum influencing these Engulfed Volurem," Sandor said.

Galterius could hear the confidence in his tone. Sandor believed what he said.

"Regardless, the Volurem are only active where fuels are available, right?" Shylo said.

"Everyone knows the Engulfed need fuel to thrive," Galterius said.

"Right, you called it the green. We need to cut through the green to get into the black," Shylo said.

"Are you suggesting we run through the flames, like your friend did back there?" Sandor asked. "Because I can assure you it doesn't work like you think it does."

"Why not? The Volurem burn into the green. What they've already burnt won't sustain them. They can't exist in a place that they've already scorched," Shylo said. "That's where we'll be safe, in the black."

"Do you see how thick this forest is?" Sandor

responded. "This won't be like a Volurem force quickly eating through grassland and dying out. They'll be burning through here for weeks."

"Not at the back of the fire, the heel," Galterius acknowledged, clearly thinking now about Shylo's suggestion.

"We can't get to the heel from here. By now, they've probably spread out in all directions," Sandor responded.

"But if there is no Pyrignum, as you suggest, natural elements are the only thing driving this army of Engulfed."

"Can you hurry this up? They're surrounding us, and we need to move," Sandor said.

"What we're suggesting is, if we can break through the green gap between the spot fire and force that's burning into Yaak, we might get to a place in the forest where their activity is less intense, right?" Shylo said.

"Exactly," Galterius said. "Given how much it rained, and the likelihood that these Engulfed are strictly wind-driven, the back side of the burn will be less active."

"You might be right. There's been a north wind for days. Without a Pyrignum the Volurem wouldn't have backburned into the wind. The only way for them to move is south, toward Yaak," Sandor said, pulling on the harquice as he started running again.

"Since the wind drives these Volurem, the spot fire in front of us will be most intense at its southern front, moving south," Shylo said.

"That's right," Galterius agreed.

"And because the wind is the primary influence in their direction, wouldn't the intensity be less on their flanks as well?" Shylo asked.

"In theory," Galterius said. "But the second Volurem force is already sending fire crowning into the trees.

Without a Pyrignum there won't be any Possessed, but I've seen an Engulfed grow to the size of one of those goliaths. The flanks of the Engulfed will be well established and potentially impenetrable."

"You've spent way too much time fighting in your precious brismil scale, Galterius," Sandor shouted over his shoulder. He angled to the left, running diagonally along the lead edge of the growing fire and toward the thin patch of darkness separating it from the spot fires of the Volurem force.

"If we can get to the rear flank of the spot fire before the main Volurem force closes the gap, maybe we'll be able to break through," Sandor said.

"We better hope the heel of the spot fire cleared creates a big enough safety zone when the front of the main Volurem force hits. Without brismil, the radiant head could still kill us," Galterius said.

"If it gets me my pay day," Sandor grumbled, doubling his speed and pulling the harquice to a gallop.

"We'll need to work together if we want this to work. Is that something you're capable of, Agunzi?" Galterius asked.

Sandor chanced a glare over his shoulder but didn't refuse.

"When we get close, I'll jump down from the harquice and lead with my brismil blade. Sandor, you follow on my heel and clear a swath wide enough for Shylo and the harquice to follow," Galterius ordered.

"I could help if you have an extra weapon," Shylo offered.

"And give you a chance to turn on us," Sandor said as he crashed through the forest like a charging lazgron.

"You wouldn't last long in those sandals," Galterius added.

"Ashes," Shylo cursed.

"Stay in the saddle. Harquice hooves are thick enough to walk on embers and their hide is tough enough to charge through low flames."

As the flames of the spot Volurem force shone through the trees and Galterius saw the front of the main fire burning closer to the rear of the spot fire, he wondered how quickly Sandor would turn on him once they made it to a safe zone. Sandor slowed the harquice to a trot. While following, Galterius wondered about the stout man's motivation. If it was money alone, Galterius still had a bargaining chip up his sleeve. Galterius saw how closely the man had been watching their earlier fight. A promise to take ownership of a brismil scale was something that might entice a bounty hunter or mercenary. Galterius tried to live honestly, but if it came down to this scenario, breaking a promise was something he was willing to do.

Sliding off the back of the harquice, Galterius quickly scouted his line of attack. The Volurem's main force now roared through the forest at an unstoppable pace. If they met much resistance at the rear flank of the spot fire, they would fry. He saw their best route. They had to punch through here.

"Hold," Galterius said, arriving at a cluster of trees and brush. He searched for a point in the forest where the Volurem were smaller and spaced out enough that two swordsmen could take them on.

Sandor and Shylo waited nervously as Galterius assessed the main Volurem front roaring through the timber.

Galterius noted the behavior of the Engulfed Volurem moving at the flank of the spot fire. They wandered slowly along the fringe of the green, weaving in and out along the edge of their burn. Their bodies were dark, like the black area of burned ground lightly smoldering beyond them. They were close enough that the trio by the trees could see their skin color shift, rolling from charcoal black to deep shades of red to match the embers at their feet. Most dragged their inky weapons on the ground while they slowly and methodically spread the fire, sprouting more Volurem between them. Beyond, where the spot fire had started, was a large area of black. It still smoldered, but not with the white-hot ash left in the wake of the fire's front. It appeared to be as Sandor predicted, this Volurem force did not seem to be accompanied by a Pyrignum.

"Sandor. Shylo. With me," Galterius whispered.

Sandor nodded, his steel great sword in one hand.

A draft of hot wind blew in from the north. The Volurem on the edge of the spot fire grew in size, now matching Galterius in height. He ran out at them. The pulse of wind couldn't have come at a better time. Though the flames of the Volurem grew, their attention turned south with the wind. Where a dozen would've come after them, now only five upwind Volurem could attack.

Galterius beat the first Engulfed to strike, hewing the flaming Ignis person with his brismil blade. His razor-sharp, dragon-bone blade passed clean through the Engulfed Volurem, severing it across the chest. The top half dropped in a pile of smoldering charcoal. Flames singed his hair and stung his cheeks, but Sandor was quickly at Galterius' side. The stout Agunzi-Rhydarian lopped the head clean off the second Volurem, producing the largest flames near Galterius.

Galterius glanced back to check on Shylo. He had hunched his head into the draco-scale surcoat as best he could and held onto the saddle.

Galterius continued cutting down more Volurem as

others behind the initial five came after them. Sandor followed on his heels, lopping off flaming Volurem limbs that Galterius wasn't able to properly address and returning them to the ashen ground. Breaking through the main flank, Galterius heard the roaring front of the main force reach the spot fire. The most intensely burning Engulfed Volurem could not veer off their course to attack these three. The wind pushed them on.

Galterius ran through the heat wave, hoping Sandor and Shylo were still behind him. Smaller Volurem smoldering in the burnt area tried to stop him, but his dragon fang slashed them before they could deliver a strike. Galterius felt relief; the heat no longer burned his face. He slowed so Sandor and Shylo could catch up. They watched the Volurem crowning through the forest, moving away from them. He'd used a strategy similar to how he and his legion fought a Volurem force. They'd start at the back and fight their way up the flanks, pinching off the Volurem at the front.

As the three here moved deeper into the burned area, Galterius noticed a new cast of Terra people lying in the wake of the burn. These were short, stunted figures akin to Rhydarians but colored a muted grey. He'd seen them before, but not so frequently or so recently after the burn. *Tarmigs?* he wondered. He knew Tarmigs were a race of people believed to have been the original native population in Tarmigan from which both Ignis and Terra people descended. *I have not noticed them like this before,* Galterius thought. He knew they could withstand fire without burning to death, as they were known to be enslaved to the Volurem and were often seen wandering the ashy battlegrounds after a fight with the Volurem.

They are slaves to these Volurem, but why are they here?

And how? he wondered, seeing them littered among the black ash of the fire, acting as if they were in a deep slumber. He muttered to himself, "You're safest in the black."

"What are those?" Shylo asked, pointing out one of the small, slender Tarmigs buried in a blanket of black ash.

"They aren't a threat to us," Sandor answered.

"How did they get here?" Shylo asked.

"They show themselves in the wake of almost every Volurem burn," Galterius said. "They're Tarmig; slaves to the Volurem."

"That's a Tarmig? I thought they were nearly extinct," Shylo gasped.

"In the Rhydarian Empire, yes. But in Volourium, they're abundant," Sandor answered.

The sight drew silence from the young man and Galterius as they continued deeper into the black. Galterius hadn't seen so many Tarmig so soon after a burn. He wondered if and how they were summoned. More disturbing to him was how they lay, unmoving in the wake of the burn. Their chests and backs lifted and fell with breath. Their bodies showed no sign of burns.

It's like they're in a deep sleep, Galterius thought.

Volurem, still smoldering in thick logs and broken stumps, attempted to lash out at the trio as they passed. The movements of these tail-end embers were slow. Galterius knew that without the strength offered by a Pyrignum, the Volurem in the burn moved slowly. Shylo's harquice spurred ahead, kicking its blunted hooves at the mini sprouting arms and heads among the coals. If the mare still had the boney spikes on her back legs, she could inflict serious damage to the dwindling Engulfed.

As they moved together, Galterius watched Sandor, expecting him to try and turn on him at any moment.

Galterius said nothing as he continued to lead them nearer to his battalion's encampment. They worked their way north through the black as the main fire merged into the spot fires near Yaak. Galterius hoped the other half of his battalion was still alive and somewhere near the north edge of the burn. If they could reach Galterius' guard, Sandor would have no choice but to surrender Shylo. Then Galterius could continue hunting for his brismil scale.

They arrived at a point in the burn where the Volurem were still actively burning along the banks of a creek. Galterius only stopped when he recognized a dip in the slope and the flat area where they'd established their camp. His battalion was not there.

He stood in the place where his two-hundred-and-fifty guards had set up tents. The only evidence of this sizeable encampment ever having been there was the odd steel blade or metal plate armor that now glowed in the ash. If any guards had survived the attack, they hadn't stuck around.

While the weight of this failure settled in, Galterius looked back toward the fire's leading edge. Between the blackened trees and field of ash littered with slumbering Tarmig, the Volurem continued to burn along the flanks and to the south. Without a forest to obstruct their view, Galterius could see the small walls of Yaak. The town glowed orange and red inside and out, as flames danced up over the rooftops. The smoke column rising into the sky was darkest there. He hoped the people had fled but doubted it. Galterius felt sick to his stomach, wondering if he could've changed the outcome and saved the town if he'd gone back with Isik.

NEW ARMOR

FOURTEEN DAYS AFTER THE EMPEROR'S DEATH

Jexsanna scored a hit on the Scaled One's thigh. This opening led to more opportunities for lethal blows. Had the Scaled One not been in the brismil plate, she would've achieved justice for the others like her and The Masters. Though she resented them, they had died in a bad way. The Scaled One stumbled from her barrage of swipes and stabs with the slight curve of her willow-leaf saber. Behind her someone shouted a warning and the man with the black dragon blade came at her. His heavy breathing giving away his position, though she was grateful for the warning, faded and unrecognizable as it was, lost in the howling wind surrounding them. She whirled to face

395

him, Galterius. Seeing the tip of his black sword stabbing at her core, she swatted it out of the way and sent him reeling.

Jexsanna didn't know why she couldn't bring herself to kill him. Galterius looked outwardly angry at her hesitation. She wanted to kill him and take his blade for herself. The High Commander asked her why she was doing this, but she couldn't answer. This was the man who Shylo was so petrified of. Killing him would be easy now, but he had a power around him of some sort. She sensed the elemental pull of his dragon blade toward the dragon scale worn by Bridger, the Scaled One. Jexsanna sensed both the Scaled One's dragon scale and High Commander's blade calling to her, driving her deepest desire to kill them both and claim them as her own.

In the fighting arena, The Masters had trained and tested her against both the scale and a dragon blade. Those did not have the same powerful element she sensed now. This feeling was only one of the contradictions that confused her about the Scaled One and the dark dragon blade. When she'd faced the Scaled One before, he had used the dragon blade, a different one that did not give off a primal attraction between the blade and scale armor or the desire for her to take the blade. Jexsanna remembered how fearful she'd felt when facing the Scaled One before. It gave her pause about claiming the brismil for herself. With the blade, all it took was one cut on her skin and she would've died from its magic. But now, the Scaled One didn't have the blade, or he wasn't using it.

She held back on her skill when fighting Galterius. He hit harder than the soldiers and guards she'd fought since escaping the arena. No doubt he drew his strength largely from his brismil blade. Whenever the black fang got close enough that she could block it from touching her skin with her saber, Jexsanna felt the sensation from within the blade overriding her fear of it. The closer it came to her, the more she desired to have it as her weapon. For some reason, she found herself pleading for The Masters to tell her that way of thinking was wrong, that she shouldn't think herself worthy of access to that type of power. As the fire of the Volurem burned closer, Jexsanna found herself torn between which she wanted more; to kill the Galterius, take his blade, and satisfy this primal instinct nagging at her, or to claim justice on the Scaled One. Given that he did not have a dragon blade, she knew she'd get an opening. The Scaled One fought better with a steel sword than he had before with the brismil blade. The Scaled One beat her once before, back when she was still fighting in the arena. But she had escaped him more recently when he took liberties with his magical protection. Those risks left openings, like the one she'd taken on the Scaled One in their second exchange, striking through a weakness in the armor at his neck.

Galterius taunted the Scaled One and attempted to get Jexsanna out of his way. She would not allow him to kill the Scaled One. He was not the High Commander's to kill. She would kill the Scaled One for taking the lives of everyone she'd known.

The Scaled One didn't oblige Galterius. Instead, pointing his index finger, he summoned the High Commander to follow. Then, surprisingly, the Scaled One turned toward the flaming Volurem front and ran.

Jexsanna watched him, torn by which she wanted more: the dragon blade or justice and to claim the scale. Before, she had feared the Scaled One. She purposely avoided exposing herself so close to his walled home. Now, though, out among the Volurem, where Jexsanna did her best work, she saw her chance to take him. As she made the choice, she heard Shylo's voice. He cried out to her, calling for her not to go. She decided that the voice was a figment of her imagination, like the one that warned her before, and the one telling her to take the dragon blade. Though she wanted to listen, take the blade, and return to Shylo, she had to use this one opportunity. She needed to kill the Scaled One. Jexsanna sprinted after the man in brismil plate, leaping through the gap between Volurem foot soldiers he'd created.

Bright yellow and orange flames surrounded her. Jexsanna darted between Engulfed Volurem, cutting through their burning limbs. Their behavior was not like that of the Possessed. They cycled back, relying on the energy of their flames to continue burning. They traveled without a Pyrignum, lacking the dragon heart needed to possess or restore them and make them intense beyond the normal flaming soldiers. As a result, Jexsanna wouldn't need to focus as much on their position. They could only be driven by the natural elements, although she noted that the fire at the front was most intense. She had never seen so many Engulfed Volurem in one place. The Masters had never put her up against a large fire in an arena with boundaries.

The Engulfed Volurem front, three lines deep, chewed through the fuels with greater intensity than their first line. Flames shot up from their bodies, climbing into the crown of the forest. They grew in size to that of the blue-and-green-skinned Zethrillians, but with the muscular girth and wide frame of the red-haired Agunzi. This third line spaced out wider than those in the first two lines but came at her with increased rage. Jexsanna dodged the first attack, ducking under an Engulfed's large glassy obsidian sword. She rolled through the fire, noticing that her tunic caught fire in the blaze. When she sprang to her feet, a second Engulfed, larger than the first, delivered a hammering blow. Jexsanna blocked with a cross guard but broke under the massive Engulfed's sword. Chips of obsidian shattered across her face, cutting her cheek and eyebrow before she deflected the blade to the ground at her side.

The first and a third Engulfed rushed her. Jexsanna sprang up into the flames, jumping into the air to contend with their height advantage. The first missed, stabbing its blade beneath her, where she'd been standing. Jexsanna used the flat of the Engulfed's blade as a steppingstone and launched herself into a backflip. As she did, she felt the rushing of the third Volurem's blade swipe at her back, catching in the hanging tail of her lazgron cloak. She heard the obsidian sword connect with the first Engulfed Volurem that attacked her. Rotating upside down through flames while she backflipped over its head, she saw the follow-through sparks shower to the side as the obsidian sword cut through one of its own. Landing in the fire around the Engulfed's feet, Jexsanna stabbed at the flaming giant, taking it in the back and ripping her saber out to the side. She spun to block another attack from the second, but its flames were carrying it on with the wind, charging to the front line.

The intensity of the fire lessened slightly. She worked her way through the Engulfed as they rushed past. Continuing her search for the Scaled One, she slew five Engulfed before the wind slowed and she spotted his metallic form in the fire. Jexsanna dodged her way through the Engulfed, noticing the trail of activity she was creating. Absent the wind driving them in one direction, the Volurem in the heart of the blaze could pursue her willingly. Suddenly those wandering the forest, dragging their weapons through the flames, turned their attention to her and followed.

When she neared the Scaled One, she found him hunkered down as if no longer wanting to face the fire. His draco-scale surcoat, worn over the brismil skin-like suit, was beginning to melt, the individual scales no longer identifiable as singular in their overlapping design. The Engulfed surrounding him struck with their obsidian weapons. Jexsanna saw several break their swords on his back as he crouched there, doing nothing to counter their attacks. Those who broke their blades slowly wandered off, dropping the useless handles in the ash.

This lack of effort confused Jexsanna, but it didn't stop her from advancing on him. She had almost reached the Engulfed surrounding him when he spotted her. Leaping to his feet, he faced Jexsanna. She wasn't sure if it was the size of the group of Volurem now following her, or the effect her uncovered body had on these people, like when Shylo saw her without the tunic, but he turned and ran. Jexsanna's leather lazgron cloak was the only clothing still weathering the flames. She chased after the Scaled One, enraged that he would not fight her. The group of Engulfed Volurem following them grew, and when Jexsanna glanced over her shoulder, she saw their size neared that of those at the front. If they caught up with her, she wouldn't be able to take them all.

Just then, the wind gusted in, carrying the sizable force of Engulfed through the burn to join the flaming front. Burnt trees snapped and crashed down into the flames, spreading smaller Volurem soldiers into Jexsanna's path. She cut through them and continued her pursuit until she found the Scaled One held up again. But not by Engulfed. They didn't seem to affect his survival in fire. Apparently, a gust of wind had broken a large salacee tree around its base. It'd fallen onto the Scaled One and temporarily pinned him. Before he could pull free, Jexsanna was on him.

She attacked through the Engulfed that had sprung to life around the burnt tree. These smaller Engulfed fell by the end of her steel saber. The Scaled One's expression was written across the fitted scales coating his face. His metallic eyes grew wide, and he pulled at his legs to free them from the weight of the massive tree. Jexsanna brought her blade down on him, connecting with the side of his neck. She placed the sharp edge of her steel saber between the crack of interlocking scales and slid it back. Where her sword dug through the last time she fought the Scaled One, now it simply sparked against the dragon scale. No blood showed between the cracks in the man's scale. Jexsanna frowned upon seeing her saber's edge dulled and bloodless. The Scaled One pulled one leg free. He grabbed his broadsword and swung it recklessly at her. She blocked, swatting it down and placing a second strike on the Scaled One's neck. This time she hit harder and pressed as hard as she could to cut through his brismil scale and draw blood, as she had before. It was then that she realized this was not the same chinked armor. He attacked her, forcing her to back into oncoming Engulfed. She fought them, having to swing her dulled saber harder to slice through them. She didn't understand why her sword would not cut through the chink in his armor.

While she fought off the Volurem around her, the Scaled One pulled free from the downed tree. A sickening feeling came over her as she added up her errors in this encounter. It was something Shylo had hinted at, but she hadn't wanted to consider as he lacked fighting experience. He seemed to believe that this Scaled One was not the same as the Scaled One she'd fought and run from before. Now she questioned whether she'd fought a different Scaled One back at the arena, the one who'd killed everyone in the arena but her. The idea was too upsetting. This had to be *The* Scaled One. He wore the same purple cloak. He had the same color armor and was the same height and build as before. She couldn't ignore the obvious though. He didn't have a bone-white brismil blade, and this scale had no fissure between the scales on his neck. If it did, her second strike would've drawn blood.

Jexsanna chased after him, the drive to claim this scale for herself dampening significantly and the need to make sure he was not the same one as before overriding her instincts. As she leapt over the downed tree, Jexsanna slew Engulfed. Embers and flames blew against her face as she charged into a headwind after the Scaled One. Whenever she got close enough to strike, he dodged, veering into a denser group of Engulfed.

Growing frustrated, she attempted to use the burning forest to her advantage. She kicked trees that were nearly burnt through at the base, trying to direct them into the Scaled One's path. The direction they'd fall was difficult to determine as the wind whipped around and pushed them to the side. Some fell where she intended, some didn't. Running deeper into the burn, she found the Engulfed Volurem decreased in size and numbers. Their activity largely focused on the leading edge and flanks of the fire.

Here, in the smoldering white ash pits of burnt tree trunks and scorched earth, Jexsanna faced the Scaled One again. She attacked with anger, crashing her willow-leaf saber into him as many times as she could, hoping to find a weakness in his armor. She noticed the man's fighting stance wasn't the same as that of the Scaled One she'd fought before. This one relied more on his stance and sword forms. The first time she'd fought the Scaled One, he'd done the same and Jexsanna lost to him. In her second encounter, she had been too focused on escaping and avoiding the brismil blade to at first notice his less precise form. She had unexpectedly landed the blow to his neck, resulting in an equally shocked reaction from him. This time, he did not react when she attacked at his neck. Instead, he went for his sword.

Jexsanna suddenly felt her confidence draining. The Scaled One began driving her back for the first time since she'd tested him earlier. Breaking away, she was distracted now by screaming. Among the voices, she thought she heard one that could be Shylo's. She turned to search for him, wondering if he had taken her advice and gone into the black. What she saw, though, wasn't what she'd expected. Along a creek bed among some green vegetation, a pocket of the draco-scaled guard similar to those in The Dirty Shame were being slain by Engulfed. The assailants' intensity wasn't so great that Jexsanna couldn't face it, but these men and women were unprepared. They dropped their steel blades before the Engulfed even reached them. Several shed their metal armor, their skin sticking to the hot surface before tossing them aside. She saw for herself what Shylo had been trying to tell her before. These people, the Rhydarians, weren't like her. They couldn't be in fire the way she could; like the others she'd trained with at the arena. They fell to ground, and the Engulfed consumed them.

When she turned back to the Scaled One, he was gone. Jexsanna looked in all directions, scanning the smoldering ground for any sign. She kicked something in the ash that glowed bright yellow. It wasn't an ember. It wasn't the same color. It wasn't a dragon heart either. This Volurem force was not traveling with a Pyrignum. Yet, its glow was familiar. Jexsanna reached into the pillowy white ash. She pulled out the round object that resembled a stone washed smooth by a river. It was a sunstone, still burning. Jexsanna glanced over her shoulder toward the Rhydarians. She noticed an absence of trees in the area where they'd probably camped. She had observed this behavior, their practice of camping in an opening near water. Jexsanna had learned how predictable their pattern was. This stone had been left on out in the forest near the camp. She wondered if any of these people had been foolish enough to leave it on in such a dangerous location – the middle of a forest that surrounded a town.

She clicked the butt end of her blade onto the sunstone to turn it off while noticing a large glow to the southeast ahead of the main fire. The spot fire was picking up intensity. The main fire had quadrupled in size. Soon their paths would merge, surrounding Yaak. The town walls were not tall enough to stop the Engulfed Volurem from jumping to town. Jexsanna dropped the now-dormant sunstone, hearing it thump onto something hollow and fleshy sounding. She looked down and was surprised that she hadn't noticed the creature before. Lying there, covered in black ash was a person, something that looked close enough to a person, she thought. It was small and slender. She brushed away the ash on its side, revealing a matt grey arm. The person didn't move, but the warmth coming from it suggested it was alive. She'd never seen this small grey person before. Jexsanna wondered where it came from and why it slept motionless in the ash. She straightened, peering across the black. Now she saw them, frequently spread across the burnt forest almost completely covered in ash.

None moved. All slept. Dismissing the oddity, she broke into a sprint, heading south toward the flaming front. She had to get through before it burned into Yaak. She had to protect Shylo. She didn't have time to explore the strange feelings she had, or the new sleeping people. Shylo was what mattered most.

"I've found a text from one of the Tarmig slaves wandering the ashfall. Seeing the woman with such a large text and nothing else immediately drew my eye. I've never heard of or met a literate Tarmig. When I attempted to take the text from her, she did not want to let go of it, but I believe this book has come into my presence by divine right. Whoever this devious creature stole it from must've been in close relation to the divinity here. I can think of no other explanation why this slave would possess such an elegant tome, for the Ignis or Tarmig people do not create literature. The language this book is written in is not of a Darian dialect I am familiar with. I've sent the text with a troop heading to the Fringe's nearest port. I hope to have a translation waiting for me when I return to Perdigon." – Sunspan 409, The Book of Volteir

ISIK

R ain showered onto Isik's hunched shoulders as she slouched in the saddle. Her feet dragged on the muddy path. Blood trailed from the holes worn through the tops of her thin leather boots. The tops of her feet hurt, but she lacked the energy to lift them off the ground. Isik listed toward the mare's neck, physically unable to raise her arms and catch herself. She fell forward, hitting her cheek on the back of the mare's skull. One of her burn blisters popped, mixing into the rainwater that dripped down her chin. Though her mind remained sharp with the increased oxygen in Old Rhydenar, she couldn't perform even the simplest physical task. Isik had gone too long without rest and food. Her body wasn't acclimated to this level of physical exertion. Not this far south. Her Zethrillian frame couldn't support the musculature required to sustain her efforts over the last day and a half.

Disappointed in her failing stamina, Isik toppled out of the saddle and onto the wet ground. Her harquice continued plodding along without her, towed on by its lead rope.

The Kai in front of her trotted for several strides before noticing his lost cargo. Slowing, Captain Bridger-Kai circled back. Isik watched the traitor from her back, wondering how the Captain could have enough confidence that he would risk using Isik as a bargaining chip. At least, that's the only rational explanation she could come up with for his capturing her and holding her as a hostage, although Isik's time in Perdigon had taught her that Rhydarians rarely acted rationally.

"Get up," Bridger demanded.

"I can't," Isik replied.

"I won't say it again," he insisted.

"Where are you taking me?" she asked for the hundredth time.

The New Rhydarian man narrowed his round eyes. Through his scowl she thought he looked like a younger Galterius-Brex, before he'd suffered the burns and scars from so many rotations spent fighting in the South. Bridger was taller, though, and it wasn't because of his longer curly black hair. He was more than the eighteen hands that his employer, Marxius Ovando-Kai, was. Bridger's lips weren't as thick as Galterius' either, she noted from the ground, but he was of similar build. Isik assumed that to be the lead guard at House Ovando, he would've had to serve in the South as well. He was stronger than most of the other guards and Isik knew she wouldn't be able to escape from him, no matter how well rested and fed she was.

So, she would have to talk her way out of whatever it was he had planned to do with her. Isik had pieced things together enough to know that Bridger's absence from the brigade and recent climb to Noble status was largely due to the young Emperor, Benton. She'd seen the letter from the Emperor summoning Bridger before Galterius found his scale on the Captain. The letter was written in Benton's hand. She knew it well after their time spent with the youthful Akai before her employment with Galterius. Combined with Galterius' actions in the face of the Volurem, it was obvious to her that Bridger was involved in Jermanus' death. She did not believe that he could've orchestrated the assassination. She understood Bridger's type, well-trained with a blade, strong, confident, and loyal to whoever offered the most coin, but not the brains of the operation. She guessed with significant confidence at where the Captain was taking her, and she would do everything in her bag of tricks to sway Bridger from dragging her back to Perdigon. Convincing a stubborn Rhydarian to listen to reason, however, was like trying to get a child to sit still. It was possible, but only for a short time.

"I don't think your loyalty to Benton will save you from what you're planning to do with me," she said in her deep voice.

"I told you to stop talking. You'll wrap your smart little brain into a knot," Bridger said.

"If you think you can blame this on Galterius and turn me in, offering me up as some kind of proof that I twisted the High Commander's mind into assassinating Jermanus, you're mistaken," she said, struggling to push herself up into a seated position.

"How do you know that I'm taking you to Perdigon?" Bridger asked.

"Why else would we be traveling north?" she asked in turn.

"To escape the Volurem on the only clear-cut path through the forest," he answered.

"With this rain, you could've crossed the road and taken me south, to your employers," Isik said.

He laughed, "You think I'd turn you over to the Agunzi rebels? How stupid do you think I am?"

"Stupid enough to get caught killing an Emperor," she responded flatly.

Bridger jumped down from his saddle. He crouched in the puddle next to Isik. She met his stare, the long side of her purple hair obstructing a portion of her view.

"Didn't you hear? House Didimo's responsible for Jermanus' death. Their guards were the ones caught by Galterius," he said.

"I never said Galterius caught you," Isik said.

Bridger held her gaze for a moment and said, "It's common knowledge by now. Everyone heard how the old Eso Commander failed to protect his Emperor when he needed him most. Galterius is nothing without his legion."

"Then why didn't you fight him?" Isik said.

"I did," Bridger said.

"If my math is correct, that's the second time you've run from him," she taunted.

"It doesn't matter now. He's dead," Bridger said.

"You don't have any proof of that," Isik said.

"When I found you, you were all alone. You were tapping your weak fists against Yaak's gate, but they weren't going to let you in. Even if they did hear you," he said.

"I should thank you, then, for saving my life, only to use me to cover your tracks."

"Don't act like you know what I'm doing. I know you can't read minds," Bridger said.

"I guess you are smarter than you look," Isik drolled on sarcastically.

"Get up. You've slowed me down too much as it is."

"Ah-ha. There it is again," Isik noised. Though she felt some strength returning, she still couldn't pick herself up off the ground. Isik wasn't used to feeling too weak to stand yet having her sharp mind fully awake. At times like this, her hyper-consciousness was maddening.

"Don't," he warned, pointing with his index finger knuckle at her.

"But how could I not? You said weren't going to tell me twice," she quipped.

"If you don't get up, I'll tie you to the harquice," he said.

"What are you in such a hurry for?" Isik asked.

When he straightened and looked up as if he was about to give up on her, she said, "Let me guess, you want to be the one to deliver the news of Galterius' failure? You'll ride in on your harquice, gleaming in Galterius' brismil scale, dragging me along as your war prize. You'll toss me down on the palace steps, claiming I was the brains behind the Emperor's assassination. Nobody would believe that

Galterius could've come up with the scheme on his own, so he employed me to help him. Without anyone from the guard to confirm the events in Yaak, you'll tell your new Emperor that we started the fire after you confronted him and told him you were sending word to the capital. You couldn't stop the blaze alone but managed to kill the traitor and take his brismil scale. Only then did you escape with me to confirm the fire's deadly grip. You'll say the assassins died along with everyone else, covering your tracks for good. Meanwhile, I'll be taken to the dungeons for the rest of my life? Do you really believe the Emperor and the Senate majority will go for that with a Zethrillian woman as your only proof?"

"You know, that's almost better than what I had in mind. No, your version does work better than telling them Galterius failed to kill the assassins and, being the skilled swordsman that I am, I bested the killers and exacted vengeance for Jermanus and his two heirs. I was going to blame the wideback Rhydarian from The Dirty Shame for coordinating the effort. I'd divulge that he was in Yaak to settle-up with the Didimo boy and assassins and receive his payment. After the dust settles on this tragedy, the war on the South will continue, giving a new Kai like me more time to fix my grip on Rhydarian power."

"So, you admit to killing Jermanus and his heirs and coming to Yaak to complete this plan?" Isik said.

Bridger shrugged.

"Maybe if you didn't have your head so far up Benton's ass you would've seen that your plan was already coming into fruition without your intervention here," she retorted.

The Captain scowled in confusion, clearly not following. "You were going to kill Galterius?" he asked.

"What? No! What purpose would that serve? He is my

employer... Never mind that. I mean, whether Galterius was successful in his search for your accomplices or not, your head of house, Marxius Ovando-Kai would've continued preparing to pass the blame of the assassination onto the South, cutting them out from the Empire. There's sure to be war among the Rhydarians and Agunzi again."

Bridger paused, thinking for a moment, then said, "If you saw this coming, then why not raise the issue with the Zethrillians? The Senators listen to their advice and would've heeded their warning to prevent the false claims, instead of allowing Galterius to search for lost possessions."

Isik at last confirmed what they'd been dancing around. Bridger *was* the one who killed Jermanus and stole Galterius' scale. Nobody but Galterius and Isik knew of his scale's absence. Galterius told her of Marxius' suspicions, but he wasn't the kind of man to offer such a prized possession to one of his own guard members. No matter how high-ranking or trusted he believed Bridger to be, when it came to a lost brismil scale between Rhydarians, loyalties dissolved into personal desire. But, however clever Bridger might think he is, Isik could tell he still didn't see the obvious. Isik refused to answer his question. If it ever got out that she told one of the Rhydarians what the Zethrillians had been trying to achieve for many rotations, she'd be killed by her own people. Besides, she'd become attached to Galterius and wanted to see him go on to lead a prosperous life, despite her people's attempts to thwart any expansion of the Rhydarian Empire.

"Don't answer," Bridger said after the silence. He hoisted her off the ground effortlessly. As he lifted her into the saddle and searched for some rope to strap her down, he added, "You've said enough."

"Why are you in such a rush to get me to Perdigon? You

haven't made sure everyone else was killed by the Engulfed. You have a scale. Don't pretend like you don't know I saw you using it," Isik said.

Bridger kept his wide jaw shut as he tied a section of rope from the binding already on her hands to the saddle horn. When he was finished, he said, "Now when you fall off, I'll drag you through the mud. The people of Perdigon love a spectacle."

Isik thought again about how best to wedge a seed of doubt into the Captain's mind. She wanted him to think he'd reached his own conclusion. That's the only way Isik saw him deviating from his plan to go to Perdigon and instead possibly let her go. After a short time on the trail again, she said, "Galterius knew his scale was in Yaak."

"How?" Bridger asked.

Isik smiled slightly. She had him nibbling at her bait. "He had a feeling."

Bridger didn't crack a smart remark as she expected. Suddenly she wasn't so sure this train of thought was the right way to convince him to abandon his goal of parading her into Perdigon. Bridger didn't look back at her, but after an uncomfortable silence he said, "I felt it, too."

Isik wondered if the residual magic drove Galterius' *feelings* about the brismil. Galterius thought he could hide things from Isik. She noticed how his *feelings* came to him after practicing his sword forms with the dragon fang. If Bridger felt the same thing leading Galterius to him, then he'd know if Galterius was still alive. "He won't stop coming for you," she said. "As long as he is alive, he will not stop hunting for that brismil scale."

"I heard your blunt honesty was why Galterius selected you out of all the advisors Jermanus offered him," Bridger said.

"Galterius selected me as his advisor because he believed I do not deceive," Isik said.

"I wonder what his reaction will be when he hears you saw this war in the south coming," Bridger said.

Isik heard his admission by speaking of Galterius in the present tense. She wondered if he'd said it to throw her off. She felt the raw spot on the top of her foot scrape across a rough stone. The pain momentarily distracted her, but she forced herself to ignore it and focus instead on the information she was gaining. "I wasn't going to admit this to you, but I never wanted to come on this hunt."

"That doesn't surprise me. Your kind is better suited to city limits where you can safely speculate about a world you've never seen."

"Wondering about the toll this Rhydarian gravity would take on me was my greatest fear of leaving the city. Galterius was determined to continue south," Isik said.

"Then why leave Perdigon? Is Galterius so incompetent without you that he can't look for a young man without his Zethrillian confidante?"

"At first I did it for the money," she said, looking ahead to see if her answer got a reaction.

The Captain perked up in his saddle.

"As I assume, since you seem to know so much about my relationship with the High Commander, that you know his wealth continued to increase even after he left his station in the South. The amount he was paying me was too great to decline," Isik said.

"What do I care what the Eso King does with his money?" Bridger said.

"But outweighing this fear of the gravity, I wondered how much faster my mind would work the farther south we rode. The allure of profound knowledge motivated me," she concluded.

"Your body would fail you. That's why the Zethrillians don't go beyond Perdigon," Bridger said.

"There are people from my country who serve as advisors as far south as the Fringe," she countered.

"And look what good their advice is doing," Bridger replied.

"Imagine what the Agunzi could do with a powerful mind of a Zethrillian leading them..." she trailed off.

Bridger didn't take her bait. Isik wondered if the South employed him at all. If he was allied with the Southerners, he would be taking her to them without any prompting.

"I expect that after you're done with me, you'll be after the brismil blade?" Isik said.

Bridger's hand drifted to his broadsword belted at his side, but he didn't respond.

"There are many legends of the powerful magic a brismil set can give a man. Have you ever read the old religious text that tells Tarmigan's story of origin?"

"The Dracolyth?" Bridger responded. "That book's ideals were disproven a century ago. Everybody knows the dragons didn't come back as the book foretold. The world is still here, and I've never seen a fire-breathing magic lizard with wings."

"Regardless of what any of us believe, at one time dragons existed in Tarmigan. Their remains are proof and the Dracolyth is the only record we have that chronicles their demise."

"That may be, but did you ever ask yourself who the author was? No Terra people of that time period were intelligent enough to write anything down."

"What they couldn't write, they drew on the walls of

their underground tunnels. And what they couldn't draw, they passed down through the generations verbally."

"Everyone knows how twisted a story spoken through many people can become. There's no truth to any of it," Bridger said.

"The brismil remains are proof. The dragons didn't break fangs, claws or spines in hunting the Terra people of that time. There was a war. Dragons fought dragons to the death, until none remained," Isik said.

"I chalk it up to territorial disputes and mating rituals," Bridger said.

"Many of the old faith believed that if a person were to possess the essence of a fallen dragon, they would acquire the powers of The Creators."

"The only dragon remains in existence that provide any proof of magic are the chunks of fractured fossils. Nobody ever finds anything of value on an entire skeleton. The magic dies with the dragon. They aren't coming back," Bridger stated flatly.

"Clearly you aren't a follower of the new religion. You haven't read, The Book of Volteir?" Isik asked.

"No, what do I need to read for? I make my living with my hands. Besides, I never cared much for fantasy. What I do and live is reality. I can see it and I can feel it," Bridger said.

"I thought you said you knew the Dracolyth," Isik asked.

"Simply because I chose not to read doesn't mean I can't. I grew up an Ai. I know how to read," Bridger said.

"Volteir claims the Dracolyth is wrong on many accounts, foremost that there weren't multiple Creators, only one that is omni-present. In his published book, he describes how The Creator's divine power showed itself to him," Isik said.

"If that's true, then why hasn't anyone claimed it for themselves?" Bridger asked.

"Volteir wrote that The Creator used dragons for a purpose in creating the Terra people. They left behind three main elements that prove the celestial power exists, or magic as we call it. Volteir believed he was chosen to bring the elements together and become a divinity. Many of his prophets believe he found the third element, which led to his ascension from this world."

"I know the legends of his ascension. It's a crock. Brismil's existence doesn't prove a man over a century ago turned into a god," Bridger said.

"Not turned into, ascended with," Isik corrected. "Did you know that there is proof of a second magical element? Only very few Rhydarians have been able to find it. And if we can believe the scholars who copied his records, no one but Volteir has come close to the third," Isik said.

"I don't care what kind of children's tale you spin at me. I'm not turning these harquice around," Bridger said.

"You can't tell me that now that you have a brismil scale in your possession, you haven't felt the magic trying to speak to you," Isik said.

"No. I've had this brismil scale for about a fortnight and I haven't felt one burning ember brighter about dragons, creators, or godly dead men," Bridger spat.

"But you felt the pull," Isik insisted.

He glanced over his shoulder at her. After a moment, he said, "That means nothing."

"I think there are elements of both that are true," Isik said. "Who's to say the brismil's calling isn't a sign the dragons are trying to return? And if they do some day, wouldn't you want to be better protected than with a single scale?"

"There's no way to prove the dragon scale I took from Galterius came from the same dragon as Galterius' blade," he said.

Without having to pry too hard, Isik had gotten him to confess to murdering the Emperor and stealing Galterius' scale. Yet she could not corral him into doing what she wanted, which was to turn back.

"Brismil blade and armor are rare enough to find in one person's possession, but a matching pair is worth a thousand times more. That value doesn't just arise from the ability to kill Volurem. The Nobles know there is truth in the old religion, despite how much they refute it to commoners."

"What are you trying to tell me, Isik? That I can believe you'd help me take Galterius' blade from him?" Bridger scoffed. "Let's pretend that everything you told me is true, all of it. Why would I risk my neck trying to take it from him again? With that white-haired monster out there and Galterius already dead or soon to die by a draco or spot Volurem fire, why would I risk the wealth this scale will bring me when I get to Perdigon?"

"Wearing the scale for too long is deadly," Isik warned. She now realized that she'd made an error in estimating how much Bridger would do for the blade.

"Oh, I've seen what the scale can do to a man. I spent my time in the South. I bet you haven't heard the rumor, that with a matching brismil set the disease takes over much faster."

Isik frowned.

"Let me put it this way," Bridger began. "I was promised a certain position in payment, and when a brismil scale fell into my lap during that effort, you better believe I took advantage of it. I'm going to get the most out of it that I can. What kind of businessman would I be if I didn't? But there's only so much I'm willing to risk to achieve wealth. I want to be around to enjoy it after I cash in. I made a decent effort to get the blade because, you're right, it does add value. But I'm not foolish enough to go back for it. I aimed to steal the capital but was given an upper-class villa. From where I'm sitting, what you're trying to get me to do isn't worth it. But I appreciate your effort to get out of this situation. I didn't intend to bring you back, but well, what can I say, I'm not a nice person. Nice people end up where you are. No offense."

"I misjudged you," Isik said.

"Most people do," Bridger smirked, then added, "you should've stayed in Perdigon."

"If wealth easily made is what you desire, I can pay you to let me go. I was not lying about the amount Galterius spends on me," Isik said.

"I have a hard time taking a bribe from someone who only had a few silver wedges in their coin purse," he said.

"I don't carry much on me," Isik replied.

Bridger turned in his saddle and said, "You said Galterius hired you because you wouldn't deceive him. How can I believe you have anything other than those two silver wedges? It's enough for a while, I'll grant you that, but it's no brismil scale."

"I said he believed I wouldn't deceive him. Galterius' money only buys so much of my loyalty. If death is where you intend to take me, then I will give you the wealth you desire," she said.

"How would you explain that to Galterius?"

"If he's alive," Isik said.

Bridger shrugged again.

Isik did not answer his question. She sensed this man was not as predictable as the deceitful Senators and the honorable Galterius-Brex. She could only hope that her words had some impact on the Captain's decision. She thought they did. He almost seemed swayed by what she said about the Dracolyth and Volteir.

They continued in silence, riding north toward Perdigon. Isik wondered what affect her time in the capital could do to disprove Bridger's story. She hoped the attention she paid the Akai and the loyalty she bought from the Esos would help her out of this situation. If it didn't, she would rot in the dungeons of Perdigon.

FROM AI TO KAI

A knock sounded on the wood-paneled door. Straightening in his chair at his desk in Perdigon's Senate Chamber, Marxius Ovando-Kai called out, "Come in."

One of Marxius' Medi trainees opened the door, and said, "Captain Bridger-Kai here to see you."

Marxius frowned, "Kai?"

His young female Medi nodded. "Should I send him in?"

"Go ahead," he said.

The man Marxius had selected to keep tabs on and follow Galterius to the bitter end entered his office. He no longer wore the lazgron-scale surcoat Marxius was accustomed to seeing him in. Now Bridger wore a draco-scale surcoat, slick with the morning's rain which highlighted recent gouges from battle. Most of the scales comprising the surcoat appeared to be melted together from prolonged exposure to extreme heat. Marxius' first instinct was theft. Bridger did not have a brismil scale to withstand such heat, though he did smell of wet coals. Marxius knew Bridger's background was in the military, though that didn't mean he was a good man; he could be capable of theft. The mention of Bridger being promoted to a Kai surprised Marxius since he had not sought such a promotion on behalf of his House Guard.

Though Bridger didn't have a single scar on his face, Marxius had seen the burn scars on his legs and torso several times. Bridger had seen hard fighting during his time served in the legions and perhaps was wearing his old uniform. Yet, however battered the draco surcoat was, Bridger's experience and skill with a sword were two reasons Marxius had promoted him to Captain over the other senior-ranking officers of his guard.

Marxius had noted that Bridger had a way of making the most of any opportunity, but knew when to hold back from the pitfalls of a major risk. It was this trait that had Marxius most concerned. Catching an unexpected glimpse of Bridger consulting with Benton in private led Marxius to his decision. The fact that he'd been promoted to Kai without Marxius' knowledge was worrisome as well. Bridger was too audacious for his own good. Marxius thought he had created the perfect solution to this challenge. Bridger was supposed to disappear with Galterius and the rest of those culled from the guards of Perdigon for this mission. Yet here he was.

"Why aren't you at Galterius' side?" Marxius said forcefully. He tried to sound as if he were scolding his daughter.

"You didn't see the column of smoke?" Bridger responded, surprised and self-assured.

Marxius planted both fists on his desk and leaned forward.

"What column of smoke?" he said, trying to keep his anger under control.

"The rain must've hit here first and blocked the City Guards' view of the Volurem force," Bridger replied.

"Why am I hearing this from you? Where are Galterius and the rest of the regulars?" Marxius demanded.

"The battalion burned or deserted," Bridger said.

"Tell me Galterius went down with them," Marxius said through clenched teeth.

"Honestly, I don't know where Galterius is. He could've escaped, but he didn't have his brismil scale."

"How do you know that?" Marxius asked, eyeing his surcoat suspiciously and wishing he could ask why Bridger was here in his office and not burnt to ash like the others. If he did, he risked others in the Capitol Building overhearing them. The door to his office remained ajar.

"He used his brismil blade, but ran after the regulars without his scale," Bridger answered.

"Galterius was pushing his luck in how often he wore the scale. Maybe he was saving it as a last resort," Marxius said.

"Trust me. Galterius does not have his brismil scale," Bridger said flatly.

"Am I the first person you've come to with this news?" Marxius asked in a hushed tone.

Bridger shook his head. "I went to the Palace first. I thought the Emperor would want to be the first to hear about Galterius' betrayal."

"Explain," Marxius said.

"Shortly after assigning the mission to Galterius, the Emperor asked me directly to watch the Eso High Commander," Bridger said.

"Something you were already charged to do by myself," Marxius stated.

"In the chain of command, his Imperial Majesty is supreme," Bridger said, leveling his gaze with Marxius'.

"Continue," Marxius commanded, inwardly concerned with his House Captain's behavior.

"While delegating Galterius' orders, I noticed the High Commander continually disappeared from the battalion for long periods of the day. After following his tracks away from the main search party, I discovered his reason for leaving. Galterius met with a cloaked individual. I wasn't sure what he was doing at first as he was walking with his brismil blade brandished but sheathed it when he and the hooded stranger met. I only saw them the one time, but I confronted the High Commander about it. He denied what I saw him doing. That night, I discovered a piece of parchment with a location and time written on it. The Dirty Shame at dusk in two spans. I didn't know what it meant until Galterius informed the group of a detour to a small town, Yaak. There we were to get the battalion food and drink at a saloon called, The Dirty Shame.

"To learn more, I went ahead of the battalion to Yaak and feigned drunkenness at the saloon so I could observe the goings on without being disturbed. First, I located a suspect, an Agunzi man. Shortly after, the cloaked individual I had seen meeting Galterius earlier and the Didimo boy entered. I waited until they sat together to discuss their treason before confronting him again. By then, the Zethrillian advisor, who was working with the Agunzi and Galterius, had already summoned the Engulfed. The Volurem were well established and burning before we knew what was happening. In the chaos of the fire and absence of Galterius' leadership, the fight was lost. I only managed to escape as I suspected the Zethrillian's involvement."

As Bridger-Kai wove this tale, the only aspect that sounded believable to Marxius was the acknowledgement of a common goal among the Zethril and the Agunzi to weaken the Rhydarian Empire.

When Bridger finished, Marxius said, "Your story is almost too convenient. It wraps up all of the suspects into such a tidy, neat package."

"That's how it happened," Bridger said.

"Did you tell all of this to the Emperor?" Marxius asked.

"A version, only what he needed to hear. You're the first to hear the whole piece from me," Bridger said. "His Imperial Majesty was at the Tourome Temple. The Magistrates told me you are now the one to deal with this kind of matter."

"Where is the Zethrillian woman?"

"Currently under Palace Guard and receiving medical attention for her burns. She'll be in a cell, awaiting Brism Court before nightfall," Bridger said.

"Did the Didimo boy perish in the fire?" Marxius asked.

"I don't see how he could've escaped the Engulfed," Bridger responded.

"Was he with the white-haired assassin?" Marxius asked.

"They met with the Agunzi and Galterius," Bridger said.

"That's not what I asked you, Captain."

"They were not together in the midst of the attack," Bridger said.

"How can you be sure?" Marxius demanded.

Bridger leveled his gaze at Marxius and said, "The white-haired assassin is the only one among them that I can be sure survived."

Marxius wondered if he knew what she was. Bridger claimed to have been away from the fire when it started, but it could've been possible that he'd seen the mutant running bare skinned through the flames like Marxius had back at the arena. Or Bridger was lying, and he had been there when the fire started. Either way, any guards that escaped the blaze would be lost in the forests now. Without the support of a large group, they'd be eaten. That meant only Bridger and the Zethrillian had reached the safety of the city walls. The mutant young woman, Galterius, and possibly the Didimo boy might've survived the Volurem; but only if they were working together, as Bridger suggested.

"How large of a Volurem force was present at the attack?" Marxius asked.

"By the time I noticed it, it must've been as long and as big as the Palace Courtyard and expanding," Bridger said.

"Where did you say the fire started?" Marxius asked.

"A small town called Yaak. It's a fairly new town, about two days' ride to the south, one if you're moving fast. The walls weren't big enough to stop the blaze."

"How did a fire that large start in this rain?" Marxius asked.

"You know how dry it's been. The Volurem could've sparked to life by any number of methods," Bridger said.

"Not this week. If Yaak is only a few spans' ride directly to the south, they'll have had the same weather that we've had. Was there a Pyrignum?"

"No."

Marxius studied Bridger's surcoat, "Were you wearing that in the fighting?"

Bridger brushed his hand over the melted scales, "No. I picked it up after the fact. Even in its damaged state, it's stronger than the lazgron scales."

Marxius didn't like the casual way in which Bridger stated taking a surcoat from a fellow Perdigon soldier. He knew there weren't very many of the guards who'd left with the heavy protection.

"There's no way a force of Engulfed grew to that size in this saturation without help. Unless someone left a sunstone on under a tree. There is no way this fire started naturally," Marxius argued.

"One of the guards could've left one on in camp before they split up to go into Yaak," Bridger now suggested.

Marxius chewed on the idea. It wasn't likely. Even the most inexperienced guard was aware of the grave danger of a sunstone if mishandled. Even within the city walls, sunstones were dangerous.

"Perhaps Isik the Zethrillian summoned the Volurem. After all, she was outside the town walls and she survived. Perhaps she left a sunstone under a tree," Bridger now added.

Marxius stared at him, studying the man who he'd made his Lead House Guard. Perhaps Bridger had learned too well from Marxius' example. "Why did my Medi call you 'Kai' just now?"

"At a time like this, it doesn't seem appropriate to discuss personnel matters," Bridger responded.

"When you left for this assignment, you were an Ai. How did you acquire land and a guard of your own while absent from Perdigon? I'm the one who pays you. You don't have that kind of money," Marxius questioned.

"I wasn't with the regulars the whole time they've been gone," Bridger admitted.

"Why not? You had orders," Marxius said.

"I received new orders to return to Perdigon for a short time," Bridger said.

"I didn't issue any follow-up orders. Who did you receive them from?" Marxius asked.

"The Emperor," Bridger stated firmly.

Marxius held any further questions. Not being included in the promotion of his own guard made him appear weak. If he wanted to retain some semblance of control, he needed to act as if the issue was of little consequence to him. He'd find out how the Sergeant gained a villa and a small armed guard after this meeting.

Pivoting away from this discussion, Marxius said, "A force of Volurem burning that intensely, after this much rain, and without a Pyrignum, does not go out in one or two spans. The rain we had today will knock it down but not out. It will smolder back to life if left unchecked."

"I heard all legions already had assignments," Bridger said.

"They have, not that it's your business, Kai," Marxius said. "There is a legion on patrol in the Apgar Forest. They will have to clean up this mess."

"Clean up what mess?" Emperor Benton Querci-Akai said as he pushed open Marxius' door without knocking.

Marxius cleared his throat as he stood up and said, "Your Imperial Majesty, I wasn't expecting you."

"Ovando, I thought I told you not to wage war without consulting me," Benton said, strolling into the office. "You should speak more softly when discussing matters of military strategy. You never know who's listening behind these doors."

Benton looked around the door to see who was standing in Marxius' office. "Bridger, just the man I was looking for," he said, pulling back the loose fabric of his dark blue toga and placing his hand on the newly named Kai's shoulder.

"Captain Bridger-Kai's return to Perdigon comes with both a development in hunting Jermanus' murderers and an issue our One Hundred and First Legion must immediately address," Marxius said.

"The rumor is true, then. Volurem are burning near Perdigon," Benton said.

"If what my Captain has reported is true, then I'm afraid so."

"I heard people talking. They saw the Zethrillian being hauled through the capital like a prisoner, hands bound and burns on her face. There's no stopping what the Nobles are gossiping about. And how embarrassing that my personal guard failed to see the urgency of the matter. They didn't dare disrupt me while I was communicating with The Creator at temple."

"I'm only just hearing of this for the first time," Marxius said, sensing an accusation in the Emperor's fretting. Something in what Benton said did not sit well with Marxius either. Tourome's Temple was one of the old religions that worshipped one of three Creators believed to have created Tarmigan.

"You heard there was a fire near Perdigon and you didn't send one of your people to alert me?" Benton said to Marxius.

"I was just —"

"Just what?" Benton snapped.

"Reviewing our options and preserving your best interests, your Imperial Majesty," Marxius said, not fully understanding where Benton's anger was coming from. "Or do you no longer desire my experience on military strategy?"

Benton visibly relaxed, letting go of his tight grip on Bridger's draco-scaled shoulder. "I believe your heart was in the right place, Ovando, but I'm afraid I'm going to have to ask you to leave this matter to me."

"Emperor?" Marxius asked.

"Did I not speak clearly? I will handle the appearance of Volurem in Apgar. Like you said, we have a legion close enough to get word to. I will take care of this mess before it gets out of hand. Now, excuse us. I have something I wish to discuss with Bridger."

Marxius forced his hanging jaw shut as he watched the young Emperor and the Captain of his House Guard leave the room, together. He waited for a moment, then went after them. If Benton was going to march on the Volurem in the Apgar Forest, Marxius was going to go with them. Especially given the possibility that the white-haired mutant and Galterius were still alive.

At the end of the corridor, he saw the duo descending the front steps of the building.

"High Commander Ovando-Kai," a passing Senator called out to him, hustling to get his attention.

Marxius ignored the woman, rushing through the rotunda between his office corridor and the exit. While the Senator called after him, Marxius stepped outside to see Benton and Bridger conversing. 'A group of the Emperor's armed guards escorted the duo across the street and into a carriage.

"Your Imperial Majesty," Marxius called after Benton. His announcement failed to reach them before they rode away. The Old Rhydarian female Senator's voice carried through the rotunda as she remained on Marxius' heels, spurring him to chase after the Emperor's carriage.

The Emperor's wagon ramped up the street and took the second right. Running up the damp gravel street, Marxius rounded the turn to see their carriage stop in front of Tourome's Temple. Marxius slowed as he approached the group of guards gathered on the stairs. Marxius recognized one of them as being a Lieutenant to a Third Class Kai's House Guard. The notion that Benton was poaching leading members of another Kai's guard didn't sit well with him.

"Hold it," the guard he recognized said.

Marxius glared disapprovingly at the guard's new cobalt-blue, Palace Guard surcoat. "Stand down, Lieutenant."

"The Emperor is in temple and requested that he not be disturbed under any circumstances."

"I'm your superior and the Imperial Majesty's right-hand man. I have a most urgent military matter to discuss with the Emperor. It can't wait," Marxius said.

"I know who you are, High Commander, but the Emperor gave me direct orders. He needs to be alone with The Creator right now."

"Cut the act, Lieutenant. I know he's in there with my House Captain. They just left my office and they didn't stop anywhere along the way."

"Can't let you in there," the guard said, putting his hand to the hilt of his sword.

"Bah," Marxius spat, turning to leave the temple.

He could hear both men's voices echoing in the empty temple, but he was too far removed to hear their words. Marxius stomped away from the temple, turning around the edge of the large stone structure. The temple had but one entrance. Marxius knew the Emperor's guard would remain stationed below the entrance at the front steps. He glanced up at the side of the rectangular building. Decorative columns lined the outside walls. Near the top just below the roof, the building was designed with gaps to allow natural light to flood in. Marxius thought about Benton's comments just after entering his office and had an idea. He waited until he couldn't see anyone passing on the street and slipped his hand into the leather pouch on his belt. His bare hand clutched his brismil scale, squeezing the fractured tip to complete his full body armor. He jumped easily onto the base of the column, fifteen hands from the ground, and slid into the gap between the wall and the roof. Placing his now-metallic ear to the wall, Marxius listened with his enhanced hearing.

Through the thick stone slab, their somewhat muffled voices sounded as though they were under water, but Marxius could just make out what they were saying.

"From what you've told me, it sounds like the plan went better than expected," the Emperor said.

"I told you, you could trust me," Bridger said.

"Trust is rare in Perdigon. It seems I'm surrounded by snakes. I can't be sure who is still loyal after what's happened," the Emperor said.

"The only things I trust are gold and silver," Bridger responded.

"Your due awaits you at your villa, Kai."

"Glad to hear it. It's been good business," Bridger replied.

"Did you see who started the fire?"

"I did. That's how I caught the Zethrillian. She burnt herself trying to escape the Volurem she conjured with her sunstone," Bridger said.

Marxius' leaned closer to the wall to hear the lie. The stone wall chipped; he had to remember his strength. The fragment of stone crumbled to his feet.

"The Council doesn't think I'm capable of handling anything on my own. Yet it was my maneuvering that got me this far. They don't even realize what I've done to get here," the Emperor said snidely.

"With all the rain, the Volurem will have been knocked down. You could lead a force to squash those Engulfed before Marxius gets the legionnaires on them. Maybe they'd respect you more, seeing you take a matter like this into your own hands. I know I would," Bridger suggested.

"I wouldn't need to if that damn Penti hadn't escaped," the Emperor said.

"I think it was your effort in planning your party that made the Advisory Council remain cool to you," Bridger commented.

Marxius waited to hear backlash. He knew if he spoke to Benton in that way, he would get a verbal lashing from the Akai.

"That is what I like about you, Bridger. You're blunt."

"Time is money, so I don't see the point in beating around the bush," he replied.

"I'll admit the party wasn't my best political move, but it won over the people. They love me more for it. You should see how they look at me when I travel through the streets. They look at me like I have ascended. Like I am The Creator reborn."

"Protecting the city against the largest Volurem army to burn this close to Perdigon in over fifty rotations is something an Akai ascended would do," Bridger said.

"And it would shut down those whispering snakes in the Senate. They would see that I wasn't given my position out of convenience. I am capable of handling my station."

"What should we do about the Zethrillian?" Bridger asked.

"I'll have her locked up in the dungeons and insist on delaying her trial," the Emperor answered.

"Why not kill her now?" Bridger asked.

"She may yet prove useful to me," the Emperor said. "As for the Eso High Commander, if he shows up alive, I'll put a price on his head and be done with this nonsense. Which reminds me, I have one other matter that Marxius and I need to deal with. Perhaps I'll have him accompany after all."

"Lovely sentiment and all, but if you're through with me, I'll be gone," Bridger said.

"Yes, leave. But Bridger, remember what my money bought you," the Emperor said.

Marxius did not hear Bridger reply, if he did before exiting the temple. He removed his hand from the brismil scale, letting his body return to normal. As he remained hidden between columns, he felt a sharp pain stinging his lower back. The sensation hit him the moment his brismil scale retracted. The blinding pain lasted a breath, then disappeared. He breathed heavily, mulling over the conversation he'd just heard. It was clear that the Kai signifier came with whatever Benton had paid Bridger to do. Ridding their world of Galterius and the Didimo boy wasn't worth that much effort. The way their mission had been designed, it would've failed without the Volurem intervention.

Emperor Benton's rapid rise to power suddenly didn't seem to be a happy accident. Marxius didn't see how he could interpret their private discussion any other way. Bridger was in Perdigon the night of the assassination. Benton clearly had established a relationship with him before they left to initially search for the escaped Penti. If Marxius was right, then Bridger had Galterius' scale. Suddenly Bridger's word about Galterius not having it and knowing the white-haired assassin was still alive made complete sense. The Zethrillian advisor, Isik, didn't start the fire, Bridger did.

MAJORITY RULES

"Halt," Galterius commanded.

Shylo froze, reacting to the High Commander's orders.

"I said, 'Stop!'" Galterius barked.

Shylo frowned. He wasn't moving. As instructed, he had frozen midway through his move to mount the harquice.

Sandor, however, strolled into view, walking away from Galterius. He didn't show any intention of adhering to Galterius' order. Sandor took up the lead rope, continuing to ignore the command.

"Get in the saddle," Sandor said, nodding at Shylo.

The sound of a brismil blade forming in the morning rain was barely audible, but Shylo heard it. Sandor hesitated. Shylo remained in limbo between the two orders, watching Sandor slowly shift his broad shoulders and thick neck to face the High Commander. After seeing the stout man heft his great sword to fell Engulfed Volurem with consistent heavy-handed swings, Shylo didn't know which one of the two men was more deadly: the more experienced High Commander with his brismil blade, or the younger, faster, stronger Agunzi-Rhydarian?

"Are you going to kill a fellow countryman with that blade, too?" Sandor asked, his wide grip cautiously drifting toward the two-handed broadsword at his side.

"I told you last night. Both of you are under arrest," Galterius said.

"You don't have the authority to bend the law, Eso. I captured the bounty legally and fairly," Sandor said, pushing on the handle of his great sword to lift the scabbard's tip from the ground, making it easier to draw. The blade was large on any Rhydarian, nearly reaching the ground when belted on, but on Sandor, the scabbard dragged through the wet ash.

"I was given an order by Emperor Benton Querci-Akai to bring him and any co-conspirators back to the capital," Galterius said.

"Co-conspirators," Sandor hummed. "You think I was with them at The Dirty Shame? That I'm bringing him south? Did you come to that conclusion because of the color of my eyes and the width of my back?"

"My opinion is not based on prejudice. Who are you to judge me so quickly? I was not the one to stand up and protect Jermanus' killers when I had them cornered at that table," Galterius said.

"This is why I refuse to fight alongside Imperials. You take your orders from a young man with no experience. Who is this, Benton? Some Akai who's never experienced what it's like to see a Volurem beyond the wall? At least Jermanus led his armies."

"There's more to leading an empire than having an emperor," Galterius said.

"It doesn't sit well with me that a young man with no experience and so recent to rule, can decide the fate of the people without any repercussions. He's been on the throne for less than a month and already the Volurem have cropped up this far north."

"Yet you're eager to take his coin for the reward," Galterius said, motioning at Shylo.

"How could I resist when something like this comes across my plate? Collecting bounties is what I do, Eso. But I never said I was taking him to your emperor. When a prize like this drops into my lap, I won't let it get away without a fight. You're not taking him. This only ends peacefully if we part ways now," Sandor said.

"He isn't going anywhere without me," Galterius said.

"What do you care who brings the Didimo boy in? You don't need the reward and he'll be in custody in Perdigon a month or two after I turn him over to the Southern Warden," Sandor said.

"This is not a negotiation. Step aside and disappear into the forest like those wandering Tarmigs, or we'll have a problem," Galterius said.

"Tell me, how much did your new Emperor pay for your loyalty?" Sandor asked.

Shylo expected Galterius to rush at him, but surprisingly the High Commander restrained himself.

"Over these last decades, you've put on quite a show for the rest of the Esos; making it into the capital and playing at being a politician. You might have them fooled, but I'm not buying it. No Eso gets the rewards of a Kai without getting his hands dirty," Sandor taunted.

Shylo had read everything he could find about Galterius-Brex. According to the literature, the man had gained wealth and status by serving admirably and even brilliantly at times in the Rhydarian Military. He had proven his loyalty to the Empire time and time again in battles against the Volurem. Shylo looked up to him. Like most Esos, he perceived Galterius to be superior in every way. Galterius broke the mold; he had proven that those who ruled the world, both politically and militarily, could rely on an Eso. Shylo thought of Galterius as a noble man, intelligent enough to work his way onto the Imperial Defense Committee, a station only held by Kai and Akai before him. Now, looking at the High Commander as a man in this setting, Shylo had a difficult time seeing how he was any different from Sandor or any other thug hoping to cash in on arresting Shylo for a reward. If Galterius simply wanted to see Shylo brought to justice, then Sandor was right. Why would he care if someone else brought him in?

Shylo couldn't believe Galterius' restraint. He was renowned for his hot temper on the battlefield. Somehow the High Commander held his stance, not responding but clearly glaring at Sandor.

When Galterius' darkening cheeks gave away his boiling rage, Sandor prodded one more time. "Never met anyone who lied about how they got their brismil. That's one way for an Emperor to leash a wild animal. We have a saying for it in the South, *bribed by brismil*."

Galterius snorted like an angry bull mongodo and jogged forward with his brismil blade in hand. Steel rang as Sandor drew his two-handed great sword.

Shylo understood that at least one of them would die if

the fight got underway, which would leave him that much more exposed and alone in the wilderness.

"Fire!" Shylo shouted, distracting the two men with one of the only words he knew would grab their undivided attention. Shylo pointed through the broken and charred remains of the forest, to where the Volurem continued to smolder at the edge of the burn. With nearly all the Tarmig slaves having awoken from the ash field and wandering into the forest, the only living sign of Volurem could be seen in the still-burning stumps and thick logs scattered across the fire scar. Small orange flames burned inside trees where the Volurem Engulfed hid from the rain. In places along the edge of the fire, enough rain made it through the canopy to slow the Engulfed, shrinking their size and intensity. At the edge of the burn, where Shylo had pointed, a small Volurem danced to life. It was hardly cause for concern as they stood surrounded by thick, black ash. Shylo used the distraction, rushing from the harquice and planting himself directly between the dueling men.

"Out of the way Didimo boy, the old timer and I have unfinished business," Sandor bellowed, seeing there were no Volurem active enough to warrant their concern.

"If an early death is what you desire, I will oblige. One way or another I'm taking the Didimo boy with me," Galterius said.

"My name is Shylo," he yelled again. "I might not look like I can take care of myself and clearly I'm not a physical match to pose a threat against a Noble Guard, but I escaped Perdigon on my own. Jexsanna and I have been evading your Imperial Guard for a fortnight. Even though she was the first to direct us into the black, I, too, contributed to the strategy that led us to safety. She burned in the fires last night and though I didn't know what it meant at the time, without Jexsanna and me, both of you would be dead too. Now, I demand your respect, at least enough to listen to my opinion."

"I'll agree with some of what you said. You two would've burned, like your crazy friend who ran into the leading edge of that fire without a brismil scale. Unfortunately for you, Shylo, we don't require your opinion for this matter. Your fate has already been decided. Who will pay and be paid for it is for me and Galterius to determine," Sandor said.

"Wrong. I am taking Shylo to Perdigon with or without you, Sandor," Galterius said.

"Will you give me a moment to say my piece?" Shylo shouted. "After I say this one thing, then you can go back to cutting each other into bits over me." Shylo held his position, shifting to stay between the two opposing men as they circled around a bit.

"If it brings this matter to a faster end, fine," Galterius said, dropping his brismil blade. It disappeared, returning to the dragon-bone scabbard on his belt

Sandor hesitated, his orange eyes shifting from Shylo to Galterius. After a long breath, he spun the great sword and planted the tip end down. He held onto the crossbar of his hilt with one hand, balancing it upright, the pommel level with his cleft chin. He gestured with his free hand for Shylo to continue.

"I already told you that I had nothing to do with the Emperor's murder, or the murder of his heirs, but somehow you think I did. Did either of you stop to consider how or why an Eso, a new member of the Penti class would do such a thing? I don't have any experience or training in fighting, let alone assassination. I'm well read, but not on that subject. I don't have any connections or true friends in Perdigon. Whoever did this would've had to have vast wealth to finance the murders. That or at least the power to commit promises worth risking being caught for killing the most important Rhydarians. For instance, bringing new people into power once they claimed independence from the Empire. Now ask yourselves, how could I have done any of that?

"I realized it the moment I recovered from the shock of seeing what had happened at House Didimo. They were set up, all those at the household. I only survived because of dumb luck. You should be looking for someone who had something to gain – power, wealth, I don't know. Find out who slaughtered House Didimo. It wasn't me and it wasn't Jexsanna. She only killed those guards to stop them from killing me! She was protecting me..." Shylo said, only stopping when he realized his emotions were causing him to ramble.

After taking a quick breath, Shylo steered himself back on topic, "What I mean to propose is this: obviously, we can't continue traveling together, and since I didn't have anything to do with these murders, we should all go our separate ways. Sandor, no offense but if Galterius scratches you with that blade, you're dead. Even if you killed him, he'd probably cut you in his dying moments.

"Galterius, you suffered massive losses before the rain returned. I don't see any sign that anyone survived. Would it be so difficult to say that I burned in the fire, too? You can go back to serving the Empire and focus on goals that are far more important than chasing me. Sandor can keep his life to hunt down another bounty. I can go free, back to Florens and live the life my father wishes of me. Nobody has to lose anything more."

"No," Sandor said flatly. "That's not the best scenario

for either of us. I don't care what proof or reasons you have for claiming your innocence. There's a price on your head and I plan to collect on it. If Galterius wants to part ways now, without violence, and head back to Perdigon, I'll take you to the South. The Southern Warden will pay just as much for you as the new Emperor. Galterius gets to live, and I get my money."

"Shylo, of course you didn't kill the Emperor or his sons," Galterius said in exasperation. "I knew that the day after the assassination. But you're the only surviving member of House Didimo, that's why they want to prosecute you and you have this price on your head. They needed a party to blame and Didimo was it.

"When you escaped, it only fueled their anger and suspicion. I saw the scene at House Didimo that morning. I'm not convinced Didimo had anything to do with the assassination. And I'm not placing the blame on the South either. The Southern Warden and I had an agreement. They wanted a deal with the Empire," Galterius said, shifting his steely gaze to Sandor.

"It was a Rhydarian who killed Jermanus," he continued. "I fought one of the killers that night, inside the Palace courtyard. In the exchange, he stole my brismil scale. Sandor, if you knew anything about a matching brismil pair, you'd know I didn't come to own my scale by bribery, as you suggest. I followed the attracting force in my dragon blade. It led me to my dragon scale. That's why I came into the saloon, and to your table. I knew someone there had my scale."

"The man fighting Jexsanna was wearing your brismil plate?" Shylo asked, knowing the man had a scale, but not of the theft behind acquiring it.

"Jexsanna. You keep mentioning her as if she were a

normal person. That monster cannot be a normal Rhydarian," Galterius said.

"She was a slave, not a monster," Shylo said, remembering what the group of Esos had gossiped about the morning he fled Perdigon. They'd said a monster was lurking in the forest. But Jexsanna wasn't a monster.

"No slave fights like that. No slave can move with the same speed as a trained Legionnaire wearing a brismil scale. I tried and couldn't even scratch the woman," Galterius said.

"Maybe you did and that's why she jumped into the flames," Sandor suggested.

"It doesn't matter now," Galterius said. "All that matters to me is my ability to prove House Ovando's betrayal."

"Ovando, not the Captain you were fighting?" Shylo said, surprised.

"They are one and the same. Captain Bridger-Kai is Ovando's Head Guard," Galterius answered. "And if you, Sandor, are truly a bounty hunter who was after Shylo and not there to meet Ovando's man, then we might have a common interest."

"House Ovando couldn't have organized the assassination," Shylo said, concluding that only the Captain of the Ovando House Guard could be at fault.

"Oh, like how House Didimo didn't?" Sandor said.

"Yes, Marxius Ovando-Kai wasn't in the capital and, therefore, couldn't have orchestrated the assassination. He'd been gone for months on the expected harvesting quota tour with Emperor Benton," Shylo said.

"The magic in my blade doesn't lie. Captain Bridger-Kai has my scale. There's no other way he could've gotten it unless he was associated with the murders," Galterius said.

"I didn't deny the Captain's role," Shylo said, remembering his interaction with Ismay outside the Didimo Villa. "I was with Marxius' daughter that night."

"Ismay?" Galterius asked in surprise.

"Like you, an Eso, could be friends with a Noble's daughter. He's lying through his teeth," Sandor said.

"Ismay Ovando-Kai is in the Penti training class. I didn't say we were friends," Shylo said, the healing wounds inflicted by Wilsall and his House Sarapio acting as a sobering reminder that he never had a true friend in Perdigon.

"Shylo's right. Ismay is in the Penti trainee class this rotation. I heard Marxius boast about her enough before he left to know Shylo speaks the truth. It's not a stretch to assume he would've spoken with her," Galterius said.

"I saw her right after I dropped off supplies at the Didimo Villa. I thought seeing Ismay there was strange because Ovando's villa is on the other side of Capitol Hill. I asked her what she was doing, and it seemed as if she was following someone. One of her father's men," Shylo said.

"That's speculation. The only hard proof is Shylo being alive," Sandor said.

"My scale is proof," Galterius said.

"Only your word can back that up. Maybe that Kai got the scale from someone else. You can't prove it's yours," Sandor said.

"I can, and I will," Galterius growled. "I'd be willing to bet Marxius' daughter knows something about it, too. I caught her snooping where she shouldn't have been before I was sent on this assignment. Shylo, come back to Perdigon with me and I'll help you. I can vouch for what happened at the Didimo Villa. Those people were killed before word of the assassination spread to the Kai."

"Yes. That's when I found them! Right *before* the bells started tolling. The whole household was already dead," Shylo said.

"Then they would've died before the Emperor was killed," Galterius reasoned.

"You believe that the Kai and Akai will listen to you?" Sandor said mockingly.

"What do you care about what happens to us? All you want is the reward," Galterius said.

"How do you expect me to collect the reward if you go to Perdigon?" Sandor responded.

"You said it yourself, the Emperor will pay as much as the Southern Warden for Shylo," Galterius said.

"They won't give a part-Agunzi stranger a reward for him. They'd lock me up with him and say I collaborated with the South in the assassination," Sandor said.

Shylo shook his head in frustration. They were getting nowhere with this arguing. He stomped his foot and said, "Enough! I'm not going back to Perdigon. If Galterius did clear me in the eyes of the court, no house would sponsor me in the trainee program anymore. Not after what's happened. There's nothing for me in Perdigon. I don't have any friends or family there."

"South it is," Sandor said.

"And I won't go with you either," Shylo said. "I don't want to go anywhere with you, Sandor. You're rude and indecent. I don't care what people are willing to pay for me. They'll just kill me or have me sent to others who will kill me. I'd rather die trying to escape from you."

"Fine. You don't have to be alive for me to collect my money," Sandor said in all seriousness.

"You would kill a potentially innocent person for a chest of coins?" Galterius asked.

"Unless you have something more to offer me than the price on his head, I'll just kill Shylo now and be on my way," Sandor said, taking up his blade again. As he did, he added, "No offense, Shylo. It's nothing personal. You understand."

"Fine, we'll do it your way," Galterius said, exposing his palms to show he wasn't going to try anything against Sandor.

"You're letting me take him?" Sandor asked.

"I won't leave Shylo, and I won't go with you to the South. I need him in Perdigon, alive," Galterius said.

"Unless you have a chest of coins buried nearby, I'm taking him South," Sandor said.

"I can offer you payment in exchange for the boy," Galterius countered.

"You don't have any money on you," Sandor said.

"Not enough to bribe you," Galterius agreed.

"Then, we don't have a deal," Sandor said.

"I can offer you something worth more than what you'd collect from the Southern Warden and the Emperor combined," Galterius said.

Sandor cracked a wide grin across his face. "You'd part with the dragon's blade for a boy you think might be innocent. He could be lying to us."

"It's not my place to decide if Shylo is innocent or guilty. I have faith in the Empire, and the court will decide his fate," Galterius said.

"Get to it already," Sandor said impatiently.

"How did you put it? That's right, bribed by brismil," Galterius said.

Sandor narrowed his vision, "If not the dragon blade, then a scale?"

Galterius nodded.

"You have two brismil scales?" Sandor asked.

"Only the one," Galterius replied.

"Let's say you did have it, why would you part with the scale and not the blade?" Sandor asked.

"You're aware of what a dragon scale does to the person who wears it, over time," Galterius said.

Sandor grinned again. "You don't want to die from the disease, like a proud Imperial soldier?"

"I have pushed the limits of wearing that scale. I am past my prime, beyond my fiftieth rotation. My days on the battlefield are limited. I would rather part from this world as burnt ash than from the magic rot brought on by wearing the scale," Galterius said.

"But you don't have the scale," Sandor said.

"I can find it again. If you help me. We know who has it and we can get from the Kai who stole it," Galterius said.

"Why don't I kill you now and take the blade? That's what you said. That it led you to the matching scale," Sandor said.

"It works both ways. The Kai with the scale will know you're coming. He'll be ready for you," Galterius explained.

"How do I know you're telling me the truth?" Sandor asked.

"You don't. You'll have to trust me," Galterius said.

Shylo forced his mouth closed to avoid disrupting this conversation. He was shocked most by Galterius' offer in exchange for Shylo's life, but also by the negotiating tactic Galterius had used on Sandor. Galterius wasn't simply a skilled military leader who won on the battlefield. Shylo wondered what the High Commander was hiding up his sleeve. Shylo questioned just how serious Galterius was about this offer.

Before Sandor could decide, a burnt tree with several Volurem huddled inside its hollow trunk crashed into the black. Shylo and the two men snapped to attention, blades at the ready. The Volurem Engulfed exploded from the burning tree, growing immediately in size with the sudden rush of oxygen. Galterius and Sandor moved to protect Shylo in case they rushed across the black at them, hoping to take hold, burning the nearest available fuel. They stopped when a flash of steel cut through the most distant Volurem Engulfed.

"Imperials," Sandor said, taking a step for the harquice.

"No," Galterius said, pointing at the downed tree.

Shylo's breath caught in his chest as he saw ash-white hair spinning from the head of a feminine figure. Her willow-leaf blade cut the Volurem down as they fled. One by one, she finished them off; the light drizzling rain slowly extinguished their smoldering remains. Shylo couldn't believe what he was seeing. He had watched Jexsanna run into the flaming front. He could see now that the tunic and undergarments she'd worn were gone. Her boots and a surprising amount of the lazgron cloak were all that remained. Somehow, though, the rest of her was unscathed.

Shylo saw the change in her expression as she spotted the three of them and ran through the hissing embers toward them.

As she drew near, Shylo saw burnt holes in her leather boots and cloak. He saw that the last several hands of the cloak's bottom hem were cut clean off. She was completely bare, cut and scratched from the fighting, but without a single burn. Even her hair was unsinged.

Jexsanna stopped two blade-lengths away from them. Shylo measured her with his gaze. The three men said nothing. For Shylo it wasn't the first time he'd seen her full body, but he could see the way the others looked at her was more than admiration of her physique and unique skin tone.

She'd been amid the Volurem, in scenarios hot enough to burn off most of her clothes. While anyone else would've perished in those conditions, she was still alive and seemingly fine.

"Jexsanna!" Shylo said, breaking the moment of awe. "How are you still here?"

"Me, how are you alive? I went to Yaak and it was on fire. I thought you'd died too," Jexsanna said, taking a step toward Shylo.

Shylo noticed the double-take she gave Galterius and Sandor before she remembered to wrap the lazgron cloak closed. It was shorter but still covered her.

"You ran into the fire," Shylo said, ignoring Galterius and Sandor and moving to embrace her. He held her tight, no longer understanding why he'd ever entertained the thought of leaving her as a desperate act of self-preservation. Just then, a chirp sounded from his surcoat pocket, startling them both.

Shylo had gotten so used to the lump in his coat, he'd almost forgotten that the borca was still with him. Shylo pulled Chirp out of his pocket and let the excited rodent bounce into Jexsanna's arms.

"How are you not burnt to ash?" Sandor asked, shattering the island of normality Shylo had felt briefly.

Jexsanna stepped in front of Shylo and flicked her willow-leaf saber to point at the two men. "Why aren't you?" she asked.

"Jexsanna, these two men did protect me. I would've burned without them," Shylo whispered, not wanting her to kill more people on his behalf.

"We cut our way through the heel of a spot fire. The Volurem here were small but still burnt our flesh," Galterius said, showing her the backside of his right hand where a bubbled blister had formed. "Shylo said it was your idea. Get to the black. We did and we survived, but only because there were no Pyrignum to send them in after us. The leading edge of the fire would've killed us had we done what you did. What are you?"

"I am like you," she said.

"You are not like us," Galterius responded quizzically. "I've never seen anyone with that color hair, or that strong of a skill set. How can you survive fire and be as fast and strong as brismil?"

"The Scaled One," she said, turning to Shylo. "He got away from me."

"Jexsanna, that's not the same person who killed your masters," Shylo said.

She nodded, "I know."

"Then why did you do that?" Shylo asked.

"What in the blazes, this isn't a reunion," Sandor interrupted. "I don't care how she's alive or why she wanted to kill the man with Galterius' brismil scale."

"You can drop the tough guy bounty hunter act, Sandor. I'm not your captive anymore," Shylo cut him off. "And if you think you can cut down Jexsanna, you have another thing coming. I've seen the way you fight."

"It's no act Didimo boy. And I thought I told you —"

"Sandor," Galterius barked. "You want that scale, then this is how you get it. I believe you saw her fighting me and the Kai. If you want to test her, go right ahead."

Begrudgingly, Sandor sheathed his sword, "What type of Terra are you anyway? I've never seen your tone before?"

"Or a Rhydarian with those eyes," Galterius said.

"She's from the far east," Shylo answered. "Whatever her culture was, she was trained to kill, and that's all you need to know."

"It seems you're in the majority," Galterius said to Shylo. "Whichever way the two of you decide to go, I will follow. With or without your approval."

"Better to keep the High Commander close," Sandor said. "That way, you know he can't bring in more Imperial forces."

"Don't think that because we're not going back to Perdigon that I forgot what you said about me, Sandor. You were prepared to kill me," Shylo said.

"I told you it wasn't personal," Sandor said.

"I take it that you want to come with us, too?" Shylo asked.

Sandor shrugged. "I'm not sticking around here to get strung up by the Imperials for starting this fire."

"Then I will not refuse an extra set of eyes for our journey south," Shylo said. "But we're not going south of Saypo." He saw apprehensive submission settle on both Sandor and Galterius' faces, wondering if he and Jexsanna really could trust them. *But what choice do we have?*

IVORY ROOM

Seventeen Days After the Emperor's Death

Palace guards stood watch outside the Ivory Room door. Marxius had never seen this level of protection inside the Palace before. The guard at the gate and several in the courtyard were usually all Emperor Benton required.

Marxius approached the Sergeants posted on either side of the bone-white door. They crossed their poleaxes, blocking Marxius from entering despite the letter Benton had sent to summon him. Marxius scowled as he looked down at the guards. The two simply shook their heads in response, motioning for him to back away.

He stepped back to stand in the hallway between the West Corridor and the Great Hall. Their usual meeting place, the Council Room, was directly behind him. Marxius stood with his hands clasped at his front for an uncomfortable amount of time. Finally, he asked, "Am I to wait here for his Imperial Majesty all day, or are you going to tell him I'm here?"

Marxius had heard nothing from the Akai the rest of the day following his meeting with Captain Bridger-Kai. Bridger, too, had failed to report when Marxius sent for him that evening.

Before the guard could knock on the Ivory Room door, the handle turned, and the door swung open. Benton exited. A young man Marxius instantly recognized, Juventius Odo-Kai, lay on the floor. Juventius, Benton's younger nephew by ten rotations, bled out, a pool of blood forming on the white marble floor. Marxius saw one of Benton's guards wiping the blood from his short sword before sheathing it. The two guards at the door entered. They picked up the young man by the ankles and wrists. Marxius had only ever seen Benton's younger nephew by Benton's mother's side. He'd learned that Benton's older brother had died of an illness shortly after Jermanus showed an interest in Benton's mother. Now, seeing this youth dying on the floor triggered a slew of questions, of which Marxius could guess at the answers. Likely, his nephew's mother had met the knife before her son. Clearly, Benton feared those who were eligible to succeed him as Emperor. Marxius didn't see any other reason the Emperor would have to kill an innocent family member.

As the guards carried Benton's nephew to the back of the room, a Sergeant posted at the entrance closed the door.

"Ovando, sorry for the wait. I was... dealing with a personal matter. One can never be sure which greedy snake will strike first."

Marxius steeled himself, trying to put what he'd just seen out of mind.

"You understand, don't you?" Benton said, flattening his expression and momentarily halting to wipe the blood from between his fingers.

"Of course. Imperial succession is not something to take lightly," Marxius replied. He thought about what it would take for him to remove one of his family members. The thought made him ill. Family was the only thing in Rhydenar that Marxius knew he could trust.

"Good," Benton said, now brushing casually at the blood on his robes. "Walk with me."

Marxius walked alongside Benton, the Palace Guard following at arm's length.

"There's a matter I wish to discuss with you," Benton said.

"Isn't it more prudent to talk in private?" Marxius asked, thinking of several topics that he and Benton could discuss, none of which should be overheard by anyone.

"We are in private," Benton insisted.

Marxius glanced at the guards behind them. They glared back at him.

"Don't worry about them," Benton said. "The only people I can trust now are those under my employ."

Marxius heard the backhanded insult but didn't say anything to further agitate the Emperor. He'd been careful while they were on the overland mission. But since returning to Perdigon, Benton's behavior had changed. He was becoming even more extreme.

"Very well, your Imperial Majesty," Marxius said.

"You've heard the expression, 'keep your friends close and enemies closer?'" Benton asked.

"Yes. I'm very familiar with the adage. However, it can

be trickier than the phrase suggests," Marxius replied, wondering if he was wise to have gone on the overland mission with Benton for that very reason.

"Which is exactly why I want you to accompany me as my personal guard on my campaign," Benton said, leading Marxius into the antechamber and toward the stairs. Benton slowed on the first step, turning to face Marxius at eye level.

"To the recent Volurem attack on the small town to the south?" Marxius asked.

"Yes. You will accompany me in my carriage as we march the best troops at our disposal to that town, Yaak," Benton said.

"Troops?" Marxius asked. "Wouldn't it be wise to take more than a few dozen soldiers? The Volurem blaze has gone uncontested for two spans now."

"Yes. Higher-quality fighters and fewer numbers will allow us to travel quickly to the burn. With all the rain we've had moving in that direction, the Volurem won't be very active. I have it on good authority that there are no Pyrignum with this fire. You don't need to do any organizing, Ovando. I've already assembled the best in Perdigon. We'll join the Hundred and First Legion at the battlefield and crush this force before it rages through Apgar. Then the people will truly see me as I am, their savior."

Marxius measured the Emperor before him, now clothed in blood-stained robes.

"Who have you asked to join us?" Marxius asked, not comfortable traveling overland into an active burn with troops he didn't personally select. Those among his own guard were mostly not ready to face the Volurem, even if it was only the Engulfed.

"Major Commander Noestriff and his personal guard,

the Palace Guard, and several members of my most loyal houses among the Senate," Benton said.

Marxius had confidence in Noestriff Landrich-Kai. He had experience serving as a Major Commander in charge of an entire Division in the Rhydarian Army. The others, he took issue with. He doubted the Palace Guard knew anything about battle formations and what to do when a Volurem front raged toward them.

"You will leave the capital in the hands of the Magistrates then?" Marxius said, thinking a step beyond their departure.

"No," Benton said. "I do not trust them to rule in my absence."

"Who will control the Senate in your stead?"

"No one. I will rule from the battlefield," Benton replied dismissively.

"This campaign could take longer than a few spans," Marxius said.

"Nonsense, Ovando. I thought you knew more about the Volurem. It is spring. We have the rain on our side. We will start in at the heel of the burn. When the Hundred and First joins us, the Volurem will be surrounded and extinguished before the new moon," Benton said.

"Perhaps I should stay in Perdigon and oversee the army. Without you in the capital, the Senate could take liberties they normally wouldn't. Our plans for the summer could be derailed. I'm sure some Senators are already trying to withdraw legions to protect their home cities after what's happened in Yaak," Marxius said.

"Ovando, I want you to be close to me. I already told you. The only people I can trust in Perdigon are those I can buy. Flash enough coin at the Senate and they'll ignore the cries for help and bring their close friends and family out of their hometowns to reside within the walls of Perdigon," Benton said.

"At least let me bring my guard. There are several who I would trust with my life in a fire fight," Marxius said.

"That won't be necessary. The men and women I have signed on are already assembling at the southern gate. There isn't time for you to gather your guard," Benton said.

"Not even Captain Bridger-Kai?" Marxius asked. He knew Benton could trust him. Bridger could be bought.

Benton cocked his head, his curled bangs shifting to the side of his face. "Bridger is needed in Perdigon."

"Your Imperial Majesty, Captain Bridger-Kai is the head of my guard," Marxius started.

"I think you'll find that my preparations are more than adequate for this campaign. You will accompany me in my coach. Be ready when I call for you at your villa," Benton said. He nodded to two guards to join them in the antechamber, the two who'd been carrying Benton's dead nephew. He jogged up the stairs toward his chambers. Two guards followed Benton while the two with bloodied hands escorted Marxius from the Palace.

Stepping up into the saddle, Marxius heeled his harquice through the Palace courtyard and out into the street. His yellow-eyed gaze instantly shot to a familiar form. Her tall figure on the back of a harquice, her thick, black hair braided out of her face ended just below her shoulders.

"Ismay," he said with surprise as she rode through the first intersection to join him. "What are you doing at the Palace? Shouldn't you be running something for Senator Basaldo-Kai's advisor? The Senate is still in session."

"Father," Ismay said. "We need to talk."

"I should think so. Does Basaldo's Zethrillian know

you're not in the balcony right now? We went over this before. Because you are a Kai does not mean you can shirk your Penti responsibilities. Another mark against you and your position in the Penti cohort could be brought into question," Marxius said.

"Please, my record with the Penti instructors is above the curve. They will let one instance of absence slide. This is more important than my responsibilities as a Penti," Ismay said.

"What could possibly be —"

"It's about why you came back to Perdigon two spans later than you said you would in your last letter," Ismay said.

Marxius quickly surveyed the Nobles and Minor Nobles who might be within earshot. There were too many pedestrians on this busy street near the Palace. If Ismay knew more than she should about what they'd done on their detour, Marxius couldn't risk anyone overhearing. As Benton had said, the people he could trust in Perdigon were running thin.

"Can it wait until we're at our villa?" Marxius said, trying to project a casual demeanor to anyone who may have overheard their conversation thus far.

"I would prefer it," Ismay said.

The rest of the trot back to the Ovando Villa was filled with polite nods to passersby, awkward silence, and a growing paranoia about what his daughter might have to say. Once home inside the purple gates, Marxius ordered the courtyard emptied of slaves, servants, and guards. When he was certain they were alone in the garden near the water fountain, Marxius said, "Tell me what you think you know." Studying her, Marxius could see she was nervous. Like her mother, beads of sweat formed near her temples and she swallowed more than was natural.

"What did you do when you and Benton left your itinerary that resulted in your return being two spans delayed?" she asked.

Marxius used the excuse Benton had told them all to say in the event that anyone asked this question. "We traveled north a day's ride to check on the mining operation in the Shield Mountains. Benton had received a request from Emperor Jermanus to gauge their progress," Marxius said.

"You visited a mine?" Ismay asked.

"Ismay, I don't have time for this line of questioning. The Emperor has decided I must guard him on his campaign to Yaak," Marxius said.

"Would mother believe your lie?" she asked straight-faced.

Marxius sagged slightly, "Your mother isn't here."

"Maybe she wouldn't have left if you told the truth more often," Ismay said.

"This has nothing to do with why your mother and I separated," Marxius said.

"At first, I thought it was strange that you wanted to go with Benton on this overland supply mission. But seeing how it all ended up for you, I can see the genius of your maneuvering," she said.

"I did not know what benefit getting closer to Benton would serve when I left for the supply mission," Marxius said.

Ismay studied him, the sweat now rolling down her slightly rounded jawline.

Marxius admired the confidence she displayed, though he could tell she was intimidated by him. She would make a fine Senator one day.

"I saw the column of smoke," she said.

Marxius absentmindedly touched the scab still healing on his neck.

"You were there. That's how you got the cut," she said, pointing to his neck as he quickly withdrew his hand.

"Ismay, it's not what it seems," he said.

"I followed Bridger that night. The correspondence you had delivered to him in secret, was it about the mine as you claim, or the money?" she asked.

Marxius frowned, not understanding what correspondence she meant. "I sent word to announce our delay, but that was all. I did not direct Captain Bridger to do anything," he said.

"Is this why Jermanus was killed? Over the money?" she asked.

"Jermanus' mine was a massive failure. There was no profit coming from it," Marxius said.

"I'm only bringing this to you first out of courtesy because we're family. I know there are others in Perdigon who knew about the mine. And a Zethrillian, too. I recognized her signature," Ismay said.

"What... How do you know this?" he asked, feeling mostly in the dark about what Ismay was inferring.

"I thought that would surprise you. After you left, I started paying closer attention to the people entering and leaving Capitol Hill. It didn't take long to figure out which of those in carts laden with chests were leaving with payment for Jermanus' mining operation."

"How did you know he had developed a mine? Jermanus kept it a secret. Very few people knew about it. I only learned shortly before we detoured to it," he said.

"It's really not that hard to learn which advisors are paying Esos to hear rumors," she said.

"But you're not an Eso," Marxius said.

"I don't need to be. You taught me better than to stoop as low to spread rumors," Ismay said.

"You learned there was a mine by deciphering rumors from a Zethrillian?" he asked, confused as to what she was suggesting.

"No, I knew there was something to be learned when I saw a Zethrillian advisor walking around the port, talking to Esos and handing them coinage out of charity. You were the one who told me a Zethrillian does not give money away because of charity. No, I heard there was a mine because I followed men carrying chests of coin from Capitol Hill to the port. After seeing the Zethrillian and putting two-and-two together, it wasn't that difficult to determine this was not an ordinary expense."

"And you overheard them talking about the mine?" he asked.

"Not exactly. They told me after inviting me on their ship," she said.

"Ismay. You don't know who those men are. You could've been assaulted," Marxius scolded.

"Why should I worry, when my father is off playing the field with the Emperor-to-be?" she said with a bit of sarcasm.

"Now you're showing off. Stop it. Get to the point," Marxius said. She was beginning to get too comfortable in knowing she had leverage. Her nervous habits had disappeared.

"Once I knew the ship, I watched for it. Once I knew which messengers were going to the ship, I paid them," she said, pulling the bag of scrolls over her shoulder so she could open it. Until now, he'd assumed they were for the

Senate as she was supposed to be in training. She pulled one out and handed it to Marxius.

Marxius opened it and skimmed the letter. It was signed in Jermanus' hand. He'd been careful not to use exact terms in discussing what he was paying the soldiers at the hidden training facility to do, but he'd made an error in labeling the units. Instead of attaching a weight measurement, he'd used the mutants' numbers. One sentence stated that Number 2841 showed promise but needed more effort to keep stable. Another mentioned Number 2331 as being too dangerous to handle after how it ended with Number 2759. Marxius rolled the scroll and handed it back to her.

"Precious metals are not identified in this way. Nor are they talked about as if they are experiments," Ismay said.

"We didn't detour to a mine," Marxius admitted.

"No. What is it that Jermanus was investing so much money in and using the Hundred and First to shuttle to the Southern Fringe?" she asked.

Marxius frowned. He hadn't known about the facility before Benton ordered him to execute the mutants and their masters. He didn't know what kind of plans the Emperor had for them. "What was being done at that facility is no longer of concern to the Empire," he said.

"I know. You burned it down with the Volurem and killed them after they destroyed the substance," Ismay said.

"The substance?" Marxius asked.

"Whatever was in the vials that the Hundred and First Legion was smuggling," Ismay said.

Marxius shook his head in confusion.

"You don't know about it?" she asked.

"I knew about the substance. That's why we were there. To destroy it," Marxius said.

"Does Bridger know? Is that why he's being paid by Benton?" Ismay asked.

"How do you know what Bridger's been up to?" he asked.

"The night of the fire, before Jermanus died. I told you I followed him. Bridger went to the North Gate," she said.

"He passed a message on?" Marxius asked.

"No, he accepted one. I thought it was from you?" Ismay said.

"Ismay, listen to me. Forget what you know about the mine," Marxius said.

"What? No! I can't. There's something going on here," Ismay said.

"Ismay. Forget it. This is more dangerous than you realize," he said.

"But I found leverage. You can use this information to keep our allies closer and our enemies in check," Ismay said.

"You still have so much to learn," Marxius said.

Without a knock, the front gate opened. Marxius heard a harquice trot into the courtyard. Out of sight from the gate, Marxius pulled his daughter closer. In a whisper he said, "You must not tell anyone about this. Do not trust anyone but me with this information you have discovered. If you try to use it as leverage against someone, House Ovando could meet its end." He let go of her arm and straightened his lazgron leather surcoat.

Striding out of the garden, he went to greet whoever had entered unannounced. Expecting to see a Palace Guard, Marxius stopped when he saw Bridger seated in the saddle, wearing new lazgron leather and a white cloak.

"Bridger, why the change of uniform?" Marxius asked.

"You won't be seeing me in purple anymore, Marxius," he said.

Marxius cringed. A few spans ago, the man was a Minor Noble. He didn't have the station in life to be calling him by name without the Kai signifier. "I did not dismiss you from duty," he said.

"No, you didn't. But I don't need to work for you anymore," Bridger stated coolly.

"We have a contract. That is binding until your time has been served," Marxius said.

"You mean this contract," Bridger said, pulling a handful of torn paper from his pocket. He threw it on the ground at Marxius' feet. "I had the Emperor annul it for us. I'm not yours to command anymore."

"You'll regret this, Bridger," Marxius said as the man steered his harquice around toward the gate.

"I don't think I will," he said, and trotted through, leaving the purple wooden gate open.

Marxius closed it before ordering his guard to have House Ovando resume their duties. Ismay's discovery of what Jermanus was doing in funneling Imperial Treasury funds into his *mine* wasn't a well-kept secret. Even Galterius had figured out that Jermanus wasn't operating a mine when no ore was produced. What was troubling was how Ismay had said there was a Zethrillian signature that she recognized in the letters she'd bribed off messengers from the Palace. That meant that Jermanus hadn't been acting on his own and had kept the details of these activities with a Zethril statesperson. Marxius understood how some Zethrillians thought they could control the Rhydarian Empire. Perhaps they were more successful than Marxius believed. Even more troubling was Ismay's confirmation about Bridger. Marxius had no doubt that the letter Bridger received that night was the signal from Benton to kill Jermanus. Why Bridger thought he was untouchable now, wasn't clear. The idea that he'd drawn public attention by capturing and arresting Galterius' advisor, and then lied to Benton left Marxius more wary of Bridger than anyone. Even Benton.

Gathering his clothing and weapons for the campaign, Marxius ordered the next person among his guard most suitable and trustworthy, if there was such a quality, to protect his house and his daughter while he was away. She entered his chambers, standing tall and anticipating his order.

"Congratulations, Noxon, you've just been promoted to Captain," Marxius said.

Noxon, an Old Rhydarian woman with slightly rounded facial features, choked while inhaling.

Before she could clear her throat and respond properly, Marxius said, "Sorry to be so informal. The Emperor is expecting me any moment."

"Yes, High Commander," she said in a higher register than Marxius anticipated.

"You're Head Guard now. Which makes you Captain Noxon," Marxius said.

"High Commander, it's my honor," she said.

"Get yourself a chevron for that uniform and let the others know. I've signed your contract. It's there on the table," he said, pointing to a scroll.

"Right away," she said, moving to the table and signing the scroll.

"I have an assignment for you," Marxius added.

"I won't let you down, High Commander," she said.

"I need you to kill Bridger-Kai," he said.

"Excuse me?" Noxon nearly choked.

"The man who used to have your position. He broke a contract with me. I need you to kill him while I'm on this campaign with the Emperor," Marxius said. When she didn't verbally confirm the order, as she had the others he'd said earlier, Marxius said, "Do I need to find a new Head Guard before I leave?"

"No, High Commander. Consider the task done. I will take care of it," she said.

"Good," Marxius said.

There was a knock at the chamber opening and a New Rhydarian servant entered. "His Imperial Majesty, Benton Querci-Akai is waiting outside for you."

Marxius ordered the man to bring his campaign clothing and gear to the coach. Before he left his chambers, he again addressed his new Head Guard, "One more thing, Noxon."

"Yes, High Commander," she replied.

"Have someone watch my daughter. Lately she's been spending time with a crowd that has a negative influence on her. I want to make sure she doesn't get into any trouble while I'm away," Marxius said.

"Yes, High Commander," she responded, visibly relieved to have this assignment.

When Marxius brought his brismil blade with him to the harquice-drawn coach, he saw that the Emperor wasn't there. When he glanced at the driver in confusion, the man nodded up the street. Marxius followed his direction to see Benton talking to Bridger. Marxius gritted his teeth and climbed into the cab. Closing the door and drawing the shade, he settled onto the padded bench seat. Across from him, where Benton had been seated before exiting, lay a simply designed, aged book. It was open, placed face down with the spine creased along its length.

The young man can't place a marker? Marxius thought, faulting the Emperor for the lack of care he used to preserve a rustic book like that. The cover was made of a hard-backed material and wrapped in black leather.

As he waited impatiently for Benton to return, Marxius took up the book. Keeping his index finger on the page where the Emperor had been reading, he examined the cover. It had no title. No description on the back. Even the spine was bare.

Is this a journal? he wondered, flipping it open to Benton's page.

The text was written in the hand of someone not trained for publishing. Marxius didn't recognize it as the Emperor's handwriting, nor did he see anything to write with in the cab. Marxius read the top line of the page Benton was on.

"Today I explored a Tarmig tunnel. The carvings in the wall depicted what I have long suspected from the dead dragons. The image showed a dragon, its head removed and carried off by a second dragon flying away. Beneath the dying dragon, droplets of its blood soaked through the ground. The blood formed a pool, or what I interpreted as a pool deep under the surface. At the pool's edge, a flaming person, a Pyrignum I believe it was, because of the flaming heart in its hand, is shown pouring something into its mouth. Perhaps the pool of dragon blood? Next to this scene on the cave wall, was a second drawing of a large person with fire and lines that suggest a beaming essence being emitted by the figure."

Marxius looked away from the page. He held the place with his finger again and went back to the cover. He flipped through the first several pages. On the third page, written at the top was, "Volteir's Book. Sunspan 1."

Benton's voice outside the coach sounded as he thanked a passerby in the street. Marxius placed the journal back on the opposite bench as it had been. He attempted to collect himself in anticipation of seeing Benton. Marxius knew of the Book of Volteir; edited copies were available to Nobles in the Capitol Hill Library. But this, this was the actual Book of Volteir. As far as Marxius knew, nobody but the select members of the new religion had read it. And Benton had casually left it sitting open on the bench seat of his coach.

The door opened and Benton climbed inside, rapping his knuckles on the wall behind the driver's seat. The coach lurched into motion and Benton picked up the book. He resumed reading as if Marxius weren't there. After a moment, Benton looked up and said, "Aren't you going to ask me what I'm reading?"

"What are you reading?" Marxius asked.

"It's an account of a man who discovered the foundation of the new religion. Perhaps you've heard of him, Volteir?" Benton said.

"Yes, I'm familiar," Marxius said.

"Are you a religious man, Ovando?" Benton asked.

"Not particularly," Marxius answered.

"Must be your Zethril ancestry that kept you from temple," Benton said dismissively.

Marxius instantly felt all the resentment and loathing that had been building up within him over months spent on the road with this self-righteous Akai return in a single breath.

"The people think I am their savior. They believe I'm The Creator returned to Rhydenar in Terra form to cleanse this world," Benton said.

Marxius studied the young man seated across from him. As far as Marxius could tell, Benton believed what he was saying, though the things Marxius had heard about Benton from other Nobles were not comments that likened him to a god. "Is that so?" he said, feeling that some response was necessary.

"Once they see me return from crushing the Volurem that are burning so close to their homes, I will ascend," Benton said.

Marxius didn't know what he meant by ascending and didn't care to find out. He ignored the comment and thought to himself, *How did this young man have the mind to pull off what he did? How did this inexperienced Akai, who failed at his uncle's every teaching, have the sense to assassinate him and his heirs while outside the city, and have everyone involved get away with it?*

The visual of Benton wiping his nephew's blood on his white robes returned, yet Marxius failed to comprehend who this person was. Earlier in the day, he'd openly and flagrantly killed one of his potential successors, just a young man. Marxius didn't understand how Benton could've pulled off what he had with Bridger over the course of half a rotation and in the next fortnight openly kill a member of his own family. Marxius knew now that there had to be more to this man than he saw at present, he just didn't know what.

"As the dying dragons' magic collected in the soil throughout Tourome's equatorial lands, gravity there intensified." – The Dracolyth

TO ASH

Shylo stood on the road and watched Jexsanna as she scaled the crack forming between the stone gate and the wall. Seeing the smooth stone now charred black and stained from the Volurem left him questioning whether he would've been safer had he stayed in Yaak. The crackling sound coming from the burnt-out tree stumps surrounding the town would've given Shylo a start only two days before. He understood now that the Engulfed wouldn't risk coming out of their stumps and into the rain without adequate fuel to sustain them. His unusual party was safe as long as they remained in the black.

Shylo glanced at the Volurem inside the stump nearest the road. It crawled from the splintered, burnt opening at the tree's base, searching for something to burn. The black-and-red glowing figure emerged from the hollow tree trunk from the waist up, feeling in all directions, clawing, and striking out with its inky black blade. The rain hissed off its body as the water shrank the creature, sending it recoiling once again into the smoldering stump.

At Yaak's gated entrance, Jexsanna fitted her toes into a narrow gap, and sprang upward with supernatural agility. Shylo caught a fleeting glimpse as she spring-boarded over the top of the wall, knowing none of them could've replicated her movements. The gate cracked, metal chains clinking while Jexsanna opened it.

Shylo led the harquice behind Sandor, Galterius bringing up the rear. For some reason Shylo trusted Galterius more than Sandor, even though Galterius had the more deadly weapon between the two men who wanted to turn him in. At least the High Commander proved that he was determined to keep Shylo alive.

Seeing smoke rising from the rubble through the open gate, Shylo felt that he, too, should be armed. He didn't have a weapon. His draco-scale surcoat offered some protection, but Shylo needed a blade to feel comfortable moving forward with this group. Not knowing how to use it was less important to him than the confidence it would bring. Shylo was beginning to understand that in his present company, a person with a sword demanded respect. And right now, he needed some respect from Sandor and Galterius.

Passing through the double-wide gate, Shylo instantly sensed the horror of what had occurred in Yaak. The charred remains in the forest seemed less haunting once he saw the burnt and crumbled buildings in the town. The staircase he'd used to flee Sandor was gone, no more than a heap of charcoal to his right. The timbers imbedded in the stone near the top of the staircase continued to smolder. From inside the two square holes,

Shylo saw the red eyes of Volurem peering out, watching them.

While looking up at the Volurem, Shylo's foot got tangled up in something heavy. He tripped, bracing himself on Sandor's broad back.

"Watch it," the brawny man grumbled, shrugging off Shylo's hand.

Shylo now noticed that it was the watchman's uniform that had tripped him up. The chainmail sleeves were blackened; the sword belt still held its scabbard and broadsword. Even the lazgron-scale armor appeared to be intact.

"Why would someone take off..." he started.

"They didn't," Galterius said from behind. "Take his blade. The Yaak watchman won't need it anymore."

Numbly, Shylo passed the harquice's lead to Galterius while he worked the belt free from the surcoat. As he did, a portion of a leather flask fell from the surcoat pocket.

"What's going on back there?" Sandor asked from up ahead.

"We should spread out. Search for any food, water, or supplies," Galterius called after him.

"Is that the level of thinking it takes to become an Imperial High Commander?" Sandor mocked.

Shylo fitted the sword belt around his waist as he walked toward Jexsanna and Sandor in the street. Once he'd cinched it down, Shylo drew the blade. He miscalculated the broadsword's length and nearly tripped himself when it got hung up in the scabbard. His struggle attracted the group's attention before he managed to free the tip.

"First time holding a sword?" Sandor asked.

Shylo rolled his shoulders back, hefting the surprisingly heavy blade. His right arm started sagging from the weight. He tried supporting the hand-and-a-half handle with his left hand as well, adjusting his posture. Shylo didn't understand how it was possible that Sandor could've fought with his eighteen-hand-long great sword for so long, never needing to hold it with two hands.

"You might want to be on the watch for a short sword considering we're heading south," Sandor said, before moving to join Jexsanna as she targeted an active Engulfed in the rubble.

"Strength will come with practice," Galterius said, nodding for Shylo to keep moving.

Yaak looked a stark replica of the town Shylo had been in two days before. Most single- and two-story townhouses had collapsed into black piles of burnt timber and broken clay shingles. A few homes had a room or two still standing, but any remaining wood burned intensely with Volurem. Shylo kept his distance, sticking to the middle of the street while the more experienced members of the group faced the threats.

"Shylo," Galterius called. "Take Jexsanna to the saloon. You two search the kitchen for any bulk food supplies."

"What are you going to do?" Shylo asked, not wanting to leave the safety of the street.

"Search for survivors," Galterius said, stepping up into the harquice saddle.

He spurred the animal forward, leaving them with Sandor. Sandor advanced on The Dirty Shame in front of them.

The saloon's wooden walls hadn't held up against the fire. Like the rest of Yaak, the building was now a broken and burning outline of the former structure. Shylo treaded lightly over warm logs, careful not to burn his feet through the holes in his sandals. He used the broadsword for balance, poking the tip into black logs and steadying himself with the hilt. Sandor started in where the bar had been, rummaging through debris and collecting coins as fast as he could. Shylo led Jexsanna toward the back of the building, where the kitchen had been. He'd been dying to ask her all of the questions that had been racing through his head since the moment she leapt from Yaak's walls, but he hadn't had a single moment alone with her since she rejoined the group.

"Jex," he whispered.

Jexsanna noted him but continued searching the pile of charcoal timbers.

She still wore the tattered lazgron cloak, wrapped closed, but little else.

Shylo quickly searched the piles of debris and spotted several marred suits of draco-scale armor. "Jexsanna," he said louder.

She straightened, looking at him expectantly. Shylo thought she might offer the explanation he'd been waiting to hear from her.

When she didn't, he said, "We can salvage these," and pointed out the depression where grey and red surcoats lay next to each other. As they cleared the debris, Shylo noted how well the draco-scale had preserved the bodies. The coats' owners were male and female and suddenly their huddling position next to each other at the back of the saloon painted a picture for Shylo. Had he and Jexsanna stayed, this could've been them. He helped fit Jexsanna into the woman's yellow tunic and dark grey draco surcoat. Since the soldier's uniform Shylo wore was still in good condition, he took only the man's weathered boots.

Discarding his sandals in the rubble, Shylo retrieved the second set of boots for Jexsanna and asked, "Why did you leave me to chase after that man in the brismil-plate armor?"

"I told you. I thought he was the Scaled One," she said.

"But it wasn't him, the one who killed the Masters," Shylo said.

"No," she confirmed, pausing in her search to meet Shylo gaze.

He saw pain in her ember eyes. Her eyebrows pinched slightly, and she held her lips tight. Dark shades of black ringed her eyes; she was exhausted.

"Why didn't you tell me what you were doing?" Shylo asked.

"When I saw him, the bright shine of his scaled suit, I felt something within me. It was like a Pyrignum took over. It forced me to go after him. I wanted nothing but to kill the Scaled One."

"Then why didn't you let Galterius help you?" Shylo asked.

"You saw?" she asked.

Shylo nodded. "I went after you." An involuntary smile formed on his lips. "I didn't even think about what I was doing. I just ran down the stairs and past the wall. I stole the Zethrillian's harquice and rode right at the fire."

"But you could've burned," Jexsanna said.

"I know, and I thought I would. But I realized something when I thought I'd lost you," Shylo said.

"Hey," Sandor called, interrupting them. "You finding any food?"

Shylo noticed the weight sagging in Sandor's surcoat pockets from the coin the man had collected.

"Nothing yet," Shylo called back.

"Probably all burnt to ash," Sandor mumbled. "I'm

moving on to the next block. Don't dawdle for too long. We should leave this place before nightfall," Sandor said.

Shylo nodded and waited for Sandor to march off.

"I realized something, too, Shylo," Jexsanna said.

"You did?" Shylo asked, butterflies swirling in his stomach at the softness in her voice.

"You can't be in the fire like me," she said.

Shylo exhaled, the fuzzy feeling disappearing with the moment. "I thought everyone knew that?" he said.

"Where I come from, all the others like me could be in the fire," she said.

Shylo again remembered the smoke column he'd seen on the day of the Emperor's death, "How far away did you say the arena was?"

"After the Scaled One killed them all, I stole their harquice. I rode through the heat of the day and into the night. I only stopped once. I kept riding through the night, until I thought the harquice would die of exhaustion. When I stopped to sleep, it was late in the morning. When I woke up to the sound of splashing in the water, I found you."

Shylo chewed on her words, analyzing them as the events of those two days had unfolded. It had all started when he noticed the smoke to the east. It had gone out quickly, but everyone, including Senator Didimo seemed perturbed by it. Galterius told them that House Ovando's guard was the one with his brismil scale. The one he'd lost while trying to stop the assassin at the Palace. Hours before, when House Didimo seemed abandoned, Ismay said she'd been following her father's guard, Bridger perhaps? Shylo considered whether it was conceivable for a single man to kill the entire Didimo Villa and assassinate three Akai in the Palace. Clearly, the guard had help. There was no denying that House Ovando was the guilty party, even with Ismay's father absent from the capital at the time.

"What are you thinking about?" Jexsanna asked while fishing a sunstone from a cast-iron stove.

"Can you tell me more about the arena?" Shylo asked her.

"The ones I came from?"

"There was more than one?" Shylo asked.

"They moved us between fighting arenas. They were different in vegetation, but similar in where we were kept. The others like me, Number 2840, number 2837…"

"Number 2759?" Shylo asked, knowing he was the one she called her, once-partner.

She nodded. "All of us were trained in the same way. We did what they told us to do."

"What the Masters told you to do," Shylo said.

"Yes. When they told us to leave a fighting arena, we did. When they told us to eat in the feeding troughs, we did. When they told us to go to sleep, we slept."

"Didn't you ever question if what they were telling you was right or wrong?" Shylo asked.

"No. They did not allow us to think for ourselves. If one of us questioned The Masters, or disobeyed, you were executed."

"That's brutal," Shylo said.

"That was the way things were," Jexsanna said.

"Before, when you told me about them, you said the masters only taught you to fight?" Shylo asked.

"Every day, we went to the arena. We sparred, trained, and in some instances were tested in live fighting rounds," she said.

As she spoke, Shylo admired how freely she spoke about her past. When she first began to speak to him, she had withheld details, only giving Shylo short answers. Jexsanna lifted a large piece of metal from the ground, uncovering a bag of uncooked rice and dried beans. Shylo helped her scoop it into a torn burlap bag that had survived the fire under the metal sheet.

"The Masters tested you in fighting to the death?" Shylo asked.

"Yes. They only wanted the best of us. The most loyal and competent fighters," she said.

"And you fought Volurem in these arenas?" he asked.

"At times, yes," Jexsanna said.

"And the others like you, could all be in the fire, without brismil?"

"Yes. We were all the same in this way."

"How is that possible?" Shylo asked.

"That is how it was," she said simply.

"Why didn't any of the others escape, like you did?" Shylo asked.

"Number 2759 spoke of it. We planned for a time, but after we were together, he changed."

"What do you mean?" Shylo asked.

"He showed too much pride. I knew it was wrong to be... intimate, but it felt right. Having our bond gave him a new determination to change things. The Masters caught onto him. They forced the others to tell them what he'd been preaching to them. That we were all capable of thinking and acting on our own."

"And they killed him for it?" Shylo asked.

She nodded.

"But you escaped when the Scaled One came," he continued.

"I was different than the others. I was like Number 2759."

"How?"

"I had, wrong, thoughts."

"You mean, you questioned the masters?" Shylo asked.

"I did not question them out loud, like my once-partner did. I only questioned them in my head. On the day the Scaled One and his companions came, the day The Masters pitted me against a Pyrignum and his Possessed foot soldiers, I displayed my skill as best I could."

"You fought a Pyrignum?" Shylo asked, helping secure the rice, beans, and sunstone in the sack.

"I took his dragon heart from him and held it up for the newcomers to see. I wanted to impress them. I wanted to show them that I was The Masters' best. But when I did, they started killing The Masters. Because I showed them my best, the newcomers acted in anger. They started killing The Masters, who didn't stand a chance against the Scaled One. I'd faced the Scaled One before and lost, but now, I don't know if he or any of the three I have now fought were the same person under that armor."

"How did you escape?" Shylo asked.

"The Master at the arena ordered me back inside the main wall after I'd shown the dragon heart. He told me to put my sword away and wait in my sleeping stall."

"The arenas were walled, like our cities?" Shylo asked.

"Yes, much taller than the walls here," she said. "I disobeyed The Master's order. I didn't put my sword away. I took it with me to my sleeping stall. And waited."

"You waited until they were gone?" Shylo asked.

"I waited as the Scaled One killed all The Masters and moved on to the others like me, stall by stall. I could hear it. They all obeyed their orders, staying still and not fighting as the Scaled One killed them with his ivory dragon blade. When he came to my stall, and saw I was armed, I attacked.

He chased me. We fought in the eating chamber. I drew blood on the Scaled One and escaped through the opening."

"You drew blood?" Shylo asked.

She nodded.

"That's not possible if he was wearing brismil plate. Steel can't cut through it. Your sword would've broken before cutting the dragon scale."

"There was a fracture in it. Right here," she said, running her index finger across the side of her neck. "My saber cut him there. That's how I knew that this man last night was not the same Scaled One. His neck plate was not fractured."

"That's why you tackled me," Shylo said, realizing what she was thinking the day he'd tried to stop Marxius and Benton. "You thought they were the group from the arena who killed everyone you knew," Shylo said.

"Not think. I know. It was them," she said.

"Not everyone who has a brismil scale is the same..." Shylo said, remembering then how he thought he saw Marxius looking through the gate with the top of his plate removed but still wearing the body suit.

"I recognized the one without the brismil. It was those men," she said.

Shylo absorbed the information. Her description provided the missing piece to the puzzle of how Shylo and Jexsanna had come to cross paths outside Perdigon. Rejoining Sandor, they continued sifting through debris as they made their way through Yaak. Near the south end of town, Shylo noticed sections of the wall that had failed in the heat of the fire. When Galterius met them with the harquice, Shylo saw he was alone. The High Commander shook his head, confirming the unspoken question about survivors. Shylo hadn't thought survival was likely but seeing the downed sections of the wall had offered a ray of hope that some people could've fled.

"Is this all you found?" Galterius asked, loading the saddlebags with the sunstone, a cast-iron skillet and the bag of rice and beans.

"And new armor," Shylo said.

"I mean for group meals," Galterius said.

"If you want to brave the Engulfed with that magic sword, go right ahead. We'll get a head start and meet up with you later," Sandor said.

"And give you the chance to slit throats and run? Not on my watch," Galterius said. "We'll head out now. That bag should last us a week if we ration it."

Once clear of town, Jexsanna and Sandor led the way, clearing a path through the burn. They moved more quickly than the day after the fire, when they were slowed down by the Engulfed burning around Yaak. With a day of rain, and Shylo's new boots, they carried on at a faster pace.

Once he got Galterius alone, Shylo said, "The day of the Emperor's murder, I spied on you."

Galterius didn't respond in the way Shylo expected. The older man studied Shylo as if he were trying to judge what advantage Shylo might obtain by admitting this to the High Commander.

"I eavesdropped on a conversation between you and several others in the Senate Chambers," Shylo said.

"The one where I asked for more support for South Saypo," Galterius replied.

"Yes," Shylo said.

"There's no harm done now. The requests were denied, and the new Emperor will continue ignoring the Agunzi's needs," Galterius said.

"Did you see the fire when you left the chamber?" Shylo asked.

"Yes. We noted it, saw it was at the base of the Shield Mountains to the east. With the snow still in the peaks, it wouldn't have gone far, though it was concerning to see fire this far north this early."

"How do you think that fire started?" he asked.

"Like this one," Galterius said. "A sunstone left out in the woods. It happens among uneducated Esos who travel overland during the offseason."

"You think a traveler started *this* fire?" Shylo asked.

"Not a traveler. It was Captain Bridger. There's no doubt in my mind. He was supposed to be my Second in Command, but he was preoccupied by overriding orders from Perdigon and repositioning my scale. Bridger was to return to Perdigon as requested by the Emperor or by Marxius working through the Emperor. Bridger must've detoured to collect my scale and I trapped him near Yaak. When I tried to ask him why he was there at The Dirty Shame instead of in Perdigon, he acted blind drunk. Too intoxicated to stay awake. He had it with him then. It was right under my nose."

"I saw you fight him. Jexsanna stopped you."

"I don't understand why she did, or how she survived the fire. She isn't one of us," Galterius said.

"When I met Jexsanna, she told me her name was Number 2841 back then. She was already outside Perdigon when I escaped."

"The night of, or the next day after the murder?" Galterius asked.

"The next day. I tried to get my friend, or classmate I should say, to help me. He just set the guards on me though. The word was already out that Didimo was responsible. What I'm trying to get at, though, is that I don't think that fire the day of your conversation in the Senate Chambers was started by a traveler leaving a sunstone on the ground."

"No?" Galterius asked, eyeing Shylo cautiously.

"Jexsanna isn't from some faraway place. She says she came from an arena a hard day-and-half ride from Perdigon. To the east of Perdigon, where that column of smoke was," Shylo said.

"You think she started it?" Galterius asked.

Shylo explained the coinciding fire with what Jexsanna had told him happened to her the day she escaped from the arena. He told Galterius about how he had tried to stop Marxius and Benton on their return to Perdigon, and about his suspicions that Marxius was the Scaled One that Jexsanna was determined to kill.

"There were others like her? How many?" Galterius asked.

Shylo shrugged, saying, "If she was Number 2841, then at least that many, I would guess."

"No. Killing that many people one at a time would take much longer than you made it sound." Galterius was silent for a time, making Shylo wonder if he should've withheld the information. "The timing and description are too close to the events that occurred for it to be a lie, though. I saw the smoke column as you did. It was already burning out, meaning a fire enclosed in a walled arena could've been what we saw. After Marxius and Benton returned, I noticed the cut on his neck."

"And his head guard has your scale, meaning he killed the Emperor," Shylo said.

"If what you're suggesting is what really happened, the plan would've had to have been thought through long before Marxius left with Benton on their supply mission. Who's to say this was Marxius' doing? Benton could've been the mastermind behind it," Galterius said.

"You know them better than I do. Who do you think is more likely the traitor?" Shylo asked.

"Marxius is strategic but knows the risks of what would come in overthrowing an emperor. Benton doesn't seem the type to think of such an elaborate plan and have the smarts to pull it off. He only lived in the Palace because Jermanus had a relationship with Benton's mother. Benton refused to take his duties as an Akai seriously and failed to learn anything from his studies. He lacks motivation. I do not believe he had the resources to do this," Galterius said.

"Then it has to be Marxius," Shylo said.

Galterius shook his head.

"But why did they need to kill all of House Didimo?" Shylo asked, ignoring Galterius' denial. "And why did they kill all of the others in the arena like Jexsanna?"

"I have my suspicions," Galterius said.

Continuing in silence, Shylo struggled to understand how Marxius or Benton would know to go to the arena in the first place.

As they neared the ground fire at the leading edge of the Volurem front, Shylo saw the flames flickering in the rain. The Engulfed struggled to climb into small trees and brush and establish a threatening presence in the drizzle. Suddenly from behind them, Shylo heard galloping. He noticed Jexsanna already preparing to defend them.

"Imperials," Sandor shouted, rushing to arms.

"No, it's only one harquice," Jexsanna corrected.

"Shylo, Jexsanna, and Sandor. Get into the forest. Be ready to support me if I need your aid," Galterius said with confidence.

Without a word, Sandor took the harquice and led them toward the smoldering front. He hewed a swath through the unsuspecting Volurem to clear a path. Just inside the green vegetation, they huddled behind a small stand of trees.

A single rider flew through the ash on her harquice. She carried no weapon, other than the dagger on her belt. She slowed upon seeing Galterius standing on the road. Shylo could see they were talking but couldn't hear.

"What are they saying," Sandor asked.

Shylo shrugged, but Jexsanna replied, "She's a messenger from the capital. Galterius is asking her if they know of the battle that happened here. Yes," Jexsanna added after a brief pause. "The Emperor is marching from Perdigon with a small force of his best military leaders to join ranks with the One Hundred and First Legion. They're going to put out the fire." Jexsanna paused again, but Shylo could see they were still talking. Galterius appeared angry.

"What's going on now?" Sandor demanded.

"She has informed Galterius that he is a fugitive of the Empire. He's wanted for his part in the murder of Emperor Jermanus," Jexsanna said.

Shylo watched Galterius stumble away from the harquice as he attempted to grab hold of its reins. The messenger rode through him, speeding past and leaping through the Volurem at the smoldering front. As quickly as the messenger arrived, she was gone. Shylo followed Sandor and Jexsanna from their hiding place, meeting Galterius.

"What was that about?" Sandor asked.

"Just a messenger from Perdigon," Galterius said.

"What did she say?" Sandor asked.

"The Emperor sent three messengers down the three roads through Apgar. They're to alert the One Hundred and First Legion of what happened in Yaak. Benton is riding out to meet them here and extinguish this Volurem force before it spreads out of control again," Galterius finished.

"Did she say anything else?" Shylo asked.

"That was all," Galterius lied. "She took off in a hurry, I don't think she recognized me."

Shylo and Jexsanna shared a worried look as he took the lead after the messenger.

"Let's get a move on. We don't want to be too close to the fire if it gains momentum," Galterius said.

Shylo felt Chirp squirm uncomfortably in his pocket. Now that they were in unburnt forest again, Shylo collected a handful of berries and leaves for the Borca to eat. He lifted the flap and the rodent chirped as Shylo tucked in the food. He noticed Sandor scowling at him.

"Seriously? Why don't you eat that thing and be rid of it?" Sandor said.

Jexsanna gently lifted the tip of her blade to Sandor, and he took a step away.

"Okay. I'll leave it alone, just don't expect me to look after it. I'll eat that thing the first chance I get," he said before following Galterius.

Shylo wondered how much he should trust either of them. Galterius claimed he wanted to keep Shylo alive, but now that he'd found out he was in the same situation as Shylo and Jexsanna, he could change his mind. Sandor had already made it known that he'd kill Shylo for the reward. Shylo had Jexsanna to protect him, but now that Galterius was wanted, he wondered if Sandor would chance taking him on for a shot at his brismil blade. All Shylo knew for certain was that they had a long road ahead.

A KNIGHT TO REMEMBER

Shylo watched Chirp bounce from Jexsanna's lap onto the surprisingly dry forest ground. The rain had let up over the last span, causing Shylo to wonder if they should've gotten more of a head start on their run from Yaak. Given their fatigue after a long day of fighting the day before, however, Shylo, Jexsanna and Galterius elected to rest for a day. Shylo assumed Galterius' motive to hold up was to contemplate what the messenger had told him. He claimed he had to wait at least one full day to see if his Zethrillian advisor, Isik, turned up.

Shylo was glad for the layover day. The way he saw it, being well rested before they continued farther south would allow them to move faster while remaining alert. He guessed that it would be a few more days until an Imperial force was able to march from Perdigon. Galterius confirmed that the One Hundred and First Legion would be further delayed than the Emperor. Galterius and Sandor agreed that once the Emperor and his force of guards reached Yaak, they'd wait for Legion support before considering sending anyone off to search for them. It would give their small group some time to find a port town and sail south. Shylo's biggest concern was to ensure that Jexsanna had some time to rest. He could see in the way she carried herself that she needed sleep.

Chirp scurried back to Jexsanna and curled up next to her. Shylo smiled at how peaceful they looked. He couldn't help but feel like it had been months since he last enjoyed a moment as worry-free as this. He knew it wouldn't last, though. Three of their group now faced accusations of orchestrating and assassinating the Emperor and his Akai heirs. He wondered if there was anywhere in the Empire where they could live a *normal* life.

"Something has been weighing on my mind," Shylo said, looking at Galterius while Sandor stirred the pan of rice and beans on their sunstone.

"You're not the only one. I've been saying for hours, we need to add the borca to the meal for flavor," Sandor said.

"No," Shylo replied. "I'm talking about what we plan to do; run away from our problems. Will it change anything?"

"It's not exactly like you have much of a choice," Sandor said.

"Why not?" Shylo asked.

"The offense you've been accused of isn't something you can just apologize for and expect to be let go," Galterius said.

"But we know who committed the assassination," Shylo said.

"Imperial law doesn't care about pointing the blame. You need proof," Galterius said. "Do you see me going to the courts and saying, 'I believe it was the Akai who suddenly came into power after such a heinous assassination?' No, because Benton wasn't in the capital. He and Marxius have an alibi placing them far from the murders. The first step is catching Bridger, the one who has my scale. My scale is proof of his guilt in this. But thanks to her, he got away."

Shylo scowled at Galterius, "You can't pass off the blame of failing to catch Bridger onto Jexsanna. You could've grabbed Bridger at the table while he was faking being drunk, but you didn't. His escape is more your fault than it is ours."

"What's done is done," Galterius said.

"Why the sudden change in perspective? A day ago, you told me you could help me secure my freedom by going back to Perdigon," Shylo said to the High Commander.

Galterius rolled his draco-scaled shoulders forward, now scowling at Shylo, and said, "I haven't changed my mind about going back to Perdigon. It's the best option for us now. If you want to get more proof, the evidence is in the capital, not out here in the wilderness. I'll lead us back and we can take our chances there. All you need to do is say the word and we'll make our move."

"Don't include me in your future for much longer. I'm only with you until I hit payday," Sandor said.

"I'm sick of running for something I had nothing to do with, but I don't see how the Empire will offer any forgiveness if I return to Perdigon. I'm done living in fear. I want some semblance of my old life back," Shylo said.

"You're an Eso, like me. Fear is unavoidable for us. I've been living in fear since I was old enough to talk," Galterius responded. "You need to learn to live with fear and not let it control you. I know it seems frightening but going back will put an end to this particular chapter one way or another. You're never going to get a chance to live a life without fear, Shylo."

"You're right," Shylo said.

"It's not going to be easy, but it's the only way you can find a sanctuary for you and her," Galterius said, eyeing Jexsanna.

Shylo followed his gaze. Jexsanna rolled onto her side, slowly opening her eyes. Shylo didn't see any sanctuary for her if they went back. She'd be labeled a monster, not fit for Rhydarian society. All of them would be locked away or killed for the Akai assassinations. Shylo knew there wasn't a life for them there.

"I'm not talking about going back to Perdigon," Shylo said.

Sandor slowed his stirring of the simmering rice and beans.

"Or to the Southern Warden," he added.

"There is no other option. Not one that I am willing to discuss," Sandor said.

Galterius leaned forward, resting his forearms on his knees, and asked, "All right, Shylo. Let's see if you've learned anything in your Penti training. I'm curious, what do you have in mind?"

"The way I see it, we're in a unique situation. One where we can do something to make sure we won't be followed any more. I'm thinking that the four of us have a chance to set things right and remove ourselves from the equation altogether," Shylo said.

"If you're saying what I think you are, it can't be done. There are only four of us," Galterius said.

"What are you scheming?" Jexsanna asked, sitting up and groggily looking at the darkening surroundings. "How long have I been asleep?"

"You've been out for most of the afternoon," Shylo said.

She blinked in surprise.

"Jexsanna, maybe you can help me get my point across. Why didn't you continue riding with me when I was injured?" he asked.

"Because you weren't able to ride," Jexsanna said.

"There was another, more strategic reason," Shylo prompted.

"Because you couldn't ride, we needed to stay behind the guards searching for us," she answered.

"Exactly, we evaded you, Galterius, for nearly a fortnight by positioning ourselves in a place where you weren't expecting to find us," Shylo said.

"And look how well that worked out for you," Sandor said.

"We're alive, aren't we?" Shylo said.

"There will be a host of guards and an entire legion in this area in the days to come. If you're suggesting we can disappear, make it look like we were killed in the flames? The ruse won't last," Galterius said.

"I'm not talking about faking our deaths and escaping. I'm talking about setting a trap on the people we know are responsible for putting us into this situation," Shylo said.

"You intend to kill another emperor?" Sandor asked.

"Whatever the Emperor's fate is as a result of what I'm proposing is not my main objective, no matter how suspect his sudden coronation looks," Shylo said. "Like Galterius said, we need proof and that starts with those who've got blood on their hands. The conductors, whether they be Benton, Marxius, or another person we haven't considered, will be exposed after."

"How do you know that any of them besides the Emperor will come to Yaak?" Galterius asked.

"Galterius, why did the Emperor send you on this mission?" Shylo asked.

"Because of Marxius. He knows I can produce results," he said.

"The battalion's worth of guards at your command didn't hold up to your reputation or the standard I have read about you. I don't pretend to know battle strategy when surrounded by Volurem but rushing out without a commander does not seem like the strategy of a well-trained battalion."

"I did not select those guards. Marxius and the Emperor did," Galterius said.

"And the Captain you were trying to kill? It seemed to me like he was there to put you to rest in the ashes," Sandor said.

"Captain Bridger was supposed to be my Second in Command. He is Ovando's Head Guard. He failed to spend even a third of his time with the battalion. Because he had my scale hidden somewhere outside the wall, I now know why," Galterius said.

"From what I can tell, Marxius hatched this scheme to get rid of Jermanus. He must've had it planned so his Lead Guard would do the dirty work, making it look like another Senator's house was to blame. Since Bridger knows we're out here, possibly still alive, he'll tell Marxius. Marxius will either talk Benton into sending him back to deal with us, or Marxius will come himself," Shylo said.

"I can't believe that Marxius is to blame for his Captain's actions," Galterius said.

"Why not? You said it yourself that Ovando's man killed the Emperor," Sandor said.

"I know Marxius' tactics. He wouldn't risk something like assassinating the Emperor. This is the Akai's doing," Galterius said.

"Ask yourself who has more experience in Perdigon maneuvering themselves into positions of power? Marxius or the forgotten Akai thought never to be in a position to rule?" Shylo said.

"Marxius had the most to gain by befriending Benton in the event that he became Emperor," Galterius admitted. "But that doesn't mean he gave those orders to his Captain."

"Regardless, do you think they won't send Bridger or Marxius out here to deal with us?" Shylo asked.

"Bridger is the most likely to return," Galterius said.

"If you're right about this, Shylo, I'll be holding you to your word, Galterius. The scale is mine to claim," Sandor said.

"We can use a tactic similar to Jexsanna's in evading Galterius; we can back through the burn to the northern side of Yaak. This will position us in a place where the Emperor and his guards would never expect to find us. If I understood what the messenger told Galterius, the Emperor will be traveling with his close personal guards and a force small enough to move quickly. Bridger should be accompanying them. They'll assume that we've fled to the South if we've escaped the Volurem at all. If we can intercept the Emperor's entourage before they reach the One Hundred and First Legion, we can corner the Captain, reveal the brismil scale, and present the facts underlying the assassination."

"Your plan has too many holes. It won't work," Galterius said.

"And you've forgotten the most important part, that I get what's owed to me," Sandor said.

"It sounds crazy at face value but think about it from this perspective. Benton is a new emperor. As far as I'm aware, Benton hadn't ever been seriously considered to take the throne. I'd never heard of him before I started training in Perdigon and commoners are always quick to gossip about who the up-and-comers are in the capital, which means he has something to prove. This Volurem burn is the largest-scale fire that's hit the Apgar Forest in my lifetime. Benton will focus on containing the Volurem. The fact that we're alive or have escaped capture will be an afterthought until he's conquered the burn."

"And if the Emperor is at fault for putting us in this situation, what then? Won't he order us executed?" Jexsanna asked.

"If he is to blame for killing his uncle and cousins to rise to power, he won't want it known to a group of Kai as large as the one he will be bringing with him. If we can expose Bridger, why wouldn't he let the blame fall solely on him? Like Galterius said, it needs to start with exposing Bridger, then the other pieces will fall into place," Shylo said.

"It's a huge risk," Galterius said. "You are right about the rest of it though. In leaving the walls to join the One Hundred and First, Benton clearly wants to prove himself as a military leader in combatting the Volurem force and especially will want to take advantage of the recent rain to make this job easier. Which is why he'll be traveling with a light force, maybe just a few troops, to get here as fast as possible. Likely he will bring senior members of the military, like Major Commander Landrich-Kai. But from what I've seen of the young Emperor, he doesn't seem to care much about his uncle's murderers, giving me all the more reason to suspect him," Galterius said.

"Isn't that a good reason why he might forget about us if we disappear to the south?" Jexsanna suggested.

"Wasn't it Marxius' influence that sent you after us?" Shylo asked Galterius.

"It was," Galterius admitted.

"What about me and what's owed?" Sandor said.

"We're just speaking in the hypothetical, you oaf," Galterius growled.

"Not for you and me," Jexsanna said over the arguing starting up again between Sandor and Galterius.

Galterius quieted and said, "What are you talking about, *for you and me?*"

Shylo wanted to stop Jexsanna before she blurted out what he knew she was going to say. She was getting better at reading social cues the more she was exposed to others outside the arena, but he knew she could let sensitive information slip. He'd done the same thing by telling Galterius where Jexsanna had come from. He held his tongue and waited to see what she would say.

"I heard what the messenger told you," Jexsanna said. "I was repeating everything to Shylo and Sandor. We know they are after you now, too. Maybe Shylo could disappear, but we can't. The Emperor will come for you just as The Scaled One will come for me," she said.

"The Scaled One will come for you, too, when he hears you're alive," Shylo said, knowing that Galterius now understood that the Scaled One was Marxius.

Galterius sat in silence for a moment.

"You can't seriously be considering this bad idea," Sandor said to Galterius. "The Emperor will have more than one troop with him, even if he's moving light. That's thirty to forty fighting men and women, and you can count on the fact that they'll be better trained than the lot they sent with you. He'll probably have Agunzi among them. And all that's betting that they aren't already heading to join up with the One Hundred and First Legion. What if the Legion is closer than you think? They could already have joined up by the time they reach Yaak."

"If Bridger told him about Jexsanna, and what you said about him being at the arena is true, he'll be with them," Galterius said, almost to himself.

"Who?" Sandor demanded.

"The Scaled One," Shylo said.

"So, what if this brismil-plated ash-stain is with the Emperor. It won't go down like Shylo suggested. You're not going to convince him to absolve all of you of your crimes," Sandor said.

"We don't need to," Galterius said.

"All we need to do is separate from the rest of those who are causing us these problems. Like I was saying before, Benton will be distracted by the Volurem. If we time it right, we can separate the troops from our targets," Shylo said.

"We would take out Bridger, but I'd be the one to confront Marxius," Galterius said.

"With Bridger gone, you'd have your proof to clear your name. You deal with Marxius and there wouldn't be anyone pressuring Benton to pursue us," Shylo said.

"You'd still be outlaws," Sandor said.

"But easily forgotten when the State of Apgar faces a

threat from the Volurem. And this current threat will escalate as the burning season intensifies," Shylo said.

"I only get paid if you survive," Sandor said.

"Or if Bridger dies," Galterius said.

Sandor focused on stirring the rice and beans for a long moment while they waited for his reply. Finally, he said, "If you managed to somehow separate these men who have brismil plates from the rest, how would you deal with them discreetly enough that the Emperor and his little war party wouldn't notice? And if you did, who's to say Jexsanna wouldn't take a scale and blade for herself?"

"I do not want the brismil. I only want the hunting to stop," she replied.

"You say that now, but things change in the heat of battle," Sandor said.

Shylo was surprised when Jexsanna didn't reply, so he filled the void in conversation. "Either way, there is a reward for you in any of these scenarios. The larger the risk, the greater the payout," Shylo said.

"You're suggesting the four of us ambush the Emperor, knowing he'll likely have a superior force and at least one brismil guard with him," Sandor said. "They won't be caught off guard very well if Galterius' blade and his scale emit their attracting bond."

"Bridger won't risk letting the Emperor know a matching scale set is nearby. The Emperor would take it from him. He'd sneak off alone. It could be how we set a trap for him," Galterius now reasoned.

"That's a pretty big assumption," Sandor said.

"The bigger the risk, the better the payday," Galterius repeated.

"What about the others? What if they catch wind of what we're doing?" Sandor demanded.

"We have Jexsanna," Shylo said.

"Yes, she's a fierce threat, but they may have more trained soldiers in brismil plate to match her. That leaves forty, maybe more armed guards for the three of us. Those numbers don't add up to us living through the day," Sandor said.

"I can beat the Scaled Ones. I've done it before," she said.

"If we need to create a distraction for the Emperor and his guard, I have an idea that might work. It would mean Jexsanna wouldn't be with us, but it would allow us to divide the groups," Shylo said.

Sandor used the hilt of his sword to strike the sunstone, clicking it off and they sat down to eat their rice and beans. Between mouthfuls, Shylo laid out the strategy for this distraction. He knew it meant using Jexsanna, but with her consent; she was more than willing to help if it meant achieving their shared goal, gaining their freedom.

That night, Shylo lay next to Jexsanna on the ground. They huddled together like they'd been doing each night for weeks, combining their warmth. With a full stomach and a somewhat solid plan, he felt the most hopeful he'd felt since leaving the Canteen all those nights ago.

"Jexsanna," he whispered.

She opened her eyes, her face pressed against the back of her hand as she attempted to fall asleep. She stared at him. They were like the hot coals broiling in the Volurem's wake. Something within Shylo burned when he looked into her eyes. Something he'd not felt before for another person.

"If tonight is our last night on Tarmigan, there's something I need to ask you," he said.

Her dark eyebrows pinched together in confusion.

"Why didn't you leave me?"

"I did leave you and when I realized what it meant, I felt strange," she said.

"Not that time. I mean, why didn't you leave me after I said all those horrible things about you back at the Perdigon gates?" he asked.

"I don't know. I didn't know I could leave you," she said.

"But you did. You left for a time, but you came back for me. You saved me after I was so mean to you. Why?" he asked.

"You weren't acting like you then. And when I saw you were in trouble, I had to come for you. Those people were worse to you than you ever were to me. Those are The Masters' kind of people. You were the first person who told me to think for myself. When you told me I should have a name, that was the first time I felt that someone saw me since my once-partner. That was the first time I knew it was okay to express my individual thoughts."

"But you hardly knew me," Shylo insisted. "I didn't think you could talk. I told you my worst secret and you didn't hate me for it."

"About the girl you lied to your friends about?" she asked.

"Yes, and I wish I could've seen it back then, that those people I lied to were not my friends," he said, realizing something. "You are the best friend I've ever had."

"You are my friend, too, Shylo," she said.

"And I like you," he said.

"I like you, too," she replied.

"No. I mean I really like you. Like a life partner," he said, leaning closer and kissing her on the lips. She didn't pull away. She hesitated for a moment, then leaned into him, kissing him back. Shylo broke away from their kiss and looked into her eyes.

"Why did you stop doing that?" she asked.

"Kissing you? I wanted to make sure it's right," he said.

"That's what you call it, a kiss?" she asked softly.

Shylo heard the lightness in her voice and sensed she felt for him in the same way he did for her.

Shylo let her lead him into another kiss. They wrapped around each other in an embrace. As he let his affection for her guide him, Shylo found himself slipping into a level of connection he'd never experienced with anyone before. He forgot everything around them. The only thing in his life that mattered was her; Jexsanna. When they finally rolled apart, snuggling under the lazgron cloak in the warmth of their bodies, Shylo fell asleep wishing that this night would never end.

BACKBURN

Nineteen Days After the Emperor's Death

The midday sun warmed Shylo's armored back. Sweat trailed from his temples, down his jaw and onto his neck. The hilt of his scavenged broadsword weighed heavily in his grip. Smoke puffing off Engulfed Volurem actively burning nearby filled his nostrils. The sound of harquice hooves clopping on the dirt path and draco scales clattering against each other forced him to a crouch behind a clump of green brush along the roadside.

"Here they come," Galterius whispered, waving a signal for Sandor and Jexsanna to get into position.

Shylo ran through their plan in his head. It would only work if the group of scouts moving in to check on the Volurem activity didn't include Emperor Benton or High

Commander Marxius. He spied the first guard riding along the road through the trees. She was an Agunzi woman with long, braided red hair. She wore a Palace Guard uniform and carried a war scythe on a pole that was at least thirty-hands long. Behind her wide frame, a handful of guards dressed in the same golden draco-scale uniforms followed, each New or Old Rhydarian.

Shylo and Galterius hid behind the unburnt thicket just a few harquice-lengths from the road. By the time they were all in view, it became apparent to Shylo that the scouting party included roughly twenty men and women, three of whom were Agunzi. Searching their faces, he did not recognize any as Captain Bridger, but looked to Galterius for confirmation. The High Commander held his dragon-fang blade, his expression taut and pointed. He shook his head, indicating the scale was not within his brismil sword's sensory parameters.

As the group slowed in its approach to the rear of the active Engulfed, Shylo spotted a familiar red cloak trimmed in white. The group trotted past them, and Shylo's heart sped up when he saw the House Sarapio man. He looked about Shylo's size, maybe a half-a-hand shorter, and thicker built. Like most of the Palace Guard before him, the young man wore a helmet with a T-shaped slot for his eyes and down the front of his face. Through the gaps, Shylo recognized those eyes. The posture he assumed when riding his harquice mare. Wilsall Sarapio-Ai was among the scouting party.

Shylo stirred nervously, thinking that if he had the same luck as the last time, Shylo would make the first move on Wilsall. A part of him wanted to abandon all caution and rush out at the Ai. Shylo had spent hours of each day since Wilsall turned on him, thinking of what he'd do when next they met. Now here he was, nearly within reach but Shylo knew he couldn't do what he wanted to. Shylo had to focus on the objective. He had to let Jexsanna do her work on the Sarapio Ai. Shylo just hoped it would be enough to give his Penti classmate a taste of what Wilsall's family guard had done to him.

"What is it?" Galterius whispered.

Shylo chewed at his bottom lip, then said, "He's the Penti who turned on me. He watched as his guards brutally beat me."

"House Sarapio, I see him now. Do you want to kill him?" Galterius asked.

Shylo glanced away from Wilsall and eyed the High Commander. He nodded slowly.

"Good. But now is not the time to strike. We must wait for the real prize. If Bridger is here, he doesn't have my scale. I can't sense it nearby. We must wait to see who the Emperor has brought on this mission. Only after can we exact revenge for other personal grudges," Galterius whispered.

Shylo nodded, gripping the hilt of the broadsword tighter. As Shylo silently waited for Wilsall to ride past, he wondered what Galterius meant by satisfying personal grudges on his behalf. Clearly Marxius had turned on him and Shylo knew now that High Commander Ovando-Kai was connected to the events that brought them to this point. Perhaps Galterius was seeing things more clearly after a few days to ponder his own situation. As far as Shylo was concerned, the coup could only be Marxius' doing. Benton was Marxius' pawn. If Galterius came around to that way of thinking, perhaps he, too, intended to exact revenge.

Shylo stared down his nemesis from the brush. Wilsall appeared confident with the fifteen others leading the way, but Shylo knew that he would likely be the first to run once Jexsanna triggered her trap. He hoped Wilsall wouldn't escape or be killed by the Engulfed before Shylo could get to him.

They waited silently in the thicket until the twenty guards had passed them and made it around the corner. It was just as Galterius and Sandor predicted. They scouted the Volurem activity on the upwind side, a tactic that allowed Shylo and Galterius time to move down the road until they located the rest of the Emperor's group. Walking near the edge of the overgrown path, Shylo trailed Galterius. They jogged on light feet, making sure not to make too much noise.

Galterius slowed before a bend and whispered, "Into the woods. We should be getting close now. Once they see the smoke chugging up, they'll send the rest of the troops in to stop the Volurem. When that happens, you know what to do," Galterius said.

"Keep behind them and separate our targets from the rest," Shylo repeated. He wondered, though, how Bridger could be separated if he didn't have the scale to come after Galterius. Their plan seemed shakier than Shylo previously believed. If they didn't get Bridger, and Marxius hadn't come with the Emperor, then they could be condemning themselves to capture and more.

Galterius broke Shylo's train of thought, saying, "This won't be easy if Bridger doesn't have his scale, or if he isn't here at all." After a concerning moment of silence, he added, "If Marxius is here, we'll deal with him. If it's only Benton..." Galterius didn't finish his thought before leading Shylo into the forest again.

Shylo walked on pins and needles now, staying near thick tree trunks and large bushes to remain concealed. He guessed at what exactly Galterius planned to do if Marxius and Bridger were not with the Emperor.

Galterius stopped, dropped to all fours, and slowly crawled to the base of the next tree. Shylo mirrored his actions, then remained still awaiting Galterius' next direction. He waved his hand, signaling Shylo to move up next to him before whispering, "There they are, the rest of them."

Through a narrow gap in the trees Shylo followed the High Commander's line of sight. In the distance, camouflaged Rhydarians on harquice sat four abreast. How Galterius spotted them, Shylo didn't know. Knowing they were there, Shylo still struggled to pick them out from the surrounding cover. Moving into a better position, Shylo struggled to count the rows of guards, but immediately spotted an object among them. In the middle of what he gauged were two troops of guards, sat a deep-blue covered coach wagon, trimmed in gold, and hitched to two winged harquice. Leather harnesses held the creatures' black wings tight against their flanks. Their spiked spurs were capped with metal sheaths. Their saber teeth hung down below their muzzles. Shylo blinked to make sure what he was seeing wasn't an illusion. The two harquice were the first of their kind Shylo had seen. These majestic creatures had not been modified for domestication. A muscular Agunzi man sat in the driver's seat. He wore gold draco-scale armor, unlike the two troops surrounding them in green camouflage draco scale. Resting next to him was a thick dual-headed battle-axe. After seeing how easily Sandor carried his great sword, Shylo could only imagine how much the dual-headed axe weighed compared to his broadsword. He prayed that Galterius wouldn't be foolish enough to go after the Emperor in the coach.

"Be ready," Galterius said. "It will take her a while

longer, but Jexsanna will be sending smoke up into the air soon."

"Is Bridger there?" Shylo asked, fear pulsing through him in anticipation.

Galterius adjusted several times, then said, "Not that I can tell. Marxius neither. But they may be in the coach with Benton. If that is the Emperor's hitch."

Shylo tried to calm his breathing. This plan wasn't going as he expected. His heart raced at the pace of a galloping harquice. He grew fuzzy on the details of what they were supposed to do next.

"What if they aren't with them? What if none of them, Benton, Marxius, or Bridger, is with this group?" Shylo asked out loud. He wondered if they'd done something foolish in trusting one messenger's word. If none of them were there, then they were attacking Benton's troops without good cause. Their primary target might still be back in Perdigon, sitting safely in his villa.

"Calm down," Galterius said, grabbing hold of Shylo's shoulder. "Don't go green on me now. Stay focused. We can do this. We just need to wait for Jexsanna to do her part."

"What if they all go running after the first wave of smoke? Ashes," he cursed. "Maybe they won't even care to send more from the troops to inspect the fire."

"Shylo, trust me. I know how High Commander Ovando-Kai works. He wouldn't miss an opportunity to face the largest Volurem force that's burned this close to his home in decades. He has Benton's trust. Marxius, at the very least will be here. And he knows how to read the battle-field. He'll believe this threat to his first troop is big enough to send a second," Galterius said.

"That would leave a whole troop of mounted guards, the coach driver, and one well-trained fighter with brismil plate, maybe two if Bridger's there, or three if Benton has one. All for you to deal with? And that's assuming Marxius is even with this group," Shylo said.

"For *us* to deal with, you mean," Galterius corrected.

"I've never fought anything with a sword," Shylo said.

Galterius cracked a slight smile, saying, "Distraction will be our ally, and that's what the spot fire is for."

"What?" Shylo said. "That's not a part of the plan."

"It's done. Sandor's taking care of it as we speak," Galterius said.

"You're letting the only person in our group who wants to see us caught do something on his own?" Shylo asked.

"Don't worry. He knows what's at risk if he doesn't cooperate," Galterius said.

"What's he doing? Starting a fire upwind with a sunstone?" Shylo asked.

"Yes," Galterius said.

"What's stopping him from waiting for us to fail and get captured? He might try to take the brismil on his own," Shylo said.

"A man like Sandor has seen enough combat to know a good deal on a brismil plate when it's offered. He'll stay on our side. Besides, I told him Jexsanna would track him down and kill him if anything happens to you."

"But he could —"

"We heard you two the past few nights," Galterius said.

Shylo flushed with embarrassment.

"Sandor understands your bond with her is a strong one. He will not risk his life by standing back and watching us fail," Galterius said.

Shylo felt as if he needed to explain himself, but the guards on harquice started moving. Their voices raised as they pointed through the trees. Shylo looked and saw the column of smoke rising. Jexsanna had kicked their plan into motion. There was no going back now.

MARXIUS SAT UP AS THE GUARDS' voices grew frenzied.

"Stay here," he told Benton and sprung open the coach door. Scanning the surroundings for whatever threat befell their troops, Marxius snapped open the flap on his side exposing bare skin. He held his hand on the leather pouch attached to his sword belt, ready to clip the scale into its harness and don the brismil-plate armor.

The men and women were still in somewhat organized lines on the path. Marxius saw no immediate danger after scanning the thick forest without seeing anything moving. No draco or Volurem had closed in on them, something he'd warned Benton about before they left the gates. Marxius felt it necessary to remind the Emperor after he saw how few guards Benton had chosen to accompany them beyond the wall. They'd traveled with fewer on their overland supply mission, but that was in the offseason and those guards were worth twice these chosen by Benton, even with the four Agunzi.

Marxius followed the troop's attention, looking through gaps in the canopy overhead. A column of smoke rose into the clear blue sky. He surmised the Volurem activity had grown in intensity with full sun and the day's heat.

"What is it?" Benton asked, cracking the door open.

"We're upwind of the Engulfed, near the fire's rear. It's as we expected, the Engulfed are still active," Marxius said.

"Where is the One Hundred and First Legion?" Benton asked.

"I don't know. Unless you received a message in private, no reply has come from them," he replied in frustration. The One Hundred and First should've been deep in the Apgar Forest and traveling the road south to Saypo. He didn't expect them to receive the news for at least another sunspan.

"Are we in danger?" Benton asked.

"It's too early to tell," Marxius answered.

"High Commander," a Rear Guard Sergeant said, riding up to the coach from the rear troop. "What are your orders?"

"Hold here," Marxius said.

"But the scouting party..." the Sergeant said.

"Fall back into your line, Sergeant. Wait there for my command," he said.

"The smoke column," Benton said, pointing to the light white plume as it swirled into the air. "It doesn't threaten us?"

"It could slowly backburn toward us. We've already sent a troop to scout it out. If it's something they can handle, we'll know in a few more moments. The smoke will slow. If it's not, the column continues to grow, and they don't make a swift return, I'll make an adjustment."

"I hope you know what you're doing, Ovando. I cannot afford to be made a fool of on my first campaign as Emperor and Creator reborn in the people's eyes," Benton said.

"Given the direction of the wind and the fact that no Pyrignum have been sighted in the area, you don't have much to worry about yet," Marxius said.

Benton closed the coach door as Marxius stood next to

it, eyes glued to the smoke column. The guards stirred uneasily as the nearby blaze seemed to grow.

"That shouldn't be," Marxius said to himself, seeing the tops of the trees bending north and the column of smoke angling similarly. He wondered if Bridger's report regarding Pyrignum was accurate. The man had seen many fire fights in his time in the legions. He would know if there were, but Marxius questioned if he could trust the Bridger's report. He'd stabbed his Emperor through the heart for the promise of Kai position and a small treasure, or so Marxius assumed.

As the fire continued to grow in an impossible direction, burning against the wind, Marxius whistled for an officer. A Lieutenant from the front rode around to the coach and saluted. Marxius dismissed his salute and said, "Take your troop north on the road. Approach the Volurem with caution. See if the scouting party has engaged them already. If the Engulfed are isolated to a pocket of green within the burn, let them blaze out. If they're back-burning, which they shouldn't be, ride immediately back to us and report."

"You don't want to us to engage?" the Lieutenant asked.

"Not if they're back-burning. That will mean a Pyrignum is nearby. Go and see what the Engulfed are doing, where the scouting party is, and only draw weapons if you need to defend yourselves during your return to the coach. Is that understood?" Marxius ordered.

"Yes, High Commander," the Lieutenant said, saluting and waiting for Marxius to dismiss her.

He did and she rode forward, relaying the order to her squad leaders before riding out. Marxius saw the youthful

Old Rhydarian Sergeant from among the Rear Guard riding forward to check in with him.

"You maintain your order to hold," Marxius said, pointing at the young man and halting him in his tracks.

Marxius rapped his knuckles on the coach door. Benton opened it, not asking what he wanted, but looking at him expectantly. "The Volurem's intensity is growing at the rear of the fire. Either they're catching in a green island of trees near the edge, or they've started back-burning in this direction," Marxius said.

"What does that mean for us?" Benton asked.

"You might get to face your first Volurem before the One Hundred and First arrives," Marxius said.

Benton fumbled for the brismil scale, forgetting to open his surcoat and undo the flap on his tunic, which exposed where the harness pressed the scale to bare skin.

"But don't put that on yet," Marxius said. "Unless you're eager to get a head start on the disease."

Benton's upper lip curled, and he lifted his hand from the pouch on his belt.

Marxius stood outside the coach, waiting to see if the smoke column ahead of them would thin to a wisp and then burn out. He thought it didn't look large enough yet to overtake forty trained and mounted guards, but it was growing. After too long a time for the second troop to have been gone, Marxius wondered if he should take this matter into his own hands. The Emperor also had a dragon scale and blade pair, not a matching set, but he would be nearly impossible for a Volurem force of this size to kill, unless there was a Pyrignum present.

"High Commander," a voice from the remaining troop called from behind him.

Marxius turned, ready to scold the Rear Guard Sergeant again for questioning his orders but he held his tongue when he saw that it was a Captain wearing House Landrich's colors. He was pointing to the blue sky behind them. Marxius followed his aim to a thin trail of smoke rising in the air. "Ashes," he cursed. "How is that possible? Something isn't right about these Volurem," he said under his breath.

"Your orders, High Commander?" the Sergeant called out to Marxius.

"Hold your position," he barked at them. "Protect the Emperor," he added.

Marxius opened the door to see Benton's surcoat opened, tunic side flap undone, and clutching the leather pouch with his brismil scale in one hand. His dragon blade in its scabbard lay across his lap.

"What's going on, Ovando?" he said.

"Something strange is happening. The Volurem are not acting like Engulfed here. I'm going to inspect the spot fire that's just started behind us," Marxius said.

"What spot fire?" Benton snapped.

"It's still small. I'll take care of it. I have a suspicion that there's more than just Engulfed lurking in the forest," Marxius said.

"What about me?" Benton said.

"You will take charge of the troops. Use Landrich's Captain for suggestions. Put on your brismil if that gives you the confidence needed to stay put. Don't go into a fight without me," Marxius said.

"You can't order me to do anything," Benton said.

"I'm not ordering. I'm telling you. If you want your guards to live, stay put," he said.

Closing the coach door, Marxius ordered an officer off

his harquice. Marxius took to the saddle and heeled the anxious animal toward the spot fire.

JEXSANNA STEPPED SOFTLY on the ash-covered ground, nearing the Engulfed Volurem flickering to life at the edge of the fire. Careful not to scare it before it saw her, she scooped it up into the bundle of dried twigs she held in her hands. Running with a palm-sized Engulfed in her grip, the rushing air fueled it, and the Volurem grew. Before it could grow large enough to attack her, she dropped it under a tree in the dry duff. She stopped long enough to taunt it into growing before leaving for the rear of the fire again. She continued to carry smoldering Engulfed deeper into the forest, growing, and spreading them out in a half-moon shape on either side of the road. She was careful not to let the scouting party see her as she worked to build the fire around them. The Volurem wouldn't burn them, not unless they were foolish enough to charge into the front of the fire. But killing these men and women wasn't her goal. She just needed to use the Volurem to block their path back to the Emperor and the Scaled One.

The group of twenty strangers didn't notice the growing fire until it was crackling into the branches in a wide swath. Jexsanna had ensured that it was too wide-spread for them to effectively target the entire burn. To her surprise, she saw the guards ride their harquice to the west. She frowned as they continued through the edge of the black and into the green forest. Whatever they were doing, Jexsanna's part of the trick was done. They couldn't return to the Scaled One on the road for hours. The route they were taking was dense, and the fire was growing to the sides in both directions. They would need to go around. It would buy her enough time. Now, she had to secure her and Shylo's freedom by killing The Scaled One.

Snaking her way through the burn, Jexsanna saw another troop of about the same size. They stopped to examine the blaze in both directions. She wondered when they would start attacking the Engulfed from behind. As they continued to stand on the road, Jexsanna picked up a burning log covered with small Engulfed Volurem trying to crawl out from the coals. She took off along the road, spreading embers into dry branches and duff under trees and thick brush. As she circled this second set of guards, she heard orders called out to not engage. She could see through the trees to the narrow road where they rode. Hooves sounded as more of armed guards rode up. She heard one in front tell the others to attack the fire, a direct order from the Emperor.

Waiting for the fire to grow in the surrounding forest, Jexsanna continued to usher new Engulfed into the half circle she was forming around the thirty or so mounted guards attacking the heel of the fire. They worked slowly, spreading out along the back edge of the Volurem. Her heart skipped a beat when she saw one of them don a metallic dragon-scale suit of armor and leap into the fire. She almost committed to attacking but noticed the sword wasn't a brismil blade. She wasn't going to make the same mistake as last time. She continued carrying out her task in Shylo's plan: to create a thick line of fire enclosing the troops as they focused on fighting the blaze in front of them.

Off in the distance, Jexsanna spotted a small, but established trail of smoke to the north. That fire hadn't been started by these Volurem. The winds wouldn't have spotted that way and there were no Pyrignum. That's when Jexsanna wondered where Sandor had gone. He was supposed to help her spread the fire with the sunstone. She didn't realize he was going to start one so far back that it could risk burning Shylo. She felt anger rising within her, burning hot like the Volurem surrounding the Rhydarians.

Holding a squirming Engulfed in one hand and her willow-leaf saber in the other, Jexsanna knew she needed to find Shylo. The Scaled One had to die today, but not if that meant Shylo would burn. She needed to find Shylo before the spot fire caught up with him.

FIRE AND SMOKE

Nineteen Days After the Emperor's Death

"Marxius is leaving the troop by himself," Galterius said.

Shylo saw that the High Commander was right. He thought he got a good look inside the coach twice and hadn't seen anyone but Benton and the High Commander. Bridger wasn't there, but Marxius was. The High Commander was leaving the Emperor with his guards and riding toward Sandor's spot fire.

"Are you ready? This is it, the opportunity we've been waiting for," Galterius said anxiously.

"Shouldn't we wait for Jexsanna and make sure she hasn't seen Bridger as well?" Shylo asked.

"Bridger is not here. You want to set the record straight, don't you? Marxius might not be the assassin, but he is closer to the truth than we are. We won't get a better chance than this, Shylo," Galterius said. "This is our only opportunity."

Shylo swallowed hard and nodded. Marxius was Shylo's main objective. This was the opportunity he hoped to achieve with his plan. "If this is it, then we should make it count," he said, putting on a false sense of bravado.

"You will not attack unless I order it. Is that clear?" Galterius said.

Shylo nodded absentmindedly. He was racked with fear about the many horrible ways this could end. He knew there was a high likelihood he'd be killed if he attacked. All it took was one scratch from the dragon blade. Shylo had hoped Jexsanna would be with him for this. He didn't have the skill to face a trained soldier, never mind one with brismil scale and blade. More so, Shylo just wanted to see Jexsanna one last time if this was to be his end. His plan, however, wasn't perfect. He hadn't anticipated that Bridger wouldn't be there. Without him they lacked the hard evidence Galterius recommended they obtain. That Marxius separated himself from the others voluntarily was a surprise as well.

"Move quickly and remember what I told you about using that blade," Galterius said.

"Only as a last resort. I'll look more threatening if I don't use it, and just hold it," Shylo repeated. He felt embarrassed saying this out loud, but it was the truth. Shylo couldn't use the steel blade effectively on such a foe.

"Sandor and I will do the heavy-lifting, if necessary," Galterius said. "Come on, we must be swift."

Shylo trotted alongside Galterius, taking in his surroundings, while focusing on saving his strength for their opportunity to corner Marxius. Yet he felt as if his body was growing sluggish and heavy. His breathing felt labored and the tingling in his stomach that fluttered up through his chest intensified as they approached the smoke from the spot fire. He slowed, as Galterius did. Galterius gave him a nod, signaling to be ready at any moment. Shylo searched the cleared corridor through the trees. He saw Volurem swaying in the underbrush. Their black-and-red ember-covered arms lashed out at anything that would carry their flames higher and give them strength. He didn't see Marxius anywhere within view. Shylo looked to Galterius, who now wore an expression of concern.

The sound of something forming in the air behind them caused Galterius to whirl on his heels, swinging his dragon fang. Shylo ducked, sprawling forward onto his hands and knees. The sound of magically sharpened bone on bone thudded as they struck sending Galterius tumbling to the ground near Shylo. Shylo looked back to see a man layered in a draco-scale surcoat with metallic brismil-scale coating his skin underneath. He bore a massive ivory dragon blade.

"I knew there was something unnatural about the way this fire was growing," Marxius said without a hint of fear at the situation. He stepped closer to Galterius as Shylo scurried away, hustling to rise to his feet.

Shylo stared at the Kai, the father of a girl he once admired. The brismil scale acted like a protective skin. Marxius ignored Shylo completely and continued past him toward Galterius.

"The spot fire gave you away," Marxius said, swinging his blade down on Galterius.

Galterius was on his feet trying to get a word in edgewise, "Marxius, we need to —" He barely brought his sword up in time. Though Shylo understood the brismil blade gave Galterius added strength, it wasn't enough.

Galterius' arms buckled under the weight of Marxius' sword.

"Where is your scale, Galterius?" Marxius asked, taking a step closer, and driving Galterius toward the growing Volurem flames.

"Your Ca —," Galterius managed to say, but again, Marxius hammered his ash-white blade down on Galterius; Galterius blocked it again.

"Before I finally get the satisfaction of killing you with no repercussions, why not make it a fair fight? Now is the time to use your scale, if you have it," Marxius said snidely.

Shylo scrambled to his feet, holding the broadsword in both hands. He took a breath, facing Marxius' back. He knew he couldn't kill the man with his steel sword, but if he could knock him off guard, then Galterius would have a chance.

"What's wrong with you, Marxius? We're equals. We share Command," Galterius said.

"You'll never be my equal. You should've died already," Marxius growled.

"It was you!" Galterius said.

"Put on your scale, Galterius!" Marxius called.

"You know I don't have it," Galterius growled. "Your man, Captain Bridger, stole it from me when you had him murder Jermanus."

"Bridger is dead; or should be by now. I did n —"

From alongside the narrow road, a flash of red draco scales flew out of the brush. Sandor lowered his shoulder into Marxius' side, knocking him to the ground. Though he could hardly follow the rapid movements, he caught a glimpse of Galterius' black dragon fang striking forward, stabbing at Marxius' armored chest. As he fell, Marxius maintained awareness of his blade, swatting Galterius' tip down into the dirt. Sandor continued his rush through his shouldering of Marxius, harrying him with his great sword and attempting to break through the fracture at Marxius' neck, the weak spot in the brismil plate.

Shylo sprang into action, dismissing what Galterius had told him. To him, killing this man meant he and Jexsanna could be free. As Shylo came to Sandor's aid, he noticed the sag in Sandor's left shoulder, the one he'd used to drive into Marxius at the start. His arm hung limp at his side. Before Galterius could stab at Marxius again, the downed Kai swiped his blade at Sandor's ankles. But Sandor jumped as if he'd expected the strike before it came, narrowly escaping the deadly bite of the ivory dragon bone.

Shylo didn't expect it. He saw the trajectory of the blade in real time as it passed under Sandor's feet and carried through, toward Shylo's legs. Tripping in fright, Shylo lost hold of his broadsword, letting it fall tip first into the ground in front of him as he fell forward. Marxius' brismil blade connected with the edge of the broadsword, carrying it with the momentum of his follow-through. Shylo winced as the steel hit him, blocking the brismil blade's edge from cutting into his leg. As a result, the steel of the broadsword did its own damage. His leather boot helped slow the cutting edge of the sword, and his knee-length draco-scale surcoat protected his thigh. Despite the protection, he felt his sword cut into his calf and the cross guard of his hilt pound into his hip. He fell to the side of the road and rolled into the brush.

While steel-on-bone, and bone-on-bone clanged from the path, the pain of his failure rang harder. Shylo looked down at his right leg to see how badly he'd been wounded. The thin slice in the calf of his boot extended up his leg. A red line showed through the cut in his trousers from mid-calf up to the top of his knee. The draco scales of his surcoat were cracked up his thigh and the scales on his hip where the cross guard hit him were missing. As the feeling returned, his leg felt wet. When he pulled open the slice in his trousers and the leather of his boot, he couldn't tell how deep the cut went. He moved his foot and found it was still working. Shylo felt around for his sword, finding it an arm's-length away in the grass on the roadside. Above, on the roadbed, Galterius and Sandor fought Marxius together, but Shylo could see that they were being pressed back into the Volurem spot fire. By the time Shylo crawled to his sword, Marxius was sprinting past him, using his brismil-enhanced speed to return to the troop with Benton.

"Ahhhh," Shylo cried in frustration as he stumbled out of the overgrown ditch. To his left, Sandor and Galterius brushed singed embers off their cloaks. Shylo met Galterius' eyes, seeing rage and disappointment. He wanted to say that he had tried his best, but he wasn't a soldier. Galterius ran after Marxius without saying a word to Shylo. Sandor stopped in front of him.

"Are you injured?" Sandor asked.

"My leg," Shylo said, noticing Sandor's left arm still hung limply at his side.

"It can't be too bad if you can bear weight on it. I need to get my shoulder back in." Before Shylo could ask how he could help, Sandor handed him his great sword, saying, "Take this."

Shylo took it from him, watching as the brute of a man sat on the ground, intertwined his fingers, and held them over the cap of his left knee. With a swift motion, he pushed his knee forward, jerking both arms. Shylo heard a pop, and Sandor exhaled with relief.

Sandor bounced to his feet, holding his left arm tight

against his side. Taking the great sword back in his right, he said, "Try to keep up and don't let that brismil blade come near you again. You only get that lucky once."

Shylo nodded, adrenaline lessening the pain in his cut leg. Before setting out after Marxius, he glanced over his shoulder to see fully formed Engulfed crawling through the forest in their direction. Some jumped to their feet, making a run before they shrank, having to turn back into the flames. Shylo knew it wouldn't be long before they burnt through the green space that lay between them and the black.

As he fell into a jog behind Sandor, Shylo heard Jexsanna cry in distress from the near distance. The sound of her shouting cut to his core. He abandoned all hesitation and sprinted toward the sound.

***

JEXSANNA USHERED one last Engulfed Volurem to life on the road behind the troop. She saw a second Scaled One don dragon scale and lunge into the flames. Jexsanna didn't let the possibility of it being The Scaled One affect her decision. Not this time. The guards were surrounded by a growing force of Volurem, yet not one of them had looked back to see this.

Jexsanna's only thought in the moment was to find Shylo. She dropped the burning log crawling with tiny Volurem on the road and took off. Sprinting up the dirt path to the north, she hastened toward the growing spot fire.

When she rounded the corner, Jexsanna almost crashed into ten armed guards as they sat complacently on their harquice in a circle around a blue, harquice-drawn carriage.

She didn't slow too much, avoiding the soldiers before they could react to strike out at her with their blades. She didn't see Shylo among them but standing next to the blue-and-gold trimmed carriage, Jexsanna noted a familiar face. She did a double-take as she continued to run past them on the road. She didn't place where she'd seen him until he barked an order at the brawny, red-haired man on the front seat of the carriage.

"Kill that mutant," he said, pointing at her.

Jexsanna only let her gaze linger for the briefest of moments. It was the stranger who'd ordered The Scaled One to kill The Masters and the others like her. She forced this distraction from her mind, though, knowing his death wouldn't be as sweet if she lost Shylo. She renewed her pace, only just making out the glint of metallic scale before realizing a brismil-plated man with a dragon blade was running directly at her. The Scaled One didn't see her until it was too late either, because they collided at near full speed. The man in brismil dropped his blade the instant before they crashed. Jexsanna felt pain from the impact the instant she and the Scaled One met. She screamed, though more from the shock of running full speed into an equally matched moving target than from the pain.

Everything flashed white, then she rolled along the roadside. Coming to a stop, she swiped away dark blood flowing from her nose and felt a tightness in her chest as she gasped for air. She still held her willow-leaf saber. Jexsanna looked back at the man she'd collided with. He was climbing to his feet. He was tall, like The Scaled One. He shook like a wet dog, summoning his bone-white brismil blade. Jexsanna blinked, trying to clear her blurred vision.

"Him," she snarled, rising to her feet.

"You," he said in simultaneous recognition.

The man who'd given the orders stood among his ten guardsmen while the Agunzi man with the double-headed battle-axe came to join the Scaled One. They were together, as they had been at the arena. He was tall, like The Scaled One who killed the others like her. He had the white brismil blade too. This was *The* Scaled One. It was Marxius, the man she needed to kill.

While the Agunzi guard behind Marxius stalked up alongside him, the axe-wielding guard pulled a scale from the pouch at his belt and fitted it into the harness under his tunic. She stood in the path, facing two scaled adversaries, one with more strength than a normal Rhydarian and one with a dragon blade. Behind them, ten mounted guards with draco-scale surcoats and swords at the ready surrounded their leader, the new Emperor. Jexsanna could see that he, too, had donned brismil-scale armor and wore a brismil blade at his hip. She had no chance of prevailing against them all. She only needed to kill one, Marxius. Shylo's absence again pulled at her thoughts, and she looked behind her. Why had Marxius been running in this direction and not toward the spot fire?

Charging through the turn like an enraged draco, Jexsanna spotted Galterius huffing as he gave chase with his black dragon blade in hand. She didn't see Shylo. Even as the sound of Marxius and the Agunzi charged her, she called out, "Shylo!"

Jexsanna spun, connecting with the battle-axe swinging at her. The clang of metal obscured her hearing, but she thought she'd heard a response. She moved with speed, dodging under Marxius' blade and blocking the axe again. The sound of charging harquice crashed around her as the two Scaled Ones forced her back.

She called out again, "Shylo!"

This time, she heard him faintly.

"Jexsanna," his voice carried over the sounds of the fighting. As she desperately fought to find a gap in the chaos through which she could exit and go to him, she continued to hear him shouting her name. The Agunzi man in brismil harassed her every time she tried to look for him. The strength of each of his swings was almost too much for her to block. She'd never fought a person with his strength while in brismil plate before. She winced as a guardsman's steel sword cut her in the side. She spun, directing her willow-leaf saber to cut clean through the Rhydarian man's exposed neck.

Another guard stabbed at her and she dodged, only to be struck in the back by the Agunzi man's boot. She crashed forward, tackling the Emperor's guard. She rolled away. The stout Scaled One's axe followed right behind her, burying deep into the downed guard's chest that she'd just escaped.

For one brief moment, Jexsanna surveyed the scene. Galterius fought with the armed guards on harquice. Each of the four surrounding him, seeming hesitant to get close to his brismil blade as he swung wildly. Sandor had joined the fighting, too. Jexsanna hadn't seen him enter the fray, but he was trading blows with two more guards. With two more dead by her sword and the Agunzi's axe, a third and fourth rushed in to fill their places.

Through it all she spotted him. Marxius walked calmly through the chaos. His gaze leveled at her as he dragged the tip of his white dragon blade through the dirt. Then, as if appearing from thin air, she saw Shylo. He ran with his broadsword held firmly in both hands, just as he'd done with a stick at the lazgron that Jexsanna killed in the burn scar. He released a cry, launching himself at Marxius' side.

The Scaled One hadn't noticed him until he was already there.

The axe came next, interrupting Jexsanna's view. She nearly buckled under its weight, letting the curved edge of the axe come dangerously close to her chest. Punching his follow-through to the side, Jexsanna pushed this stout Scaled One out of the way. But she wasn't fast enough to stop Shylo from facing Marxius. The two mounted guards came between them as Shylo's sword deflected off Marxius' surcoat. She was too late.

MARXIUS NOTICED the young man again when he heard him shouting, giving away his position. He knew the Didimo boy didn't have any fighting skill. He'd heard as much from his daughter, but that was reenforced when he saw the young man trip and drop his broadsword as he tried to attack Marxius the first time. Apparently, Shylo had gotten lucky and not been cut by Marxius' blade. If he had been, the young man wouldn't be on his feet. But he wouldn't be lucky twice.

Shylo's broadsword hit Marxius in the side as he turned to face him. Marxius didn't let the metal blade faze him. It couldn't do anything to hurt him, not in this Eso's hands. He caught Shylo by the throat, holding him easily at arm's length. Shylo dropped the sword, trying to pull Marxius' grip away from his neck. Marxius didn't understand why this young man, an Eso who was smart enough to get into Penti training, would do something so foolish as to attack a man in brismil with nothing more than a steel blade. Then the desperation of the mutant's voice rang in his ears. She was calling to him and fighting to break through the guards to get to Shylo.

Jexsanna? he thought, realizing that was the name the Eso had been shouting before. *Why does that name sound familiar?* he wondered. It didn't matter though. Marxius knew that sound of desperation in each of their voices and he now knew how he could bring the mutant woman crawling to him on her knees.

Marxius released his stranglehold on Shylo, taking him under his arm and carrying him like a child through the fray and toward the side of the road where Benton stood watching. He'd abandoned his coach in the charge and was hanging back near the fighting. Benton stood near the fray now, his blade in hand, awaiting an opportunity to use his brismil. Marxius held Shylo tight, placing him on his feet next and holding him still as he stood next to the Emperor.

"What are you doing, Ovando? I want that mutant killed," Benton demanded.

"She's not a mutant! She's a person," Shylo snarled.

"Who is he, and why isn't he dead?" Benton asked Marxius.

"This is the Didimo boy."

"My name is Shylo," he said, trying to wriggle free.

"Kill him, Ovando," Benton said.

"He has been with the mutant since he escaped. I found him and Galterius-Brex at the spot fire. They tried to surprise me, but this trap of theirs has been sprung. They failed to kill me," Marxius said, seeing over Benton's head that Jexsanna, as Shylo had called her, had killed another of the Emperor's guards. The Agunzi guard with Benton's extra brismil scale was doing well, preventing the mutant from breaking through to help the other two. Galterius continued to swing his brismil blade wildly, keeping the guard at bay. The other one, a man who appeared to be a Rhydarian-Agunzi mix, fought one guard while one lay near death at his feet. Marxius didn't fear them. They didn't have dragon scales. He would let the Volurem burn them down if he had to.

"They're only trying to kill you so they can get to me. Kill this Eso and deal with the mutant. That's an order, Ovando," Benton said.

"He's been with the mutant long enough that they share a bond. If we keep this Shylo alive, she will come to us and give herself up," Marxius said.

"Why would we want her? I already told you they need to die," Benton said.

"Don't you see how useful she could be to the Empire? Surely you must've wondered why your uncle would keep them secret?" Marxius said.

"They will only destroy what Rhydenar has already established. I don't care what my uncle was planning to do with them. I gave you a direct order, High Commander," Benton said.

Marxius considered. With the Volurem burning around them and a group of traitors trying to kill him, Marxius didn't see things as his Emperor did. Marxius knew he could control this situation better by using Shylo as collateral.

"The man's a traitor, your Imperial Majesty," Shylo said.

"I know what Galterius is," Benton said.

"No. Marxius is the traitor. He was the one who orchestrated Emperor Jermanus and his heirs' murder. Look to his Captain of the Ovando House Guard for proof," Shylo said.

Marxius' curiosity at how the young man came to this

conclusion drove him to allow Shylo more time for explanation.

"The High Commander created the elaborate plot, charging his man, Captain Bridger-Kai, to act as Marxius' hand in the Akai assassination. While escaping the Palace after the murder, Bridger stole Galterius' brismil scale. Marxius timed the murders so they would happen while he was away, giving himself an alibi. Captain Bridger and the others he must have contracted slaughtered all of House Didimo before the warning bells even began to toll. I didn't get back to the villa until the massacre had already occurred, which is why I survived. I speak the truth, you have to believe me," Shylo said in nearly a single breath.

By the time he'd finished telling this story, two more guards had fallen to Galterius and his companion. Jexsanna was still trying to get through the Agunzi guard to reach Shylo and Marxius.

Benton chuckled, "Can you believe that, Ovando? This Eso is trying to give *you* credit for assassinating the Emperor and putting me in power."

Marxius didn't answer. He felt the aching sensation pinching his gut. The one he'd felt the last time he wore his brismil. Marxius ignored the pain, focusing on how Benton typically reacted in situations like the one he faced. He wasn't pleased that Marxius was getting the credit for his plan. Yet, Marxius didn't know how he'd come up with the idea and executed it without more suspicion. Benton acted so impulsively. He was turning out to be less of a puppet that Marxius could control and more of a delusional Akai with too much power.

"That's why we're doing this. We're trying to kill Marxius, not you, your Imperial Majesty," Shylo said naively.

"You admit to trying to murder my personal guard?" Benton asked.

"We want justice for Jermanus. Place us all under arrest and let the evidence prove who really organized the Emperor's fate," Shylo said.

Benton leaned in and whispered in Shylo's ear. Marxius' brismil-enhanced hearing could hear clearly what the Emperor intended only for Shylo, "You won't get justice for my family's murders by killing Marxius because he isn't smart enough to pull off what I did."

Marxius felt Shylo grow rigid in his arms.

"That's right, Didimo boy. I did this to you. I did this to all of you and before the sun sets, you will die by the poison of a brismil blade or burn in the fire of the Volurem. Whichever it is, I don't care. When I return to Perdigon, having tied up every loose end to these murders, I will ascend. The people of Rhydenar will finally see me as I really am – a Creator," Benton whispered. When he pulled away from Shylo, Benton smiled at Marxius.

Marxius held Shylo from squirming free, but having heard what Benton said, and seeing that Benton believed his admission was spoken in private, was disturbing.

Marxius understood when he first decided to go with Benton on their overland supply audit that Benton wasn't the average Akai. He'd refused to take seriously the training that his uncle forced on him. Marxius understood now that there was no controlling Benton. He'd lost that trust and could see the Akai turning on him as he did repeatedly on his own family. He wondered how long it would take Benton to realize that Marxius was using him to put himself in a better political position. However, being attached to the loose cannon that Benton had become came with serious repercussions. What would happen when the Senate saw what Marxius saw in Benton now? That he seriously believed he was going to become a god. That he believed he was better than every person in Rhydenar and that they should perform blindly everything that he commanded. Marxius wondered what that would mean for his daughter's future. If Benton threatened Marxius' house, he was threatening Ismay as well.

"Do it, Ovando. Kill the Didimo boy," Benton ordered.

Marxius noted the flames of the spot fire spreading through the surrounding forest. It wouldn't have to run far before it met the burned area to the south. The wounded and dying guards with them wouldn't escape the surrounding Engulfed. Galterius and the man in red draco scale were gaining momentum against those left standing. He searched for the mutant, the one he'd known as Number 2841. Marxius spotted her. She was bloody, with a mixture of her own inky blood and the crimson blood of the guards she'd slain. She no longer held her willow-leaf saber. The young woman held a double-headed axe in her hand and was hammering down on the Agunzi guard in the brismil plate. She hadn't killed him yet, but when he saw her reach down to the place where the scale attached to the guard's flesh, Marxius decided. He pushed Shylo to the ground in front of him and summoned his blade. Marxius watched Jexsanna's keen awareness notice his move. She stopped before grabbing hold of the man's brismil scale and waited to see what Marxius was about to do. In one fluid motion, Marxius turned to face Benton and stabbed his ivory dragon blade through the Emperor's chest, not stopping until the hilt's cross guard touched his armor.

Marxius held the Emperor's shocked gaze, taking the scale from his harness and ripping it free. Benton's knees grew weak, falling as he tried to form the question 'why' on his lips. Marxius let him fall to the side, dropping off the end of his blade. He let go of it, crouching to retrieve the Emperor's brismil blade before doing anything else.

Not forgetting his other opponents, Marxius looked out at the ten dead guards laying at the feet of Galterius, Jexsanna, and the stout Rhydarian. They looked at him in shock. Galterius was the first to charge, rushing with his black dragon fang.

Bursting through the forest behind him, Marxius heard members of the Emperor's troop crashing onto the scene. To his right, on the road, he saw a flash of brismil as two more dragon-scale armored soldiers led a handful of burnt and charred guards back to the Emperor's position.

Before they noticed the Emperor lying dead at his feet, Marxius bellowed, "Galterius-Brex has slain the Emperor!"

Marxius pointed at Galterius, stopping him in his advance. Shylo joined him at his side, equally confused. As the fire burned closer around them, Marxius knew the members of the guard were even more confused than those who'd seen what happened. Only one among them was an Imperial Guard and as Marxius' gaze fell on the Agunzi man pinned under Jexsanna's foot, she tore his scale free and buried the axe into his back. Before the life left the man's body, Jexsanna trained her sights on Marxius and threw the axe.

"After breaking Brisrome's dragon army, Tourome continued north. His dragons hunted and killed the remaining lesser dragons. When they were victorious, Tourome used his magic and his dragons to go after his brothers. The Creators cannot be killed, but that did not stop Tourome from dismembering them. He separated Brisrome and Pyrome into three parts. Their hearts apart from their bodies, and their bodies apart from their magical essence. He scattered these parts across Tarmigan, making sure they would not find their way back together again." – The Dracolyth

TAKEN

Minutes After the Emperor's Death

Shylo heard the words as the guards broke through the forest behind him and Galterius.

"Galterius-Brex has slain the Emperor!" Marxius bellowed.

A moment later, Jexsanna hurled the battle-axe at Marxius and ran from a dead Agunzi's side toward Shylo. She scooped up her discarded willow-leaf saber in the process. Shylo was still trying to process what had just happened. One moment he thought he was going to be killed by Marxius' dragon blade and the next he was witnessing the Kai stab the Emperor through the chest, killing the Akai he was supposed to protect.

Jexsanna helped him up and they ran.

"There're too many to stop," she said.

Shylo had seen the other two brismil-plated guards rounding the corner and heard the stomping of hooves on the road behind them.

"To the coach," Sandor said, matching their speed.

Shylo heard Galterius' labored effort in trying to keep up with them. The two brismil-plated guards new on the scene posed a threat. Shylo saw that he could beat the handful of guards to the coach as the draco-scaled guards on foot were moving slower than the two in brismil. Shylo glanced over his shoulder; those still on harquice merged onto the road. He saw they were too far away. They wouldn't catch them before they loaded into the coach. Among the gold surcoats on harquice riding to Marxius' command, Shylo spotted a red cloak flapping behind his former Penti classmate. Marxius continued to bellow accusations about the Emperor's death.

Shylo met Wilsall's determined look. There was no surprise in his eyes, only hatred. Though Shylo hadn't gotten the chance to confront Wilsall, Shylo could see from his former classmate's expression that he understood Shylo had played a heavy hand in this ambush. Shylo took joy in seeing the Ai lack any control over what he'd been charged to do, guard the Emperor. Because of what Shylo, Jexsanna, Galterius and Sandor had done, this Emperor had met his deserved fate. Wilsall had failed and the look on his face showed that he understood it was because of Shylo's actions. Shylo cracked a smile. Wilsall drew his sword and charged after them, but Shylo knew he was too distant to catch them.

The only serious threat that would hinder their plan to use the Emperor's coach for an escape ran toward them: two soldiers in brismil. Fortunately, they looked charred and weathered from fighting their way back through Jexsanna's fire.

Jexsanna and Sandor spurred forward, distracting the dragon-scaled guards while Shylo and Galterius weaved around them to the coach.

Once Shylo released the wing harnesses, the harquice pulling the coach would take flight. He hopped onto the driver's bench, finding the leather strap attached to their wing harnesses. Meanwhile, the High Commander began pulling up two staked lengths of rope at the back that kept the coach in place. Now free, the harquice pulled the coach forward.

"Jexsanna," Shylo shouted in warning.

Hearing him, she ducked away from the brismil-scaled guards they'd been holding back and pulled Sandor along with her. Sprinting to the coach, she allowed Sandor to climb into the coach while Galterius pulled from the inside.

The coach now headed directly at another clutch of Imperial guards on harquice returning from Jexsanna's fire, but they peeled off the path, jumping out of the way of the Emperor's coach while Jexsanna grabbed onto the handrail next to the driver's seat.

"Climb inside," he said to her, ready to pull the ripcord and release the wild harquice wings at a moment's notice.

"Take my sword," she said, handing him her blade and dropping the brismil scale she'd taken from the Agunzi guard on the floor.

As she hopped up to join Shylo, he pulled the ripcord.

He grabbed Jexsanna's hand, helping her the rest of the way onto the driver's seat. Shylo couldn't force the smile from his face when the harquice lifted into the air with Jexsanna sitting beside him. He couldn't believe that after how poorly his plan had gone they still appeared to be making it out alive.

Just then, a flash of silver entered Shylo's peripheral vision. Behind and below Jexsanna's smiling face, he saw Marxius.

"No," Shylo blurted out, trying to grab hold of Jexsanna before it was too late.

Jexsanna's smile broke, and she looked down. Marxius' brismil arm was wrapped around her waist. She held on, but the harquice was flying up through the opening in the canopy. Shylo grabbed her arm and held onto her. The railing Jexsanna held onto ripped free, still held tightly in her grip. Shylo felt Jexsanna's arm slide through his hand and her grasping fingers slip from his. Jexsanna fell from the coach back to the ground, held in Marxius' arm. Landing on the road, Shylo saw the other two brismil-plated guards and Wilsall with his red cloak descending on her.

"Jexsanna!" Shylo cried. He stepped to the edge of the coach. The forest canopy was beneath them, and he moved to jump. A wave of hot air, thick with black smoke and orange flames splashed up his chest, pushing him back onto the bench seat. The harquice flapped through the flames. Everything around Shylo clouded with a thick plume of black and grey smoke. His eyes stung and he coughed, searching for the reins. When he'd found them, he pulled on the right, steering them out of the rising smoke column. Looking out across the sky, Shylo saw how quickly the harquice had climbed. They now circled high over the forest. The Volurem below were erupting with violent intensity on all flanks. Shylo struggled to find the small pocket of green where they'd been fighting. He had to return for Jexsanna. The harquice veered away from the fire and Shylo struggled to direct them back.

"Shylo, what happened?" Galterius sounded from directly behind him.

Shylo saw the High Commander's face through a thin woven screen window in the coach. "Marxius, he got her. They took Jexsanna. I'm going back."

"Hold on," Sandor barked from the side door.

Shylo saw he was clinging to the side of the coach, climbing toward the front where Shylo sat. Shylo heard the brismil scale Jexsanna dropped on the floor rolling near his feet. Quickly, Shylo snatched it from the ground, using his tunic sleeve as a covering and stuffed it into the pocket opposite Chirp's den.

Sandor gripped the remaining handrail and hauled himself onto the driver's seat next to Shylo. "What's your plan here?" Sandor asked over the rushing wind.

"I'm going back for Jexsanna," he said, fighting against the harquice to point them back toward the fire.

"The fire's growing. We can't land where they took her," Sandor said.

"I'll land behind them," Shylo said.

"There're too many of them. We'll have to come back for her later," Sandor said.

"No!" Shylo shouted. He plucked Jexsanna's willow-leaf saber from the floor. "We're going back."

Sandor stared at the blade in Shylo's grip for a short time. "If we're going to do this, think it through. How will you not kill us and save her?"

"Jexsanna will fight them off," Shylo said.

"With what? You have her blade. I looked down as we

climbed through the trees. Three of them in brismil plate were pinning her down. They overpowered her."

Shylo shook his head. "I won't leave her. I can't."

Sandor didn't object. With a grimace, he helped direct the harquice down toward the upwind edge of the fire.

"Where are you taking us?" Galterius called through the screen.

"Where do you think, old timer," Sandor shouted.

"There," Shylo said, picking out a gap in the trees and seeing the road.

"We're going to land, Galterius. Be ready for another fight," Sandor shouted.

"The risks are too great. We need the element of surprise. It's over now. We'll come back for Jexsanna later," Galterius shouted.

"I still need what was promised, Galterius. Its either land and fight, or we go south, and I cash in on both of you," Sandor said.

"Ashes with you," Galterius cursed.

Their conversation fell like white noise over Shylo's ears. He focused on following the road leading north from the fire. Through the trees he saw glints of metal and gold. "There they are," he said, angling the coach toward them.

"Hang on," Sandor said. "We can't land now."

Shylo ignored him. The harquice kissed the flames at the rear end of the fire. Shylo lined them up with the road and focused in on the opening where he planned to touch down. They'd be blocking Marxius and the guard.

"Shylo, look at the road," Sandor said.

"I know where to —" Shylo saw glinting green and silver armor shimmering as the figures filed into the opening. Trailing the mass of soldiers, Shylo could see they extended deep beyond the clearing in the road. Shylo's heart sank when he realized it was the One Hundred and First Legion. Six thousand armed soldiers congested the length of the road, about to merge with Marxius and the Imperial Guard. Shylo hesitated for an instant before reacting. He did what he thought Jexsanna would do. He dove the harquice down, directly at Legion's leaders.

"What are you doing? There're too many. We'll all die, Shylo. What good will you be to her then?" Sandor demanded.

"She may be dead for all I know. I've got nothing left but her," Shylo said, tears welling in his eyes.

"They didn't kill her," Sandor barked.

"Pull up before we all die," Galterius shouted through the window.

"No!" Shylo cried. He knew it wasn't logical, but logic was not driving him now. He needed Jexsanna.

Sandor grabbed the reins. The harquice responded instantly, pulling up as the wheels of the coach skimmed the forest canopy. Shylo abandoned them, knowing if he jumped now, with the scale, he'd live long enough to be captured with Jexsanna. He shifted to the edge of the bench seat.

"Don't," Galterius called after Shylo.

Shylo spotted the purple cloak trailing behind Marxius. He carried Jexsanna on his harquice. She was draped over the front of his saddle, not moving, and bound. Shylo pushed off the coach out into open air. As he did, a firm grip took him by the back of his surcoat. He hung in the air for a moment before Sandor hauled him back onto the coach. Shylo struggled to break free, but the brute of a man overpowered him. Sandor twisted his wrist, forcing Shylo to drop the blade on the floor.

"Stop. We have to get Jexsanna," Shylo snapped.

"Galterius, do something," Sandor shouted.

"Shylo," Galterius said from within the coach. "Jexsanna is not dead. Marxius will keep her alive. We are not finished with them, but we must live another day if we're going to help her."

Shylo tried resisting Sandor, but it was no use. He pinned Shylo to the seat as he let the harquice escape farther from the fire. Shylo considered grabbing the scale with his bare hand and leaping from the coach, but Galterius' words were sinking in. He might survive the Volurem, but he wouldn't survive the Legion. He needed the element of surprise to help Jexsanna now. "Promise me we will return for her," he said.

"I promise you, Shylo. I will not stop trying to expose what Marxius has done today, nor will I give up on my duty to my Emperor, Jermanus. Bridger must pay for his part in Jermanus' death. I will not stop until I have my scale and you have Jexsanna."

Shylo held still through the pain. *Facing an entire Legion alone will only get me killed,* he told himself. *She'd still be captured, and I can't do anything to help her if I'm dead. I need to live so I can get her back.*

"I hadn't considered that the magic capabilities in the Pyrignum opal gem and the brismil fossils we use to fight the Volurem could be used by both species. When the Pyrignum grasped the brismil, it retreated. I do not know if it works for the Volurem the same way it does for the Terra people. I feel called to test these theories. To answer this call, I will need to end my journey south. I believe divine intervention will not allow me to continue. The gravity has taken a toll on the Legion as of late. I believe this to be a sign. The divine presence I sense here seems to be stealing our ability to breathe with each day. Evidence suggests that those of us in brismil armor should be able to capitalize on this oxygen-rich environment, yet even our brismil seems to be weak in the presence that resides in this heavenly place." – Sunspan 430, The Book of Volteir

PERDIGON

Marxius ignored the gut-wrenching pain twisting his insides as he rode ahead of the One Hundred and First Legion. The pain continued to worsen each time he donned his brismil scale, but he wouldn't let this pain show now. Hundreds of thousands of people lined the streets of Perdigon. Rhydarians, Agunzi, and Zethrillian; Eso, Ai, and Kai flocked to see the harquice-drawn hearse as it passed.

News of Emperor Benton Querci-Akai's death preceded their arrival by several days. Marxius was determined to squash every Volurem threat in Apgar before returning. The One Hundred and First Legion was the only available military force able to react to Benton's strike force in Yaak. For some unknown reason, they'd been much closer to Perdigon than their last reported position.

Marxius again thought about his daughter's words suggesting that the Legion was smuggling something from the arena. He left the fire fighting to answer the Palace's request for an Imperial funeral. With Galterius, the Agunzi-Rhydarian, and Shylo spotted flying over the road, Marxius didn't want to run the risk of traveling without access to military support. He knew these renegades were waiting for Jexsanna's transportation to attack. With roughly one hundred soldiers to escort him, however, Marxius successfully scared the three off of another attempt at an ambush.

Jexsanna, or Number 2841 as he called her again, was more important to Marxius than seeing the Emperor's body safely returned. She was unlike anything Marxius had seen. She wasn't a Rhydarian. She was the product of an experiment, one conducted in a facility tucked away at the base of the Shield Mountains. The 2,841st of her kind, if he were to guess the reason for her identification number. Following the return of Benton's body to the Palace, Marxius intended to find out exactly how Jermanus created them. If Ismay had found a paper trail, he could uncover what Jermanus was doing with these mutants in the arenas he'd built, and why.

Hushed voices and sobs sounded from civilians and the Noble class as Marxius led the funeral train, followed by a string of ash- and charcoal-stained soldiers. Marxius ordered the Legionnaires to follow the hearse with Number 2841 chained to a supply wagon. He wanted her on display for the people to see just as Bridger-Kai had done with the Zethrillian traitor, Isik; only Marxius' procession was more dramatic in every way.

Sunlight glistened off the eggshell-white buildings on Capitol Hill. The smoky scent they carried only added to the whispered gossip among the Noble classes. Marxius felt a strange sensation as he presented himself to be the Hero of Perdigon, safely returning the body of the Empire's fallen leader, with a looming victory against the Volurem threatening Apgar to boot.

Cresting Capitol Hill and riding through the row of Palace Guards into the courtyard, he approached a gathering of Rhydenar's most important citizens. The first person Marxius searched for was his daughter, Ismay. Yet he did not see her among those from his House Guard in attendance. Even more to his disliking, Marxius noticed the absence of his newest Captain, Noxon. He accepted what it meant. Bridger was still alive. Among the many leaders of the Senate and the Council, and the members of the Emperor's and Senate's various committees, Marxius didn't see Bridger or Ismay.

He did notice, however, that both Magistrates were in attendance. It took only one of them to decree the promotion he expected to receive, that of Major Commander in charge of an entire division of the Rhydarian Army. He envisioned being held in higher esteem than anyone else on the Advisory Council. Surely his opinions would carry more weight on the Defense Committee now. Marxius expected the next Emperor of Rhydenar would listen to his counsel above all others.

Marxius dismounted his harquice at the Palace steps. The black hearse had its shades drawn to mask the Emperor's bloated corpse. Several days in the elements, with nothing more than a canvas tent and wool blanket to preserve him, left Benton in a hideous condition. At Marxius' request, the Palace delivered a casket with the hearse before they rode into Perdigon. Wearing his military surcoat and clad in draco scales with brismil blade belted around his waist in a heroic display, Marxius approached the Palace steps. None of the remaining members of the late Emperor's family were present. Rumors had reached Marxius in the field that their lives had been threatened by Noble houses now relieved of the many threats Benton had issued so cavalierly.

Troop leaders from the One Hundred and First Legion opened the hearse and carried the casket. Magistrates Inyez Bynum-Kai and Lucerro Ventous-Kai ushered Marxius and the casket-bearers up the Palace steps, through the entrance and antechamber, and into the Great Hall. Combreti flowers adorned the massive opening, their black petals an iconic decorum for funerals. The long-stemmed flowers hung sorrowful heads of rippling, wide petals. Their green leaves had been trimmed off and scattered on the marble floor. At the heart of the Great Hall, the Legionnaires placed Benton's casket on a pier. The tradition of leaving the Emperor's casket open would not be observed in this case.

Once the casket was securely placed on the stone pedestal, Marxius stood respectfully at attention as council and committee members filed past to pay their respects. The display was a show, and even though some of the Senators and advisors wept, Marxius knew none of the tears were genuine. Benton would be forgotten. His short reign as Emperor had lasted less than three weeks. He was a blip in the timeline of Imperial succession.

As he stood tall, chest forward at attention, Marxius sensed the one question on every mourner's mind: Who would be the next Emperor? Many only wanted to know how to position themselves in the coming political shift. Some would leave Perdigon before an assassin's knife slit their throats or a cup of poison was served in their villa. Some would risk it all, hoping to do what Marxius had been able to do and come out on top.

When the crowd wound down and the Senators began to disperse, Magistrates Bynum-Kai and Ventous-Kai approached Marxius. This was it; he could feel it. They'd award him his promotion to Master Commander and he'd be issued a new villa, one larger and closer to the Palace.

"Marxius Ovando-Kai," Magistrate Bynum-Kai said. "There is a matter we need to discuss with you."

"I'm available now," Marxius said.

"As you know, we've been busy processing the events that have occurred since you left Perdigon," Magistrate Ventous-Kai said.

"It is paramount that the Empire must not go without a leader in this time of uncertainty with the Agunzi," Magistrate Bynum-Kai said.

"The decision regarding just who is next in line to lead our great empire is not one we take lightly, especially when we have no heirs to step into the role," Bynum-Kai added.

"It's a matter that requires careful consideration to be sure. If you wish to have my official endorsement of a new candidate, I have several Senators in mind who would surely provide excellent leadership," Marxius said.

"The Senate came to us with a proposed candidate yesterday," Ventous-Kai responded.

"I see. So, you want my advice on proposing an opponent? One you would rather have win the good graces of the Senate?" Marxius asked, a bit thrown off guard.

"No," Bynum-Kai and Ventous-Kai said together.

"The candidate the Senate adopted by majority decision, though unorthodox as we have no suitable Akai from which to choose, is the candidate we recommended," Bynum-Kai finished.

"Who?" Marxius asked, assessing the seriousness of the Magistrates with concern that he and his family could potentially be in danger because of this selection.

"You," Ventous-Kai said.

"We have considered all the Senators and found you to be the most suitable and agreeable to step into the role as the next Emperor of Rhydenar," Bynum-Kai said.

Marxius' jaw dropped. He had not expected this as there had only been Akai chosen to lead the Empire since the third Emperor of Rhydenar. He questioned whether he wanted this position. What threats would Benton and Jermanus' relatives pose in the future, when cousins and nephews came into adulthood? It was not his life he worried about. Considering his internal pains from applying his brismil scale too often for too long, he could feel his end approaching. How best could he secure his daughter's future? As a Major Commander, possibly forced to march into battle, or as Emperor of Rhydenar?

While remaining collected externally, Marxius attempted to weigh the costs and benefits of what he was being offered. It wasn't expected, but Marxius felt he would be foolish to decline. He nodded to the Magistrates, still struggling to find the right words to offer as a response.

"We will announce the transition of power tomorrow. Congratulations, Emperor Marxius Ovando-Akai, you will be the eleventh Imperial Ruler of Rhydenar," Bynum-Kai said.

JEXSANNA STRUGGLED against the chains that twisted around her body. She couldn't break through them. Not with her arms pinned at her sides like this. The wooden platform rolling her through Perdigon came to an abrupt halt, throwing her off balance for a moment. She tried to examine her surroundings, but the restraints were too constrictive. She could only see what was directly in front of her. The dark night in the city was lit by the lumistones inlaid in the stone walls. The air was dank, reminiscent of her stall at the arena. But she was far from the arena now. She'd just been hauled through the streets of the city like an animal. Jexsanna couldn't appreciate the towering buildings, swaths of new people, and mixture of fresh smells. The experience of entering a walled city, the one Shylo spoke of so fondly, instead was fraught with danger as she arrived at the hands of The Scaled One, Marxius.

Soldiers led the harquice-drawn wagon away from the rest of the group once they had climbed the hill to a place where the buildings turned white and were built on a grander scale than the walled villas they'd passed below. She was taken through a door on the lower side of a building and carted through faintly lit twisting corridors. Now that they appeared to have arrived somewhere, she wondered if this was the place where they would try to kill her.

The soldiers opened a heavy cell door. The cell was created with metal bars rather than solid walls like her stall at the arena. If this was to be her destination, she knew she could break free. The metal used to build this cage likely was the same metal used to construct the arena. If they removed the chains, Jexsanna could and would break through the bars, kill the soldiers with their own weapons, and escape the city as Shylo had done a month before.

When the soldiers removed her from the wagon, however, they didn't remove the chains. Instead, they set her in the metal cell still tightly bound. When the soldiers then locked the door and turned to leave, Jexsanna shouted after them, "Let me go, or I will kill you all."

They did not take her seriously. When they'd gone, only the faint light of the lumistones remained. The stone floor was cold and damp. The wet was soaking through the trousers the soldiers had forced onto her. Jexsanna again tried to push through the chains. Her muscles and bones felt bruised and bloodied by the chains and her continual effort to free herself over their rushed journey to Perdigon. This metal didn't break.

Now, in the silence of the dark cell, she huffed a defeated exhale. She missed Shylo. She missed being outside any walls where the air was clean, and her survival depended on sustenance, shelter, and her ability to kill. Here, she couldn't do anything.

To her right, Jexsanna heard a scuffle, followed by the sound of flesh slapping around the metal bars of the cell next to her. A deep feminine voice spoke. Jexsanna recognized it as similar to that of the tall purple-haired man she'd met in the group around the cooking pot on the night of her escape from the arena.

"Aren't you a specimen to behold?" this woman said. "What did you do to get wrapped up like that?"

Jexsanna struggled to break free again.

"Don't worry. You can trust me. We can be friends down here. Maybe even work together to break free... I've engineered more impossible scenarios, or fates rather. Though in those instances, I had more time to manipulate the Akai."

"Who are you?" Jexsanna asked, tired but interested.

"My name is, Isik. What's yours?"

EPILOGUE

FEELING THE CARNAGE

Seven Days After Emperor Jermanus' Death

Rain smattered her face, mixing with the sweat from her brow, and stinging her eyes. Kayda struggled to see clearly as she rode the stolen harquice through the evening drizzle. The burning in her eyes came as a much-needed distraction from the aches in her feet, hips, and stomach. Pains that arose during her panicked flight through the Apgar Forest. Getting back to the legion was all she could think about. It was the only thought she could focus on since fleeing the fire.

When the stinging in her eyes passed, her stomach took over. It felt as if it were sucking inward from the lack of food she'd had since racing away from the dying Volurem. She didn't trust anyone enough to stop, not after what she'd witnessed. The only person Kayda knew who would believe her was a week away from where it had happened. A week's ride away from the meadow where the white-haired woman killed her companions. The Volurem got two of them, but the strange woman had summoned the Engulfed Volurem. By accident or on purpose, Kayda didn't know if the white-haired woman used the Volurem against the envoy or killed them all out of fear. All Kayda knew for certain was that no

551

Terra person could stand in the fire without being burned. But that's what the white-haired woman had done. She'd killed with the speed of an Agunzi but was the size of a Rhydarian. The memory of that night haunted Kayda, driving her toward a single goal, to return to the One Hundred and First Legion.

Glowing lights appeared in the distance. Kayda squinted, trying to determine if the light was coming from a distant town or her longed-for army encampment. Kayda hoped this was her legion at long last. In her panicked flight through and away from the forest outside Perdigon, she didn't know exactly how far she'd traveled while regaining her mental faculties. She'd run until she couldn't. Then she'd walked until she found a town and stole the harquice. Kayda knew the legion was south somewhere along the road to Saypo. She rubbed her eyes, clearing them enough to make out the clear spread of individual lumistone and sunstone lighting a widespread encampment. A wave of hope hit her. Finally, she'd reached her legion.

Slowing her harquice, she approached the officers on guard at the road.

"Whoa! Who goes —" the legionnaire started, but then cut himself short when Kayda's green draco-scale uniform became visible by his light. "Lieutenant?" he asked, raising a lumistone embedded into a staff to better see the visitor.

Kayda imagined she looked a mess, her straight black hair greasy and slicked flat from the rain. Her skin was cracked and dry from a week of hard travel. Her stormy grey eyes were bloodshot and underscored with dark bags. She did not dismount her harquice. In a scratchy voice, she said, "I need to speak to Commander Nolstram-Kai."

"Where is the rest of your envoy, Lieutenant?" the officer asked.

"There was an attack. I escaped. The Commander needs to hear my report without delay," she said.

"Was it to do with the Emperor's death?" the officer asked.

Kayda blinked in surprise, "The Emperor is dead?"

"He died about a week ago. A messenger flew in on harquice to deliver the news four days ago... Hey, are you okay? You don't look so good."

"I'll live. Where's the Commander?"

"Command tent is near the center of camp, on the east side of the road. Right next to an old growth tsuga tree; you won't miss it," he said.

Kayda rode past, deeper into the Legion camp. Few soldiers lingered in the light as a steady rain fell. Those outside their tents were mostly Agunzi. They stared at her with fiery-orange eyes, hollow expressions on their broad faces. She almost thought to stop and tell them to go inside where it was dry, but she had more pressing concerns.

As she hitched the harquice to a low-bowing branch of the big tree outside Commander Nolstram's tent, she heard the door flap open. "Who's riding out there?" Nolstram said, his higher-pitched voice sounding awkward coming from his stout body.

"Lieutenant Kayda, Sir. I have urgent news," she said, hurrying toward the opening where Commander Nolstram blocked the entrance. His legs were squat and muscular, while his torso was similar in size to the average Rhydarian build. His arms were longer than Kayda's and lanky. Kayda put him at an estimated height of fourteen-and-a-half hands, shorter than her fifteen. His neck was shorter and thicker than Kayda's, too, while his head was longer and oval-shaped. The Commander's nose was pressed flatter than Kayda's, and his eyes sat farther apart above his high cheekbones. Nolstram's magenta hair waved in loose curls on top of his head while he kept the sides fingernail length. Where Kayda's eyes were shades of grey, his eyes were a rich yellow, flecked with orange.

"Why are you alone, Lieutenant? Do you realize how late your envoy party is? It's lucky for you that we rerouted to the north upon learning of the Emperor's death, or you would be even later. Do you have his reply? You know I won't get another now that he's gone from this world," Nolstram said, showing little concern for the state of his Lieutenant and forcing her to stand outside in the rain.

Kayda frowned, wondering if he was going to notice her haggard appearance.

Nolstram sniffed the air between them and said, "Is that smoke?"

Kayda gave a quick nod.

The Commander shot a glance to either side of the tent and said, "Come inside. Explain why you are alone and smell faintly like wet ash."

Kayda stepped over the small drainage trench surrounding the canvas tent and walked inside. It was well lit with lumistones and warmed by a sunstone burning inside a cast-iron box in the center of the room. Rugs spanned the floor and a single cot stretched along one side of the tent while a table was set up along the other. Two chairs were tucked into the table where a single map and neatly placed paper and quill lay waiting for notetaking. On the table next to the map sat a wooden crate filled with tightly rolled maps and neatly stacked parchment. Between the cot and the table hung the Commander's armor. The freshly polished draco-scale surcoat, helmet, and sword belt hung on a rack, as if on display.

Relishing the warmth inside the tent, Kayda began to

tell her story: "We'd stopped a few hours' ride outside the Capital. The Zethrillian, Agus, wanted to eat and rest before traveling farther south. After we'd cooked our meal, a woman appeared from somewhere in the forest. She came alone and walked right up to us without any of us hearing her until she was standing on the edge of our circle.

"She had a saber, but nothing else. She was nude and looked unlike any Terra person I've ever seen. Her hair was white as ash. Her skin, black as soot, with splotches of red that weren't scarring. She didn't speak but it was clear to all of us that she needed help. She put down her sword willingly, didn't act like much of a threat. We gave her a blanket. She was eyeing our scraps of the food like she hadn't eaten in days. We told her she could have the rest that remained in the pot. She walked up to the sunstone and grabbed it with her bare hands."

Kayda took a short breath, reliving their surprise, and continued, "She picked it up like it was nothing, like it didn't burn. Her fingers didn't blister, the skin on her hands didn't melt off. She held it like it was nothing to fear, and we reacted. She spooked and dropped it. At least, that's the way it seemed to go. That's when the Volurem came. And the killing started."

"Did you receive the Emperor's reply?" Nolstram asked, seeming to ignore all of Kayda's more important facts. Most notable to Kayda and her now-deceased fellow travelers was that this person was not like any Terra anyone had ever seen.

"No," Kayda said. "Helmer, Pyter, Robson, and I only escorted the Zethrillian to the Palace as instructed. We were not permitted to enter and afterward he didn't tell us what they discussed or if any message was in his possession."

"You didn't see Agus with a letter or some type of document?" Nolstram pressed.

"If he had one, he died without telling us about it or showing anyone that he had one," Kayda said.

"Did you search his body? What about the saddlebags? Do you have his harquice with you?" he asked.

She shook her head. "Commander, we were attacked off guard in dry grass by Volurem. Agus was the first to die. They sprouted in the grass at his feet and burned him before he could escape."

"His body burned?" the Commander asked.

"He died, but the Volurem did not burn out of control. She killed them before they ran wild," Kayda said.

"So Agus' body is still there, where he died?"

Kayda scowled, "I would expect so, unless something has eaten it. It's been days."

"A week. Probably too long, but there's a chance we could find his robes. What about the harquice he rode? Do you have it?"

She shook her head, "No."

"What is wrong with you? Why did you leave without them?" Nolstram snarled.

"Because I watched a mutant Terra person stand naked in the fire. The Volurem did not burn her skin, not even a little. She moved faster and with more strength than any Agunzi. She killed them all, and not just the Volurem. Robson, Helmer, Pyter and the Volurem, all dead. I ran for my life. I did not stop running until I found a harquice to steal and I did not stop riding until I found the Legion and I came directly here to report this to you. Commander, this woman is not a normal Terra person. She is unlike any fighter that we have known to exist. She can't be burnt by the Volurem or overpowered by the Agunzi. It is as if a Creator is in her. As if she's —"

"Stop," Nolstram nearly shouted. "I will not allow you

to suggest that a dragon god has returned to Tarmigan."

"The old religion tells of a Creator's magical ability. Couldn't a being as all-powerful as this return to our world in Terra form?" she argued.

"No. You will forget what you saw in the wilderness, Lieutenant. There are things in this world that you cannot comprehend and this is one of them. There is not a dragon god among us. This is something else entirely," Nolstram said.

"Forget it? How can I? I saw her holding the sunstone without burning herself. I watched her move unaffected among the flames. I saw her kill an Agunzi and one of our best swordsmen with ease. She did not speak. She did not know what we were."

"I'm not asking, Lieutenant. You will forget what you witnessed. If you tell anyone what you saw, I'll execute you for treason. Is that understood?" Nolstram demanded.

"Commander, how do you know this isn't what it looks like?" she said.

"I know far more about what that thing was than you can imagine. It was not a god. It was not a Creator. She was not a dragon. I'll only say this one more time to you: If you open your mouth about this or I hear that you're preaching the old religion to the soldiers, you'll be executed," Nolstram said.

Kayda stiffened, looking directly over the top of his head at the canvas wall. "When they ask me what happened, what do I tell them?"

"Tell them Pyter turned traitor. He killed Agus first, in his sleep, then Robson. You woke up to his dying breath only to see him struggling with Helmer, who was mortally wounded. You did what you had to, killing the traitor. Pyter destroyed the communication Agus had for me."

"Pyter was an innocent young man. He didn't deserve to die and his memory doesn't deserve to be stained with this lie," Kayda said.

"Fine, Helmer was the traitor. Nobody liked the burn-scar anyway. His family's all dead and gone in the South Apgar wars. He won't be missed," Nolstram said.

"It's still a lie," Kayda said.

"You don't have to tell anyone anything. But they'll start to think you're guilty of their deaths. It's up to you, Lieutenant. You know the consequences."

"What about the harquice?" she asked.

"Lazgrons or dracos got them. It happens often enough with the domestic equines in small groups, take your pick."

When Kayda didn't offer a reply, the Commander said, "Go to your squad's tent. Get some rest. We're marching north in the morning."

Kayda pressed her right hand to her heart in salute. Nolstram returned the gesture and she walked out into the drizzling rain.

She passed an Agunzi man sitting in the mud outside his tent. "Get inside your tent soldier," she said. The man looked at her for a moment, opened his mouth to reply, decided against it, then walked into the tent. As Kayda searched through the camp for her squad's flag, she wondered what the envoy mission had really been about. She was shocked to learn that Commander Nolstram-Kai was not the least bit concerned about the dangerous woman running free in the wilderness. Whatever Nolstram wanted from Jermanus either died with Agus and the Emperor, or was lost somewhere near the meadow where the Volurem sprouted. Whichever it was, Kayda intended to find out exactly what was going on.

SEEKING OUT CONNECTIONS

Two Days Before Emperor Benton's Death

The sprawling dirt avenue stair-stepped past tightly packed buildings of brick and wooden siding that cascaded from the city skyline down to Perdigon's port. Ismay smelled the briny water rolling in on a breeze from Brism Bay. She realized she hadn't been down to the port since the last ship had sailed to Florens with Jermanus' final payment to the *miners*.

Ismay's suspicions had been confirmed when she spoke with her father earlier in the morning. Whatever Jermanus' people were doing in remote locations along the Shield Mountains, it wasn't mining. Marxius had called it "the substance." Ismay didn't know what that meant, but she guessed it had something to do with the military if Benton had wanted Marxius to deal with it.

Ismay's inclination to return to the sprawling Eso neighborhood wasn't driven by what Benton and her father were attempting to cover up, rather more by her father's reaction to something she had said. Ismay doubted that her father even caught onto the inconsistency about the Captain of the House Ovando Guard, Bridger-Kai. When she asked him what he'd directed Bridger to do on the night of the assassination, his response didn't follow what she'd seen Bridger doing.

Ismay remembered the night well. She'd returned from the day's training on Capitol Hill and was preparing to tell those among her family guard who she directed as their Kai to take the night off when she saw Captain Bridger suspiciously leaving through the back gate. She thought it odd, and instead of heading directly to the Canteen as she had planned, Ismay followed the Captain to a Kai neighborhood. He met a man there. Someone with a written message. Bridger accepted the parchment, opening it to read its contents. That's when a strange light from a neighboring villa distracted her. It flashed blue for a moment, or she thought it had. Though, the more she thought about it, no light source she knew of in Perdigon had a blueish tint. She rationalized that it must've been lightning. The white flashes of energy from a storm that could summon the Volurem sometimes appeared light blue, but the skies were clear that night. When Ismay returned her gaze to Bridger, he was gone as was the stranger he'd met. She left the spot confused and guessing at the message's contents, likely sent in private for the Captain from her father. However, it was the way Bridger received the message that wasn't normal. She remembered walking up the hill after the fact toward the Capitol Hill Canteen, trying to puzzle out why the message was sent in this way. Lost in thought and growing angrier at her father's strange trust issues, she was relieved when she saw a fellow Penti classmate, the Eso from House Didimo.

Now, as she walked toward the port while trying to process who the note would've been from if not her father and why Bridger went to a neutral location to receive it in private. Here, Ismay's thoughts drifted again to Shylo and what had happened to him in the days after the Emperor's death. A poor fate, even for as bold an Eso as Shylo had been. He had the confidence to lie to an older Ai about sleeping with one of the Novi trainees. She wondered if his lying, in part, gave the Nobles reason to distrust the Senator's House and target Didimo so quickly in retaliation. It hardly seemed reason enough to Ismay, but some Kai houses would look for any petty excuse to move up in the political standings.

Out of all the murky lies people spread about who was really pulling the strings behind the Akai murders, Ismay found the disconnect between Bridger's suspicious actions and her father's lack of awareness about it the most disturbing. To further deepen the shadow growing around Bridger's loyalty to House Ovando, she'd heard recent rumors about him leaving this post for good. They said Captain Bridger-Ai was now Kai of the Fifth Class. Though many Kai houses whispered their suspicions that Didimo wasn't solely to blame, all acted in public as if the Emperor's death was a tragedy that had been resolved.

Over the last several days, Ismay had begun to think House Didimo wasn't tied to the murders at all. She had a feeling the deaths were linked to the amount of money Jermanus was spending on a fruitless mine. Growing up as a Kai, Ismay understood the motivations that sent houses into blood feuds. Money and adultery were top of the list. Jermanus had openly married a second wife early in his reign as Emperor and had also been openly affectionate with his brother's widow for almost a decade before his own death. That anyone noticed how much money he was hemorrhaging for the so-called mine, to Ismay's knowledge, had only just surfaced in recent years.

A passing harquice-drawn wagon splashed mud from the recent rain onto her lazgron cloak. "Ugh," she said in frustration, seeing that some had splattered under the brown cloak that hid her expensive dress. "Excuse you!" she shouted after the driver, but the two Agunzi men didn't turn around. "Dullards," she murmured and crossed the median separating the two lanes of traffic.

Ismay located the fish cutout that she was looking for. The sign hung over the door of the shop Bridger had entered. The Customs area at the port was still a few more blocks down the avenue. Ismay was glad she wouldn't be snooping down at the docks again. More than a few ships' crews had ogled her and made passing comments when she'd been down there. To Ismay, looking was one thing, but lewd comments were much worse.

She chanced a sweeping glance over her shoulder to make sure the new acting Captain of the House Ovando Guard wasn't still on her trail. Noxon was easier to lose than she expected, but Ismay didn't want her to see what she was doing in confronting Bridger. Arriving at the shop front, Ismay spotted Bridger through the window. He was leaning on the counter, scribbling on a scrap of parchment. The shop attendant, a brawny New Rhydarian man with nappy black hair, well-formed muscles, and scarred features, shook his head after reading the note. Ismay hesitated. The shopkeeper looked meaner than any of the Ovando Guards, including Bridger. What this man was doing working at a tackle shop in the port-side neighborhood, Ismay didn't understand. He looked like the type to be fighting alongside Agunzi infantrymen at the Fringe.

Despite this appearance, he would be a witness. As would all those who passed by the large shop windows along the busy avenue. Ismay fought back her doubts about confronting Bridger here. If he tried anything, she would have an audience, and of all people, Bridger knew what kind of trouble House Ovando could bring.

Ismay entered the shop.

"And you'll set it up for me, Nayt?" Bridger asked.

The muscular attendant eyed Ismay briefly with green and golden eyes, then shook his scarred head, saying, "Nah. I don't broker for anything this high risk."

"You worked with me before…" Bridger continued but trailed off as Ismay cleared her throat.

"What can I do for you, Miss?" Nayt said.

"I'm here to talk to the Captain," Ismay said, making sure to stay more than an arm's reach from Bridger.

"Ismay," Bridger said as if they were old friends, causing Nayt to eye her more thoroughly now.

She ignored Nayt, knowing she was well concealed for any inappropriate imagination. "Funny that you don't use my full title now."

"Your father didn't tell you? I resigned from my post as Captain this morning. I'm not your dog anymore."

"I heard. Rumor is you're a Kai now. Still low class, but a Kai," she said,

"A Kai all the same. I'll use your proper title if you use mine," Bridger said.

"Excuse me," Nayt said, pointing at Ismay. "Where did you get that cloak?"

"This old thing," she said, casually looking at the descaled lazgron cloak wrapped around her. "I don't remember. My father probably got it for me. It's hideous but keeps away prying eyes."

"I had one just like that. Harvested it myself. Someone stole it from my shop about three weeks ago," Nayt said.

"Trust me," Bridger interjected. "Ismay wouldn't have stolen something like that. She's more the honest type. Aren't you, girly."

Ismay felt the hairs on the back of her neck rise. "No,"

she said firmly. "I don't steal things and I don't deal with strange men in secret. I always pay for my information, ask any Eso informant."

"Nayt is hardly a strange man. He's a businessman. Dealing legal merchandise, clearly in plain sight," Bridger said, gesturing to the windows.

"I've heard enough. Take your quarrel and leave my shop," Nayt said.

"Fine," Bridger said. He slid the paper he'd been writing on into his pocket and started for the door. Before leaving, he said, "Don't try to get a hold of me if you change your mind, Nayt. I'm not staying in Perdigon for long."

Ismay made to walk out the shop door. There was something about the way Nayt eyed her cloak that spoke to her sympathetic side. "Here," she said, taking off the lazgron cloak. "Take it."

"No. I can't. It's not right," he said, gesturing and Ismay noticed the copper bracelet he wore. It was much the same as ones she'd seen Senators wearing on Capitol Hill.

Ismay placed the cloak on the counter and said, "This is compensation for whatever disturbance I caused your business."

While rushing after Bridger, she heard Nayt call out, "Thank you!"

Ismay made a mental note about Nayt's tackle shop. If Bridger came to Nayt to broker something, a deal that seemed outside the tackle shop's regular business, Ismay might use his services in the future, whatever they might be.

"Leave me alone," Bridger said, as Ismay caught up with him on the avenue. He abruptly veered off the main street.

"What was in that letter?" she asked. Ismay didn't see any reason to beat around the bush with this man.

"That wasn't a letter. It was a scrap of parchment for

notes. Go pester the new Captain of your family guard. I don't want anything to do with you."

"Not that paper you have now. I'm talking about the letter I saw you receive from a stranger on the edge of the Third Class Kai neighborhood. You remember the one, it happened on the evening of the Emperor's assassination."

Bridger slowed, looking at the Esos along the street who now stared at them. "It was a message from your father. Now piss-off before you make me do something I might regret."

"My father didn't send you that message. I think it might've had something to do with —"

Bridger broke stride and pinned Ismay up against the brick wall of a building in the narrow side street. He put his mouth directly alongside her ear and said, "I don't give a burning ember what you think you saw. You and I didn't have this conversation. You and I don't have anything to do with each other. I don't know what possessed you to come down here and confront me about something you think you saw, and I don't care. I'm leaving Perdigon for good. I did what your father asked of me and now I'm done. I don't work for you or him anymore. I work for myself now."

Ismay quivered, tucking her chin in close to her neck, trying to avoid Bridger's aggressive stance. He pushed away from her and continued walking.

"How did you do it?" she asked.

He stopped, glancing over his shoulder at her. "I don't know what you mean."

"How did you become a Kai. You don't have the money."

"Maybe that Zethrillian you were speaking with near the docks will tell you," he said, distancing himself from her. "Don't come looking for me, Ismay," Bridger called back. "Bad things happen to people who do."

"You're a mongodo, Bridger," she said through gritted teeth, unable to resist getting a last word in. He didn't turn back, instead he rounded the next corner and disappeared up the street.

Straightening her light purple dress and adjusting her hair, Ismay noticed some Esos still staring at her. Lifting her chin, she left the side street for the avenue and flagged down the nearest harquice-drawn wagon.

"You need a ride?" the Old Rhydarian driver asked.

"Do you know where the courts are?" she responded.

"Which one? District or Imperial?"

"Imperial," she replied, climbing the steps onto the bench seat next to him.

"All the way up to Capitol Hill will cost you. I'm not a hansom. I'm a delivery carrier," he said.

"Did I mention I was Kai?" Ismay said.

Instantly the driver put the empty wagon in motion. As Ismay rode up the avenue, she saw her new House Guard Captain searching the side streets for her. Their eyes met briefly before Noxon passed from view. Ismay heard her calling her name for a block, but the woman's voice faded quickly. Ismay smiled. She considered how Bridger might have known about her dealing with Isik. She wondered if Bridger tortured Isik for the information while she was his captive, or if he had tricked Isik into talking. Ismay had to admit Bridger didn't seem the type to outwit a Zethrillian. Few Rhydarians could. But if she was going to get the answers she wanted from Isik, Ismay was in for a challenge.

ORDERED TO LIE

Two Days Before Emperor Benton's Death

"This is where it happened, yeah?" the Sergeant asked, emerging from the trees into the charred clearing.

Kayda recognized the soldier immediately. He was an Old Rhydarian who had served in Helmer's squad.

"This is where he tried to turn on you?" he said, sauntering closer, drawing the attention of the two dozen or more soldiers around them who'd headed up the rest of the legion as they entered this new camp.

Kayda ignored their questioning glares, forcing the painful memory from her mind. She thought being here again, where *it* happened, would answer the questions eating at her. It might offer a clue that would bring the bigger picture into focus. But seeing the charred grass where her companions died only dredged up the horror of it all, leaving her more confused than ever about her Commander's reaction. Kayda turned away from the Sergeant and returned to the job at hand, erecting her squad tent.

"I asked you a question," the Sergeant demanded. "I want to hear the words from your traitor mouth."

Kayda understood she outranked this man and could order him to stand down. But she knew by the venom in his voice that he wouldn't obey. With Helmer dead and having yet to fill his Squad leader position, Kayda would be forced to seek out another Troop Leader to enforce any disciplinary measure. Either that or she would have to report the insubordination to the Battalion Leader, Captain Livingston. A move like that would discredit her authority as a Troop Leader. Legionnaires didn't respect someone who couldn't control the crew under his or her command. She had a feeling this wasn't going to end well.

"You're out of line, Sergeant. Return to your squad tent."

The Sergeant looked to the other soldiers who had stopped setting up camp, no doubt to gauge his support. Kayda understood the rumors circulating about her, but she refused to lie to the men and women of their Legion. She couldn't dishonor the loyal legionnaires who had died by the white-haired woman's saber.

"I served with Helmer for ten years. Sure, he was rough around the edges, but not a turncoat. It doesn't add up, Lieutenant."

Kayda stopped pounding in the tent stake and faced the Sergeant. At least fifty other soldiers now watched them, waiting to see what she would do. Kayda noticed another Troop Leader three soldiers back in the crowd, watching in silence, not offering any effort to check their insubordination. "I never said Helmer turned on us. Whoever you heard such rumors from is a liar," she said.

"I heard that's what Commander Nolstram-Kia is telling everyone. Word is you went directly to his tent after you returned. Told him everything as it happened," the Sergeant said.

"I did go directly to his tent and tell him everything that happened. Nobody in the envoy turned traitor. The

Volurem came up out of nowhere. They killed the others," she said.

"And you expect us to believe that four trained legionnaires, one of which was an Agunzi, couldn't defend themselves against a handful of Engulfed?" the Sergeant responded.

"There were more than a handful," Kayda said.

"Not many more. Look at the size of the burn scar. Look at the green grass coming up. Any Terra person worth a burning ember knows that means the Volurem's intensity was low. The Agunzi alone should've been able to handle it."

"The fire started while we slept. It caught us off guard."

"I don't believe that for one second. Before we started setting up, we found blankets, the gear pile. None of it touched by the fire."

Kayda held her tongue. She couldn't tell them what really happened, no matter how badly she wanted to. She questioned if her silence was worth it. With the rumors that she was the killer spreading like wildfire through the Legion, would they believe any other story, truth or not?

"How long have you been with the Hundred and First?" he asked. "Longer than the recruit that came with you, but not as long as any of the others in the envoy party. Especially not longer than Helmer."

"I never said any of them were traitors. They died saving my life. They were killed by the enemy. That's the truth. Anyone who says otherwise is a liar," Kayda said.

"Are you calling the Commander a liar?" the Sergeant demanded.

Kayda didn't respond. She wouldn't directly answer that question as she couldn't lie to them about this. The Commander was a liar. He was hiding something, she knew it. It had something to do with why they'd been sent with the Zethrillian envoy in the first place. Knowing now that the Emperor died that very night, she suspected whatever they'd been there for was related to Jermanus' murder.

"Lieutenant Kayda," she heard a new voice speak up.

She saw her superior, Captain Livingston, winding his way through the camp on his grey harquice.

The Battalion Leader came onto the scene sternly eyeing the gathered soldiers. He didn't ask, but Kayda could tell from the look on his face that he understood what was happening. "The Commander demands your presence," Captain Livingston said.

Murmuring could be heard among the soldiers as they began to turn back to their duties in establishing camp. The Captain didn't offer any hint as to their suspicions.

Kayda felt a sense of relief for Livingston's timely interruption. Simultaneously, she felt a wave of anxiety about why the Commander might want to see her. He hadn't asked to see her at any point during their march toward Perdigon. That he wanted an audience with her now, the very afternoon they arrived at the burn scar where her group had been attacked, left her with a pit in her stomach.

She followed Livingston away from the meadow. He led Kayda a short distance up the road to the Commander's tent. She thought it strange that Commander Nolstram-Kai had chosen to erect his tent away from the rest of the camp. Typically, the Commander stayed in the center of their Legion to keep an eye on the troops and enjoy their protection.

When the Commander's tent came into view, Livingston stopped. Before he left her, he said, "Thought you should know going into this, I was with the scouts when we came onto the scene this morning. The bodies were still there, on the edge of the meadow as you described. We found the harquice deeper in the forest. They'd been killed by dracos. And scavenged by lazgron by the looks of the markings. The beasts didn't touch the other bodies with the envoy, though. I don't know what you told the Commander, but only the Zethrillian was killed by the Volurem's fire. There was no sunstone, but your cooking stand and pan were there. I believe I found the fire's point of origin. It came from the sunstone, didn't it?"

Kayda nodded.

"None of you, even the new recruits are foolish enough to drop a lit sunstone in grass that dry. And I refuse to believe that any of my Troop Leaders were traitors. That leaves the Zethrillian... But the Volurem move much faster than a Zethrillian at this longitude. There's no way Agus could've walked that sunstone away from the safety zone and dropped it in the grass and returned to where the fire got him. He couldn't have moved that quickly."

Kayda didn't confirm or deny his suspicion.

"Then there were the tracks and bloodstains on top of the dead Volurem and their ash. Agus burned to death, and Pyter was killed by a Volurem blade, but the other two..." he said, his New Rhydarian features darkly creased with concern. "They were killed after the fire was out."

Kayda nodded, knowing that by doing so, she was acknowledging the Captain's suspicion. If their Commander learned this, he'd have reason to kill her.

"The rain over the last few days made reading the tracks next to impossible, but I know a mortal wound delivered by a Volurem when I see one. Those on Helmer's neck and through Robson's chin did not match the black stains on

Pyter. They were cut down with a narrow blade. The cut on Robson, a curved blade, like a saber," Livingston said.

Kayda screamed yes in her mind, but only blinked in response.

"I don't know what you told the Commander. I don't know why he's telling others that Helmer turned traitor, but whoever killed them walked away with Helmer's armor. His body had been stripped when we found him," Livingston said.

Kayda hadn't expected to hear this discovery, but after considering the white-haired woman's appearance, taking Helmer's armor over Pyter's made sense. Pyter's armor was damaged. The other two had armor that remained intact. And though Helmer's armor wasn't the best fit for that woman's body type, the Agunzi's armor wouldn't have done her any good.

As Livingston heeled his harquice into motion, Kayda said to him, "Captain. Thank you."

He gave a half-nod in reply, acknowledging her situation, but presumably not fully understanding why the Commander had kept quiet about the truth of the soldiers' deaths. If the Commander was planning to take her out of the equation now that he'd arrived at the scene, at least Kayda knew someone else understood she wasn't to blame.

After taking a moment to prepare herself for whatever the Commander wanted from her, Kayda entered the tent.

"And before The Creator left Tarmigan for good, he shed a single scale." – The Dracolyth

DIGGING FOR DETAILS

Two Days Before Emperor Benton's Death

I smay dug through her coin purse. She offered the Eso driver a square lazgron piece in exchange for the ride to Capitol Hill.

"No, Miss. I can't take that as payment," he said.

"Don't be silly, this is worth more than a day's pay, even for my guards," she said.

"I can't exchange a lazgron-minted coin in my business. I'll take a round steel piece instead," he said.

"Take three," Ismay said, fishing out three round steel pieces.

"Three?" he asked, clearly not knowing the exchange for this coinage.

"Unless you'd rather have nine triangular steel pieces, or what about twenty-seven square steel pieces?"

"Twenty-seven square steel pieces?" the man blinked.

"That's the going exchange for steel to lazgron," she said. "If it were me, I'd take the single square lazgron piece."

"I'll take the three rounds," the Eso said.

Ismay placed the three round steel pieces in the man's hand and climbed down from the wagon bench. He drove away quickly, possibly anticipating that Ismay would realize she'd overpaid him for the ride even though she'd had to school him about exchange rates. She hadn't expected that an Eso would be inexperienced in dealing with money of higher value than the more common ore-minted coinage. It surprised her that even the lowest of the scale-minted coins, a square lazgron piece, was something the Eso would not accept. In her mind, Ismay would much rather carry a coin with a higher value. It took up much less space and covered the cost of most of her daily needs.

Standing before the Imperial Courts, Ismay tried to recall which of the serving Court Councilors had graduated their training under House Ovando sponsorship. The alumni of Ovando's Medi classes almost always gained honorable positions if they elected to stay in Perdigon. If she wanted to speak directly with a prisoner charged with being a traitor, then she'd need inside help.

The Imperial Courthouse was built directly over a deep, expansive underground prison system, a system Ismay understood she couldn't bribe her way into. Security was tight at the dark, dank, underground cells, and access in and out was limited. There were two points of entry; one on the main floor of the Imperial Courthouse, through which prisoners were brought to and from their trials, and a second, broader entrance on the downhill side of the Courthouse. Escape through either of these entrances was nearly impossible. Ismay had never heard of an instance where a prisoner awaiting trial had managed to break out of the dungeons.

Approaching the tubular façade with two-story columns adorning the rounded stone courthouse entry, Ismay heard a commotion arising from somewhere behind the building. The Imperial Courthouse spanned half the length of the Capitol Building. She couldn't see around the sides to understand what was causing the scraping and banging noises. She heard shouting before she heard the twang of ropes snapping and a crushing boom reverberated through the stone steps. An Old Rhydarian woman, exiting through one of the building's three double-wide doors, searched the space around her as if worried something were about to fall on her. Ismay rushed to her, asking, "What in the Creator's name was that?"

The middle-aged woman calmed quickly, shaking her wavy hair in annoyance. "That must be the renovation. For a moment, I thought the building was collapsing."

"Renovation?" Ismay asked.

"Yes, dear," she said. "Emperor Benton Querci-Akai approved the renovation design for additions to the Courthouse a week ago."

Ismay now noticed that this woman seemed somewhat familiar. She wore a long light blue tunic, with simple trim and a prim design. Her wavy black hair fell neatly around her shoulders. She carried an armful of documents tightly secured with twine.

"Pardon me, but aren't you a Councilor?" Ismay asked.

"Yes," the woman replied. "Councilwoman Gilden-Kai."

Ismay remembered her now. She'd attended an event her father had hosted at their villa before leaving on his supply mission with Benton. She was one of twenty-seven Imperial Court Councilors living in Perdigon. The remaining two-hundred and twenty-seven councilors served on the ten district courts in the city. "My name is Ismay Ovando-Kai," she introduced herself, ignoring the shouts echoing from the back of the courthouse. Clearly something in their construction project had failed.

"You're Marxius' daughter?" the woman asked.

Ismay smiled.

"Aren't you supposed to be in the Capitol Building with the other Penti trainees today?"

"I am, but my father authorized me to carry out a personal matter here at the court. You see, he's just been summoned by the Emperor to protect his Imperial Majesty on their defense of the Apgar Forest," she said.

"Yes, of course. We only just voted on the request and sent it through to the Magistrate yesterday," Gilden-Kai acknowledged.

"My father had hoped to interrogate the Zethrillian advisor before leaving, but unfortunately didn't get the chance," Ismay said.

The Councilwoman raised her eyebrows at Ismay and said, "And he sent you in his place?"

"Oh, no," Ismay replied with a frown. "My father wishes to wait until he returns to take the matter into his own hands. You see, it's personal for him, with his close ties to Galterius-Brex and their command."

"Naturally, I understand. But if I may, what are you doing at the Imperial Courthouse?" Gilden-Kai asked.

"Before I'm to return to my training, my father asked me personally to set eyes on the Zethrillian prisoner," Ismay said.

"I can assure you that isn't necessary. The prisoner has been processed and is locked securely in a cell."

"I told father this was a ridiculous and unnecessary request, but he insisted," Ismay said, feigning frustration. "He wants to ensure her condition isn't compromised before he's had a chance to interrogate her."

"I see. But your father knows you haven't the clearance to enter the dungeons," she responded.

"Yes, and unfortunately he couldn't acquire it before the Emperor unexpectedly summoned him away. Before I return to my training, I'll need proof that I tried to gain entry. When my father orders a task completed, he expects results, and he isn't the forgiving type. As his only child, he holds me to a higher standard, so you see I must do my due diligence. The sooner I see this matter through, the sooner I can return to the Capitol Building. It's been a pleasure, Councilwoman Gilden-Kai. If you would be so kind, will you point me in the direction of the authority I'll need to speak with," she said.

"Right," Gilden-Kai said, looking over her shoulder and back through the antechamber she'd just exited. Clicking her tongue against the roof of her mouth, she returned her gaze to Ismay, and said, "I believe I have a few moments to help you. Do you have your documents?"

"I never leave our villa without them," Ismay said, patting the coin purse in her dress pocket.

"Follow me."

Ismay strode behind the Councilwoman through the door and into the main hall. They crossed the mostly empty room, feet echoing slightly on the stone floor. Passing through large wooden doors, Gilden-Kai led Ismay into the now-vacant main courtroom. Ismay had been in this Imperial Courtroom before, but it had been years. Despite the rotations, it appeared identical to the last time she'd been there. Rows of wooden benches filled a third of the room. A path between them ran down the middle, heading toward a large desk where a magistrate presided over legal cases. On both sides of the magistrate's desk were the desks where the council observed each case before casting votes for the magistrate to consider. The walkways were carpeted with cobalt blue rugs, one leading to a series of doors behind the magistrate's desk. Ismay followed the councilwoman behind the desk and through the second door from the left.

Lacking natural light, the hallway felt narrow and constricted to Ismay, though it was twice her height and wide enough for three people to stand shoulder-to-shoulder. They wound down staircases that sloped deeper beneath the Court. The corridor opened into a well-lit room. There, five Agunzi Imperials guarded a secure doorway. Each stout guard had a pouch on his sword belt, indicating they were armed with brismil armor. A barred window opened to a Zethrillian and two Rhydarians seated at desks in a dimly lit reception room. Councilwoman Gilden-Kai walked up to the barred window, "Access request to prisoner in dungeon block D."

As the man recorded the request, studying the Councilwoman and Ismay's identity documents, Ismay eyed the Agunzi guarding the single scale-plated, steel door. Ribbed with draco scales somehow adhered to or fabricated into the thick steel door, the entrance into the dungeons appeared more heavily guarded than any other entity in the city, including the Imperial Vault. Seeing nothing for the Agunzi to sit on, Ismay wondered how often they changed shifts. Did they share scales? Or did they each own one? And if they didn't own them, why wouldn't they think to use them to their personal advantage? She'd always been told of the Agunzis' limited mental capacity while in Rhydenar. Those she'd seen speak to the Senate, though, didn't seem as dull minded as her father made them out to be.

"Here're your documents back. You're allowed one hour maximum," the Zethrillian behind the barred window said.

"She won't need that long," Gilden-Kai said.

"Make sure you're back before the time's up. You don't want to get left in there with the likes of them prisoners for any longer than necessary. The stench alone is enough to drive anyone mad. Just ask Chels here if you don't believe me," the Zethrillian said.

Ismay cringed as one of the Agunzi guards strained under the weight of the brace, locking the door's wheel-like opener. He spun it, and it clicked into place. Heaving, he pulled it open.

"Miss Ovando-Kai," the Councilwoman said, gathering Ismay's attention. "Don't forget to sign the access document on your way out after you've seen the prisoner. Chels will lead you to the cell."

"Thank you. I will find a way to repay you for your kindness," Ismay told the woman.

"We must look out for one another in this city. As Kai, and women of power, we stick together," she said.

"This way," Chels, the New Rhydarian guard said while stepping through a smaller door and into the main dungeon opening. Eyeing the stout Agunzi guards with some reservation, she passed into the secure antechamber. The door behind her closed and locked. For a moment Ismay stood alone in the small chamber with the husky man, Chels. Lit by the lumistone lamp he carried, she could see his grey robes were stained and unclean. The visual was quickly followed her detection of his foul odor. A second, equally heavy-duty door on the inside of the chamber opened and a wave of new smells washed over Ismay. Musky clothing mixed with sewage burned her nostrils; Chels' stench seemed almost pleasant in comparison.

Ismay walked slightly behind Chels as he led her down a main corridor. Cells constructed of metal bars divided by thick stone walls lined either side of the hallway. The few people held in these cells rushed to the bars, watching, and waiting for some kind of announcement or handout. Ismay clutched her coin purse as she tried to avoid looking at them.

Just as Ismay wondered if they'd ever reach an end to the row of cells, she spotted the opening. They came into a vaulted room and in its center stood a table scarred with countless divots and gouges. On one side sat a single chair with chains and steel clasps bolted to it. Various tools, ranging from rounded hammers and clubs to any size of blade with sharp edges, rested in racks on the walls. Chains with hooks and cuffs hung from the raised ceiling. Ismay cringed at the bloodstains on the floor. The room had openings to four corridors.

Chels led her straight on through to the next corridor, which ended in a similar central room. These rooms all matched; they were equally stained and equally horrifying. Chels made sure to call out which block they were passing at each intersecting room. On the fourth, he said, "This is block D. The prisoner you want to see is down the third corridor. Don't get lost on your way back."

"You're not going to stay?" she asked.

"No. You can get lost, but the only way out other than the main entrance is the way you came in. Follow the signs," he said pointing to the wood posting on the wall in the open room.

"I don't have a light," she said.

Chels exhaled, frustrated. He searched his stained robe pocket and pulled out a small lumistone. "Don't lose it," he said handing it to her.

He left her standing in the dimly lit dungeon. Lumistones on the walls were so widely spaced that visibility was extremely poor.

Ismay clicked on the light by smacking it against the stone wall. She located corridor three and followed it. Each cell she passed was empty. She was beginning to doubt the cell keeper had led her to the right cell block and corridor when she heard shuffling feet.

"Isik?" she said, her light voice carrying down the hollow corridor.

A scratchy, dry voice much lower than hers, but still feminine, responded, "Who's asking?"

"My name is Ismay Ovando-Kai," she said.

"Ismay," Isik repeated. "If you have come to mock me —"

"I'm not here to mock you. I'm here for your counsel," she said.

Isik chortled, "Why would you want advice from a Zethril advisor who's been imprisoned by Rhydarians? Are the Kai really so shortsighted?"

"That's why I'm here. To learn what you know about Captain Bridger-Kai."

"You want to know about Captain Bridger-Kai? I'm not sure I'm the right person to answer your questions. Your father would know more about his man than I," Isik said.

"My father left the city late this morning. He's gone with the Emperor to stop the Volurem army that you summoned into existence," Ismay replied.

"Hmm. So, Bridger would go with that explanation. I was wondering which lie he was going to tell the Emperor."

"Explain," Ismay said.

"Straight to the point, I like that... Bridger could explain things to best serve himself, couldn't he? After all, it seems there are only two of us who made it back to civilization. Until now, I was wondering which tale he had used. Both made him out to be the hero. He rehearsed them aloud while bringing me back here as his captive."

Though her voice was steady and wavered little, Ismay could see the Zethrillian advisor had been beaten down. Her body was bruised and covered with scabs. She stank like Ismay's father's armor when he returned from battle. "Why did you do it?" Ismay asked.

"I'm sorry, darling, you'll have to be more specific. I understand they intend to try me for multiple offenses against the Empire," Isik said.

"Why did you and Galterius-Brex turn against the Empire? Why try to sabotage the guards under your control when you could've used them to help your cause? Galterius' wealth would've been enough to buy an army, but instead, you set the Volurem on them."

"I thought you were here to talk about Bridger-Kai?" Isik replied.

"I am. I suspect you know more about who he truly is. More than the loyal Captain my father and I believed him to be. I guess I want to know what happened to him, to you, to Galterius-Brex, and everything that got so twisted around after you all left the Capital," Ismay said.

"For that, we should start at the beginning, back when you first came to me, posing as an Eso girl," Isik said.

"What does that have to do with how you got here? All I did was help supply information to you in exchange for your knowledge about the letters," Ismay asked.

"You came to me with information that could've only come from within the Kai social circles. No servants or slaves gave me the detailed information that you did. At best, the servants recounted gossip, which is useful, but nowhere near as accurate as the conversations a Kai is privileged to hear in private.

"That is why I decided to point you toward the ship and feed your curiosity about the letters passing from Jermanus to the mine operatives. After all, they didn't reveal anything. They were simply the reports to and from a frivolous mining operation that infuriated almost every Kai who knew about it. Jermanus played it as though it was a hobby he couldn't let go of. My employer, Galterius-Brex, was most enraged by Jermanus' ability to waste Imperial funds, but nobody could convince Jermanus to stop. Your father gave it up more quickly than Galterius. He distanced himself by going on the supply audit tour with Benton. Galterius couldn't let it go, the same way you weren't satisfied with the one letter you managed to steal from the ship captain's quarters."

"You admit my father was right. Galterius-Brex had the motive, the means and opportunity to kill Jermanus. And he did, faking the attacker that he claimed to have fought," Ismay said.

The Zethrillian shook her ovular head. "If it were that simple, we wouldn't be here. Bridger wouldn't have been involved. I would've stayed here in the capital."

"You say Galterius didn't do it? And I'm assuming you'll now tell me that you are innocent as well, though my father's guard caught you red-handed," Ismay said.

"I can't claim complete innocence. All of us are guilty in some capacity. You, by snooping into Jermanus' letters and inadvertently rousing suspicion. Your father by helping the Emperor-Elect on his supply audit journey. Galterius, by withholding information from his peers. As for the Akai assassinations, none of us wielded the knife," Isik said.

Ismay frowned. What Isik said didn't make sense. Isik was trying to confuse her on purpose; she was trying to distract her for some reason.

"Some are more guilty than others. My father may have played a role in the destruction of Jermanus' so-called mining operation, but he did not turn on the Empire. He was following orders from an Akai. You could've stayed in Perdigon and not gone along with Galterius and his plan to betray the Empire."

"Galterius had no plan to betray the Empire. That is nonsense. He, too, believed he was following orders from the Emperor and your father."

Ismay frowned. She could sense the Zethrillian was trying to twist her perception of things. "You said I bear some guilt for snooping into those letters. If you believe that, why did you give me more letters?"

"I didn't, remember."

"No, that's what you told me to say, and I did. I went to my father with them. I told him how I repeatedly went to the docks and persuaded them to give me the letters, but that's not how it really happened. I only stole the one, any more would've raised too much suspicion. You gave me the others. By your logic, you're the one who encouraged me to snoop, which would make you more guilty than me."

"We had an agreement. I honored it. Leaking a few letters is hardly as harmful as destroying an operation, like your father did. But that's not what this is about. I underestimated you. You figured it out through those letters, didn't you?

Ismay felt herself flinch ever so slightly, then quickly regained her composure.

"Clever. That's why you went to your father with the letters," Isik said.

"Never once did the author of those letters write the name of a mineral or an ore. The elements were always classified with a set of four numbers. They were written as if the assigned numbers were something they needed to control, not something that is part of a normal mining operation. What miners have trouble controlling the ore they are mining? They seemed to refer to the numbers as though they were living beings," Ismay said.

"Your father denied knowledge of this?" Isik asked.

"He didn't lie to me when he said he didn't know what the facility was really working on. I can tell when he's lying. About this, he wasn't. Just like he wasn't lying to me when he said he only sent one letter during the week of his return, yet I saw Bridger receive a second. The second arrived in private on the evening of Jermanus' murder."

"I see. This is why you've come to me about Captain Bridger-Kai," Isik said as if his name were something sour in her mouth.

"Not Captain. Not for House Ovando at least."

"Really?" Isik asked, the corners of her moth curling up slightly.

"Yes, he claims he's leaving Perdigon for good," Ismay said.

"I'd love to see the look on Benton's face when he hears about this," Isik said.

"The Emperor?"

"You still can't see it? That Bridger is a sword for hire. He rose up rapidly under your father's employ, but he is a man of opportunity. Benton offered Bridger that opportunity. How else could he have become a Kai so quickly, if not granted the status by an Akai?"

"You're suggesting that Benton paid off Bridger? But what about the letter I saw him receive? What did it say? How does it fit into this business with the mine and the other letters? And if you know so much about all of this, how did you end up here?"

"My knowledge of the events as they unfolded was all-encompassing, but as it happened, there were minor aspects that I couldn't control. For instance, I underestimated Bridger. You see, Galterius couldn't have killed the Emperor because he was still outside Jermanus' chambers while Jermanus was being murdered. The other Akai were already dead before he arrived at the Palace. There are plenty of witnesses to attest to this. Though Galterius had motive, he liked Jermanus and enjoyed his favor. Galterius was not the killer nor the mastermind behind it. His goals were focused on healing and empowering the Rhydarian Empire, not destroying it."

"After I learned what the Emperor-Elect ordered my father to do, he is suspect. He gained the most from it all, but Benton was not in the city when the assassinations occurred either. And he didn't employ Bridger until after he took control in Perdigon," Ismay reasoned.

"You're overlooking something important in the time-line of events. When I say Benton supplied the means for Bridger, I did not say the Captain entered Benton's employ after they returned from the supply audit," Isik said.

Ismay understood what this implied, but she still couldn't see how it all fit together with the mine and what her father had done.

"You mentioned a second letter that arrived on the night of the Akai murders. How did you learn about this message? Did Bridger tell you about it?" Isik asked.

"No, I followed him. He went to a different Kai neighborhood to receive it. It was near House Didimo."

"And the missing piece falls into place," Isik said.

"I have my assumptions, but explain your train of thought," Ismay said.

"Galterius and I knew someone in the Kai or Ai class was responsible. Or so we suspected. Your father, along with the rest of the Kai thought the Agunzi delegation that we met with were to blame. It was all part of masterful timing though. You're right to suspect Benton. He couldn't hatch the plan on his own, so he was influenced into orchestrating a flawless insurrection. Whoever planted the ideas in his head must have made him believe they were his own thoughts, which is genius on their part," Isik said.

"That would imply someone close to the Akai, someone smart. Like an advisor from Zethril," Ismay surmised.

"Very good," Isik said.

"Maybe someone like you," Ismay said.

"You're saying that because I am here, in a dungeon. There are more than a handful of Zethril advisors who were closer to the Akai than me."

"You're still avoiding what I really came here to ask you about," Ismay said.

"We're working up to Bridger's role in this."

"Fine, I'll entertain you. You were telling me my suspicions are correct. That the new Emperor, Benton, was responsible for all this. The one who enacted the plan to kill Jermanus and his sons?"

"Benton only needed to execute the murders at a time when he wasn't in the capital. He covered his tracks by quickly blaming and slaughtering a Noble house. That it was Senator Didimo-Kai's was random as far as I can tell.

That it happened when the Agunzi delegation was in Perdigon, and on the night they were set to sail, was intentional."

"Why would Benton want to kill his family members, those providing him with a free ride through life with no expectations or responsibilities? Why would he want to start a war with the Agunzi?" Ismay asked.

"Benton's motivation is selfish. He wanted to create a state of panic so the Empire would have a reason to rally around a new leader. Let's face it, he was not anyone's first choice. They could've picked one of Benton's younger cousins, but Benton understood the motivations of the Senate and the Magistrates. Given his lack of interest in politics, they thought they could distract him with the pleasures of being an Emperor and use him to get their way. And they were right about that in some regard. But they failed to see how Benton's selfishness would extend into his politics once crowned. Besides, being leaderless when the Agunzi are demanding more freedom could've caused a ripple of instability in the Empire. Benton chose chaos to make sure his transition to power was flawless and effortless. Once he was Emperor, Benton could act as he pleased."

"But that's what Benton was doing before Jermanus died. Why would he want to change his comfortable lifestyle?"

"Because Jermanus *was* making him take on more responsibility. The training period of Benton's Akai life was ending. Jermanus was requiring more responsibility from him, like the supply mission," Isik said.

"What about Bridger?"

"He was Benton's right hand while Benton was away. You said the communication he received in private came after your father sent word of their delay," Isik said.

"Yes."

"The letter was from Benton. It was his signal to go through with the strike," Isik said.

"The strike on House Didimo?"

"Yes, House Didimo and the Akai assassinations."

"How do you know it was Bridger?" Ismay asked.

"Because Bridger now has Galterius' brismil scale," Isik said.

"My father suspected Galterius had lost his scale," Ismay reflected.

"Exactly. Galterius wasn't supposed to be there. Benton arranged for Bridger to have a clear escape, but Galterius unexpectedly arrived at Jermanus' chambers the night he was murdered. Galterius walked in just after Bridger had stabbed Jermanus. He used his scale to jump off the balcony, but he dropped it when he hit the ground and Bridger stole it. He used it to escape Galterius and hid the scale in the forest. Whether he knew it or not, he hid it just far enough outside the walls that Galterius didn't sense it."

"Galterius had a matching brismil set?" Ismay said.

Isik narrowed her eyes. "Not many people know about how the pair works."

"My father has one. I know how it works."

"Galterius assumed I didn't know, but I know a lot of things about Galterius that he doesn't suspect."

"Bridger was in on this with Benton before he left on the supply mission?" Ismay asked.

"Now we know the price. Benton promised him Kai honors," Isik said.

"And Galterius' scale?"

"A bonus," Isik said.

"He didn't mention the scale to Benton?" Ismay asked.

"No. Bridger kept it a secret. He moved it a few times while they were all out searching for your classmate, Shylo."

"Did you find him? Is he still alive?" Ismay asked, suddenly realizing that she now had confirmation that Shylo hadn't been involved. She didn't ever truly believe Shylo had something to do with the coup. He was just an Eso with a dream. She liked how bold he'd been on the night of the assassination; Ismay almost forgot he was Eso.

"I can only say for certain that Bridger and I escaped the fire alive," Isik said.

"Is he why you started the fire? You and Galterius were trying to trap Bridger with the scale?"

"I told you, child. I didn't start the fire. I thought it was obvious to you now. Bridger was only with our group for a few days. Between the Emperor calling him back to work out his payment for his services and Bridger moving Galterius' scale, we hardly saw him. We didn't know it was him, but finally, Galterius cornered Bridger in Yaak. Yet by then, we'd walked into a trap. One devised by the Emperor and your father."

"My father did not have anything to do with this," Ismay stated emphatically.

"Your father was the one who forced Galterius into leading this mission and because of it I am now here, where Benton and Bridger should be," Isik said.

"Blame anyone but my father for your misfortune," Ismay said.

"Believe what you want, but I will tell you the truth. Your father wanted Galterius dead. He was the one who told Benton to use Galterius as a scapegoat. Marxius wanted to make Galterius disappear. It was their plan that sent Bridger back into the forest to start the fire. Bridger survived because he had Galterius' scale. The rest of us were left to fend for our lives. Had Bridger not needed someone to haul back and blame for the fire, I'd be missing like everyone else," Isik said.

"So Shylo is dead?" Ismay said. She'd assumed he would've died in the first hours after escaping Perdigon but reports of him slipping away had continued to trickle in ever since House Sarapio was attacked by the white-haired assassin.

Isik shrugged. "He was in Yaak that night. He was there with that young woman your father didn't kill."

"What? What young woman?"

"One of those numbers from the *mine*. On Benton's orders, your father killed all of them, except for her. Or so I can only assume since no response came from the facility after Benton returned. She escaped, somehow, and they conveniently blamed the Akai killings in part on her, Shylo, Galterius, and now me. They say we're working for the Agunzi. And it's all because of what you found out about Jermanus' mine. This information is dangerous, Ismay Ovando-Kai."

"No," Ismay said. "These are lies. You're lying to me, so I'll help you. Well, I'm not that gullible. I'm not going to help you, Isik."

"I don't need you to help me. I need you to know exactly what your father's role in this was. You were the one who came here asking about Bridger. He learned from the best, your father. You wanted to know about Bridger's connection between us. He's the one who has turned on me and now on your family as well. If what you said is true, that Bridger is not with House Ovando anymore and is leaving Perdigon for good, he got what he wanted, didn't he? He'll disappear with Galterius' scale. Bridger didn't need to save me from the fire. He could've let me burn, but he needed proof so that he could receive a hero's welcome and then disappear with his money. And I suspect after the fire he sensed that Galterius was still alive with his brismil blade."

Ismay remembered what Bridger had said to her. That he was done, that he was leaving for good. Before she left this dungeon to try to catch him, she needed to hear what happened to Shylo. "You said you saw Shylo?"

"Yes. He was alive the last I saw him."

"Did you speak to him?"

"No. I saw him, though. A few times. The first time, when he snuck into a saloon in Yaak with his young woman friend. And again when he left Yaak to follow her toward the fire. He stole one of my harquice," Isik said.

"Shylo left the safety of the walls for her?" Ismay asked.

"Yes. He ran right toward the flames where Galterius and Bridger were fighting. She was there, too. She went into the fire after Bridger. Shylo appeared distraught. He let a bounty hunter capture him. They wouldn't have escaped the fire. It was too widespread and fast-moving. It's possible they fought through to safety if they were with Galterius. They weren't among the survivors who fled Yaak's southern walls though," Isik said.

Ismay stepped away from the cell door.

"Before you go, and since it seems as though Benton will most likely have me executed upon his return, tell me what you will do with this information?" Isik asked.

"Because you are Zethrillian, and because you are in this position, I can only trust what I know to be the truth," Ismay said.

"It was all the truth," Isik said.

"Maybe. But I know Bridger is leaving Perdigon and I

think I have a way to stop him," she said, taking another step away from the cell.

"When your father returns, ask him for the truth. Ask him what role the One Hundred and First is playing in Jermanus' *mine*," Isik said, her voice echoing through the dungeon corridor after Ismay.

As Ismay fled cell block D by the light of the lumistone, she hoped Noxon was still searching for her. The woman was her best chance at stopping Bridger before he escaped.

UNFORSEEN OPTIONS

TWO DAYS BEFORE EMPEROR BENTON'S DEATH

"Lieutenant," the Commander said.

Kayda saw Nolstram swipe something small from the table and place it into his armored surcoat pocket. She examined the remaining items, trying to discern what it was he didn't want her to see. Several open letters lay in an organized stack. The Commander's short sword and hatchet lay before him, attached to a belt and ready for wear. An ornately carved dark wooden box lined with silk was propped open and appeared to be empty. Kayda's gaze lingered for a moment as she wondered whether Nolstram had a brismil scale nobody knew about. The box was the wrong size, however. Much too small, more the size of something used for jewelry. Dragon scales varied in size depending on which part of the dragon's body they came from, but they were typically slightly bigger than the average Rhydarian's palm.

The Commander took up the sword belt, taking the hatchet out of its hanger.

Kayda stiffened. "Commander Nolstram-Kai. If this is about what happened here, with the envoy. I haven't told anyone."

"No. I knew you wouldn't. If you were going to, you

would've already done it by now. We found the harquice, by the way. Killed by dracos and scavenged by lazgrons," he said.

"And the bodies of the others?" she asked, testing to see if the Commander would offer the same details as Captain Livingston.

"Yes, hardly recognizable after the lazgrons had fed on them."

"Commander, if I may speak bluntly?" Kayda said.

"Go ahead."

"If this isn't about what happened here two-and-a-half weeks ago, why have you called me to your tent?"

"The harquice's saddlebags did not contain any response from Jermanus. If there was one, it was on Agus when he burned and is now lost."

"What does that have to do with me?"

"As you know, I changed our planned return to the southern Apgar border after the Emperor's death. I hadn't made our detour known to anyone after what you told me happened here."

"The events you expressly told me to forget," Kayda said.

"Exactly. Our primary duty is to protect the people of Apgar from Imperial threats. What you saw, in combination with the tragedy that occurred in Perdigon and in such close proximity to one another, it's all connected," Nolstram said.

"Why are you telling me this now? Why not share with the rest of the Legion what really happened here?"

"The objective of your mission is too delicate a matter to be made public, even among those of us serving in the Hundred and First Legion. What Agus carried as you returned from his meeting with the Emperor was for my eyes only."

"Then why tell me?"

"I can tell you this now because you've seen something that you weren't supposed to see. Something that relates to the nature of what Jermanus was trying to accomplish and something that I believe resulted in his assassination," Nolstram said.

"Something of this magnitude should be shared with others in power," Kayda reasoned. "Surely there is someone in Perdigon we can communicate with."

"That's what I've been working on these last few weeks. It's no secret that I have Zethrillian and Agunzi ancestry. It was for this reason that I reached out to a Zethrillian within the walls of the capital. Through our brief communications since I received news of the Emperor's death, I have become aware of reports of a white-haired assassin. This person is believed to be involved in the Akai killings and has been witnessed killing Kai guards beyond the wall. They believe this person is helping whoever killed the Emperor to evade capture. These bad actors are loose in this forest somewhere."

"I'm confused. What do you want me to do?" Kayda said.

"Yesterday, I sent a message to Emperor Benton Querci-Akai alerting him to our presence outside the city. I told him of my situation. This morning, I received a response from the Emperor. His Imperial Majesty is marching to fight a group of Volurem believed to be summoned by High Commander Galterius-Brex, who apparently has orchestrated the Akai murders. He is said to be the person responsible for allowing the white-haired assassin you encountered to escape."

"The High Commander? Are you sure?" Kayda asked. She'd never met him, but she was well aware of his stellar reputation in serving the Empire and improving the lives of Esos. Kayda couldn't imagine someone with his reputation turning against the Empire so aggressively.

"These words came directly from the new Emperor. I have no doubt of the letter's authenticity," Nolstram said.

"Do the Captains know about this?" Kayda asked, still struggling to understand why he wouldn't have Livingston or Thompson convey this information to the Lieutenants along with orders to take some action.

"I told them only what they need to know. They believe we're stopping for one last rest before we carry out the Emperor's orders to join him and fight the Volurem. They know that the Emperor is riding ahead and plans to wait for our reinforcements outside the town of Yaak. They don't know that the Emperor is sending an envoy of his own to handle the matter that was left unresolved when Jermanus died."

"The matter that concerns the white-haired woman?" Kayda said, beginning to understand why she was asked to the Commander's tent.

"What I, or we rather, need to do is settle this matter that fell to the wayside upon Jermanus' death."

"I'm the only other person in this Legion who knows what really happened in this meadow. I'm the only person here you trust with this because you think I'm too afraid to talk? To talk about her impossible ability to remain unburned?" Kayda asked.

"That's about the size of it, what you need to know at least. I want you to join me now, to meet the Emperor's messenger. Your purpose is strictly to serve as my back-up. In response to the Emperor's message, I disclosed that I would meet his envoy alone. I have not made it this far in my career to put my blind trust in any Imperial official I haven't met."

"And you want someone with a weapon hiding in the brush in case it's some kind of trap?" Kayda said.

"What I have to work out with this new Emperor is something others have already been killed over. I don't trust anyone at present, least of all a stranger."

"But you trust me?" Kayda asked, thinking that she would never trust someone she'd recently threatened to kill, as he had in trying to persuade her to remain silent.

"If I had more time to prepare, I wouldn't drag you into this. Seeing as we're marching toward a Volurem burn tomorrow morning, my options are limited. You know too much about this already," Nolstram said.

"How long do I have to prepare?" Kayda asked.

"Didn't you hear me, Lieutenant? This is happening now. I see you have your sword. That's good but you'll need this," Nolstram said, retrieving an enormous bow and several spear-like arrows from the corner of the tent.

Kayda held the bow, its wooden handle nearly too thick for her to grip. "You expect me to shoot this? This is an Agunzi bow."

"If you can't draw it with your arms, use your feet. I know we've trained you for this."

"For emergency situations! I don't know if I could even hit what I'm aiming at if I use my feet to support the bow and pull the string back with both hands," she said.

"I don't expect you'll need to use it. But I want you to have it, in case," he said. "Come along. I don't want to be late."

"What if somebody comes looking for you and you're not in your tent? Won't they spread an alarm?"

"I made it clear to the Captains that I did not want to be disturbed this evening. They're spreading orders to the other Lieutenants as we speak."

Nolstram checked his pocket, the one Kayda had seen him drop something into when she first arrived. She awkwardly held the Agunzi bow. The arrows posed another challenge; they were nearly as long as her body. While attempting to manage this gear, she considered what the Commander was asking of her.

She'd wondered earlier why the Commander often sent an envoy along with protection to Perdigon on foot. This seemed especially odd when she learned of her selection to accompany the party that included a Zethrillian, given their physical disadvantages in Rhydenar. Agus was the Emperor's personal representative who had been carrying extremely sensitive information, apparently. Kayda had wondered even then why they hadn't flown on winged harquice. She knew the Emperor could have provided such transportation. Now that she knew that mission had been related to the white-haired woman, as the Commander had just admitted, she needed to find out what it was the Commander and this new Emperor were trying to work out. What secret burned when Agus was taken by flames? What could possibly be so important that they wouldn't ride with the Emperor-Elect and his entourage directly to the active fire burning in Apgar?

Kayda followed the Commander's directive, leaving through the back flap of his canvas tent. They tracked east for a short distance before the Commander turned parallel to the road. Apparently, he hadn't assigned soldiers to guard his tent or they would've been spotted.

Now she wrestled with various suspicions about what the Commander had put in his pocket. Although normally she would be on high alert for draco and lazgron active in the area, at this point she was more curious about the Commander's secret activities than awash in fear of the creatures in the forest.

He veered back to the west, and they bushwhacked their way back onto the cleared road. The recent rain had left the forest damp. A set of recent draco prints cutting across the road sent an eerie shiver down her spine. She hoped the harquice the draco had been eating were enough to tide them over for a day or two.

As the sun dropped lower in the sky, they approached a fork in the road that Kayda assumed was their meeting place. One direction headed off through the Shield Mountains; the other led to Perdigon.

"Go into the forest," Nolstram commanded. "Keep a visual on me until I reach the fork in the road. I'm meeting the Emperor's man at dusk. Get into a position that would allow you a clear shot should you need to use that bow. Once the meeting is over, I'll wait until the Emperor's envoy leaves before I head back. You can merge with me on the path, and we'll return to camp."

"If something does go wrong and I need to use the bow?" Kayda asked.

"Don't miss," he said bluntly.

Kayda waded into the thick undergrowth alongside the road. As nighttime approached, she moved into position. The road was within view but not clearly. Kayda shifted until she could tell for certain that the Commander was alone before she crept closer. The vegetation was so thick that she had to move to within a stone's throw of the junction before she gained a good vantage point. From here, if she had to, Kayda thought she might have a chance at hitting a still target with the oversized Agunzi bow. She knew from practice that she wasn't strong enough to pull back an Agunzi bow without using her feet.

Kayda cleared a spot so she could sit down. She found that the moisture was only knuckle-deep beneath the thick grass. After multiple days of rain, she was surprised how little had saturated the ground.

From this position, she could see the Commander standing on the road, his short sword and hatchet at his sides. Nolstram was fidgeting with his pocket. Whatever it was had to be something he intended to use during this meeting. Yet, she could only think of a few things that would warrant a situation like this, and brismil wasn't a part of the equation.

The sound of harquice hooves alerted her to the arrival of the Emperor's envoy. Kayda placed the Agunzi bow into position, the flat of her feet on either side of the grip. She nocked an arrow and pulled on the bowstring with both hands, testing its draw weight. If she needed to use it, Kayda would need to pull with all her strength. Aiming accurately wasn't something she could do with her feet. The harquice hooves slowed. The animal's labored breathing sounded just beyond the brush.

"What's all this?" Kayda heard the Commander say. He faced the Emperor's envoy. The hooded figure sat on a bench at the front of a wagon apparently bulging with chests and crates that were covered by a loosely flapping tarp.

"I'm carrying on after this," the man said.

"To join the Emperor in Yaak?" Nolstram asked.

"If that's what you need to hear to move this along, then, yeah. I'm going to Yaak," he responded.

Kayda thought there was something familiar about this envoy's voice. She adjusted her position, straining to see him more clearly in the dim light. Though he was seated, Kayda could tell he was tall, New Rhydarian by the look of his face. He dug something out of a bag and clicked it with the butt of a dagger. The soft white light of a lumistone illuminated his features. She recognized him, but Kayda didn't remember where from.

"In his letter, the Emperor wrote that you would be informed about what I have," the Commander said.

"The Emperor says a lot of things; remind me what it is again?" the man said.

"Are you serious?" the Commander responded.

"Is it for sale?" the man asked. In that moment, Kayda remembered where she'd seen him before. He was at the Palace the day they left Perdigon. Kayda was with Helmer, Pyter, and Robson waiting to escort Agus from the Palace, beyond the city, and to the One Hundred and First Legion. The man acting as envoy for this new Emperor at the time seemed to have been showing someone around the Palace grounds. She remembered hearing him tell the Old Rhydarian he was with about the layout of the courtyard.

"Captain, I don't think you realize exactly what I have and exactly what this means for the Emperor. I know something bad happened at the facility in the Shield Mountains. Bad enough that one of them escaped and is killing Rhydarians in the forest," Nolstram said.

"Oh, Benton knows about the white-haired assassin. He was the one who ordered that facility to be shut down. Killed them all," the Captain said.

"Did Jermanus know about this? Is that why he's dead?" Nolstram asked.

"No, Jermanus didn't know what Benton was doing to his operation. I thought you would've heard by now. Jermanus died because of an Agunzi separatist coup. They killed him and his heirs with assassins and fled to the South. Galterius-Brex is the one who orchestrated it and now he's on the run, setting fires in the forest. That's where you're heading next, to deal with the traitor."

"Captain Bridger —"

"It's Bridger-Kai," he interrupted.

The Commander leveled his gaze, "Captain Bridger-Kai."

"I'm not a Captain anymore," Bridger said.

"Am I to believe that what you just told me is correct, that Emperor Benton does not want this program to continue?" Nolstram asked.

"That's right. He wants the creation of the mutant Terras to end with Jermanus," Bridger said.

"Then why did he send you to meet me here? Why not avoid this charade and tell me himself in private once we reach Yaak?" Nolstram asked.

"Because he told me to destroy what you have. He said, destroy it with whatever means necessary," Bridger said.

"And you expect me to just hand it over?" Nolstram said, pulling his hatchet from his belt.

"No need to turn on me yet," Bridger said. "I'm a businessman. I think there's something we can do to reach an agreement here."

"What's in this vial is worth more than anything you could possibly offer me," Nolstram said.

A vial, Kayda thought, realizing that's what Nolstram had in his pocket and was likely what had been in the ornate box on his desk.

"I don't know, Commander. I've been told there are few Legion Commanders in the Imperials anymore who have a brismil scale for protection," Bridger said.

"Do you honestly think that I'd give you what's in this vial for a brismil scale?" Nolstram asked sarcastically.

"If you want to live, yes," Bridger said.

Kayda understood where the conversation was going. She affirmed her fitting with the Agunzi bow and attempted to get a clear shot at the envoy.

"I'm not going to sell you this for a scale just so you can destroy it," Nolstram said.

"I don't want to destroy it. Simply because the Emperor told me to, doesn't mean I will," Bridger said. "This business with the element you've got in that vial, it doesn't have to die here today. Sell me the vial for the scale and we can both walk away from this. Benton will not be the wiser. I'll tell him I destroyed it."

The Commander thought about the option for a while longer than Kayda expected. He pointed to the wagon behind the Kai, and said, "You're not going back to Perdigon."

Bridger shook his head, "For personal reasons, I'm moving house to a new city. Maybe Sprague or Sularo."

"Does the Emperor know about this?" Nolstram asked.

"This is the last job I'm conducting for Benton. The only thing the Emperor needs to know is that this vial was *destroyed*. It's not my fault, or yours, that Zethril or Agunzi separatists discovered a formula similar to what Jermanus had created," Bridger said.

"And you get rich off my labor? I don't think so," Nolstram said.

"You realize the position I'm in, right? I've got a brismil scale. I know you don't have one. The Emperor will believe whatever I tell him. I don't need to make a deal with you at all. I could just kill you now and take the vial," Bridger said.

"How do you know I have it with me?" Nolstram said.

"For the same reason you've been eyeing the scale pouch on my belt. It's in your right pocket. Unless it's a scale you have in there that you've been fidgeting with this whole time."

Kayda pressed her feet against the Agunzi bow. She strained as she pulled on the string to bend the bow. Her training took over and she found herself staring down the shaft of the taught arrow, pointing it as best she could at the envoy.

"I'll show you mine, if you show me yours," Nolstram said.

Kayda shook under the weight of holding her aim. She wondered at the repercussions if she took the shot. What would come to pass if she killed the Emperor's envoy? What would happen if she didn't take the shot? What would happen if she took the shot and missed? What would happen if she let Nolstram deal with this situation on his own?

Kayda only saw this playing out two ways. The Commander wasn't going to let the Kai take the vial. That's why he'd made Kayda accompany him, to attack in case this very scenario occurred. Then it was Kayda's choice, she realized. Which brought her around to what this Bridger-Kai had said. The only people who knew about this meeting were these two facing off on the road and the Emperor, and unknown to Bridger and the Emperor, Kayda as well.

If her Commander had been willing to kill her if she told anyone in the Legion about what happened to their fellow soldiers, she wondered whether Nolstram now planned to kill her when this meeting was over. How hard would it be for him to say that she had wandered off from camp, never to be seen again? Nolstram said himself that he hadn't come this far in his career by placing his trust in others. He was ruthless. And yet so was this Bridger-Kai.

It was time for Kayda to embrace the same philosophy. If she didn't shoot at Bridger and remained hidden, the Kai might kill the Commander for the vial. Kayda imagined returning to the camp, pretending she didn't know what happened. Questions would arise. Captain Livingston knew she had been summoned to the Commander's tent. All of the soldiers were already calling her guilty for the murders of Helmer, Pyter, and Robson. This would feed that fire. Even if they didn't condemn her for the Commander's death, only one person in the Legion knew a hint of the truth about the demise of those in her earlier mission. Did Captain Livingston know enough to save her?

Her mind raced as she struggled with the bow. Kayda saw that this moment on the road in the woods was her chance to break away from it all. Start a new life. She could disappear. All she had to do was let the two Kai kill one another and she could go. But the Legions were all she knew. She'd served in the military her whole adult life. She didn't have documentation to prove her station in society. But then she knew that with enough money, she could buy whatever she wanted, documents, a new life, start a business perhaps. She could do all that by taking the vial or the scale. She could do that by taking them from Bridger or the Commander once one was done killing the other.

A man in brismil scale wasn't impossible to kill. She understood even those with scale needed to sleep and this one would not expect to be attacked on the road. Kayda could kill the man in his sleep and take both the scale and the vial. But a stolen scale only brought more death. She knew that as well. A scale needed to be bought legally or found in the wild to gain respect. Stolen scales were dangerous. Others would kill to keep them in circulation on the black market.

These thoughts swirled through her mind in a matter of seconds. Kayda released slack into the bow. This was Nolstram's mess, not hers. He had only shown her ill will. She didn't want to help him get away with it.

Kayda saw the Commander glancing into the forest while the Kai took out the brismil scale, being careful not to touch it with his skin. Nolstram was expecting Kayda to shoot now. When she didn't, and Bridger revealed the brismil scale, Commander Nolstram-Kai had no choice but to expose the vial.

"See. Neither of us is bluffing," Bridger said.

"Now what?" the Commander said, vial in one hand, hatchet in the other.

"You give the vial to me, and I won't kill you," Bridger said.

"What about the scale? I thought you were going to give it to me in exchange?" Nolstram said.

"I will. But not here, not while you can still follow me. I'll take the vial and return to Perdigon. I'll give the scale to an associate of mine who will be waiting for you tomorrow morning outside the gate," Bridger said.

"No. I don't think so," Nolstram said.

Bridger gave a half shake of his head. "You should've taken —"

Nolstram threw his hatchet at Bridger with lethal intent.

Kayda blinked, seeing Bridger press his bare hand to the scale before the hatchet's blade sank into his chest. The Commander's aim was true, and the hatchet would've killed him had he not donned the brismil plate. The steel edge sparked as it cut through the leather surcoat and deflected off the brismil underneath. The hatchet fell to the wagon floorboards before the Commander was able to draw his short sword and attack. Bridger moved much faster than Nolstram could react. He was down off the wagon and driving his dagger into the Commander's throat before Nolstram had unsheathed his blade. His gasps for air gurgled with blood. Bridger caught the Commander before he fell, dragging him off the road. And into the brush. He was coming directly for Kayda. She held still, the bow still strung, but not aimed or drawn. She knew it wouldn't do her any good now that Bridger was in brismil plate. Kayda held her breath as the Kai dropped her dying Commander in the vegetation just beyond where she hid.

She remained perfectly still, not making a sound while the gurgling and twitching Legion Commander died a few yards away. Kayda watched the Kai saunter back out onto the road, almost casually pocketing the vial the Commander had dropped. Bridger secured the scale back into his leather pouch and went to work scuffing the ground where he'd stabbed and dragged Nolstram. Kayda understood the decision she faced. She could either sit, do nothing, and watch the most valuable assets she'd ever been close to be carried away, or she could try to kill Bridger. She prepared the bow. Bridger snapped to attention. Kayda held her poise, not sure if he'd heard her, or if something else had caught his attention. A half a breath later, she heard harquice hooves pounding. Bridger rushed to the wagon. As he sat down in the driver's seat, Kayda took aim. The wagon lurched forward with Bridger's harquice responding to his directive. Kayda let the arrow fly. The sound of galloping harquice overshadowed the rushing of her arrow. The Agunzi shaft soared through the darkness, missing Bridger as the wagon pulled away.

Kayda cursed under her breath as the Kai glanced over his shoulder, but he was not able to see or know what had just missed him. He continued down the road, calmly riding in the direction of Saypo, toward the Legion camp. Kayda held her position, not sure what to do next. She stirred upon seeing a lone rider in the darkness. The rider was dressed in armor, draco-scale armor. A purple cloak trailed behind her. Her broadsword was drawn. In a blur, she flew past the fork in the road, shouting, "Bridger!"

Kayda sprang from her seat, leaving the bow and running alongside the road under the cover of the forest. She rushed to where the armed woman now blocked Bridger's path. Kayda slowed, careful not to make too much noise as she watched the two arguing from the cover of a tree trunk.

"Noxon, what the ash are you doing out here?" Bridger said.

"You have some explaining to do, Bridger," Noxon said.

"Really? Like what? I'm not Ovando's dog anymore. I don't owe him anything," he said.

"You owe me an explanation," Noxon said.

"Yeah?"

"Yes. I need to know why you suddenly came back into town telling everyone you're a Kai and you've quit the guard. How is it possible?"

"You came all the way out here to ask me that? You could've written it in a letter, for Creator's sake," Bridger said.

"No, I didn't come out here to tell you that. I came out here because High Commander Ovando-Kai gave me an order."

Bridger dropped the reins on his harquice. Though this guard, Noxon, might not have understood what he was reaching for, Kayda did. She held her breath, but the Kai didn't don the scale. Instead, he held his hand near the pouch and said, "What order?"

"He wants you dead, Bridger. He told me to kill you," Noxon said.

"If that's the way he is going to play this, so be it," Bridger said.

"I don't want to kill you, Bridger," Noxon said. "We've served together for six rotations. I followed your orders until the High Commander up and made me Captain of the Guard."

"Marxius is on the wrong side of things. The Emperor is only keeping him around until he gets word of what I'm procuring for him. Then he's going to make some serious changes to the way the Empire is run. It's why I'm getting out. So should you," Bridger said.

Kayda frowned. That wasn't the story Bridger had just told her Commander. He said the Emperor wanted whatever was in the vial destroyed.

"Get out? Bridger, listen to yourself. I don't know what you've gotten yourself into, but whatever it is, you can't just disappear," Noxon said.

"Let it go, Nox," Bridger said.

"Marxius Ovando-Kai will not just let this go. If I fail in his first order, I'm next. He'll make sure I go back to the bottom. He'll take everything away from me and what I've struggled so hard to build for my family," she said, becoming despondent.

"You can't win against me, Nox. You know it as well as I. I'm better with the sword than you," Bridger said.

"You might be if you put on that brismil scale. But you're not without it," she said.

"That's always been your shortcoming. You don't know your limits," Bridger said.

"If you want to keep that scale, I'll let you go. Only if you promise me that House Ovando will believe you're dead and gone forever. Never let him hear that you're alive," Noxon said.

"I can't make that promise, Nox. Marxius does not scare me and neither do you," Bridger said.

"You're forcing my hand," Noxon said, dismounting her harquice.

"I'm not. Marxius is. You don't have to die," he said.

To Kayda's surprise, Bridger squared off with Noxon without donning the brismil scale. He drew his broadsword from the wagon and paired off with her on the road.

"Last chance to walk away with your life," Noxon said.

Bridger shook his head and Noxon attacked.

Steel rang on steel as the two New Rhydarians fought in the road. Kayda crept closer, no longer worrying about how much noise she made. If she got close enough, she could surprise Bridger and kill him and take the vial and scale. The two exchanged heavy blows. Bridger drew blood first. He landed a strike to Noxon's left arm. She ignored the injury and doubled down her attack. Bridger blocked, somehow managing to land another strike to Noxon's right thigh. The fight was not going to last much longer. Kayda had seen many duels. Rarely did one with Noxon's wounds and inferior skill recover for a victory. Kayda needed to strike.

Noxon rushed Bridger, peppering him with strikes and not worrying about blocking. She overwhelmed him on the attack but suffered a stab in her side. Noxon tackled Bridger, his sword still stuck into her side. She screamed, hammering him in the face with the brunt of her forehead. Kayda hunkered down near the edge of the road, her short sword drawn, waiting to see if Noxon was going to win. Kayda noticed that the way in which Noxon had pinned Bridger, he wasn't able to grab the scale on his belt. Bridger worked the blade that he still gripped, trying to inflict more internal damage as Noxon hammered his face with the square of her forehead. Kayda realized they might just kill each other. Noxon, her face bloodied with Bridger's, peeled away from him as he pushed her off. Kayda rushed out from the edge of the road, seeing her chance.

The Kai pulled his sword out from Noxon's side, pointed it at her, and said, "It was a good try Nox, but you're dead."

Before he could stab her again Kayda side-punched the pommel of her short sword directly into Bridger's exposed head. The handle of the blade cracked into his skull dropping him like a pile of bricks. He collapsed, unconscious. Kayda went to finish him off, but hesitated. Bridger was not a threat for the time being, but the woman was. She moved to the female guard who was crawling for her sword. "Stop," Kayda commanded.

Noxon froze, blood seeping from the wound on her side.

Kayda trained the tip of her short sword onto the female guard.

"This is a dirty trick, Bridger," Noxon said. "Having me ambushed."

"I'm not with him," Kayda said.

"Ashes with that. You aren't just out here alone. I might be dying, but I'm not stupid," Noxon said.

"I'm not with this man. I'm here for something else," she said.

"The scale?" Noxon coughed. "It's cursed. You won't

outrun its owner."

"What do you mean?" she said.

"That scale was stolen from Galterius-Brex. He owns the matching brismil blade. The blade will lead him directly to the scale. He'll kill you or anyone who has it," Noxon said.

"Why didn't you just let Bridger leave with it then?" Kayda asked.

"He was my Captain for six years. I couldn't talk sense into him before he left the gates. I decided to try to take it from him. Hide it somewhere for Galterius to find. I don't know? I didn't think he'd actually kill me," Noxon said, feeling at her side.

Kayda rummaged through Bridger's pockets finding the small white crystalline glass vial that he had taken from her Commander.

"What's that? What are you doing?" Noxon asked, her voice weakening.

"It's nothing. Forget that you saw me. There's a legion camped not far away on this road. They'll help you if you can live long enough to make it to them," Kayda said.

"Why should I believe you?" Noxon said.

"Because I'm trying to help you," Kayda replied.

"Help me?" Noxon spat. "I know you're with Bridger. I'll send the legion after you."

Kayda let a heavy exhale escape her chest, then sprang at Noxon. The larger woman tried to block her, but Kayda stabbed her short sword into the soft spot of her armor. She drove the blade through Noxon's armpit, severing her artery. The woman wailed and attempted to crawl to her sword. The blood loss hit her quickly and Noxon never made it to her weapon.

Kayda eyed Bridger. She'd hit him hard. He wouldn't

likely wake up for at least a few more minutes. Possibly longer. If what Noxon had said about the scale was true, it was better that Bridger stayed alive. If Galterius-Brex owned that scale, he'd come for it. If Galterius died, there'd be others who would come hunting for the scale.

Kayda saw her options laid out in front of her. One, return with the vial to the Legion and tell Captain Livingston the truth. She could give him the vial, tell him who the culprits were, and hope for forgiveness from the Legion. Or she could run. She could take the vial and go. She didn't know who would buy it, or if she could sell it, but whatever it was, if Bridger lived, it was worth more to her. Its authenticity would increase.

Kayda hitched Noxon's harquice to the wagon and drove Bridger's loaded wagon away, back toward Perdigon. It seemed Bridger didn't want to return there, so that was where Kayda was going. She could start her life over there. With the money she made off the vial, she hoped to have it all, provided she wasn't murdered first.

THE BLUE LIGHT

THE DAY AFTER EMPEROR BENTON'S DEATH

Shylo leaned against the wall inside the coach. He glanced up as he turned the page in the book he'd found. Sandor averted his gaze. Shylo sensed he was uneasy about what they planned to do next. Shylo bowed his head, reading the passage in Volteir's journal for the second time.

"I've made a groundbreaking discovery, a discovery which I will use to found this new religion. The Dracolyth got it wrong in teaching that the magic of the dragons is dead and gone from Tarmigan. We now have proof that the chipped pieces of dragon teeth, claws, and spines contain remnants of the magic that existed in our world's predominant species in centuries past. That we can use these rare pieces of dragon remains to brave the blazes set by the Volurem offers us a godlike power; but I have uncovered an even deeper layer.

"I have performed extensive tests on the Pyrignum that we encapsulated and brought to the far north in Zethril and I have discovered the source of its magic. The dragon hearts, as we have come to call them, are elements of magic left behind by the dragons who used to roam Tarmigan. Like our brismil elements, these opal gemstones have preserved a form of magic that I hypothesized had descended from a magical dragon. As previously stated, after my last series of tests I found that when the dragon heart is taken away from the Pyrignum, the super-powered being becomes nothing more than an Engulfed Volurem.

"The strangest thing happens when the dragon's heart is taken away from the Pyrignum. The brilliant blue light emanating from the opal gem slowly burns out and the glassy heart-shaped stone grows a thick stony exterior. It appears indistinguishable to me when compared to other sedimentary stones. Rhydarians of either race, Zethrillians, and Agunzi are unable to pick it out of a pile of comparable rocks with any measurable success. The Volurem, however, find it every time. I have tested this on a number of Volurem that we have captured in the North and kept alive for my studies. Each picked out the dragon heart and turned Pyrignum, allowing the opal essence of the stone to return.

"When I remembered from my journey south how the Engulfed Volurem passed over brismil scales without notice, I conducted a test fashioned similarly to the previously mentioned test for recognition of the dragon hearts. I reached my conclusion yesterday. It appears that Terras can spot brismil scale when discarded on the ground while the Volurem cannot. Conversely, Volurem can spot a dragon heart when discarded on the ground while Terras cannot. Both of these elements contain magical qualities, yet one appears to be invisible to one species while the other is obvious. This evidence-based realization now enables me to prove my hypothesis that both magical elements have come from the same extinct species.

"While the Volurem were in their Engulfed and Pyrignum states, I presented them with brismil scale scattered among other similar-appearing fossils and rocks. The brismil was passed over without interest by the Engulfed. The Pyrignum, however, went directly to the scale. The creature picked it up and something happened. It took the combined strength of me in brismil plate and my Agunzi security guard to remove the brismil scale from the Pyrignum. While the Volurem are an eighth their normal size here in Zethril, I do not want to test this hypothesis again. But if these are some of the elements that form The Creator's power, I need a second confirmation to prove my hypothesis.

"Following my experiments, I have no need for the Volurem. I took the dragon heart from the Pyrignum and donned my brismil scale. I cannot quite describe the raw power I felt surging through me. I knew that I could control things with a magic that I had never thought possible. While holding the dragon heart, I spoke through my mind's eye to my Agunzi guard. He obeyed my commands without a word said aloud. As I held the heart while in my brismil-plated armor, I noticed faint lights. They lay scattered on the ground, glowing a light yellow. I cannot know what they meant, but I felt a need to get to them. In my yearning to discover what they were, I dropped the dragon heart. The lights disappeared. The power I had while holding the dragon heart was lost. And I could not find the dragon heart again. I have piled up the rocks and am going through them one at a time, hoping to locate that blue glow of the opal gem again, but I fear that without a charge the Volurem must be able to give it, I will not find it again. Even while in the plate, it seems that Terra eyes are just as useless at picking out the opal gem. My only hope is that it will reveal itself if I happen to touch the dragon heart while in my brismil plate. For I could see and feel its unique difference when I held it while in brismil plate before."

"Shylo, Sandor," Galterius said through the window from the driver's seat. His voice broke Shylo's concentration on the book. "Get ready. We're approaching the port."

Shylo set the book down and retrieved Chirp from the pile of spare clothing the borca used as a nest. Setting him into his pocket, Shylo peered out the window. Past the water's edge, beyond the forest, Shylo saw steady columns of smoke in the air in the distance. The stone wall surrounding his hometown, Florens, came into view on the river delta below.

Tucking the journal under his arm, Shylo thought through the passage from Volteir again. The author had been enamored of the blue glow of the dragon heart. The heart had given Volteir the power to manipulate someone with his mind alone; the same effect the Pyrignum were said to have on the Engulfed Volurem, making them Possessed Volurem. Shylo then thought of the blue light he'd seen emanating from Senator Didimo-Kai's villa. A dragon heart could've caused everyone in the villa to have gathered to be slain. Shylo did not know how this was possible, considering that Volteir died a rotation after he wrote of his discovery, centuries ago. He never discovered the dragon heart again. While there were no Pyrignum in Perdigon the night of the massacre, there was a blue glow in Senator Didimo's chambers. Shylo now suspected whoever it was had used a dragon heart.

He forced the theory to the back of his mind. Shylo needed to rescue Jexsanna first. And to do that, now that she was locked away inside the walls of Perdigon, he and his unlikely team needed to enlist some help. Shylo wasn't looking forward to returning to Florens, but Sandor had connections in the area. Shylo just hoped that when they were on the ground again, none of them would be recognized. Though, with the scale he hid from his companions, Shylo knew he could always run. He could run back to Perdigon and find a way into the city. But if they could enlist the help of trained Rhydarians and Agunzi who were willing to rail against the Empire, then he'd gladly join in. Shylo wasn't done with those in Perdigon who'd wronged him, and he wasn't going to give up on Jexsanna. He couldn't give up, not yet.

LEAVE A REIVEW

ENJOY THIS BOOK? YOU CAN MAKE A BIG DIFFERENCE

Consider posting your review.

Leaving a book review is a very powerful tool when it comes to getting attention for my books. As an independently published author, I don't have the connections or financial muscle of a New York publisher. Getting my books to the front of the bookstore or in full-page ads in the newspaper is something I'm not able to take advantage of, not yet anyway.

But I do have the advantage of speaking directly to you, the reader. Spreading news about my books by leaving a review not only proves my story's worth to others who might enjoy it, but word-of-mouth and social prof can be more powerful than anything New York publishers can offer.

Honest reviews of my books help attract other readers. If you've enjoyed this book, I would be very grateful if you would spend just five minutes leaving a review — it can be as short as you like.

Thank you so much. Happy reading,
A J Walker

NEWSLETTER SIGN-UP
GET YOUR FREE BOOK

Sign up for my newsletter and you'll never miss another A J Walker book launch. You'll receive my prequel novellas, ebook promotions, monthly writing updates and more.

Building a relationship with my readers is the best part about being an independent author. I send out a bi-monthly newsletter with details on new releases, special offers, and other updates concerning my writing progress.

When you sign up for my newsletter, you'll get an exclusive book:

Dragon Wars: War of the Magicians

To get your free book, go online to ajwalkerauthor.com and enter your email address in the sign-up box.

About the Author

A J Walker is an emerging author of epic fantasy. This is A J Walker's tenth book.

A J Walker grew up in Bozeman, Montana. In his youth, writing fiction and becoming an author was a distant dream, something a young dyslexic didn't think was achievable. A J was diagnosed with dyslexia at a young age. He struggled through most of his education with an elementary school reading comprehension level. When he was sixteen, A J found neurofeedback therapy. With the help of this new technology, he quickly learned how to read and write to the level of his high school peers. Before striving to become an author, A J's love for whitewater kayaking and the outdoors led him to study at the University of Montana. In his university years, A J worked as a wildland firefighter and graduated with a bachelor's degree in the Science of Forestry. Currently, A J lives along the Yellowstone River near Columbus, Montana, with his wife and their dogs.

A J Walker loves hearing from readers, so please feel free to contact him on social media or by sending an email to ajwalker@ajwalkerauthor.com.

Thank you for reading. :-)